THE INGENIOUS MR STONE

Then Miss Trubshawe was in the room. Actually I believe she was up those precipitous stairs before the third shriek. Dr Plummer must have been close at her heels, but I knew nothing of that at the time. All I could do as I lay twitching and convulsed on the bed was to cling desperately to Miss Trubshawe's hand.

Also in Arrow Books by Robert Player

The Homicidal Colonel
Oh! Where are Bloody Mary's Earrings?

Robert Player

THE INGENIOUS
MR STONE

OR

THE DOCUMENTS IN THE
LANGDON-MILES CASE

ARROW BOOKS

ARROW BOOKS LTD
3 Fitzroy Square, London W1

An imprint of the Hutchinson Publishing Group

London Melbourne Sydney Auckland
Wellington Johannesburg Cape Town
and agencies throughout the world

First published by Victor Gollancz 1945
Arrow edition 1974

Made and printed in Great Britain
by The Anchor Press Ltd,
Tiptree, Essex

ISBN 0 09 909160 7

Contents

Part One

being a foreword by Adam Muir, Esq.,
Writer to the Signet, of The Little Doon
Farm, Dalmellington, in the County of Ayr

When, in the Spring of 1931, Miss Philippa Langdon-Miles, headmistress of Easton Knoyle School, Torquay, fell dead on the platform of a London lecture hall, the affair could hardly have been kept out of the newspapers. The world, however, was in the midst of the great financial crisis and if Miss Langdon-Miles's death served as a sensation for a day, it was soon forgotten by the great public.

When, a few weeks later, Miss Langdon-Miles's sister, Mrs. Harold Warburton, died quietly in her sleep at a hotel on the Northumberland moors, there were very few who connected the two events, although there was at the time some rather sensational and ill-informed talk about what came to be known as 'The Langdon-Miles Tragedy.'

The story which follows has been compiled by me at the request of my old friend, Mrs. Alexander Soutar, of the Coquet Hall Hotel, near Rothbury in Northumberland. The tragedy occurred over ten years ago, but the facts have never been laid before the public. At the time, indeed, every possible effort was made to avoid publicity, for the sake not only of Mrs. Soutar and of Easton Knoyle School, but also because of all of us who were concerned naturally shrank from the vulgarity and notoriety which would undoubtedly have resulted from any sort of public statement. Even now, when the story is no longer what the reporters call 'news,' I am far from convinced that Mrs. Soutar's decision is entirely wise, although her motives are, I must admit, altogether praiseworthy and correct.

Once again, she tells me, lies and malicious rumours are circulating in the Coquet Dale and further afield. These must be scotched, and to publish the truth has seemed to Mrs. Soutar to be the most effective and dignified form of doing this. It would, in any case, be difficult for me to refuse her request; she is a very old friend and I have had charge of her affairs for nearly a quarter of a century—ever since Colonel Alexander Soutar was killed on the beaches at Gallipoli.

Mrs. Soutar was the eldest daughter of Dr. Carlyle of Corstophine—for over thirty years the minister at the Roxburgh Square Chapel—and I know of few women who command greater respect. It was a great grief to us all when it was found, after Colonel Soutar's death, that she would have to earn her own living. Daughters of the manse are not usually blessed with worldly riches, and Mrs. Soutar had been one of a family of ten. I myself played some part in forming a small private company which—after much discussion as to ways and means —installed Mrs. Soutar, with her niece, Miss Amy Carlyle, to assist her, as manageress of the Coquet Hall Hotel. As was to be expected, the hotel was a great success under such capable supervision; by its regular clients it is indeed regarded as unique.

I still have some little business interest in Coquet Hall. Solid material reasons, therefore, as well as loyalty to an old friend, having weighed with me in acceding to Mrs. Soutar's plea that a statement should be compiled in order that the good reputation of the hotel may be preserved.

I have thought it best, in the interests of absolute truth, that I should limit my own narrative to those events in which I personally played a part; I shall confine myself to that extraordinary summer at Coquet Hall. What happened at Easton Knoyle, in London and elsewhere must be described by others. I have told Mrs. Soutar, however, that I accept full responsibility for the compilation and editing of the whole story. While it is only right and proper that parts of this story should have been told by others— by those who were in a position to know the real facts—it was a method which I adopted only with considerable trepidation.

Miss Sophie Coppock and Mrs. Bradford will forgive me if I say that neither of them has had the necessary experience for casting their narrative in proper legal form. To my dry and perhaps unduly legalistic mind there is much in what they have written that is mere hearsay and speculation. Miss Coppock herself insists that she is 'no story-teller,' and I feared at one time that Mrs. Bradford's great age—she was over eighty at the time of the tragedy —might have impaired her memory. In this, I am glad to say, I have been proved wrong. Mr. Stone himself was able to fill in many gaps in the story of how he solved his problem.

Although the documents that follow are deplorably diffuse from a legal point of view, and quite unsuitable for presentation in court or as the basis of a brief, I am satisfied that Mrs. Soutar's purpose has *been served. The shadow of a calumny has been lifted from Coquet Hall, and the truth, the whole truth and nothing but the truth concerning 'The Langdon-Miles Tragedy' is at last presented to the world.*

Part Two

in which Miss Sophie Coppock, B.A.,
Secretary and Bursar of Easton Knoyle
School for Girls, Torquay, tells how Mrs.
Carberry and Mr. Pym visited Easton
Knoyle in the winter of 1930.

I

Really, I hardly know how to begin! I feel quite bewildered at the thought of the task I have undertaken. It is such a complicated story, such a maze, so difficult to tell. The whole affair was so tragic and so distasteful, so completely outside my normal sphere and—I think I may truly say—so utterly foreign to my upbringing and to my whole nature. Then there are the feelings of so many friends to be considered; I do hope that I shall offend none.

My long life—I am sixty this year—though not untouched by sorrow, has on the whole been pleasant and, I trust, useful; but it has also been limited and protected. I am, therefore, quite unfamiliar with many aspects of the events I have to describe. I know nothing of the niceties or phraseology of the law, although Mr. Adam Muir of Dalmellington has promised to correct me in such matters, and to edit my whole story when I have finished it. Having undertaken so reluctantly to write this little narrative, I owe it both to the memory of Miss Langdon-

Miles and to dear Nellie Soutar to be quite truthful. I foresee that, in describing the events of ten years ago, this will not be easy. I can, however, assure my readers that I shall do my utmost—truthfulness and complete sincerity have ever been my guiding stars.

When Mr. Muir wrote asking for 'an unvarnished account' of the facts as I knew them, I felt quite overcome and my first impulse was to refuse. Indeed it was more than an impulse; refusal seemed to be the only course. Even had I set my personal predilections on one side, it was still my duty to refuse—a duty which I owed both to the girls—past and present—of Easton Knoyle and to the dear memory of Miss Langdon-Miles. After all I am still Secretary and Bursar at Easton Knoyle and if I can keep the fair reputation of the school free from stain, that I must do.

The whole affair was so at variance with all that is truly gracious and ladylike, in such utter contrast with that unsullied atmosphere of purity and beauty with which, for so many years, Miss Langdon-Miles had striven to imbue our little community, that silence seemed at first to be the only course. I was sure, too, that the Governors—to whom, when all is said and done, I owe my first allegiance—would hardly thank me for reviving once again the perils of publicity.

Then, above all, what would dear Miss Langdon-Miles herself say? This probing into the events surrounding her own passing! No, it would never do. She would rather we held in our hearts only two memories of her: the one, that summer afternoon of 1931 when we said our last farewells on the lawn outside the chapel, the air heavy with the scent of flowers, many of them tributes from the highest in the land; the other, of the busy woman of affairs, working untiringly and unceasingly for the realisation of her ideals—always so truly noble! No, it would never do—this raking up of the past. In any case, I said to myself, the whole horrible affair is surely long since over and done with. Let the past bury the past, say I.

Yes, it is all long ago and, one had hoped, forgotten. Over and done with—and very fortunate we all were that it was no worse. Tragic and unutterably sad it was, but at least we escaped the ghastly nightmare, the vulgarity, of becoming *dramatis personæ* in a *cause célèbre*. That, I think, would have been worse than death itself. I cannot conceive of anything more terrible. Neither Nellie Soutar's hotel at Coquet Hall nor dear Easton Knoyle could have survived *that* shameful fate.

So I wrote to Mr. Muir refusing to take any part in this stirring up of the mud. Then, the very next morning, there came a letter from Nellie Soutar—Nellie Carlyle as she will always be to me—begging me to do as Mr. Muir asked. She had, I think, guessed how I should feel and wanted to add her word to that of Mr. Muir. The Coquet Dale, she said, was full of rumours and malicious lies—some of them lies of a very terrible character about herself and her niece. Dreadful stories were being raked up about the old tragedy, some of them great nonsense about corpses under the cellar floor and about the exhumation. Some of these stories were just those half-truths which are the most dangerous of all. It was becoming intolerable, she said, and none too good for business. So she had decided to publish the true story and would I help her? Well, if you are to understand my tale you must know why it is that there are very few things in this world that I could refuse to Nellie.

It is nearly fifty years since she and I used to walk together through the cold windy streets of Edinburgh, to Mrs. Drysdale's Academy in Charlotte Crescent. My father was a hard-worked country doctor, away in Nithsdale; he was marvellously good to his patients, but was not, I think, very well off. I was an only child and he and my mother were determined that I should have a grand education, so that I could take advantage of the opportunities which were beginning to be opened up to women. So, at the age of ten, I was sent off to live with my granny in Edinburgh.

Nellie and I almost grew up together and I often went to play with her regiment of brothers and sisters in the rather dingy little manse at Corstophine—and what grand times we had! It is a far cry from those happy days to the riding lessons and winter sports and the visits to Glyndebourne and Paris which the girls at Easton Knoyle take so much for granted—but if you gave me my choice I know well what my answer would be.

Old Dr. Carlyle was kindness itself to me, and when I was a little older he coached me for my exams and there was never a word about payment. I was not at all a clever person and I am afraid that he had an uphill job, but I got my degree in the end. Then, just after the last war and a few months before he died, the old minister used his influence with some friends in England to get me the post at Easton Knoyle. By that time I had been drudging away for some years as a teacher for the London School Board, and so you can imagine what this new work meant to me.

It was not easy for a simple Scottish lass—for that is what I always call myself—to plunge into the rather sophisticated little community at Easton Knoyle, but I have been there twenty-five years next September, so I do not think that Dr. Carlyle would be ashamed of me.

It was the kind of debt that can never be repaid, but I have always done what I could for Nellie. When Colonel Soutar was killed and Mr. Muir helped to set her up in the hotel at Coquet Hall, I sent her quite a number of clients from among the people I met at Torquay. Canon and Mrs. Fish of Exeter went there for many years, and my dear Aunt Bertha, old Mrs. Bradford, still spends three or four months there every summer; and then, of course, there were Mr. and Mrs. Warburton....

There were many little ways in which I was able to be of help to dear Nellie. There was, for instance, the rather peculiar case of Hypatia Crowe. Crowe, as we called her, was the daughter of a Brixham fisherman and a Plymouth Sister. She was a kitchenmaid at Easton Knoyle, but soon after I first went there she was accused of hitting one of the junior girls with the back of a scrubbing brush. The child was rather badly hurt and there was trouble with the parents. Crowe was a dark, sour creature whose very appearance was against her. In this particular case, however, I felt sure she was innocent —but she had to go. She felt that Miss Langdon-Miles had been unfair to her, and was rather bitter about it. She wanted to leave the district and as Nellie, at that time, was looking for staff for Coquet Hall, I sent Crowe to her. Crowe remained at Coquet Hall for many years, becoming a most excellent chambermaid.

But I really must not let myself run on like this, writing about the old days and about Nellie Soutar, when I ought to be setting down my 'unvarnished account' of the tragedy at Easton Knoyle. But you can see how difficult it would be for me to refuse Nellie's appeal. In any case, since she had decided to give the facts to the world, refusal is useless; if I do not tell the story, another will. So I have written to Mr. Muir a second time, telling him that I give way—although I do so with very grave doubts.

2

There is another reason why I should have refused Mr. Muir's request. I am no story-teller. You must realise that when I became 'secretary' to Miss Langdon-Miles it was not because I could claim any special literary ability—in writing letters or lectures or anything of that sort. On the contrary, it was tacitly but clearly understood that my duties would be social rather than clerical.

Miss Langdon-Miles usually dictated almost her entire correspondence—and a very considerable correspondence it was—to our competent stenographer, Miss Bussey. The solicitor to the Board of Governors, Mr. Paston, was a Torquay man, which was a great convenience as he was able to look in every Thursday morning, usually remaining to take lunch with us at the high table. He and I went carefully through the books, and he would then advise us on any business matters about which we might consult him. He was always most helpful, quite a tower of strength.

On more serious matters of policy—specially in the spiritual sphere—we were indeed blessed in having the advice and good counsel of Canon Fish, our visiting chaplain. He was a real saint, but a man of the world too. He took his duties at Easton Knoyle very much to heart and was a great comfort to Miss Langdon-Miles and, may I say, to myself. Although many disapproved of him as an extreme ritualist, I was able, despite my Presbyterian childhood, to see the sterling qualities which lay beneath the outward show. Moreover, as the years went by, the colour and music which pervaded the services in our school chapel quite took possession of my soul.

I do not doubt that, to the girls, Canon Fish was an inspiration that would endure throughout their lives. I regard it merely as one more deplorable sign of the times, and as an indication of how difficult it is to counter bad home influences, that I should have discovered that the girls were referring to Canon Fish as 'the old red mullet.' True, he had a rosy countenance, but it was not the kind of thing that one expected of our nice, well-bred girls at Easton Knoyle. I tracked it down to Felicity Carhampton, but I never reported her, for I knew that Miss Langdon-Miles would only have been pained and cut to the quick. Moreover, I am sure that throughout the school Canon Fish was really quite revered. The Carhamptons were a horsey, Irish lot, and Felicity suffered accordingly.

Whenever he was in residence at Exeter, the dear Canon would motor over to Torquay on Saturday afternoons, and would spend the night in our guest wing at Easton Knoyle. At an early service the next morning he would administer the Eucharist in our chapel, and would return to Exeter in time to officiate at Matins. A full life, but a very lovely one, I think.

After tea on Saturdays there were often the Confirmation classes. The evening was devoted to consultation and inspiring converse; two or three Sixth Form girls being usually invited to the drawing-room to meet the Canon. During the last hour of the day, he and Miss Langdon-Miles would enjoy a very precious *tête-à-tête*.

Canon Fish's visits were always something of an occasion at Easton Knoyle. In a school such as ours it is always necessary, I need hardly say, to set a very high standard of daily conduct, but on these Saturday evenings we so far relaxed as to have wine served at the high table. A bottle of Burgundy was placed before Miss Langdon-Miles and she shared it with Canon Fish and Frau Lauprecht, our German mistress. It was offered to all at the high table but this was a mere formality as neither myself nor any other members of the Common Room ever touched intoxicating liquor of any kind. Perhaps it was the survival of some instinct from my childhood—'inhibition', I think, is the fashionable word—that always made me feel a little uncomfortable on these occasions.

There was a good deal of discussion about it among the mistresses. Frau Lauprecht was not English and must, therefore, be judged by a different standard. Canon Fish was a man, and that again makes a difference; but it did go against the grain to see our beloved Miss Langdon-Miles consuming alcohol. Miss Bell—a vegetarian and, therefore, abnormal in such matters—roundly condemned the practice on hygienic grounds; Miss MacTaggart, on the other hand, said that if it had been beer she would have had some herself. Fancy that! I used to say that perhaps we might regard the little ceremony as symbolic of the fact that Miss Langdon-Miles belonged not only to us, but that she was also a woman of the world. I always tried to be a peace-maker in the Common Room—with but variable success. I must admit that my defence of Miss Langdon-Miles was just my loyalty; I was never really reconciled to seeing that bottle uncorked in full view of the girls.

Canon Fish's care for Easton Knoyle was boundless, and Miss Langdon-Miles frequently consulted him on all manner of things—secular as well as spiritual. The chapel was, however, the great bond between them and the planning of the services and the hunt for new treasures to beautify the little building were a constant joy. I very much fear that the highly ritualistic nature of our liturgy and the beautiful sacerdotalism which so permeated our lives, cannot have met with the universal approval of either the Governors or parents. On more than one occasion there was trouble, and General Lucas went so far as to remove his three daughters from the school at very short notice. So perhaps—in going bravely on—Miss Langdon-Miles and Canon Fish felt that they shared a common martyrdom.

In this, my sixtieth year, I have turned irrevocably to Rome, but ten years ago I certainly saw much of which I could not entirely approve. Canon Fish, I believe, heard Miss Langdon-Miles's confession regularly, and she once confided to me that their comradeship was touched by a very lovely mysticism. It was, nevertheless, very wrong that tongues should wag and foul scandal be put about. I am sorry to have to put it on record that, both in Torquay and Exeter, there was some most unpleasant gossip. It was so unedifying that I can only pray that it never reached the ears of the girls. No doubt it was all great nonsense, although there is, of course, no smoke without fire.

Mrs. Fish, a distressingly plain woman, was many years older than her husband and was a constant invalid. One would like to take the charitable view and dismiss the idea that she was a hypochondriac. She was a very stay-at-home person, excessively domesticated, and she played no part in the Canon's public life. She was said to be of a very mean and jealous disposition, but I knew nothing of life in the Close and I do not propose to repeat what is mere hearsay. Perhaps I have said too much already. During all the years that I was at Easton Knoyle, Mrs. Fish visited us on only one occasion—two days before Miss Langdon-Miles's death!

3

I must now say a little about my own duties at Easton Knoyle. What with Mr. Paston and Canon Fish visiting us so regularly, it is clear that we did not lack male advice. Miss Langdon-Miles had usually dealt with her correspondence before prayers. Miss Bussey could then be trusted to handle the affairs of the office until lunchtime, thus enabling Miss Langdon-Miles to turn undivided attention to her true sphere—that of the intellect. She was wont to spend an hour visiting the classrooms; then she

would read until lunch, prepare her lectures or de-
vote an hour to her beloved Sixth Form, moulding
them, as she put it, to become 'gracious English
ladies.' I have even known her spend a whole morning in the chapel in meditation. In some ways a
strange woman!

All this meant that I often had to deputise for Miss
Langdon-Miles in the drawing-room. I interviewed
parents and I often presided at our 'At Homes.' I
think that my early training in a simple Scottish
family enabled me to play my part with dignity on
these occasions, although many of the Easton Knoyle
parents were from the highest ranks of what the
papers call 'Scoiety.' I remember that once, when
Miss Langdon-Miles was abroad, I had to entertain
a very high personage indeed. It was a great honour
and I can only hope that I did not make too many
faux pas.

My main duties were really domestic. I had to
supervise and engage the kitchen staff—all so much
more difficult than in the good old days—and to pay
their wages and deal with the tradesmen. On three
occasions—shall I ever forget?—I had to take Miss
Langdon-Miles's place at a Governors' meeting, always held at White's Hotel in Albermarle Street.
Somehow I stumbled through Miss Langdon-
Miles's report, but for at least a week before I was
quite prostrate with nervousness. Miss Langdon-
Miles was very kind and spared me this ordeal when
she could. But I was often in London on sundry
errands—escorting girls from Paddington to one of
the other termini, accompanying them to the dentist
or visiting the Army and Navy Stores about their
clothes or our school uniform. It was altogether a
very full life. It was because of these frequent visits

to London that I happened to be with Miss Langdon-Miles when the end came.

My duties were not lessened by the fact that Miss Langdon-Miles's activities extended far beyond Easton Knoyle. She was a leading figure in the world of higher education and among the Church laity. This often meant meetings and conferences at the universities or elsewhere. As a lecturer she was in great demand, and in 1926 she spent several weeks on a tour of the United States. This led to quite a little American connection for Easton Knoyle —which was very delightful. Miss Langdon-Miles visited several American towns, lecturing on her favourite subject: 'The Importance of Material Beauty in the Spiritual Life—with special reference to the Higher Education of Women.' It was a unique course of lectures—or 'talks' as she modestly called them. They were excellently received both at Harvard itself and by the general public in Boston; less well, I believe, in Chicago.

One result of this tour was that quite a number of Boston girls came to Easton Knoyle in the succeeding years. There was Zoë Denvers who—in spite of the fact that she was not English—actually became our hockey captain! The Lodge girls were also a great asset. I think that these American girls regarded Easton Knoyle as a sort of stepping stone for their first visits to Europe, and Miss Langdon-Miles always made a point of including one or two of them in those wonderful little tours on which, each year, she escorted some specially chosen seniors. They would usually spend a few days sight-seeing in Paris and would then go on, perhaps by way of Bayreuth or Oberammergau, to Florence. There, under Miss Langdon-Miles's inspiration, they would worship at the shrine of the *quattrocento* with—as Miss Bell, our mathematics mistress, rather tartly remarked—Baedeker in one hand and Browning in the other. One year, I remember, the tour was extended to include Vienna and Venice, and I was asked to accompany the little party. I cannot pretend that I cared for the foreign food—or certain other things; I recall being involved in a most unpleasant contretemps with the *valet-de-chambre* at Basle over my hot-water bottle. He was most unreasonable. However, I had never been abroad before and it was all a great thrill.

Miss Langdon-Miles maintained that these tours not only broadened the mind, but that international relationships were cemented. In view of the present sad state of Europe, I fear that I must remain a little sceptical about this. She and Canon Fish had most ambitious ideas; there was the year when they planned the famous 'Pauline tour.' The Sixth Form had been studying the 'Acts' and the idea was to follow in the Apostle's footsteps. I spent many weary hours wrestling with Thomas Cook's. Alas! It was found that—by Easton Knoyle standards—the hotel accommodation at Ephesus was severely limited, and the whole scheme was abandoned in favour of the Bernese Oberland. Canon Fish had arranged to accompany us in order to expound on archaeological matters, for he was a great Hellenic scholar. It leaked out later that the hotel difficulty was not the only one; that Mrs. Fish—very selfishly to my mind —had taken up an obstructionist attitude. It was very unreasonable, and Miss Langdon-Miles was quite bowled over by the disappointment.

Well, there I go again—prattling about school affairs instead of getting on with my story. I must

23

now describe the various buildings at Easton Knoyle, so that my readers may follow my account of several most unpleasant incidents which occurred towards the end of the Winter Term of 1930, about six months before Miss Langdon-Miles's death.

4

The buildings at Easton Knoyle, apart from the chapel and the Brownlow Library, consisted of four large stucco-faced villas, built about a century ago when Torquay was just becoming a fashionable resort. The rooms were large and airy—most suitable for school purposes—and several of them opened into quite spacious conservatories, which served as hygienic sun-traps. I am told that, according to current notions, our buildings were hideous, but to me they seemed excellent in every way.

The smallest of the four houses was The Firs; this was our junior school, quite self-contained under the altogether admirable jurisdiction of Miss Wheelwright. Miss Wheelwright often joined us in the Common Room but generally speaking The Firs had little to do with the rest of the school. Then there was St. Mary's and Torrington House; these had been linked together by a new range of classrooms and were both under the care of Miss Buchanan. I say nothing against Miss Buchanan, but a sad lack of discipline was evident in both houses—and one could not but draw one's own conclusions. Finally, there was School House, directly under Miss Langdon-Miles herself.

The gardens of all four houses had been thrown together and we were very proud of our extensive grounds, with their undulating lawns, broken by large clumps of rhododendrons and laurels. The botany class did not fail to benefit from the specimen conifers planted by former occupants. To these grounds Miss Langdon-Miles had made a most artistic and inspiring addition—The Poets' Garden. Here bloomed every flower referred to in English verse. Could one conceive of a more charming idea— or more original?

Most of the classes were held at School House and all the girls—except the little ones at The Firs— could be accommodated in the Assembly Hall there, for Easton Knoyle, in spite of its fame, was not a large school. This arrangement involved much going to and fro, much use of mackintoshes, umbrellas and goloshes—but we were all, thank God, singularly free from colds. In a separate wing, on the first floor of School House, Miss Langdon-Miles and I each had a sitting-room with a bedroom adjoining, and our own bathroom just across the corridor. It was all very sunny and pleasant as our windows looked across the tennis courts and The Poets' Garden to Torbay.

The chapel was not completed until 1926, but Miss Langdon-Miles had dreamt of it ever since Easton Knoyle had moved from Eastbourne before the last war. The building of the chapel, I remember, had given relief to her sensitive mind at a time when the perpetual internecine squabbles inside the Langdon-Miles family had reached one of their periodical crises. It was largely American money that had made the chapel possible, but gifts came from many sources. Miss Langdon-Miles was indefatigable in

her efforts and I once heard Canon Fish describe
her as 'a veritable princess of beggars.' When one of
the Governors referred to her in a speech as a 'sound
commercial traveller,' I thought that that was a very
crude and coarse way of saying much the same thing.

The chapel was a separate building and since it
had been felt—quite rightly, in my view—that the
Victorian stucco of the older houses would be both
unsuitable and unsightly for a religious edifice, no
attempt had been made to harmonise it with the other
buildings. It was of a rosy brick, in the free Gothic
manner, having been designed by an architect much
in favour with the ritualistic clergy. Skilful planting
of ampelopsis and laurel under Miss Langdon-
Miles's direction had almost completely hidden the
chapel, thus minimising the architectural discord.

I was not strictly correct when I said that the
chapel was a separate building. From the vestry, on
the north of the chancel, a short passage had been
built, joining the chapel to School House. This passage was merely a covered walk with glass sides but
it had somehow become known, rather magnilo-
quently, as 'the cloister.' Canon Fish assured us in
his jocular way that the more correct ecclesiological
term would be 'slype,' but this never caught on with
the girls.

The chapel stood on higher ground than School
House and consequently the slype, while leading
out of the vestry at one end, opened at the other on
to the first-floor corridor of School House—as it
happens, on to the corridor of the suite occupied by
Miss Langdon-Miles and myself. This arrangement
was always a great pleasure to Miss Langdon-Miles.
It meant that she and I virtually had a private
entrance to the chapel, since the girls were strictly

26

forbidden to use the corridor outside our rooms. Miss Langdon-Miles and I could, in a moment, when the gong went for prayers, pass from our own rooms through a door at the end of our corridor, along the slype and so by way of the vestry to our stalls in the choir. I fear we were also tempted to make use of the chapel as a short cut to the big lawn and so to the other houses. However, Miss Langdon-Miles's chief pleasure in the slype was, so she said, derived from the ease with which she could escape from the weary strain of the study to the peace of the chapel. Miss Langdon-Miles was a very devout woman and I scorn those who questioned her sincerity.

Upon the little chapel there had been lavished the very best that artists could produce. The Burne-Jones window, brought from the old buildings at Eastbourne, looked very lovely in its new setting. He is my favourite artist. Miss Langdon-Miles was always very nervous about safeguarding our treasures. There were our vestments and altar frontals, so exquisitely embroidered for us by the Sisters of St. Anne—an Anglican Order, of course—at their convent on Dartmoor. These were locked in the oak presses in the vestry. The Denvers altar plate and the little fourteenth-century pyx which Miss Langdon-Miles brought back from Nuremberg were kept in the safe in Miss Bussey's office. But there was always the Bellini.

Curtained off from the chancel on the north side was the lovely little Lavers Memorial Chapel—really just a small niche with a blue vault, fretted with silver stars. Here there hung the greatest treasure of Easton Knoyle, an 'Assumption of the Virgin' by Giovani Bellini. The pride which Miss

Langdon-Miles took in this, and indeed the pride of all at Easton Knoyle, may be imagined. I believe that Mr. Lavers paid quite a fabulous sum for the picture at the famous Reinbecker Sale in Philadelphia. That it was genuine has never been questioned.

As soon as Mr. Lavers made his gift I interviewed a police officer who had called to advise us as to what precautions could be taken against possible marauders. I felt that he took his duties very lightly. Clearly he had never heard of the gentle Giovani and considered us alarmists. However, Miss Langdon-Miles remembered the fate of the Mona Lisa and was taking no risks. Only when I mentioned the insurance company's valuation did the man become a little more helpful. In the end a special type of lock and an electric burglar alarm were placed on the great west door which opened on to the lawn. It was arranged that the alarm should sound in Miss Bussey's office and outside my room. The chapel windows were all of stained glass in iron frames, and it was not considered necessary to take any special precautions about the door from the vestry, since this only led, as I have explained, by way of the slype to the upper floor of School House. There were no other doors to the chapel. In spite of our precautions, we always felt deeply our responsibility as guardians of a treasure which was visited by connoisseurs from all over the world.

It would have been easy to keep the chapel locked, except when in use for services, but this—to Miss Langdon-Miles's mind—would have defeated its main purpose as a place of rest and meditation set apart from the turmoil of school life. Canon Fish strongly supported this view and so the west door was always open during the day; with girls and mistresses constantly passing across the big lawn, the risk was quite negligible. It was the duty of Totterdell, our trustworthy handyman, to lock the door at dusk, to switch on the burglar alarm and to hang up the keys in Miss Bussey's office. He was an excellent fellow and carried out his duties with unfailing regularity. Unfortunately he lived in the town; a great pity as it would have been most comforting to have had a man on the premises at night.

5

It seems sad to think that the work of adding beauty to such a precious building should produce discord and jealously but such—alas!—was the case. Our art mistress, Miss Trubshawe, thought that the choice, and even design, of all the furnishings, embroideries and so on was her province and that she should be consulted. Unfortunately Miss Trubshawe's views on art and those of Miss Langdon-Miles were diametrically opposed. Moreover, Miss Langdon-Miles regarded the chapel as her personal concern and would brook no interference and take no advice—except that of Canon Fish. This led to real friction and when passions are aroused, cause for quarrelling over other issues will not be far to seek. We spinsters are often inclined to make mountains out of mole-hills but Miss Trubshawe was sadly in the wrong, setting herself up in a very presumptuous manner.

I remember one horrid clash. Miss Trubshawe,

who took her work very seriously, was accustomed to pin up in the Art Room, from time to time, prints and photographs to illustrate Art Down the Ages. One morning, Miss Langdon-Miles entered the Art Room to find, to her horror, disgust and astonishment, that the walls had been plastered with an array of amazing productions—the works of, I think, Picasso—all absolutely incomprehensible. There were others of the modern French school; some of them—alas—only too comprehensible. You can imagine that Miss Langdon-Miles, with her high ideals of Purity and Beauty, was simply appalled; she told me afterwards that she had had the greatest difficulty in restraining herself before the girls. There was an atmosphere at the lunch table that day which one could have cut with a knife, and after lunch, in the Common Room, there was a 'stand-up row'. It was very painful and I was in an agony of embarrassment lest the raised voices should be heard beyond the Common Room door. Both women used words which, I am sure, they regretted later. Miss Langdon-Miles spoke of 'indecency' and 'degenerates'; Miss Trubshawe retaliated by saying that Miss Langdon-Miles, for all her intellectual snobbery, was nothing but a philistine. She then went further and, with an oblique reference to the confession box—which I considered unpardonable —she spoke of emotional spinsters being unduly influenced by their priests. Miss Langdon-Miles lost her temper, with a violence which was quite terrifying, and finally stormed out of the room. When she had gone there was an awful silence. Miss Trubshawe had gone very white, but calmly—although with shaking hand—poured herself out a cup of coffee and began to read *The Times*. We all took this as a signal to say no more, and drifted away to our afternoon duties.

I always try to be strictly impartial in these matters, but it was clear to me that Miss Trubshawe was entirely at fault. Modern art is quite outside my orbit, but when I compared the daubs in the Art Room with the perfect products of the Medici Society which adorned our classrooms I could not but be amazed at the wrongheadedness of a—presumably—well-educated woman. In any case Miss Langdon-Miles clearly had a right to the last word as to what should or should not be taught in her school. I therefore felt quite bowled over when, on the subject being reopened over the tea cups, I found that I had not the entire support of my colleagues. There are few things I dislike so much as lack of loyalty.

Miss Wheelwright considered that both Miss Trubshawe and Miss Langdon-Miles were guilty of riding their hobby horses. Now, in those days enough of my nonconformist tradition still clung to me to make me disapprove of a good deal that went on in the chapel. Nevertheless, to describe our liturgy—however 'high'—as Miss Langdon-Miles's 'hobby horse' seemed to me most improper, and I did not hesitate to say as much. Miss MacTaggart was wholeheartedly for Miss Trubshawe and accused me—incredibly—of currying favour. Fortunately MacTaggart's pronouncements never cut any ice. Miss Bell, with her usual acidity, remarked crudely that any art, to her mind, was more wholesome than 'the red mullet's pantomime.' I replied that while there might be room for disagreement, there was no need for blasphemy. Miss Bell's reply was not printable, but I went up to my room feeling quite out of touch with these younger women, and sadly bewildered and put out.

I was very astonished and rather touched when, later in the evening, Miss Trubshawe knocked at my door. She said that I was the only one to whom she could come for sympathy. I was quite overcome and rather gratified. I told her that I could never agree with her about the pictures, but that I did think Miss Langdon-Miles had been very hasty, speaking out as she did in public, and that the violent loss of temper had been unpardonable—whatever the provocation. Miss Trubshawe had felt quite humiliated, she told me, and then the poor thing broke down. In spite of her mistaken ideals, she was really very sensitive; she told me that she had had a very lonely life and had put everything in her work—of which, apparently, she took a very high view. The art classes had meant a lot to her and now she felt that her professional ability had been called in question. She doubted whether she could go on. I could not follow her in all her theories but I gathered that she had wanted to show the girls that Art was a living thing—not merely an affair of picture galleries. It was all Greek to me. The old masters, to my eye, reproduced Nature more truthfully than did these modernists and were, therefore, better painters—and that was all there was to it. However, I kept my opinions to myself and we had a very cosy heart-to-heart chat over our cocoa, parting the best of friends.

The next morning I tried to pour oil on troubled waters; intervening with Miss Langdon-Miles as tactfully as I could. She was still very distrait and I got a distinctly chilly reception. It was not, she said, the insult to her religion that had angered her—she was always prepared to suffer in silence for that; but what Miss Trubshawe had done in the Art Room was the very negation of those ideals for which she had striven so hard—ideals of sweetness and light. I also suspected that Miss Trubshawe's remarks about Canon Fish were rankling. There seemed to be little that I could say and a few weeks later there was another terrible scene—over Epstein, I think—and after the holidays Miss Trubshawe did not rejoin us. She and I were to meet again in most curious circumstances.

Well, I never intended to record the tittle-tattle of the Common Room and I really must get on with my story of all the queer things that happened at Easton Knoyle that winter. Mr. Muir has asked me to be very accurate and I should, therefore, like to record that although ten years have passed I have been able to verify many dates and facts from the School Log Book, so carefully written up each day by our competent Miss Bussey. The volumes lie before me now. I find that it was on the eighth of December, 1930, that we received our first visit from the mysterious and objectionable Mrs. Carberry.

6

Miss Langdon-Miles and I were at work in Miss Bussey's office, which overlooks the drive, when a large canary-coloured Rolls Royce car crunched over the gravel and stopped beneath the *portecochère*. To my mind the whole equipage was just a little too smart—vulgar in fact. The chauffeur, who proceeded to peel off several layers of rug from the car's only occupant, wore a mustard-coloured livery. Eventually, when the unwrapping process was complete, out stepped Mrs. Carberry, clasping a small black pug.

'Oh dear!' I said, and Miss Bussey raised her eyebrows and glanced at me as if she knew only too well what Miss Langdon-Miles's opinion would be. Miss Langdon-Miles gave a severe sniff of disapproval, and I heard her murmur *'Nouveau riche!'* As it turned out, she was very right.

Parkinson entered with a card: 'Mrs. Roderick Carberry, 62 Cosgrave Mansions, Knightsbridge, S.W.1.' Mrs. Carberry awaited us, seated regally in the centre of the drawing-room. She was rather a gorgeous creature and I suppose that many would have called her handsome; certainly she was statuesque—if rather *embonpoint*. I am afraid that—to use a common phrase—she was not my 'cup of tea' at all. The strong perfume which she used was discernible as soon as we entered the room. She ignored me completely, turning to Miss Langdon-Miles.

'I presume that I am speaking to Miss Langdon-Miles. You will, I know, be delighted to 'ear that my daughter Jennifer is to join you after Christmas. . . .'

'Really, Mrs. Carberry, that would be very delightful'—Miss Langdon-Miles had her own way of combining politeness with determination—'but I am not at all sure that it is possible.' Mrs. Carberry gasped. 'Perhaps you had not realised, Mrs. Carberry, that vacancies are few and far between at Easton Knoyle. May I ask where—er—Jennifer is at school at present?'

'Jennifer,' announced Mrs. Carberry, ' 'as been educated privately. No expense 'as been spared—of

that I can assure you. You will not find 'er backward
—far from it.'

'Expensive governesses, in our experience, Mrs.
Carberry, are not the best preparation for school
life. But that is neither here nor there—the real
difficulty is the vacancy.'

'My 'usband 'as to spend a year in Buenos Aires
and Rio,' said Mrs. Carberry pompously, 'and I
am to accompany 'im. We 'ad quite decided on
sending Jennifer to Easton Knoyle. I don't mind
tellin' you, Miss Langdon-Miles, that Roderick will
be really vexed.'

Clearly Mrs. Carberry was convinced that we
ought all to have been delighted to have her Jennifer
at Easton Knoyle, and was amazed at Miss Langdon-Miles's attitude. Miss Langdon-Miles, I knew
well, was thinking that Jennifer would probably be
quite impossible, and must be prevented. Mrs. Carberry rose. I have said that she was statuesque, but
she was almost impressive. She gathered her
leopard skin coat around her and settled the asth-
matic pug under her arm. Her use of jewellery and
cosmetics rivalled her use of perfume. Her elaborate
coiffure, its deep auburn tinge not unassisted by art,
showed from beneath a toque of violets.

'We will,' she announced, 'inspect the buildings.'
Mrs. Carberry was almost comic in her vulgarity, but
she was also offensive, and I suddenly felt a quite
irrational but overwhelming fear of the woman. I
had an instinct that there was something evil; here
was no former barmaid or chorus-girl with the proverbial heart of gold. This woman was as masterful
and ruthless as she was ignorant and ill-mannered.
I felt very frightened.

'Really, Mrs. Carberry,' said Miss Langdon-

35

Miles, 'is not this rather waste of time. Miss Coppock and I are both busy women, and I can assure you there is no vacancy.'

'Miss Langdon-Miles, I 'ave come to Torquay specially to see Easton Knoyle. I am at the Sheldon for a week and cannot 'ave my visit wasted. We leave for South America early in the new year—and we must get Jennifer fixed. As for the vacancy—I can assure you that Roderick will not bicker about fees. We can come to an arrangement, Miss Langdon-Miles.'

Miss Langdon-Miles winced. This outrageous suggestion of bribery must have hurt her delicate soul. Besides, fees were not things which one discussed at Easton Knoyle. It was true that they were extremely high but, except in the case of daughters of the clergy, for whom we had a most generous system of endowments, they were taken for granted.

But Mrs. Carberry was not to be got rid of easily. With a weary sigh and a shrug of resignation, Miss Langdon-Miles led the way. Perhaps a glance at the chapel would satisfy the wretch. But no! Mrs. Carberry insisted on going everywhere and seeing everything. Her inquisitiveness was outrageous and inexplicable. Even if the miserable Jennifer had been coming to Easton Knoyle it was altogether inexcusable—this poking and prying into every nook and corner. I really got quite hot with anger and embarrassment. Our morning, too, had been completely wrecked. I found myself asking why on earth this woman should want to explore Easton Knoyle in this manner—and I could find no answer.

Everywhere that Mrs. Carberry went she wounded Miss Langdon-Miles's deepest feelings, scoffing at our dearest schemes. When we came to the chapel I had to remain outside with the pug, but Miss Langdon-Miles told me afterwards that it was almost the only part of the school to which Mrs. Carberry paid but scant attention. She strolled around in a most irreverent fashion and our treasures obviously meant nothing to her. Her only comment was that they must have 'cost a pretty penny.' We came to our Gallery of Fame—our collection of portraits of the great women of history—and she dismissed it with a vulgar laugh as our 'Chamber of Horrors.' Poor Miss Langdon-Miles was on the verge of tears. Mrs. Carberry insisted on inspecting every classroom, interrupting the tenour of our morning studies, speaking to the mistresses and causing, of course, sniggering among the girls. She asked innumerable and apparently pointless questions about our time-table and about Miss Langdon-Miles's personal activities. It was insufferable. She went over the entire kitchen quarters, discussing her own domestic difficulties in a loud voice and making us look foolish before the maids. For two hours we traipsed wearily round Easton Knoyle.

Finally, to crown all, Mrs. Carberry fainted. It was on the second floor of School House where we were inspecting the girls' bedrooms. Mrs. Carberry had already decided that Jennifer must be under Miss Langdon-Miles's personal care at School House—neither St. Mary's nor Torrington House were good enough for Jennifer. She had even come to a final conclusion as to which should be Jennifer's room—balancing the rival claims of the view over Torbay and proximity to the fire escape—when suddenly she gave a gasp, a little scream and subsided in a crumpled heap on the floor.

Neither Miss Langdon-Miles nor myself were the

sort of women who lose their heads. I, for one, would willingly have let Mrs. Carberry lie where she was, but of course something had to be done. Miss Langdon-Miles plied her with smelling salts from her own handbag and dashed water in her face, while I hurried off to the first-aid box for a dose of brandy.

When I returned Mrs. Carberry had regained consciousness and was even having the grace to apologise. A few moments on the drawing-room sofa, she assured us, and she would be perfectly all right; her heart had always been a little troublesome and she had been up and down too many stairs during the morning. One might have retorted that that was nobody's fault but her own. Well, we assisted her as far as the first floor and then, in the corridor outside Miss Langdon-Miles's rooms she again collapsed—this time in a fit of sudden giddiness. By now she was in most pitiful disarray. Her make-up was blotchy, her toque removed and her elaborate coiffure sadly disorganised. Her *savoir faire* had completely vanished. There was nothing else for it; she must lie down either in Miss Langdon-Miles's room or in mine.

At that moment the gong sounded for luncheon, so an invitation to the high table—which I had been dreading—was at least avoided. Once more I took the wheezing pug in order to hand him to the mustard-liveried chauffeur, while Miss Langdon-Miles took charge of Mrs. Carberry. At last the pug was deposited in the car and Mrs. Carberry on the bed. Miss Langdon-Miles and I sat down to our lunch in a state of complete exhaustion. What a distressing and fatiguing morning it had been. The tone of the school, moreover, is not improved when, in front of the girls, the headmistress is compelled to dance attendance on such a harpy.

When Miss Langdon-Miles and I entered the dining-room, several minutes late, I was extremely pained to find distinct traces of amusement and even giggling among the girls. Most of our colleagues had sufficient tact to converse of other matters, but Frau Lauprecht immediately rushed into voluble comment. Really I could hardly blame her, for Mrs. Carberry, when visiting Frau Lauprecht's classroom, had made indiscreet remarks about the Germans.

Miss Langdon-Miles tried to dismiss the whole affair philosophically, but later she confided to me that she shared my feeling that there was something evil about Mrs. Carberry and that there was really something quite mysterious and inexplicable about her inordinate curiosity. However, Miss Langdon-Miles had a proper sense of her duties as a hostess, and between the courses she asked me to slip upstair to see whether Mrs. Carberry had recovered sufficiently to take a light lunch or a cup of coffee.

Then there happened a curious thing; perhaps it was not important but it left me with an uncomfortable feeling that all was not well. You may think that I am just a foolish old woman, and that it is very old-fashioned to write about a woman's intuition but I can assure you that mine has seldom misled me. It may all have been harmless and trivial but my uncanny intuition told me otherwise—and I don't mind saying that I hardly slept a wink that night.

I opened the door of Miss Langdon-Miles's bedroom as quietly as I could since I thought that Mrs. Carberry might be asleep. But evidently she had recovered for she was not on the bed at all. She was standing by Miss Langdon-Miles's dressing-table, looking out of the window on to the Poets' Garden. Now the tall mirror in Miss Langdon-Miles's room was placed cornerwise, diagonally opposite the door; as I entered Mrs. Carberry had her back to me, but I could see her profile clearly in the mirror. I could swear solemnly that, the instant Mrs. Carberry realised that I was there, she bit her lip and a look of intense annoyance came over her face. If a woman will insist on covering her face with a disgusting coat of paint it is difficult to judge, but I feel certain that she went quite crimson with anger. In a couple of seconds she had recovered herself and was making a pretence of adjusting her complexion—but I could not forget what I had seen.

'Miss Langdon-Miles sent me, Mrs. Carberry,' I said, 'to see whether you felt better. Perhaps a cup of coffee . . .'

'Nothing, thank you, Miss Coppock.' Then, very oddly, she began to gush. 'Really nothing at all; you are too kind, too kind. I have wasted far too much of your precious time already.'

This was undoubtedly true but it seemed a little late for these effusive apologies.

'If you have rested sufficiently, Mrs. Carberry,' I said, 'perhaps you would like to say good-bye to Miss Langdon-Miles before you go.'

'Miss Coppock, on no account. You must thank 'er for me, and please, I beg you, apologise to 'er. I must have wasted 'er 'ole morning—and such a wonderful woman. Now I must get back to the Sheldon for lunch—I'm late already.'

Mrs. Carberry continued her effusive thanks all the way down to the front door. I was quite glad not to have to disturb Miss Langdon-Miles again, and Mrs. Carberry now seemed satisfied with the vaguest of assurances that, should a vacancy occur, we would write to her.

'If it should 'appen, Miss Coppock, if it should 'appen, of course Jennifer will be as pleased as Punch, and Roderick. But I can see your difficulties. And now I mustn't keep you another moment. Good-bye, Miss Coppock, good-bye.'

The mustard-liveried chauffeur once more wrapped the rugs around her and planted the pug on her lap, and once more the canary-coloured limousine crunched over the gravel. But that was not the last of Mrs. Carberry.

7

I returned to the high table to report this extraordinary conclusion to Mrs. Carberry's visit.

'Most peculiar,' I said, 'but at the end she was really apologetic—almost anxious not to give further trouble. By the way, Miss Langdon-Miles, it was kind of you to let the creature rest in your room; mine was, of course, available.'

'But, Coppock dear, she used your room, I left her on your bed. We came to the door of your room first and she looked like collapsing again.'

'But, Miss Langdon-Miles, she was up and was using your dressing-table.'

I had noticed that Miss Langdon-Miles's bed had not been disturbed but I had given Mrs. Carberry credit for having put everything straight again. Miss Langdon-Miles and I looked at each other and each knew what the other was thinking. Mrs. Carberry had been left on my bed, why should she be in Miss Langdon-Miles's room at all?

Never to think ill of others is always my motto, but try as I would I could not find a charitable explanation of Mrs. Carberry's conduct. Perhaps—feeling better—she had started to find her way downstairs but, still bemused by her giddy fit, had accidently gone through the wrong door, thus finding herself in Miss Langdon-Miles's bedroom. This was really a most unsatisfactory solution of the problem and I knew, in my own mind, that it was no solution at all.

Miss Langdon-Miles and I, as I have explained, had our own rooms in a self-contained wing. We each had two rooms, a sitting-room and a bedroom. Between sitting-room and bedroom, in each case, was a door; each of the four rooms also opened on to the corridor. Between Miss Langdon-Miles's rooms and mine, however, there was no intercommunicating door.

Mrs. Carberry must have got up from the bed in my room and—either directly or by way of my sitting-room, reached the corridor. It was quite a short corridor and at one end, on her left as she came out of my little suite, Mrs. Carberry could not have failed to see the main staircase. Even if she had still been a little dazed, the big oak newel posts were plainly silhouetted against the tall stairway window. Opposite her, across the corridor, would be two doors, one to our linen-room and one to the bathroom. This bathroom was shared by Miss Langdon-Miles and myself, but was used by no one else. At the other end of the corridor, that is on Mrs. Carberry's right, was the handsome copper-studded door which led to the slype and to the chapel.

That Mrs. Carberry should turn to the right, away from the staircase, and then a second time to the right into one or other of Miss Langdon-Miles's rooms seemed quite incredible—however faint or giddy she might be. No, the more charitable explanation must be rejected. Even a couple of hours of Mrs. Carberry's company had shown clearly that mere vulgar curiosity could not be ruled out. It was dreadful to think that the woman, in the few minutes that she was alone, had been prying and poking around our rooms. But what else could I think? The angry face which I had seen for a moment in the mirror certainly fitted in with such an explanation. I had caught Mrs. Carberry red-handed in her explorations and she had, not unnaturally, been annoyed. It was very unpleasant. And even if curiosity was the explanation—what was the motive? Mrs. Carberry had recovered from her malaise with suspicious rapidity and it was beginning to dawn upon me that her whole visit was excessively odd from beginning to end.

After lunch I went up to my room and was disgusted to find that the odour of Mrs. Carberry's perfume still hung in the air. I flung open the window. There was no doubt about it. Except for the little drop of *eau de Cologne* in which I indulge when suffering from one of my bilious headaches, I never use scent of any kind, and to Miss Langdon-Miles it was abhorrent. In any case, it was forbidden to the girls and an example must be set. I investigated further; in both my rooms and in both Miss Langdon-Miles's rooms the odour was very plain. I crossed the corridor; it was also to be traced in the bathroom. It was clear that Mrs. Carberry had thoroughly investigated the entire wing.

I hope that my readers will not think that I have a suspicious nature when I admit that, having re-arranged my bed, which Mrs. Carberry had left in a chaotic state, I looked in my dressing-table drawer to see whether my jewels were intact. I am afraid that it must sound rather pretentious to speak of my jewels in that way. But there was the little silver crucifix which Miss Langdon-Miles and the girls had given me in Venice; I also had two or three rings and the antique topaz pendant and earrings which my dear, dear Aunt Bertha, old Mrs. Bradford, had given me on my 'twenty-first'—thirty years ago! There were also a few other gew-gaws which I had accumulated through the years—mostly just of sentimental value. Everything was quite intact; neither the drawer nor the jewel box had been tampered with. No doubt I had been absurdly sus-picious, but I was very relieved.

I tried to dismiss the whole Carberry affair from my mind, but the ghost would not be laid. I kept turning the facts over and over, but no satisfactory explanation could I find. The whole horrid business was a discord in the sweet harmony of existence at Easton Knoyle, and I went about my afternoon's work with a heavy heart.

8

First on my list was an appointment with Miss Wheelwright at The Firs. Mrs. Adams, the cook at The Firs, was becoming rather difficult after many years of faithful service. Dr. Potts had recently placed the junior girls on a regimen based on the latest dietetic principles, and Mrs. Adams was proving most recalcitrant. In consultation with Miss Wheelwright I had to decide whether a change must be made.

Now, although it was forbidden to the girls, I must admit that if Miss Langdon-Miles or I wanted to reach any of the other Easton Knoyle houses from our rooms we often made our way through the slype and the chapel, emerging by the west door on to the big lawn. This was quite a short cut compared with the alternative of going down to the ground floor and out of School House by the main door. Miss Langdon-Miles never quite liked using the chapel in this way, as a sort of corridor, but it was a great saving and I am afraid that it had become a regular habit. Miss Langdon-Miles always genuflected most reverently when she crossed the chancel. As for me, I always slipped quietly down the side aisle, thus avoiding what I always felt to be an embarrassing dilemma.

Having tidied my room and put on my goloshes I set out for The Firs. I passed through the copper-studded door at the end of the corridor and into the slype. The slype windows were all closed and the door ahead into the vestry was shut, so I suppose the slype was not very well ventilated. At any rate although half an hour had passed, once again I could detect the odour of Mrs. Carberry's perfume. I sniffed. It was quite distinct. I went on into the vestry. There it was again. In spite of the traces of incense which hung in the air, there could be no doubt about it. It was very odd. During the morning the chapel had been the only building in which Mrs. Carberry had taken only a perfunctory interest.

Now it appeared that she had been exploring it in secret.

I thought that perhaps I would ask Miss Wheelwright's opinion; she certainly had more sense than many I could mention in the Common Room. Then some instinct which I cannot explain made me change my mind. I decided that, for the moment, I would keep my own counsel. I went on my way through the chapel.

Everyone at Easton Knoyle was expected to rest for a full hour after lunch. With the little ones at The Firs this rule was strictly kept and I knew I should find the house quiet and that Miss Wheelwright would be in her room. Like myself, however, she was not one of those who took to her bed during our 'siesta' and I thought that this would be a good time for a chat.

As I crossed the lawn I felt glad that I had put on my goloshes; there had been a slight frost during the morning but now the grass was distinctly damp. I went in, out of the cold air, to find Miss Wheelwright's room in a state of complete 'fug', with the gasfire blazing away. Miss MacTaggart, our new English mistress, was there and both women were smoking over their after-lunch brew. Frankly, I was not altogether pleased to see Miss MacTaggart; she was a young woman about whom the words 'brilliant' and 'progressive' had been used when she joined the staff. I never knew on what authority. New brooms sweep clean. Personally I found her meretricious and flippant; perhaps her good qualities were reserved for her work and were thus hidden from me. She waved a tea cup at me as I entered the room.

'Hurray! Coppock. Scandal at Easton Knoyle at

last! Wheelwright has seen a sinister man accosting the girls. It will just about be the death of Miles.'

I took off my wrap and goloshes in silence. I was aghast but was not going to show it. How any decent woman could treat the matter in this frivolous fashion was quite beyond me. I settled myself in Wheelwright's arm-chair with a cup of tea before saying a word.

'What on earth do you mean, MacTaggart? Naturally Miss Langdon-Miles will be horrified—who would not be? But what is it all about?'

'Oh, it's Wheelwright's story; I won't deprive her of the pleasure of telling it, but you'll be terribly shocked. I bet, though, that the parents know more that we do already; the little devils would never leave that out of their letters.'

Miss MacTaggart had a most astonishing way of looking at things. A sinister man accosting the girls! If true it was terribly distressing. On top of the Carberry mystery too! It will be readily understood that at a school such as Easton Knoyle we always had to be most cautious and circumspect about things of this kind. Such delicate matters were never referred to—naturally—but it was always tacitly understood by us all, or so I believed, that our sacred guardianship of the girls' lives carried with it, as a first obligation, the warding off of all taint or suggestion of the more unsavoury things of this world. That, surely, goes without saying. I was truly shocked at Miss MacTaggart's attitude. Like the rest of her generation she seemed to lack all right feeling in these matters and to have no proper sense of her vocation.

Although I was shocked I was not altogether surprised that immoralty should have reared its ugly head in this way. Miss Langdon-Miles had what some called enlightened views about the liberty which should be allowed the girls; it was intended, I was told, to create responsibility and good citizenship; but liberty, in my experience, soon becomes licence—then where are you? I suppose I am old-fashioned—I am not ashamed of the fact. The little ones from The Firs, were of course, always escorted on their expeditions to the shops or the beach, but on half-holidays the older girls were allowed to roam the town as they pleased. True, we had always regarded Torquay as a very 'safe' place—but then, as I always say, you can't be too careful. And here was the proof. . . .

The previous afternoon had been a half-holiday; after lunch Miss Wheelwright and I had been to the shops together. When I had matched some wool and we had both changed our library books I left her, as she had an appointment at the hairdresser's, and returned to have tea in my own room. Presumably it was after I had left Miss Wheelwright that the incident of the sinister man had occurred. I ignored Miss MacTaggart and turned to Miss Wheelwright for details.

'It was after you left me, Coppock. I bought my new stockings and then I had a shampoo.'

'I can see that,' I said.

'Then I went to Mellor's for an early cup of tea. It was only about half past three and the café was almost empty. But there, at a table in the window at the far end, were Gay Clintock and Prudence Lloyd, munching hot-buttered toast and Devonshire cream. . . .'

'How thoroughly indigestible . . .' I began, but Miss Wheelwright went on with her story.

'As I say, the café was nearly empty and I took a table near the door. I am sure that neither Gay nor Prudence saw me. Then, after about five minutes, in came "Mr. Pym." '

'Mr. Pym!' I exclaimed.

'Oh, that's not his real name—that's what the girls call him. He made a bee-line for their table as though he had arranged to meet them. He was a dapper, elderly little man, very well dressed and, I must admit, quite gentlemanly looking.'

'Well, that's something,' I said. I had been expecting to hear the story of some ruffian.

'Depend upon it, Coppock,' said Miss Mac-Taggart dramatically, 'that was just a mask. It's a clear case of attempted abduction, if ever there was one!'

I gasped—and then I caught Miss Wheelwright's eye and said no more. If Miss MacTaggart thought she could pull my leg, then she was barking up quite the wrong tree.

'He hailed the girls from the other side of the café,' went on Miss Wheelwright, 'he was most friendly and familiar. "Well, well, here we are again—all bobbish and cheerful," that was how he greeted them. It was only too plain that they had all met before. I heard one of the girls say: "Oh, Mr. Pym, we haven't seen you for ages and ages." Then they all sat down and "Mr. Pym" ordered ice-cream concoctions all round.'

'Fancy!' I said, 'on top of hot-buttered toast. . . .'

'I picked up my cup of tea,' continued Miss Wheelwright, 'and moved a few tables nearer, but the café was beginning to fill up and I would only hear a word or two, now and again. What I did hear

49

certainly sounded quite harmless. "Mr. Pym" was asking them about school life, games and so on.'

'Ah!' said Miss MacTaggart, 'that was just his cunning. Mark my words, Coppock, he was trying to gain their confidence.'

I was not to be drawn; I ignored the woman pointedly, and Miss Wheelwright went on with her story.

'There was so much noise going on in the café including a beastly loud-speaker—that I really couldn't hear what they were saying. But I sat on till after five o'clock. At last "Mr. Pym" got up to go, but not until they had each had two more ice creams.'

It all sounded very ominous and quite contrary, of course, to School Rules. But I suppose it might have been worse; it seemed as though the girls' digestions might have suffered more than their morals. But Miss Wheelwright had not finished.

'After "Mr. Pym" had gone,' she said, 'I went over to the girls and tackled them about it. They didn't mind having been caught, in fact I think that they thought I was making a great fuss about nothing. I said that surely they knew that they mustn't talk to strangers. "Oh, that wasn't a stranger, Miss Wheelwright," Prudence said, "that was only Mr. Pym." Well, to cut a long story short,' went on Miss Wheelwright, 'it seems that the whole school—except of course the wretched staff—knows all about "Mr. Pym." Lots of the senior girls have met him, and Prudence and Gay and Miranda have all been to Paignton with him on the tram.'

'Good Heavens!' I said.

'If you want to know my opinion,' said Miss Mac-Taggart, 'I think it's pretty bloody the way we never know what goes on.' I nearly retorted that we didn't want her opinion, but decided to hold my tongue.

'Surely,' I said, 'the girls must know how unwise they were. How did this "Mr. Pym" business start?'

'It was difficult to get the whole story,' said Miss Wheelwright, 'you know how Prudence will giggle when she's trying to tell you anything, but apparently the first time they met him was on the beach last summer, and as MacTaggart was with them at the time they thought that that made everything all right.'

'Really, MacTaggart,' I said, 'what were you thinking of? You may well have incurred the gravest responsibility. . . .'

'Well, he seemed quite harmless,' said Miss Mac-Taggart airily, 'and anyway he only had his bathing dress on; how could I know that he was a White Slave Trafficker? . . .'

'Oh, do be quiet,' I said, 'you don't seem to realise that there has been a grave breach of the rules. Miss Langdon-Miles will be horrified when she realises that this may have been going on for weeks. Why, the police may have to be informed!'

'Now, Coppock, don't panic,' said Miss MacTaggart rudely. 'I expect our "Mr. Pym" is just a harmless, friendly little chap—feeling a bit lonely.'

'You are hardly in a position to take a light view of the matter, MacTaggart. If anything really dreadful happens—and, please God, it won't—the blame will lie fairly and squarely on your shoulders.'

'Oh, don't talk rats, Coppock.' The woman's manners were deplorable, but I think I had shaken her. I turned to Miss Wheelwright again.

'And why, may I ask, is this suspicious character called "Mr. Pym"?'

'The girls have christened him "Mr. Pym",' said Miss Wheelwright, 'because he keeps coming and going; they see him one day at Mellor's, then he disappears for perhaps two or three weeks, and then turns up on the front or in the town.'

This explanation got me no further and it was only later that I learnt that 'Mr. Pym' was a character in some piece which was playing on the West End boards just then. There seems to be very little, nowadays, that the girls do not know.

Clearly something must be done and without a moment's delay. Miss Langdon-Miles, to my mind, should call a staff meeting. Apart from Miss Mac-Taggart's palpable guilt in failing to nip 'Mr. Pym's' intrigues in the bud, I was quite unable to accept her irresponsible view that the less fuss we made the better. The whole reputation of Easton Knoyle might be at stake; half the Sixth Form, apparently, had been gallivanting round Devonshire with this unknown *roué*. Anything might have happened, and Heaven knows what exaggerated version might have reached the parents! Meanwhile the room was getting quite airless, and as rational conversation with Miss MacTaggart was not possible I decided to abandon my discussion with Miss Wheelwright about the new cook. I therefore returned to School House, leaving the two women to continue their gossip and tittle tattle if they chose.

I got back to my own little sitting-room feeling quite distracted. It had been a truly terrible day! To rid my mind of both 'Mr. Pym' and Mrs. Carberry I set about the washing of stockings and woollies—but in vain. I was quite exhausted and was very glad when Parkinson at last arrived with my tea-tray. I was allowed this little privilege in deference to my age and position, and never had I been so glad to escape the chatter of the Common Room. It would, I think, have been more than I could bear.

I settled down cosily with my feet on the fender, and began my weekly letter to my dear Aunt Bertha —finding it a great relief to set down my thoughts on paper. Dear Aunt Bertha—old Mrs. Bradford of Bath—she is over ninety now but is still a very queenly old lady, with such beautiful dresses and such magnificent jewellery. For over thirty years she had been almost more than a mother to me and ever since my mother's death I have written to her every week. I never missed, except, of course, for that wonderful fortnight which I spent with her at Coquet Hall each summer. My letters to her must have formed quite a detailed diary of my life and of events at Easton Knoyle. I told her everything. Certainly on that particular occasion there was no lack of news, and I remember writing a long, long letter to Aunt Bertha—all about Mrs. Carberry and 'Mr. Pym.'

Well, I never meant to start telling you all about Aunt Bertha in this manner. And I find, on looking back over my story, that I have quite forgotten to mention that two weeks later Miss Wheelwright and I found 'Mr. Pym' hiding at the bottom of a pew in the chapel—a most perilous episode.

9

Miss Langdon-Miles was a strong-minded woman; having once come to a decision she seldom changed her mind. I was, therefore, surprised and shocked when, on coming downstairs the next morning, I was greeted with the news that Jennifer Carberry would have to come to Easton Knoyle after all. Miss Langdon-Miles, sensitive soul, was almost in tears.

'All we can hope for,' she said, 'is that the governesses have made her a little more presentable than her mother.'

'Why!' I exclaimed. 'Whatever has happened to make you change you mind like this? Mark my words, Miss Langdon-Miles, the tone of the school will suffer—we have more than enough *nouveaux riches* already.'

'You're right, Coppock, you're right, but what can I do? It's all the fault of this horrible American crisis. The banks and stockbrokers are going down like ninepins. Zoë Denver's sister has cried off and so have the Van Huysen girls. They say that if they manage a month in Europe next summer, it's all they'll do. It's really too bad. That leaves at least three vacancies, and if Jennifer Carberry is next on the list we have got to have her.'

'In my opinion,' I said, 'it's a most short-sighted policy; I have never agreed with the Governors in the matter. How can the social tone of the school be preserved if we let in the children of every Tom, Dick and Harry! But, of course, it's not for me to say. . . .'

Really, the morning was going badly. Miss Mac-

Taggart had started the trouble before breakfast. I had begun to hope that she and Miss Wheelwright were no more than a couple of alarmists. I was glad to think that I am among those who can keep calm while others are losing their heads. It was, after all, quite probable that 'Mr. Pym's' intentions were honourable, or at least harmless; and if Mrs. Carberry had been unpardonably inquisitive—well, what of it? Probably, I had been thinking, we shall never see her again. I considered, therefore that Miss MacTaggart was merely being impertinent when she greeted me on the stairs in her usual familiar way.

'Good-morning, Coppock. Been dreaming of our little friend and his White Slave gang?'

'Really,' I said, 'I don't know to whom you refer.'

'They use a hypodermic, Coppock dear—and when their victims come round, there they are in a South American brothel. Or perhaps he's a Mormon!' I had passed on in dignified silence, only to be greeted by Miss Langdon-Miles with this additional bad news.

'We must hope for the best,' she said, 'but I decline to deal with Mrs. Carberry herself. Be a dear, Coppock, and telephone her later at the Sheldon; say how delighted we shall be to have dear Jennifer —but it must be St. Mary's, I won't have her at School House.'

'Very well,' I said. 'And oh! Miss Langdon-Miles, have you heard about "Mr. Pym"?'

'If you mean have I heard about the man in Mellor's café; yes, I have—and I don't wish to discuss it.'

I felt rather snubbed. I suppose that Miss Wheelwright must have spoken to Miss Langdon-Miles the previous evening; I couldn't help but feel that it should have been left to me to tell her about 'Mr. Pym.' After all, I was her recognised *confidante*—or so I had always believed. However, some people are always anxious to be the bearers of bad news.

Just before our 'elevenses' I rang up the Sheldon and asked for Mrs. Carberry.

'No, madam, there is no Mrs. Carberry stopping here.'

'Carberry,' I repeated, 'c-a-r-b-e-r-r-y.'

'I heard the name the first time, madam. No Mrs. Carberry on our books at all.'

'Most extraordinary!' I said. 'Most extraordinary! Perhaps the rooms were reserved in another name. Pray find out whether you have a lady at the Sheldon with a yellow Rolls Royce car.' There was a buzz at the other end of the line, and I waited.

'No, madam. Our garage man says there has been a black Rolls in at the week-end, but no yellow one. . . .' I rang off sharply. My intuition had not betrayed me.

'Well,' I said, 'whoever heard of such a thing?'

I flatter myself that I know how to act in a crisis. I turned to Miss Bussey.

'Bussey,' I said, 'will you please send a telegram to Mrs. Carberry, 62 Cosgrave Mansions, Knightsbridge, saying how delighted we shall be to see Jennifer next term.'

Later that afternoon, when I was crossing the hall, I saw a telegraph boy cycling up the drive. I waited and took his message myself. It was not a telegram; it was a little blue form: 'Your telegram to Carberry has not been delivered . . . address and addressee unknown.'

'Well!' I said.

Miss Langdon-Miles was actually rather pleased to think that the Jennifer problem had been so easily solved. She considered that we had done our duty towards Mrs. Carberry and were well rid of her. I could not share this complacency, and I confess that once again I had a sleepless night.

10

The last day of the Winter Term began and ended disastrously. It was the day of our Christmas play and was always something of an occasion. Of course the principal event of our social round was Speech Day in June, but quite a number of parents managed to get down to Torquay for the play. That year there was to be a little ceremony in the Assembly Hall before the curtain rose, and it was here that our misfortunes began.

Miss Langdon-Miles had, to my mind, done an extremely rash thing. A new and beautifully carved Honours Board was to be unveiled and Miss Langdon-Miles had actually invited Captain Carhampton to speak! I was astonished. The man had never been to Easton Knoyle before, but what one had heard did not redound to his credit. It was true that Felicity's name was the first to appear on the new Honours Board, with an Exhibition to Girton; I suppose the child had more brains than manners. It was also true that Captain Carhampton, although leading a very loose and gadabout life, had recently been returned as Member for Bournemouth West—in the Tory interest I believe. Moreover he was an extremely wealthy man. Snobbery, however, even by the malicious, could never have been regarded as one of Miss Langdon-Miles's failings. The whole thing was most incomprehensible.

I had spent a hectic morning, supervising the packing of the girls' trunks, arranging train schedules and seeing to it that Parkinson had the tea arrangements well in hand. Miss MacTaggart's absurdly elaborate contrivances for the setting of the Christmas play—and the resulting mess—had thrown all Easton Knoyle into a state of utter chaos. Why Miss MacTaggart was allowed such licence was beyond me. I sat down to lunch—to a very scratch meal—quite prostrate with exhaustion. Then Miss MacTaggart, unable as usual to keep her tongue still, threw the first shadow across the proceedings by informing the table at large that, when visiting her dentist, she had come across a portrait of Captain Carhampton in the *Tatler*, dining at a place called, I think, Quaglino's with a woman other than Mrs. Carhampton. He was moreover, referred to as 'Captain Reginald ("Bongo") Carhampton.' All this was most ominous and I also disapproved of Miss MacTaggart gossiping in this fashion—such things are better left unsaid.

This lunch-table discussion was in full swing when the young man himself drove up, a full hour before his time, in a noisy, crimson 'sports' car. Then Miss Langdon-Miles actually asked me to entertain the Captain for an hour by showing him round the school. I was dumbfounded, but I must say that he soon put me at my ease. His manner was familiar, but he was decidedly good-looking with his smart military moustachios. His gay badinage made me feel quite youthful and I wondered whether my suspicions had not been ill-founded. I dare say that many of the things said about him were calumnies. Felicity hung on to her father's arm, addressing him as 'Bongo' and so far forgetting herself as to call me 'Coppy dear!' The climax came when she and the Captain wanted to pack me into the crimson car, if you please, and take me off to the Sheldon for a 'cocktail'!! I began to wonder whether they were not having me on, as the saying is. When three o'clock came and we were all safely gathered into the Assembly Hall I was in quite a whirl.

Then came Captain Carhampton's speech—a ghastly disaster. I watched Miss Langdon-Miles biting her lip, twisting her lorgnette chain nervously between her fingers and visibly growing paler and paler. As for me, I got hotter and hotter. Our visitors kindly tried to laugh off the whole affair, but a terrible impression must have been made. He began by saying that he had had the pleasure of being shown round the school by 'Miss Coppock, a very charming young lady'—and me past fifty! Well, of course, I hardly knew where to put myself. A very audible remark from the MacTaggart woman about dark horses kicking over the traces, only shows you how little mutual loyalty there was in the Common Room. I had explained to Captain Carhampton that the carved border to the Honours Board was composed of lilies—for purity—intertwined with sprays of amaryllis—the emblem of Easton Knoyle; a most charming and suggestive symbolism. To that man, however, nothing was sacred. It was news to him, he said, that an amaryllis was a flower, he had always regarded it as something with which one sported in the shade! He would have to go back to school and—by Jove!—didn't he wish it could be

Easton Knoyle! So he ran on, dropping bricks by the cartload. At last he seemed to have reached what I suppose must be called his peroration—only to wind up by congratulating Miss Langdon-Miles on her admirable success in—if you please—'grooming fillies for the debutante stakes!' Miss Langdon-Miles told me afterwards that the room positively swam before her eyes and that she seriously feared lest she would collapse. Canon Fish, I observed, fixed his gaze on the ceiling, all the colour drained from his usually ruddy complexion. By the Mercy of Heaven I was near the door and was able to slip out as the Captain finished speaking. I was quite prostrate with embarrassment and felt that I must retire to the Common Room for a few moments to regain my calm. Then a very odd incident occurred.

As I crossed the hall the building seemed quiet. The maids were in the drawing-room, putting the finishing touches to tea, everyone else was in the Assembly Hall. I soon felt a little better—at one stage I had feared lest I should faint—and as I did not wish to miss the play, I returned to the Assembly Hall. As I passed the foot of the staircase I stopped, quite frozen with horror. A slight noise had made me look upwards and there, I was almost certain, I saw between the balusters—just disappearing from view—a trousered leg! It was extremely alarming! No doubt it was one of our visitors, but why should one of them be slinking off to the upper regions in this fashion? My first impulse—for I do not lack my share of physical courage—was to seize the gong stick and follow the leg. Discretion, however, is often the better part of valour and I decided to consult Miss Wheelwright first. Unfortunately, in pushing my way through the crowd in the Assembly Hall, I got jammed well to the front and to have extricated myself would only have caused an embarrassing disturbance.

You can imagine my state of mind! Exhausted by showing Captain Carhampton round the school, bowled over by his dreadful speech, and now in a twitter of alarm as to what might be going on upstairs, I was pinned against a radiator, unable to move. Then the curtain went up and—to crown all—the play itself departed sadly from Easton Knoyle traditions. Throughout the term—ever since I had known that Miss MacTaggart, as English mistress, would be responsible for the choice and mounting of the piece—I had had grave fears. The first part was excellent. The little ones from The Firs, under Miss Wheelwright's artistic direction, gave four Shakespearean *tableaux vivants*. Nothing could have been in better taste than the fairies poised gracefully in the moonlight around Titania, and a most vivid and macabre representation, in a green glow, of Banquo's ghost, quite brought the house down. Then, however, came what was intended to be the *bonne bouche*; it seemed endless. Why on earth Miss Langdon-Miles had ever sanctioned Miss MacTaggart's plunge into Restoration drama was quite beyond me —perhaps she had assumed that there would be judicious expurgation. But no! Captain Carhampton's guffaws only emphasised what might otherwise have passed unnoticed. I am a loyal subject but never, never have the strains of 'the King' been so welcome. I thought they would never come, and the radiator, meanwhile, was getting very hot indeed.

At last everyone began to drift through for tea. Spying Miss Wheelwright, I made a bee-line for her, only to be buttonholed myself by the MacTaggart, who hissed melodramatically in my ear.

'Friend "Pym" is about!· He must have slipped in with the crowd.'

'My God!' I said, and passed on ignoring her completely. It seemed a lifetime before I could detach Miss Wheelwright from the group around her. We decided not to raise a general alarm, and so slipped quietly upstairs, Miss Wheelwright with the gong stick and myself with a riding crop. All seemed quiet and we felt a little foolish going through the empty bedrooms in that fashion—armed *cap-à-pie*! Nothing seemed to have been disturbed. Miss Langdon-Miles's trunk and my grip, both strapped and labelled ready for the morrow, were just as I had left them before lunch. True, the little medicine cupboard in the bathroom was open, but that was really immaterial as Miss Langdon-Miles and I had packed everything that was in it; it might, in any case, have been left ajar during the morning's rush. Everything seemed in order. Miss Langdon-Miles, I had noticed, was wearing her pearls, and my few jewels were packed; so that was all right too. Miss Wheelwright and I went on through the slype; the far door into the vestry was wide open and the incense from the Advent services hung heavy in the air.

It was the year's shortest day and the chapel, although it was barely four o'clock, was very dark. Even on the brightest day the stained glass and the heavy stone tracery produced that religious gloom so dear to the heart of Miss Langdon-Miles and Canon Fish. At this hour the effect was even more awe-inspiring. Normally Totterdell should have locked up by now, but he had been instructed to leave it a little later than usual, since so many parents liked to inspect our treasures. The crib and manger near the west door, built by the little ones at The Firs, had attracted much attention; its success, I remember, had almost reconciled me to the awful mess made by the straw. Looking down the chapel from the vestry, Miss Wheelwright and I could see out through the west door and across the big lawn to the drive. There had been a powdering of snow and as the beams of car headlights fell across the white grass it seemed lighter outside than in. The sounds of Christmas excitement and departing cars reached us through the frosty air.

Inside the chapel the altar candles, the sanctuary lamp and a few tapers round the crib could hardly pierce the darkness and the incense clouds. A shudder of mystical emotion ran through me, and then I turned to the business in hand. Suddenly Miss Wheelwright clutched my arm; she thought she had seen a movement away in the gloom at the far end of the chapel. I whispered to her to take the central aisle, while I took the side one. We advanced cautiously on tiptoe down the chancel steps. I remembered that I was uncovered and put my handkerchief on my head, signalling violently to Miss Wheelwright to do the same. Whether the handkerchiefs would remain in position if the gong stick or riding crop were brought into action I could not say —but we had done our best.

We got half-way from the chancel to the west door. Suddenly we both stood transfixed, petrified! A man's head was slowly rearing itself up from the depths of a corner pew. The pew was right at the back of the chapel, beyond the diffused glow of the tapers around the crib, and it was difficult to see what was going on, but undoubtedly it was a man. He must have seen us too, for slowly the whole figure emerged and 'Mr. Pym', if it was 'Mr. Pym', skipped nimbly across the chapel, silhouetted for a moment against the white lawn outside.

'Hi!' I shouted, feeling both ridiculous and irreverent.

My voice echoed strangely in the empty chapel. The man hesitated and then, with considerable presence of mind, knelt down and began to pray. This was most disconcerting. After all, Miss Wheelwright and I were acting on the vaguest suspicions; the whole affair might be a mare's nest and although prayer, in any shape or form, seemed strangely at variance with the sinister *roué* of Mellor's café, one hardly cared to interrupt anyone's devotions. It might even be—who knows?—a sign of repentence. I signalled to Miss Wheelwright to sit down and wait.

The minutes passed and still 'Mr. Pym' remained on his knees. Now and again the flash of headlights flitted down the distant drive, and a draught coming in through the west door would make the candles flicker. I could hear Miss Wheelwright breathing in little gasps. I began to feel very nervous and wished that someone would come. Then it occurred to me that if this man was really the owner of the trousered leg which I had seen disappearing upstairs, just before the play began, he must have been hidden in the depths of that corner pew for nearly two hours. Then, when he saw us advancing with gong stick and riding crop he must have realised that the game was up—and revealed himself.

Feeling more and more desperate I began to creep

across to Miss Wheelwright to tell her what I was thinking and to concert our plan of campaign. Then another idea struck me and really put me in quite a panic. 'Mr. Pym' may have intended to remain hidden at the bottom of the pew until after Totterdell had locked up, leaving him there for the night. A cold sweat came over me as I realised that, in that case, the way back through the vestry and the slype to my room and to Miss Langdon Miles's room would have been open to him! He might quite easily have murdered us in our beds—and God knows what else! Clearly we were face to face with a very ugly customer. Hurriedly I whispered to Miss Wheelwright all that I was thinking.

'I can't hear a word you say,' she exclaimed. 'Do speak up, Coppock.' This was unkind and I began to sob.

'Mr. Pym' must have seen us whispering. I fear that the wretch was never really praying at all, but was watching us all the time between his fingers. How despicable! Then he suddenly leapt up and, before we could collect our thoughts, bolted out of the west door and sprinted off across the lawn. We tore after him but—alas!—I was baulked. I had on my new patent leathers with the cut-glass buckles and to have ventured across the lawn would have ruined them. Miss Wheelwright was more daring. The snow had begun to fall again and I sadly feared lest her green velvet should be wrecked, but she charged on very courageously. Most plucky!

Then everything seemed just like a mad dream— literally like a dream, all crazy and mixed up. Far away beyond the tennis-courts, across the bay, the light-house kept blinking and there was still a lemon-coloured streak in the sky; to the right, from under the *porte-cochère*, came laughter, shouting and the noise of cars being started. Behind me were the candles, the incense and the gloom. Ahead, in the light which streamed from the front door, Miss Wheelwright was scurrying across the white lawn on tiptoe, waving her gong stick, her handkerchief still on her head. On the far side of the lawn, hatless and with his overcoat flying, 'Mr. Pym' was plunging into the rhododendrons.

I had been sobbing, but suddenly I sat down on the chapel steps and began to laugh. I laughed and laughed. I choked with laughter . . . and then I was on my bed and Miss Bussey was throwing water in my face and Parkinson, kind soul was holding my hand. I heard someone use the word 'hysterics' and I felt thoroughly ashamed of myself. I don't mind owning, after all these years, that I had behaved very foolishly. I suppose that Captain Carhampton and Congreve and 'Mr. Pym'—all in one afternoon—had been too much for me.

I heard no more of 'Mr. Pym' that night; when last I had seen him he had been diving through the bushes in the direction of the stables and the back drive. Someone must have given me a sedative, for I slept soundly. I came down to breakfast the next morning feeling a little sheepish, but everyone was too concerned with luggage and taxis to bother with my adventure. Miss Wheelwright was a little cold and distant; it was very unfair but I think she thought I had deserted her in a critical moment. It was in the middle of breakfast that Miss Mac-Taggart, in her rude manner, shouted at me down the table:

'Coppock! My bike's a gonner.'

'Really,' I said, 'I don't understand what you mean.'

'My bike, Coppock! Your friend "Pym" went off on it—stole it. Bell saw him from her window, pedalling down the back drive—very wobbly and without a hat.'

'Well!' I said. 'Whoever heard of such a thing?'

Three days later the wretched MacTaggart's bicycle was found by the Torquay police, all twisted and smashed up, at the bottom of the Babbacombe cliff.

Part Three

in which Miss Sophie Coppock resumes her narrative and describes how she herself was in great peril at a Cotswold inn, and how Miss Langdon-Miles came to meet with sudden death in the early summer of 1931

I

The Spring Term passed uneventfully. We were all back to the busy round before the end of January, and although the events in the chapel would remain engraved on my memory for ever I was surprised and a little hurt when I found that my colleagues seemed prepared—in a most light-hearted manner—to forget all about both Mrs. Carberry and 'Mr. Pym'. I was not altogether sorry, therefore, when on the very first evening of the term Totterdell administered a cold douche by raising the question once more.

That first evening was always a busy one and Miss Langdon-Miles, Miss Bussey and myself were all at work in the office when Totterdell came in on his evening round, stoking the fires and drawing the blinds.

'Good-evening, Totterdell,' said Miss Langdon-Miles. 'I trust you spent a pleasant Christmastide.'

'Thank you, ma'am, same to you. The missis and I, we stopped quietly in Torquay.' Totterdell threw a bucket of slack on our fire. 'And about 'im as the young ladies call "Mr. Pym," ma'am. Well, he's all O.K. and above board.' Totterdell gave the fire several pokes. 'I thought as 'ow you might care to know.'

'I find that difficult to believe—how do you mean, Totterdell?'

'Well, ma'am, I'll tell you. On Christmas Day it was so warm and sunny like, that before church the missis and I took a bit of a stroll along the 'prom— a thing as we don't do twice a year, ma'am.' Totterdell drew down the blind. 'Quite an 'appy crowd enjoyin' the sunshine, ma'am.'

'Quite, Totterdell—very pleasant. But you were telling us about "Mr. Pym" you know.'

'Well, ma'am, we strolled along, the missis and I, to the far end of the 'prom, and there we sat in the shelter for maybe ten minutes, or maybe it was a quarter of an hour, ma'am; no, more like ten minutes it was.' Totterdell pulled the left-hand curtain. 'Then we started back, not wishin' to be late for church—for as the missis says to me: "If we can't be punctual, Jo, on this day of all days . . ."' Totterdell pulled the right-hand curtain. 'Is there anythin' else as you'll be requirin', ma'am?'

'Nothing, thank you Totterdell. But about this wretched "Mr. Pym." . . .'

'To be sure, ma'am. Well, we were about 'alf— or maybe it was three-quarters—no, it must 'ave been about 'alf-way back to the town when 'oom should we meet but 'im as the young ladies call "Mr. Pym", ma'am.'

'Oh dear!' exclaimed Miss Langdon-Miles. 'I am

afraid that doesn't help us much, Totterdell. I hoped that the man had left Torquay altogether.'

'Oh, you needn't worry about "Mr. Pym", ma'am. He's all O.K. an' above board. There he was, ma'am, as dapper as ever, and the lady with 'im dressed to the nines. Just a leetle too smart ma'am—my missus says—even for Christmas Day. Mutton as lamb, ma'am, that was 'er view. But it was all right, ma'am, because I spotted 'er straight away as the one wot comes up 'ere in the yaller Rolls—an' there was our "Mr. Pym", ma'am, with 'er on 'is arm— both of 'em as smart as paint. I thought as 'ow you'd like to know, ma'am, as "Mr. Pym" was with the lady out of the Rolls, because it just shows, doesn't it, as 'e must be O.K., 'an as it can't 'ave been 'im 'as Miss Coppock 'ere found in the pew— or if it was, ma'am, then 'is hintentions must 'ave been quite hinnocent like. Well, ma'am, if there's nothin' else I'll be sayin' good night, ma'am. Good night, Miss Coppock. Good night, Miss Bussey. Glad to see the young ladies back to the grind, ma'am. Good night, ma'am.'

'Well!' I said, when Totterdell had gone. 'Whoever heard of such a thing? Mrs. Carberry and "Pym" hand in glove!'

Of course Totterdell's story brough back all my old doubts and fears. The next morning I rashly mentioned the matter in the Common Room. I might have known that Miss MacTaggart would make capital out of it.

'There you are, Coppock, what did I tell you? The Carberry woman openly admitted that she was off to some South American haunt, and now she's found to be on intimate terms with your White Slave friend. She's just the sort of painted old harridan one would find in that game—a typical procuress!'

'MacTaggart,' I said, 'there's no need to be disgusting. You do no good with this poisonous talk. If Mrs. Carberry was—what you say she was—why should she send her own daughter to Easton Knoyle?'

'Really, Coppock, you're very simple. How do you know that there ever was such a child as Jennifer Carberry?'

Well, of course, Miss MacTaggart had me there. It might well be that Jennifer had been invented by Mrs. Carberry as an excuse to get inside Easton Knoyle and explore our rooms. But why?—I kept asking myself. Why? Why? Miss MacTaggart's wild theories, apart from being indecent, were obviously the figments of an overheated and morbid imagination. But I had to admit that there was a mystery to be explained, and a very nasty one. That Mrs. Carberry and 'Mr. Pym' were acquainted, so far from providing an explanation, merely made the whole affair more sinister. I confess, I was flummoxed. It really did begin to look as though there was some plot being hatched against Easton Knoyle. It was easy for people of the MacTaggart brand to play on one's fears by hinting at terrible things, things which might be worse than death. I knew that such ideas were utterly absurd—such things simply do not happen—but I also knew in my heart that in this case they were not so easy to refute.

There *might* be an innocent explanation of Mrs. Carberry's visit and even of 'Mr. Pym's' antics, but when one heard that they had been seen arm-in-arm then indeed there was cause for alarm. I was amazed that Miss Langdon-Miles should so resolutely refuse to consult the police, although I had to admit that if they were no more helpful than they had been over the Bellini, then little good would have been done. Throughout the term I never lost my sense of foreboding, although the more complacent members of the Common Room took the line that both Mrs. Carberry and 'Mr. Pym' must have left Torquay soon after Christmas. True, they were not seen again during the term but then one never knew when they might turn up again. I felt quite haunted and began to suffer from nightmares in which they played a part. My only consolation was that I had an unusually delightful Easter holiday to which I could look forward—or so I thought.

2

So far I have tried to keep myself out of this story; it is my duty to make a record of facts, not to express my opinion about this or that. Now, however, I have to tell of something which, as my readers will see, deeply affected me and which, indeed, made a lasting impression on me, so frightening was it, and so unaccountable. It all began with a letter from Miss Trubshawe.

I was really most surprised. True, we had sometimes exchanged confidences when she was at Easton Knoyle, but she and I had really very little in common. I was some twenty years her senior and I had never concealed my disapproval of her 'advanced' views, both on Art and other matters. When, after her final disagreement with Miss Langdon-Miles, she had left Easton Knoyle I had thought that I should probably never see her again. It is so often the way. Many times have I heard departing members of the Common Room promise to write to their colleagues, only to pass out of their lives for ever—to be caught up, I suppose, in the whirl of other activities. I had also been under the impression that Miss Trubshawe—after telling Miss Langdon-Miles once and for all what she thought of her—had wanted to shake the dust of Torquay from her shoes and have no further truck with us. I was, therefore, astonished to see her handwriting and even more astonished when I found that she wanted me to spend a couple of weeks with her in the Easter holidays. Her proposal was that we should tour the Cotswolds in her Austin Seven.

After leaving Easton Knoyle she had, so she told me, taken a post at an Art School in the Black Country, where she could have full scope to develop her theories and where she would be happy because she would be doing useful work. What an odd woman! I simply could not understand her rather bitter references to the 'insipid gentility' of Easton Knoyle and to 'Miss Langdon-Miles and her priest'. I should have thought, too, that in artistic matters there could be no comparison between the inborn good taste of our really nice girls, coming as they did from such cultured homes, and the rough types with which Miss Trubshawe must have to deal in her new work. I think that she was convinced that she had some mission in life; I had always found her so earnest, her bonnet so very full of bees. That she was sincere and kindly, none could deny; and I thought that if controversial subjects could be avoided she might perhaps make a satisfactory holiday companion. Also, to be frank, her invitation rather solved a problem for me.

My holidays were always a problem. For the greater part of my life I have been a rather lonely person. Apart from dear Aunt Bertha I have not a relation in the world; perhaps that explains why I have always written to her so regularly. Easton Knoyle was really my only home. Of course there were always those few glorious weeks which I spent each summer with Aunt Bertha at Coquet Hall, motoring over the moors in her big Daimler. At other times it was rather difficult to know where to go—quite a problem for a lonely spinster. The Venice adventure had not inclined me to visit the Continent again—at any rate not by myself—much as I should have enjoyed the churches and galleries. I had completely given up suggesting holiday plans to my colleagues; however early in the year I did so I invariably found that their arrangements were already made. It was very odd, but I had no wish to push myself where I was not wanted.

In recent years I had made a habit of stopping at a little private hotel in Leamington—the 'Balmoral', kept by the Misses Johnson. The Jephson Gardens were most delightful and sheltered on a sunny day, one could always take one's knitting and listen to the band. But I am bound to confess that a little motor tour in the Cotswolds did sound a most attractive— if rather adventurous—alternative. The district was quite new to me, but it was well spoken of, so after very careful consideration and with some doubts, I wrote to Miss Trubshawe and accepted her offer.

I hope my readers won't think that I have a deceitful nature when I confess that I hid from Miss Langdon-Miles the fact that I was to spend my holiday with Miss Trubshawe. Miss Langdon-Miles was not always very tolerant about the private lives of her staff—after all the reputation of the school must be guarded—and as she still felt strongly about the events of the previous term I thought it more tactful, from every point of view, to say merely that I was going away with 'a friend'.

At last the Spring Term came to an end, and my ill-starred escapade began. I packed my grip and set off. I had arranged to meet Miss Trubshawe at Worcester, and although I had had some trepidations about the whole adventure I must admit that it was very reassuring to see her standing on the platform. She was a substantially built woman, rather square in general outline, and in her russet brown tweeds and sensible brogues she looked a comforting companion. She welcomed me quite effusively—for her —and carried my things out to the Austin Seven. Then came the first shock. The back seat of the little car was piled up with her own bags and painting impedimenta and with what, to my horror, appeared to be a tent! Miss Trubshawe had—rather dishonestly—never mentioned anything of this sort in her letters and I had certainly envisaged nice, clean little hotels. I felt that I had been misled and that it was the first cloud. However, I had no wish to start by being a wet blanket—there might be plenty of those later, I reflected—so I held my peace for the time being.

We were soon chugging merrily along through Worcestershire orchards. The fruit blossom was out and I think that perhaps the spring sunshine had got into my blood. Be that as it may, when I discovered from Miss Trubshawe's map that we were passing within sight of Bredon, I rather foolishly spouted a couplet from Housman, only to feel rather squashed when Miss Trubshawe explained severely that, as a poet, he was quite *démodé*. That kind of thing makes conversation so difficult. Later, when I was in grave trouble, Miss Trubshawe was so very, very kind that I hesitate to criticise her. I suppose the fact is that when two women are cooped up all day in a little car, there is bound to be a clash of temperaments. No doubt she found much to criticise in me too, but whatever my faults I can at least claim that I am a very patient person. In some ways Miss Trubshawe was a most irritating companion but I am sure that I never let her know that I felt this.

Apart from her extraordinary views she had some most curious mannerisms of speech, always speaking, for instance, of 'hedgerows' and 'countryside', whereas all my life I had spoken quite simply of 'hedges' and 'the country'. It is surprising how these little things rack one's nerves after a time. She also had an affected way of referring to the most ordinary stretch of road as 'the King's Highway'. On the whole I think she tried, as I did, to avoid controversial matters, but they kept cropping up in the most unexpected places. When I exclaimed at the beauty of some lordly seat she would treat me to quite a diatribe on the uses to which she would put such places—homes for the aged poor, summer schools for youth movements—whatever they may be—and so on. There was no end to her fantasies. I hardly know whether we should have 'hit it off,' as they say, for two whole weeks, but as you will see, the issue was never put to the test, for our holiday was brought to a most untimely end.

We soon passed through the orchard country to the foot of the hills.

'Well, Coppock,' said Miss Trubshawe, as we pulled up in the village street at Broadway, 'here you are in the heart of Merrie England!' Miss Trubshawe had not been there before, any more than I had, but evidently she was to act as self-appointed guide.

'Hm!' I said. 'Merrie England seems to have been one vast car park.'

'Oh! Come, Coppock, you must use your imagination. Strip off the modern excrescences and think yourself back to the old days—when England was wool, and wool was England.'

This cryptic utterance left me so flabbergasted that I hardly knew what to say.

'Very well,' I said meekly, 'I'll do what I can. Certainly it's a very pretty street—quite a picture post-card.'

'A wonderful mellow gold,' said Miss Trubshawe.

'It looks just yellow to me, but it's very pretty,' I said. After we had been into the post-office and sent off cards to our friends, I plucked up my courage and spoke out.

'There's just one thing I've got to say, Trubshawe. I'm awfully sorry to disappoint you, but—it's no good—I just can't and won't sleep under that piece of canvas you've got in the back of the car. It might let the rain in, there might be a bull in the field—and, in any case, I'm too old for such goings on.' To my relief she only laughed.

'All right, Coppock. I thought that I would sling the tent into the car, just in case. . . . But I had a feeling you might draw the line somewhere. Don't you worry, we'll "take our ease at an inn".' This sounded like a quotation and aroused my deepest suspicions. For the moment I said nothing, the tent business was settled and that was something.

Soon we were up in the hills, among what Miss Trubshawe insisted upon calling 'Ploughland and Coppice.' It was certainly bracing and when the huntsmen in their red coats went trotting by with their dogs, I had to exclaim that it really was most picturesque—quite like a Christmas card. Alas! Once again I had said the wrong thing, for Miss Trubshawe had some pretty pungent remarks to make, both about 'blood sports' and Christmas cards! It was going to be very difficult if one's most innocent remarks were taken up in this way, and I decided to maintain a strict silence—unless spoken to. Presently we pulled up in a side lane and Miss Trubshawe produced a picnic lunch from the depths of her sketching bag. I always think that an alfresco meal has its attractions—provided that the weather is satisfactory in every possible way—and as I was quite hungry after my early start from Torquay, I raised no objections and, indeed, thanked Miss Trubshawe for her forethought. We did full justice to the potted-meat sandwiches and cake which she had provided. There was also a thermos of coffee—most welcome.

Since I had so flatly rejected the idea of the tent Miss Trubshawe suggested that we should find our quarters for the night, leave the car at the inn, and get a tramp during the afternoon in order—as she said—to get up an appetite for a ham-and-egg supper. In spite of my suspicions about the 'inn', I was forced to agree with this scheme since there seemed to be no alternative. I had a horror of hunting round for a bed after dark—with the possibility of being stranded. Moreover we both like a good walk

—although why Miss Trubshawe should keep calling it a 'trek' was beyond me—and we had both come provided with walking-sticks and good, strong shoes.

We trundled along for a few miles across the uplands, towards a village which the ominous word 'inn' was marked on the map. The country was very open and looked pleasing enough in the spring sunshine, but I decided that in the winter it would be most bleak and treacherous. Every now and again I had to jump out of the car and open a gate—a very inconsiderate arrangement. We soon came to a bosky hollow in the rolling hills; Miss Trubshawe shut off the engine of her car and we ran quietly down into the village of Nether Fordington—a name I shall remember to the end of my days—and pulled up outside 'The Harrow Inn.'

'Ha! ha!' said Miss Trubshawe, 'this is the real thing, Coppock.' I was quite stunned.

'You're surely not suggesting that we should spend the night here,' I said. 'It's completely primitive.'

'Nonsense, Coppock. You obviously don't know the English inn. Haven't you read Chesterton. We'll spend a thoroughly cosy evening in the bar, chatting to the yokels and getting really close to the soil. You leave it to me.'

'It may sound very romantic . . .' I began, only to be interrupted.

'Well, of course, if you want to go on to the Metropole at Cheltenham, say so. . . .'

'Look here, Trubshawe,' I said, 'don't be silly. This place might look very well in the middle distance of a sketch; but the curtains are quite yellow and—if you want to know what I think—I think the whole place looks fly-blown.'

It was no good; Miss Trubshawe had heaved herself out of the car and was knocking at the door. She knocked again and again, while I sat in the car, hoping against hope that she would get no answer. Then an upper window opened and a large red face, haloed by curling-pins, shot out.

'Openin' time's six.' The window was shut with a bang. Miss Trubshawe knocked again, and again the curling-pins appeared. Miss Trubshawe explained that we did not want a drink, but were seeking accommodation for the night.

'Accommodation? Oh Lor'!' The head again disappeared and there was a long interval during which my hopes rose. Then there was a prolonged drawing of locks and bolts and the door opened. The curling-pins and the red face now reappeared above a gay but greasy frock.

'Accommodation? Just the two of you? Well, I don't know I'm sure. We don't reckon to, ye' know.'

'With supper and breakfast, of course,' said Miss Trubshawe.

'Oh Lor! I don't know I'm sure. There's only the double feather, an' I don't suppose tha'd suit you.' Even Miss Trubshawe had begun to waver, so I stuck my head out of the car and attracted her attention in a stage whisper.

'We'd better go on somewhere else,' I said. 'This is quite hopeless. I can't sleep in a double bed, and what's more I won't.' It was high time to put my foot down. I have said that Miss Trubshawe was substantially built; possibly this was rather less than the truth. At any rate to have shared a bed with her would have been a most unequal partnership. I had never slept in a double bed in the whole of my life, and I wasn't going to start now; it would have been too absurd. Suddenly the 'curling-pins' disappeared and we heard them shouting to someone in the back quarters.

'Tom! When you've finished doing the Ford, here's two ladies as wants accommodation. Can you put up the camp-bed? The double feather won't suit them.' Tom said that the camp-bed was in the loft, but he would see what he could do. I felt that my last chance of escape was slipping away. The 'curling-pins' came back.

'Well, if you don't mind sleepin' on the camp, miss, ye' can bring ye' things up.'

'And about supper?' said Miss Trubshawe. 'I suppose you can manage ham and eggs.'

'Oh Lor'! No. Nothin' like that. I can manage some nice pickles with ye' cold, or if ye'd prefer it I can open a tin of nice co-op salmon. But ye' see it's a bit difficult like. Yvonne's gone off on the back of Trevor's motor-bike to see *Two 'Earts Aflame*—and anyway, everyone knows as 'ow we never cooks on Tuesdays.' Even Miss Trubshawe seemed a little subdued, I thought, as we lugged the bags and sketching impedimenta up the precipitous staircase; as for me, I was beyond speech.

' 'Ere y'are. This is the room, and Tom'll get up the camp later.' I was utterly bowled over. I also blamed myself; I should have been firmer with Miss Trubshawe. The English inn, indeed! The English pot-house! Apart from the 'double feather' the only furniture was a chair and a very tipsy wash-stand. A vivid representation of 'Daniel in the Lions' Den' could easily have been dispensed with in favour of a chest of drawers. The bed itself looked singularly uninviting, the sheets were far from snowy and—if the truth must be told—I had the very gravest suspicions about fleas! Later developments proved that I was fully justified.

As a concession to Miss Trubshawe's substantial build we had tacitly assumed that she would occupy the double bed, and that I—being quite a little thing —should have the 'camp'. I felt thankful that I had made it a lifelong rule never to travel without my spirit lamp; at least I should have a hot-water bottle as a protection against damp sheets. As soon as the 'curling-pins' had left us I opened the minute window; it was somewhere down on the floor. This was urgently necessary as the stench of beer was everywhere; it must have crept up through the floorboards from the bar-parlour below, and it was not less obnoxious because Miss Trubshawe called it 'ale.' Later, on making a very natural enquiry as to the geography of the inn, I was informed that it was 'down be'ind the 'olly'ocks.' This was the last straw —or so I thought at the time.

After a four-mile tramp to the next village, where we managed with great difficulty to get a most disappointing pot of grossly over-stewed tea, we both felt a little more cheerful—but only a little. The discovery—too late—of a really clean and attractive hotel did not raise our spirits. I tried to tell myself that one could survive almost anything for one night, but I knew that I should never sleep a wink. As for Miss Trubshawe, she was very quiet; probably she felt guilty at having rushed the whole business in such a precipitate manner and at having failed to take my advice. I left her to her thoughts, perhaps later she would have the courage to admit herself in the wrong. We passed a very beautiful and ancient manor house—Fordington Court. It was quite a dream and I visualised to myself the aristocratic life within, going on, no doubt, much as it had done for generations. But even this beautiful sight did not cause us to break our silence and we returned to Nether Fordington without a word being spoken on either side. To make matters worse I began to suffer from one of my severe bilious headaches, but after the stress and strain of the day this was really to be expected.

When we got back to 'The Harrow' the bar was open. The bar-parlour, as it was called, was apparently to be our supper room. A hot bath and a change would have been welcome, but as it was obviously hopeless even to think of such a thing, we sat ourselves down on a window bench. The table was badly stained with the rings of former beer glasses and was bare save for an ash-tray advertising the local brewers. I had with me the latest Walpole and Miss Trubshawe produced her *Time and Tide*, but it was very difficult to concentrate. Two callow, sickly-looking youths were the sole representatives of Miss Trubshawe's Chestertonian yokels. For the first half-hour they kept interfering with the switches on the wireless apparatus. The appalling screeches and squeals which resulted had a disastrous effect in my poor head. Then they turned their attention to filling in 'football coupons'. I gathered from Miss Trubshawe's rather hazy explanation that this was some easy-money gambling scheme. I felt that it was our duty to warn them not to be so foolish and wicked, but Miss Trubshawe said it was not our business—and I was in no mood for arguing.

Only when 'Trevor' returned from the pictures were we left alone for a few moments, while the youths went outside to join in a committee meeting round the motor-cycle. We scarcely spoke the whole evening. Trubshawe did once attempt to join in the general conversation, volunteering some remark about the turnip crop; this was not very well received and I distinctly saw the two youths wink at each other. Most impertinent; Miss Trubshawe had meant well. The hours passed and still there was no supper. My headache, meanwhile, got worse and worse and I knew that, in spite of a light lunch and a poor tea, I should never be able to swallow the cold mutton and pickles which we had chosen in preference to the 'co-op salmon'. I was obviously in for a very nasty bilious attack. Miss Trubshawe, on the other hand, took no pains to hide the fact that she was ravenous, and she got more and more restless as the evening wore on.

About nine o'clock a large cruet appeared; probably the supper arrangements had had to await Trevor's and Yvonne's return from *Two 'Earts Aflame*. By this time the evening was getting very chilly and a request for a fire produced—very reluctantly—a small and smelly oil stove. Shortly after nine a few more local people drifted in and although the bar-parlour was but a pale reflection of Miss Trubshawe's 'English Inn,' it did become a little more lively—and more noisy! Never have I heard such language!

Among others was a gentlemanly-looking young man in riding breeches, who impressed me as being handsome if a little too ruddy. We thought he might have been out hunting and Miss Trubshawe whispered to me that perhaps he was 'the squire'. We learnt later, however, that he was a Dr. Plummett, the resident medical officer at a private mental home, recently started at Fordington Court. I recalled my vision of aristocratic life behind those mullion windows—and felt that another illusion had been smashed. Dr. Plummett consumed his drinks in silence and very rapidly. Poor man! I do not want to be uncharitable; it must be a great strain living with lunatics—you never know what they may do next—and perhaps, too, he was thirsty; but after he had had three glasses of whisky I really did begin to get rather frightened. I have always been exceedingly nervous about intoxication—anything may happen. I kept my eye on him so that I could skip upstairs if he began to get quarrelsome or to start any horseplay.

At about half-past-nine a young woman—presumably Yvonne—came in with our supper, crashing the tin tray down on the table. I have never been able to decide whether it was the sight of cold mutton or of the deep crimson tinge of Yvonne's finger nails that brought to a head my final decision to be sick. Possibly it was the juxaposition of the two. Be that as it may, I gave a wild gulp and fled.

I got upstairs in the nick of time—Miss Trubshawe in my wake. I am afraid that I must put it on record that I was violently sick—twice. I must say, Miss Trubshawe was a brick and saw to everything. I have been a lifelong martyr to headaches, so I knew from experience that, unpleasant as it was, I should probably be all right the next morning. Never, however, had I suffered in such a deplorable environment; I remember one very nasty attack in a stuffy *wagon-lit*, just outside Venice, but even that was preferable to 'The Harrow' at Nether Fordington.

Thank God the camp bed was ready! Miss Trubshawe had me cosily tucked up within a few minutes; then she got my spirit lamp going and soon had my hot-water bottle filled. Finally she burrowed in my grip. For a moment I dreaded lest I had left the aspirins in the bathroom at Easton Knoyle; however, Miss Trubshawe soon found them and, after swallowing a couple I lay back and shut my eyes. In spite of the buzz of conversation and the vulgar din of the wireless vaudeville, both of which floated up from the bar-parlour below, I think that after a few minutes I must have dropped asleep, or into an uneasy doze, and that Miss Trubshawe must have returned to her cold mutton.

Then it happened!

Suddenly, quite suddenly, I sat bolt upright in bed. My face was twitching in an unaccountable manner. I felt extremely ill—not as if I was going to be sick again, it was quite different now—but extremely ill indeed. Then the most awful and terrifying agony swept over me—in wave after wave. I was racked and doubled up with pain; it shot through my whole body in an unimaginable manner. Never, never had I conceived of anything so awful as this. I sweated. I groaned. The room swam before my eyes. I could hardly see, but—alas!— oblivion would not come. Then I lost all control of myself; I gave a wild shriek. It must have rung through the inn. I gave another and another. . . .

Then Miss Trubshawe was in the room. Actually I believe she was up those precipitous stairs before the third shriek. Dr. Plummett must have been close at her heels, but I knew nothing of that at the time. All I could do as I lay twitching and convulsed on the bed was to cling desperately to Miss Trubshawe's hand.

'Oh! Trubby, Trubby,' I sobbed, 'I'm going to

die, I know I am.' Dimly, very dimly, I heard her reply.

'Stuff and nonsense, my dear, stuff and nonsense!'

Then, for two whole days and nights, there was blackness, almost complete blackness—broken only by delirium and nightmare.

3

I was in the hands of my Maker, and indeed it was a miracle that saved my life. How inscrutable are the ways of Providence! If Dr. Plummett had not embarked upon a fourth whisky, and if Trevor's motorcycle had not been standing outside the inn I should certainly not have survived for an hour.

When I became convalescent Miss Trubshawe told me the whole story. Dr. Plummet took one look at me and then, in a flash, he was across the road at the post office, telephoning to the matron at his mental home. Trevor—frightened but obedient—was rushed off on his motor-cycle; in ten minutes he was back from Fordington Court with Dr. Plummett's bag. What, meanwhile, had been happening down in the bar-parlour Miss Trubshawe hardly knew. When I gave my first shriek there was, I gather, a terrified silence while they all stood with ears cocked, listening to my groans and cries. When they heard that I was merely ill and that my throat had not been cut—as they had at first hoped—interest waned. They turned their attention to Yvonne instead. She had started a fit of violent hysterics and this, according to Miss Trubshawe, went on intermittently until closing time.

What Dr. Plummett did to me was all just part of my nightmare. No good purpose is ever served by the recital of nauseating details—the modern school of literature I abhor. In any case I had been so sick an hour before that no sensational consequences could be expected from the administration of an emetic. I know that my readers, one and all, would choose death rather than be victims of the stomach pump. However, I had no choice—I was in a coma—and it was this that saved my life.

Looking back over my story I find that I have made one or two rather sharp remarks about Miss Trubshawe. I do hope that these won't be taken too seriously. During the weeks that followed she was an absolute tower of strength, a real Christian. She nursed me night and day, snatching a few hours sleep when she could and never handing me over for an instant to the tender mercies of the 'staff' at 'The Harrow'. I rather think that, with the support of Dr. Plummett, she pretty well took over the domestic affairs of the inn. Neither the 'curling-pins' nor Yvonne ever appeared in my room. Miss Trubshawe did everything for me. Goodness knows how many times a day she heaved her substantial figure up and down those precipitous stairs.

Of course the bedroom remained very desolate to look at, but the oil stove found its way upstairs and so did one or two sticks of furniture. And there was always a bowl of primroses. After a few days, when I began to eat again, quite appetising dishes began to arrive from the kitchen—obviously far beyond the skill or imagination of 'The Harrow'. In her queer modern way Miss Trubshawe said that I was providing an outlet for her suppressed maternal instincts. Be that as it may, it must have been a dismal time for her—living in that dreadful inn—apart altogether from the fact that her holiday was completely ruined. She would never listen to my thanks, but I can say here that I shall be grateful to her to the end of my days.

Dr. Parker, from the village, had officially 'taken over' my case from Dr. Plummett. He was a very kindly old man, but just a little bit past his work. I remember that he got very fussed and worried about the mysterious cause of my seizure; he couldn't make it out at all and was honest enough to admit it. Dr. Plummett kept up an interest in my case and frequently looked in. As a doctor he was rough and ready, but I quite got to like him after a time. He would burst into my bedroom in his riding clothes—most unprofessional—greeting me at the top of his voice in an exceedingly cheerful manner. The loud voice was rather trying, but he was extremely handsome, even if all the whiskies did keep him on the ruddy side. I think that his heart was more in his hunting than in his work. It was for the sake of the hunting, he told me, that he had accepted the appointment at Fordington Court. I dare say, however, that his poor lunatics found his breezy manner most exhilarating and cheering.

About ten days after I had been stricken I was sitting up in bed one morning, sipping the beef-tea which Miss Trubshawe had prepared for me—most delicious and sustaining—when I heard the voices of both doctors talking to her, down in the bar-parlour. I could not hear what they were actually saying— it rather sounded as though they were deliberately speaking in a low tone—but they certainly had a long consultation. Then, to my surprise, Miss Trubshawe came upstairs alone.

'Coppock darling,' she began, 'I am going to ask you a very strange and intimate question—please don't be hurt with me. I want to ask you, Coppock, have you any secret unhappiness or sorrow?' Well, as you may imagine, I was a bit flabbergasted.

'Whatever do you mean, Trubby? Of course not. I am a most happy and contented person—a little lonely sometimes, perhaps, but most happy and contented. . . .'

'That's what I thought, dear. But—I must ask you just one thing. Please don't be cross with me. You didn't, did you, try to kill yourself the other night?'

'Well!' I exclaimed. 'What an extraordinary idea! No, of course I won't get cross with you, Trubby, but really . . . why, I've always regarded suicide as most wicked—most wicked and reprehensible. I am sure that we are not intended to escape from our earthly troubles, they are sent to try us. But, really, whatever has made you think. . . .'

'That's all right then,' she said. 'I knew that's what you would say—but I had to ask you.' Then, if you please, she actually kissed me and slipped out of the room before I could say another word.

'Well,' I said to myself, 'whoever heard of such a thing?'

I felt quite stunned, but before I had time to collect my scattered thoughts Miss Trubshawe was back again with both Dr. Parker and Dr. Plummett. Then there was quite a little committee meeting. I went on sipping my delicious beef-tea, Miss Trubshawe sat on the foot of my bed, old Dr. Parker took the one chair and Dr. Plummett sat on the edge of the 'double feather', slapping his cloth gaiters with his riding crop—really he looked more like a vet than a doctor, but his cheery face was very reassuring.

'Now, old girl,' he began—he always spoke like that and somehow I didn't mind—'we want you to to tell us all about last Tuesday week, the day you were taken bad. You see, Dr. Parker and I can't quite make out what gave you such a nasty upset. Tell us what you had to eat.'

'Well,' I said, 'I got up quite early to get my train from Torquay to Worcester and—let me see now it was the school holidays, so Parkinson as a great treat brought my breakfast tray up to my room. It was just my usual, a very lightly boiled egg, very lightly boiled, and two pieces of thin bread and butter. And, of course, a pot of China tea.'

'Never mind about breakfast, Miss Coppock,' said old Dr. Parker, 'too early in the day to make any difference—much too early. Nothing else till lunch?'

'No,' I said, '—or let me see. Yes, I had a cup of coffee—black—in the restaurant car, just after we had passed Taunton. Very poor coffee it was, too. Then nothing more until Miss Trubshawe and I had our sandwiches...'

'The sandwiches were all right,' interrupted Dr. Plummett, 'Miss Trubshawe sent to her "digs" in Wolverhampton for the remains of the potted-meat still in the jar, and the analysis showed nothing wrong....'

'Analysis!' I cried. 'Oh dear! You are being thorough. I thought that I had had just a very nasty gastric turn; you don't mean to say it's food poisoning, do you?'

'Now, my dear lady,' said Dr. Parker, 'Pray don't upset yourself. Dr. Plummet and I want to make sure—that's all. Now the cold mutton and pickles—

you're quite certain that you never touched them?'

'Oh! Quite certain. Why, as soon as I saw them I rushed up here and was sick immediately.' Dr. Plummet turned to Dr. Parker.

'I don't know what you think, Parker, but it beats me. Here's a patient who's violently sick, and half an hour later I have to empty the stomach all over again to save her life.'

'Oh dear!' I said, 'do tell me what you are all talking about. . . .' By this time I was getting quite agitated; the very word 'poison' is so terrifying, isn't it? Dr. Plummett, in his breezy way, tried to calm me.

'Now, old girl, don't you fret yourself. In another week you'll be as right as rain, and out and about—and that's what matters.'

'That may be,' I said, 'but I would rather know the truth, please.'

'Very well,' said Dr. Plummett, 'I suppose you've got to know some time. You see, we sent the results of the emetic and all that to Cheltenham to be analysed. Well, you know it's a jolly good thing for you, old girl, that loonies sometimes do odd things to themselves; I mean to say—that's why we always keep a stomach pump about the place, don't you know. It really was a bit of a miracle—that is if I believed in miracles which, of course, I don't. Anyway it was a chance in a million—wasn't it, Parker? Another quarter of an hour and . . . but there, you needn't worry any more, Miss Coppock.'

'But the analysis . . .' I said.

'Well, Dr. Parker and I can't quite make it out. It's very odd, but there it is. At the Cheltenham hospital they found almost two grains of strychnine —and that, I can tell you, is quite a lot more than a fatal dose. So you see, old girl, when I called it a "miracle", I wasn't far wrong!'

'Well,' I said, 'whoever heard of such a thing?'

4

A week later I was back at Easton Knoyle. Oh, what a relief it was to get away from that horrible pothouse! I had quite a send-off; as we chugged away up the hill and round the bend, Trevor and Yvonne, the 'curling-pins' and Dr. Plummett all stood waving at the door of 'The Harrow'. Miss Trubshawe had wrapped me up well with rugs and coats in the Austin Seven—she was most kind—and by teatime we were safely in Torquay. Miss Trubshawe and Parkinson saw to it that I was cosily tucked up in my own dear bed, and then Miss Trubshawe kissed me—for the second time! —and left me. I could understand that she had no desire to linger at Easton Knoyle. Fortunately there was a week to go before the Summer Term started and so Miss Langdon-Miles was still away. Embarrassing encounters were thus avoided.

As I lay in my own cosy room, with all my pretty things around me, you can imagine my feelings. There was Torbay glittering in the sun, and there was Parkinson, so kind and good, to bring up my dainty meals. One of the first things I did, the morning after my return, was to slip on my nice quilted dressing-gown and totter through the slype to the chapel. There I gave thanks on my knees for the miracle which had saved my life. To think—if it had not been for that stomach pump I might have been laid in my coffin at 'The Harrow'. I shuddered at the very thought of such a fate.

Then I got back into bed and wrote a long, long letter to dear Aunt Bertha, who was spending Easter at Buxton. What a lot I had to tell her! From Nether Fordington I had been able to send her only two or three postcards—scrawled in pencil. Now I wrote a full account of my holiday and my illness, in much the same way as I have tried to tell the story here.

The next evening, when Parkinson came up with my supper tray, she brought me a telegram. It was from Aunt Bertha. I was astonished. Not that it was unusual for Aunt Bertha to send a telegram; on the contrary it was one of her habits to send the most extravagant telegrams upon the least provocation. But really, this telegram! I read it again and again, scarcely able to believe my own eyes. Even at that time, you must remember, Aunt Bertha was over eighty and, although I don't like saying it, I really did wonder whether her mind was not giving way—just a little you know. Of course I couldn't possibly do as she suggested, I should have looked foolish. Besides, whatever would Miss Langdon-Miles have said? A most extraordinary telegram—this is what it said:

'Suggest that you destroy immediately all drugs and medicines at School House. What a very warm spring we are having. By the way where does Mr. Pym buy his hats? Much love, dear, and many, many happy returns of next Monday.

Aunt Bertha.'

5

Miss Langdon-Miles had always been wont to suffer from fits of melancholia, and she returned from her holiday in a terribly despondent mood. She was barely fit for her work and spent many tearful hours alone in the chapel. In these circumstances I thought it best to make as little fuss as possible about my own illness, and Miss Langdon-Miles was far too deeply sunk in her own troubles to ask me how my holiday had gone; the Nether Fordington episode was barely referred to. I am also compelled to admit that I still concealed from Miss Langdon-Miles the fact that my holiday companion had been Miss Trubshawe. I saw no point in probing old wounds. Fortunately by the time the Summer Term opened I was on my feet again and, although I had to watch my diet very carefully, I felt quite prepared for the busy daily round.

The principal reason for Miss Langdon-Miles's spiritual crisis and deep depression was revealed to me on the second evening of the term, when she confided to me that her elder sister Beatrice had decided—at the age of sixty, if you please!—to get engaged to a perfectly unknown and not very attractive fellow nearly fifteen years her junior—a certain Harold Warburton. It was almost indecent. He was said to be both a pianist and an Australian—neither of which were very creditable—and the wedding was being rushed through in the most extraordinary manner. How unaccountable people are! Miss Langdon-Miles might well feel despondent and melancholy.

Personally I felt that it was most unfair of Miss Beatrice Langdon-Miles to behave in this outrageous way—upsetting everybody and everything. She was, as I say, sixty, whereas Miss Philippa—my Miss Langdon-Miles—was only forty-six. On the death of Sir Stuart Langdon-Miles the greater part of the vast Langdon-Miles fortune had passed to Beatrice, and on her death it would have come to Philippa. Now, presumably it would go to the worthless Warburton. Miss Langdon-Miles had not yet met him and knew nothing of him, but who could doubt that it was the money he was after?

I have given a very false idea of Miss Langdon-Miles's sweet nature if any of my readers—like some of the cats in the Common Room—should think that her gloom and melancholy was due to a mere change in her own worldly fortunes. To wealth and to the social standing which it brings she was ever indifferent. It was, however, no secret that Miss Langdon-Miles had provided in her will for the further adornment and extension of the Easton Knoyle chapel, and that the greater part of the Langdon-Miles fortune would pass, one day, to the coffers of the Sisters of St. Anne, to whose wonderful Devonshire convent Miss Langdon-Miles had so often gone in retreat, and behind the walls of which she intended to end her days.

Beatrice Langdon-Miles had, therefore, by her marriage struck a blow not only at her sister Philippa and at Easton Knoyle, but at the very Church itself. It was all most dishonest and unfair and, I could not help but think, symptomatic of a definitely irreligious feeling. However, when an elderly woman allows her head to be turned by a younger man—God knows what may happen!

Robbing the Church—and it was really nothing less
—was not what one would have expected of Beatrice Langdon-Miles, in spite of her many idiosyn-
crasies, but I suppose that Mr. Warburton had
alternately flattered and dragooned her.

The last few days of Miss Langdon-Miles's holiday, which she had spent with her sister at Hampstead, had evidently been very painful. The 'wedding'—if you can call it such—was to take place at a
London register office! Miss Langdon-Miles, with
her high, severe ideal of the marriage sacrament,
could hardly be expected to condone with her
presence such a farcical proceeding. When the two
sisters parted, relations had, I gathered, been
distincly strained and it was only with difficulty that
a compromise was reached. The Warburtons were to
be married early in May. They were then going to
spend a week in Normandy, after which they were
going to Coquet Hall for a couple of months while
the Hampstead home—where the young man was
going to 'hang up his hat'—was redecorated. As they
passed through London on their way north—on May
19th—there was to be a small family dinner-party
at which Miss Langdon-Miles would meet her
'brother in-law'. Of course Beatrice had sung her
Harold's praises fulsomely, but she was necessarily
biased and Miss Langdon-Miles must have hesitated
before agreeing to face the young adventurer. Unfortunately it was known that on May 20th she had
a lecture engagement at the Cranmer Hall, so she
would in any case be visiting London. This made
it very difficult for her to refuse to go to the dinner-
party, but you can imagine that she looked forward
to it with dread.

My readers may well wonder why, on the death of

her father, the Langdon-Miles fortune had passed to Beatrice, and why Sir Stuart had dealt so hardly with his other children. Perhaps I had better explain a little. A glimpse of the Langdon-Miles family will also enable my readers to appreciate better the grim background to that fatal dinner-party of May 19th.

They were an unusual family. Sir Stuart Langdon-Miles had two sons and two daughters; he quarrelled with them all and, on and off, they all quarrelled with each other. They were all individualists, with strong views and strong passions. Often their ideals were high, but they were ruthless in seeking to achieve them. If that ruthlessness had been inspired by more ignoble motives I shudder to think of the consequences. My Miss Langdon-Miles, of course, was sweetness itself—as a rule. But even in her I have sometimes glimpsed the sleeping tiger of the family bad temper.

Sir Stuart Langdon-Miles was in his day a notable man in the world of Liverpool shipping. He was immensely rich and a 'self-made man', if ever there was one. Such men are often proud of their humble origins, but not Sir Stuart. He was always out to cut a figure in Liverpool society and he took great pains to hide the fact that he was the son of a County Durham coal-miner and had been born in a Gateshead slum. I always like to take a kindly view and I think that perhaps, poor man, he merely wanted to forget the far-off days when he and his fifteen brothers and sisters—not to mention their mother—had been soundly thrashed every Saturday night.

Certainly Sir Stuart Langdon-Miles was a pious man and a philanthropist. He was a stern Evangelical and brought up his family in an atmosphere of plain living and high thinking. Even to me who had known the life of a Scottish manse Miss Langdon-Miles's childhood, as she described it to me, sounded strict and repressive. I have been told that forty years ago there were stories current in Liverpool that Sir Stuart—like his drunken father—had been guilty of actual physical cruelty to his two sons. I rather suspect that there was a good deal of exaggeration. When some cause appealed to his better nature, Sir Stuart Langdon-Miles could be a philanthropist on a most generous scale; the 'Langdon-Miles Refuge' in Liverpool's slums is well known, and the Borneo and China missionaries owe him a debt which is, I believe, boundless. I must, therefore, dismiss as absurd the whispered tale that in Sir Stuart Langdon-Miles there ran an inherited streak of sadistic insanity.

Although both Edward and Fortescue had been omitted from their father's will, it must not be thought that either had been cut off with the proverbial shilling. Sir Stuart's vanity among his business colleagues would never have permitted that. In spite of violent quarrels he saw to it that both his sons should be well started in life and both, in their own way, made brilliant careers for themselves. I think that it was not until their father's death in 1925 that either Edward or Fortescue knew of their disinheritance, and by that time both were wealthy men of established position. It is true that neither of them were on speaking terms with each other or with Beatrice and Philippa, whom indeed they had not seen for some thirty years. But in the Langdon-Miles family that kind of thing was to be expected.

The break between Edward—the elder son—and his father was not altogether inexplicable. Sir Stuart, like many men who have given their lives to the pursuit of money, was dimly aware that there were better things, and he had decided to send his sons into the professions, Edward to the Church and Fortescue to the Bar. Edward, however, like a true Langdon-Miles, had his own views on the matter. After a year at Oxford he came home one Christmas to announce that he had no inclination for the Church and had decided on a commercial career. A most violent scene followed, Edward making things no better when he had the impertinence to try to justify himself by theological arguments. The break with his father was almost complete and was only patched up with difficulty and only—as it turned out—for a few months.

Of the episode which ultimately caused Sir Stuart to ship Edward out of the country, Miss Langdon-Miles—very naturally in view of its delicate nature—had told me but little. The family were at that time—it must have been about 1900—living in a large country mansion out on the Wirral, so that the girls might be isolated from the distraction of the city. Sir Stuart had found Edward some sort of berth with an insurance firm and the boy—if you please—had recklessly struck up an acquaintanceship with a mill girl whom he saw each morning on the Mersey ferry-boat. Probably the girl was pretty enough in her common way—the Langdon-Miles boys always had an eye for that kind of thing—but she must also have had all the wiles of a little gold-digger, for Edward was anything but weak. Well, the inevitable happened and Edward, in a fit of misguided chivalry, married the girl. That, of course, as far as Sir Stuart was concerned, was the end. But he was still determined to keep up appearances as far as possible, and Edward reached New York not only with his golden-haired mill girl but with business introductions such as only a Liverpool shipping magnate could give him. Five years later the stockbroking firm of 'Langdon-Miles and Gabbitas' was one of the most substantial on Wall Street. When Edward had left Oriel he had, at any rate, known his own mind; the ruthless hunt for money can, I suppose, be inherited, like any other vice. In the thirty years that followed, Beatrice had one or two letters and, when Sir Stuart died in 1925, Philippa had a very brief note, but otherwise there was silence.

The quarrel with Fortescue, the younger brother, was more inexplicable. Any normal father, one would have thought, might have tried to patch things up—not so Sir Stuart Langdon-Miles. It is true that Fortesque began to sow his wild oats almost as soon as he got to Oxford—there was one very nasty story about cruelty to a dog in the course of some wild undergraduates' jape, such as was common in the 'nineties—but he ultimatley took his degree with considerable brilliance. Wild oats, however, were neither dreamt of nor tolerated in the philosophy of Sir Stuart. There was a violent quarrel and Miss Langdon-Miles told me that she cried herself to sleep that night, for Fortescue was her favourite brother. Fortescue's career, after he left Oxford, was what is known as 'meteoric.' His father would boast to his Liverpool business friends about his son's achievements, but father and son never spoke to each other again. Fortescue eventually became perhaps the most eminent judge on the Indian Bench. His correspondence with his sisters was limited to an annual Christmas card. One or two unpleasant stories, reminiscent of the Oxford days, found their way back to this country; one told how recalcitrant natives had been forced to crawl in the mud past the judge's bungalow, and there were others telling of the imposition of savage sentences. I have made it clear, I hope, that I am most firmly opposed to the repetition of malicious gossip, and I dare say that these stories were without foundation. Nevertheless, there is—as they say—no smoke without fire.

Fortescue, just before he went out to India early in the century, got married. Unlike Edward he married well; but Sir Stuart was unrelenting and flatly refused to meet his wife. Fortescue had one son, Hallam. Like most Anglo-Indian children Hallam was sent to England to be educated and I must say that Beatrice played her party nobly *in loco parentis*. Through all the years that Hallam was at Marlborough, she invited him regularly in the school holidays, either to her Hampstead home or to her Cornish cottage. I believe that there was quite a genuine affection between aunt and nephew. At the time of which I write he was at Cambridge and was, I had been told, a most attractive boy, and quite brilliant if a little wild. In many ways, in fact, a typical Langdon-Miles. It seemed to be most unfair that this nice boy should also be deprived or an ultimate share in the Langdon-Miles fortune; there seemed to be no end to the consequences of Sir Stuart's spiteful nature. Hallam was being allowed to come up to Town to meet Harold Warburton— his new uncle!—and to attend the family dinner-party. It was there that I met him for the first time.

I have described the Langdon-Miles family because I want my readers to realise what a peculiar lot they were. There was always, to my mind, something a little frightening about them. Even Beatrice and Philippa had been comparative strangers for over twenty years. Neither of them, it is true, suffered from the dangerous passions and vices which had so afflicted Sir Stuart and his sons, although in both the sisters I had sometimes suspected hidden depths which were rather terrifying.

So long as Sir Stuart was alive it had been almost impossible for Beatrice and Philippa to meet even if they had wanted to do so. Beatrice lived with her father—a most uneasy existence I imagine—whereas Philippa had quarrelled with him irrevocably. Only after his death did the two sisters start meeting once more, and then only on rare occasions. They had never openly broken with each other but —both by temperament and in interests—they were at opposite poles.

The family squabbles and, indeed, the whole atmosphere of the great gaunt mansion on the windswept Wirral, must have been almost unbearable to a sensitive and high-minded girl such as Philippa. Lady Langdon-Miles had died when the children were quite small—a meek woman for whom one cannot but feel a deep sympathy—and almost before she left school Philippa had found her one consolation in the arms of the Church, and in the colour and emotion of a particular kind of Church. Gradually it leaked out; she had been to confession, she had done this, that and the other. Sir Stuart, for a time, dismissed it all as a school-girl's passing whim. Then, when Fortescue went to India, she held the threat of a convent over her father's head. There were terrible scenes but, in the end, Philippa had her way— she would! Of course the convent had never been much more than a threat—what she really wanted was a career. She, like her brothers before her, left home for ever—but with a pretty substantial allowance, for Sir Stuart was not going to have it said in Liverpool that his daughter was living in a Bloomsbury attic. He would not let his children disgrace him —he would punish them after his death. Philippa, like Edward and Fortescue, was both brilliant and determined, and while still in her thirties she became Headmistress of Easton Knoyle. Sir Stuart, however never relented for indeed it was not in his nature to do so.

As long as their father was alive the estrangement between the two sisters was complete. Since Philippa neither spoke nor wrote to him, while Beatrice kept house for him, this was not unnatural. Beatrice's life was not easy, however, for no Langdon-Miles was ever content with a purely domestic existence, and she soon flung herself into charitable work in Liverpool and into wildcat schemes of all sorts. Some of these were far from meeting with Sir Stuart's approval, and a fourth family quarrel was only just averted at the time of the suffragette movement, when Beatrice lost her head and behaved in a really disgusting manner, pouring ink into pillarboxes, and goodness knows what else! Many people, I understand, considered that she was charming, as well as being 'progressive', whatever that may mean, but as I never really knew her I cannot vouch for this and I am afraid that I must put it on record that she was, in actual fact, a 'red' and an atheist into the bargain. I suppose we must try to see the good in everybody and it is just possible that Beatrice was sincere, but the fact that no sooner was her father dead than she moved to London and took to addressing meetings in low parts of the East End, shows her up, I think, in a very ugly light.

And now—to crown all—she had taken it into her head to marry this mercenary little pianist. Really, it was to preposterous that the mere chances of Fate and the squabbles of forty years ago should have concentrated the vast Langdon-Miles fortune in Beatrice's irresponsible hands. She had always squandered large sums on her pet schemes and protégées, and now the whole fortune would pass out of the family for ever. It went without saying that the wretched Warburton fellow would coerce his wife into making a will in his favour. In view of the great difference in age between the two sisters, the money—if it had not been for this disastrous marriage—would almost certainly have come to Philippa in due course, and so ultimately to the Sisters of St. Anne. Who can doubt that this was God's intention? I do not say that He would have grudged a modest competence for Hallam, that nice-looking boy at Cambridge, but in the main it was the Church that should have benefited.

I was the only person at Easton Knoyle to whom Miss Langdon-Miles had ever confided the sad story of her family affairs, and so it was to me—and to me alone—that she revealed her grief and disgust at Beatrice's marriage. I was ever her *confidante*, and if that caused some jealousy in the Common Room it was not my fault. I alone knew the reasons for Miss Langdon-Miles's gloom in the first weeks of that Summer Term, but that she was not herself was clear to all the Staff. As Miss MacTaggart vulgarly asked at breakfast one morning: 'What's bitten Miles?' I could have enlightened her but, needless to say, I did not do anything of the kind.

Looking back, ten years afterwards, on the weeks which preceded Miss Langdon-Miles's death, I sometimes think that I really did have some sense of foreboding. I am sure that Miss Langdon-Miles did, for many were the hours which she spent alone in the chapel. Whether the girls felt that something was wrong I never knew, but the queer and ugly gloom that pervaded Easton Knoyle was everywhere and it was unmistakable. In those last weeks it became quite oppressive and I remember that we all got very touchy. Mrs. Fish's visit plunged us into even deeper depression, and the only relief was when a rather amusing little artist came along wanting to copy the Bellini—a Mr. Francis Toplady.

6

In describing the last days of Miss Langdon Miles's life I must be very accurate. She died on May 20th, so it must have been on the 16th that Mr. Toplady came to Easton Knoyle. He sent a note round from his hotel, introducing himself as Francis Toplady, R.A., of Fowey in Cornwall. He had, he said, been commissioned by a wealthy patron to make copies of Old Masters for the walls of some mansion that was being built in the Home Counties—and would Miss Langdon-Miles give permission for him to copy Bellini's 'Assumption of the Virgin'? Might he call and discuss the matter? Miss Langdon-Miles naturally felt that Mr. Toplady's patron should have written to her in the first place; she was always very particular about procedure—and quite rightly so to my mind. However, Mr. Toplady's request was innocent enough, so later in the day he called, at Miss Langdon-Miles's invitation, and took tea with us.

I must say that when I entered the drawing-room I was quite startled—not because Mr. Toplady presented an altogether unexpected appearance, but rather because he did look so precisely like the popular idea of the artist. I really could not help smiling. He wore a tweed knickerbocker Norfolk suit, a flowing silk tie and a neat grey Vandyke beard —only the easel and the camp-stool were missing. In manner, however, there seemed to be little of the dreamer or the poet or, I was relieved to find, of the Bohemian. You never quite know where you are with artists, but Mr. Toplady was rather a jolly little man, and for an hour he cracked jokes with us in a most roguish manner. Over the Bellini he went into ecstasies. Indeed he praised and admired everything —quite winning our hearts.

Miss Langdon-Miles told him that she had no objection to the Bellini being copied, but could the work be done, she asked, in the school holidays? Mr. Toplay said that that would never do; all the other Old Masters had been copied, only the Bellini remained, and his patron was getting impatient. For three years Mr. Toplady had been working away, copying pictures in the Louvre, the Uffizi and elsewhere; this was the last and he had promised it by the end of the summer. Of course, Miss Langdon-Miles could rest assured that the chapel services would not be disturbed in any way—that, said Mr. Toplady, would be his first thought.

Finally we agreed as to whereabouts in the Lavers Memorial Chapel the easel should be set up, and I must say that Mr. Toplady made no difficulties about the arrangements; he was most accommodating. Miss

Langdon-Miles mentioned that she would be in London for a few days but that there was really no reason why Mr. Toplady should not start work immediately. Rather to our surprise, since his patron was in such a hurry for his Old Masters, Mr. Toplady said that he had come to Torquay only to make arrangements for copying the Bellini, and that he would not be starting work until the end of the month. I could not help thinking that the arrangements could quite easily have been made by letter, and that Mr. Toplady had travelled to Torquay rather unnecessarily. I said as much, but Mr. Toplady assured us that his visit had been a joy and a delight to him and that he was, in any case, taking a holiday in Devonshire. He was quite exhausted, it seemed, by the winter's work in Italy and he had promised himself a fortnight's holiday. He was not going far—only to Simonsbath on Exmoor. There, he told us, he would—in spite of his sixty-odd years —tramp twenty miles a day over the Moor, and in two weeks he would be back at Easton Knoyle with renewed vigour, prepared to spend many happy hours in front of the Bellini.

So we said good-bye—for the time being—to Mr. Francis Toplady, R.A. He was quite a refreshing personality and his departure, although he had been with us only an hour, seemed to deepen the pervading gloom of Easton Knoyle. I spent the evening in my room in a state of complete depression, finding but little comfort in writing my weekly letter to Aunt Bertha who had now gone north to Coquet Hall for the summer months.

After all, I could hardly foresee that, three days later, I should meet Mr. Toplady in a railway train —and in the most odd circumstances.

7

Mrs. Fish was the plainest woman I have ever seen. It was on the afternoon of May 18th—just forty-eight hours before Miss Langdon-Miles's death—that Mrs. Fish and her husband arrived at Easton Knoyle. It was the first time that I had ever seen her and I was shocked and embarrassed.

Canon Fish, I had always thought, was the very epitome of Christian manliness. He was over six feet, of rubicund complexion and with hair rather prematurely white. He was so, so handsome, if rather ascetic-looking, and with that deferential stoop when talking to the weaker sex which was so comforting and so becoming in one of his profession. And she—poor woman—what a contrast! She was dwarfish and, I think, slightly hunch-backed; that could have been forgiven—but those prominent white eyes behind their rimless pince-nez, the hooked nose, the mean, tight-lipped mouth, the receding forehead from which the scanty ginger hair was drawn tightly back, and that extraordinary chin—these were all quite repulsive; I could scarcely remain at ease in her presence.

Mainly, I think it was the chin. If it had not been for that chin Mrs. Fish might have been just a poor, pitiable creature. But that prognathous jaw betrayed the vice and malice that were within, giving a simian cast to the whole head. Even so, one could not but feel a very deep pity; certainly pity must have been uppermost in the Canon's profoundly Christian mind when he took this woman to be his wife. What other explanation could there be?

It was an additional misfortune that Mrs. Fish should have chosen so perversely to dress in a fashionable manner. If she thus hoped to minimise her physical misfortunes—what a blunder! The smart but tasteless clothes, the jewellery and the gaudy colours in which she persisted were merely *outré* and grotesque on such a figure, and the high-heeled shoes gave to that dwarfish body a forward stoop which only added to its malevolence.

I had always known that Mrs. Fish lived in great retirement at Exeter, taking no part in the life of the Close or in her husband's social activities. Now I realised why! It was small wonder, too, that—in a cathedral town—the clouds of malicious gossip should gather round such a creature. Who can blame the Canon—I can imagine those old cats saying—if he seeks comfort outside his own home? How much those visits to Torquay must mean to him! The spiritual and intellectual companionship of a kindred soul such as Miss Langdon-Miles must provide a real escape. And—I was forced to admit—it might be only too true. I may be an old spinster myself, but gossiping—thank God!—is not one of my failings. Nevertheless, if tongues wanted to wag, there was certainly fuel for the fire.

Now, too, I realised why Mrs. Fish, in all the many years that the Canon had been our chaplain, had never been to Easton Knoyle. Canon Fish was most gentle and affectionate towards his wife—or so it appeared—and her distorted mind must have been in constant dread lest that affection should be stolen from her. She may have sensed, if she did not know, the cruel things that were said about Miss Langdon-Miles and her husband; to have visited Easton Knoyle might have shattered her last illusion.

The whole time that she was with us she was morose and silent. Not once did she smile, and again and again I saw her watching Miss Langdon-Miles—sometimes furtively, sometimes as a cat watches a mouse.

Why then had Mrs. Fish broken the habit of years? Why had she visited Easton Knoyle at last? How often she had been invited and how often she had refused! Perhaps she could bear the suspense no longer and must know the truth—even if it did mean the shattering of an illusion. Perhaps, however, there was some more definite motive, although it was difficult to imagine what it could be. Anyway, her past absence was naturally not referred to and the reason for her present visit remained—for the time being—a mystery.

The immediate excuse for the visit was not sufficient to account for Mrs. Fish's changed attitude; had she chosen she could easily have avoided Easton Knoyle—as she had always done. The Canon had been to some ecclesiastical conference at Truro, and as his wife was—for once—to accompany him, he had suggested to Miss Langdon-Miles that they should break their return journey at Torquay. Miss Langdon-Miles, always ready to forgive, had welcomed the idea and had insisted on their spending the night at Easton Knoyle. Mrs. Fish suffered from very severe headaches—or claimed to do so—and never motored long distances; she and her husband were, therefore, on this occasion travelling by train.

To tell the truth, it was all a little awkward. Miss Langdon-Miles and I were leaving for London early the next morning—for that dreaded Warburton dinner—and the Fishes had most kindly insisted that they, too, should rise early and travel with us as far as Exeter. A further complication, I could foresee, would be Miranda Gladstone. I had nothing against Miranda; she was one of our nicest and prettiest Sixth Form girls, although sometimes I did think that Miss Langdon-Miles had got her knife into the poor child. Well, Miranda had to go to Tilbury to meet her parents, returning from the East, and I was to hand her over to an aunt at a Kensington hotel. Miranda was, therefore, travelling to London with us and I foresaw that her presence might place an awkward constraint upon the party—between Torquay and Exeter. By the next morning we were all so embarrassed by each other's company that, when it came to the point, Miranda's presence made little difference and the few jokes which the Canon so very kindly cracked with her even came as a relief. But I am running on ahead of my story.

When they arrived I conducted Mrs. Fish to our guest-room. This was close to the staircase, just at the end of the corridor leading to our rooms and to the slype. It was a large and sunny room with a big bay-window looking over the Poets' Garden. Conversation was difficult, and in an effort to break the ice I made a few commonplace remarks about the pleasant prospect. Mrs. Fish and I stood for a moment by the window, gazing across to the blue and purple bay. It was very warm and the window had been flung wide open. From below there came the sound of voices; Miss Langdon-Miles and the Canon were just beneath us—stooping together to look at their dear flowers. To each plant was fixed the appropriate verse, and the Canon's deep voice came up to us, reading:

' *"The myrtle bush grew shady,*
Down by the ford"—
"Is it even so?" said my lady.
"Even so!" said my lord.'

Both so tall and so handsome, standing there
among the delphiniums and poppies in the summer
sunshine—they looked at each other and smiled. I
glanced at poor Mrs. Fish. What a contrast! A terrible thought came into my head, a memory of the
hideous gargoyles of Notre Dame, spewing down
evil on the fair city beneath. At last she turned back
into the room, and for a few moments there was
silence. Then she spoke.

'Tell me, Miss Coppock, my husband is often here,
is he not? I know so little about what he does, you
know.'

'Yes, Mrs. Fish, often here—almost every week.
But then he is our chaplain.'

'I had forgotten. Yes, of course. He hears Miss
Langdon-Miles's confession, I suppose?'

'Yes,' I said—for what else could I say. That was
almost all that passed between us, but it left me—
I really hardly know why—in a state not far short of
terror.

When at last the gong sounded for dinner it was
a great relief to leave the constrained atmosphere of
the drawing-room for the general company of the
high table. But even there I knew that all eyes were
on Mrs. Fish, and I was almost as embarrassed as if I
myself had been their object. It was ridiculous but it
was so. The bottle of wine was on the table, as always when the Canon was with us. Miss Langdon-
Miles offered it to Mrs. Fish:

'No, thank you, Miss Langdon-Miles,' Mrs. Fish

smiled, 'neither Hector nor I ever touch alcohol of any sort.' It was an awkward moment. An audible guffaw from Miss MacTaggart was quite uncalled for, but the general smile that went round the table was understandable. As Miss MacTaggart so vulgarly put it afterwards—'Hector evidently tipples on the sly.' Frau Lauprecht was away—she had been ill for some weeks—and so Miss Langdon-Miles alone drank wine that night.

I hardly know how we all got through the evening. The Canon made most noble efforts to break the long and difficult silences, but I think we were all thankful when Miss Langdon-Miles suggested that, in view of our early start the next morning, we should go to bed. I was quite exhausted but, as is so often the case, exhaustion did not mean sleep.

Hour after hour passed, and each quarter I heard the school clock chime. Do what I would, my mind went round in a whirl, worrying and worrying over the events of the day. Three o'clock struck and a few minutes later I may have begun to doze. Then, suddenly, I found myself wide awake and alert, thoroughly alarmed at what I had heard. The great copper studded door at the end of our corridor had been closed—not with a bang but with a slight thud, as though someone, not realising its weight, had tried to close it quietly. The thud, I thought, had not been sufficient to awaken a sound sleeper, but to me it had been unmistakable. There might, indeed, be no cause for alarm, but my nerves were badly shaken and I felt that the mystery must be solved.

I did not get in a panic—that is not my way. I put on my pink quilted dressing-gown and quietly opened the door on to the corridor. I looked to the right, towards the slype and the chapel. The copper door was closed; perhaps—I reflected—someone had passed through to the chapel. I looked to the left; towards the staircase, where a dim light always burned through the night. I gave a little gasp and then held my breath. Silhouetted against the light was a limping, dwarfish figure. The door of the guest-room was quietly opened and closed, and the corridor was empty again. Mrs. Fish—and fully dressed—at three o'clock in the morning!

8

It was a relief to get away from Easton Knoyle, and even the hubbub and stir of the journey were welcome. Travelling with Miss Langdon-Miles, however, was never easy. A railway journey always throws me into a twitter; there are so many things to remember, and as soon as we reached the station —which, in spite of every precaution, we did only just in time—I had to run on ahead to secure seats for us all. I was quite hung round with parcels, cushions, books, rugs and a variety of objects which could hardly be entrusted to the porters, and— though I deprecate criticism of those who have passed on—I could not help feeling a little hurt when, as we got out of the taxi, Miss Langdon-Miles said to me: 'Now, Coppock, don't fuss'—in front of the Fishes and Miranda too! I wasn't fussing, I was trying to be helpful, which is what I am paid for, and I could have cried.

Miss Langdon-Miles and I—especially if accompanied by one of the girls, usually arranged with the Torquay stationmaster to have a compartment labelled 'Ladies only'. The presence of the Canon had wrecked this comforting arrangement and so, beyond Exeter, one could only hope for the best. After twice enquiring whether I was on the correct platform I found that the first-class compartments would most fortunately be near the centre of the train—so much safer, I think, if the train telescopes in a smash. The moment the train came in I made a wild dive and secured an empty compartment. It was all very well to talk about 'fuss', but there are times when it pays. I soon had our impedimenta spread over the seats, and then stood guard awaiting the others, fretting a little lest the whistle should blow. At last they came—quite a picture as they walked down the platform in the early morning sunshine— Canon Fish as handsome and clerical-looking as ever, and Miss Langdon-Miles a striking figure in her new grey tailor-made. She wore no jewellery save her lorgnette chain, but there was the tinkle of hidden bangles. She carried only a slim volume of verse and a rose, as I had relieved her of everything else. Almost as tall as Miss Langdon-Miles was dear Miranda, dark and apple-cheeked, all aglow with the excitement of the journey and very chic in her school uniform and her big boater. The Canon, I could see, was chaffing her a little. Then, a few paces behind —like an evil dwarf attendant upon some medieval king with his queen and princess—came Mrs. Fish —conspicious in green and orange.

As for me, I wore my best grey alpaca and my white straw with the cherries. For the occasion I had had a little diamond brooch made into a clip to fasten the black velvet band at my throat. I had a new watered-silk ribbon for my eye-glasses and I was wearing the Aunt Bertha earrings. Under my goloshes were my new patent leathers. So altogether, you see, save for that one tragic figure, we were a very presentable party.

At last we were all seated, but not in an entirely satisfactory manner. Miss Langdon-Miles and Mrs. Fish had the two corner seats facing the engine, but when I came tearing back from seeing the luggage safely deposited in the van, I found that the Canon had seated himself between them. Possibly he did this with the kindly intention of leaving the other two corner seats for Miranda and myself, but I suspected that he had a different motive. In any case it left me with my back to the engine and I could only pray that I should not be sick before we reached Exeter.

We left Torquay at 7.30 a.m. It was a painful journey. We had breakfasted at Easton Knoyle and so even the diversion of a meal on the train was denied us. The Canon told Miranda a few amusing limericks—at which we all tried to laugh—and gave her some very sound advice on what to read in preference to the arrant rubbish which finds its way into the school library nowadays. Miranda, usually quite bright and chatty, said 'Yes', and plunged back into her rubbish again, remaining with her hair hanging over her eyes and book until we reached Exeter. There was another difficult silence. I said how pretty the sea looked. Miss Langdon-Miles who, rather rudely, was absorbed in the *Church Times*, made some pungent remarks about an article advocating equality in education. Since Miss Langdon-Miles was a recognised expert in the educational field, it seemed sheer impudence on Mrs. Fish's part to suggest that there might be something to be said on both sides. In any case Miss Langdon-Miles's remarks had been addressed to the Canon. I heaved a sigh of relief when the Cathedral towers at last hove in sight.

I leapt out of the train as Miss Langdon-Miles's bidding—'Coppock, The Canon will need a porter' —and rushed off to the van to secure the Fishes' luggage. Thus it was at the ticket barrier, and not in Miss Langdon-Miles's presence, that I finally said farewell to them. During their visit to Easton Knoyle I spoke scarcely a dozen words to Mrs. Fish and I was, therefore, amazed and touched at the affectionate and, indeed, tearful way in which she pressed my hand, 'You've been so kind,' she said, 'so very kind. I don't think that I could have borne it without you.' Then I had to scurry back, lest the whistle should blow, but as I climbed into the train again I found myself murmuring—half aloud: 'What a very strange woman! What a queer creature!'

We reached Taunton at 9.0 a.m. Hardly had the train pulled in the station, when the door was opened on the corridor side, and a man's voice said: 'Well, ladies, what an unexpected pleasure—and so soon too. May I intrude?' My first thought was that we were being accosted by a stranger and that we must either change our compartment instantly or summon the guard. Then I looked up and recognised the intruder. It was—if you please!—Mr. Francis Toplady, R.A., complete with Vandyke beard, carpet bag and knapsack.

We had to be civil but, frankly, it was a nuisance. Miss Langdon-Miles was deep in her book and was, I knew, in no mood for small talk. She was always nervous before lecturing and for some days she had been quite overwrought at the prospect of the Warburton dinner-party. She had looked white and strained ever since the Fishes' arrival the previous afternoon, and to have to chat to a comparative stranger all the way to Paddington would quite wear her out. As for me, I had begun to doze and was irritated at this intrusion. However, there seemed little we could do about it, and Mr. Toplady settled himself down in the seat next to Miranda.

'What a pleasant surprise this is!' he exclaimed, evidently prepared to chatter. 'Who would have thought that we should meet again so soon? A delightful surprise!'

'An unexpected pleasure,' murmured Miss Langdon-Miles.

'I had such a grand time at Simonsbath. A really comfortable inn, and the moors at their very best just now. I feel a new man already. Really it's most annoying—having to break into my holiday like this. . . .' I made a sympathetic sound, but he rattled on. 'My patron down in Sussex wants advice on some stuff coming up at Christie's—a nuisance, but I shall be back in a few days. A glorious morning—I was up early to get the connection from Minehead—a most glorious morning. After a year in Italy I still say—give me Exmoor on a May morning. . . .' Miss Langdon-Miles rose.

'Mr. Toplady,' she said, 'Miss Coppock and I left Torquay at an early hour and were thinking of taking a cup of coffee in the restaurant car. Perhaps we might leave Miss Miranda Gladstone and our bags in your care; it would be most kind if you would, most kind. . . .'

As I followed Miss Langdon-Miles along the

swaying train I reflected that she had extricated herself from the situation with skill, but I also reflected that we really knew very little about Mr. Toplady and I hoped that Miranda would be safe under his care. As we sipped our disgusting railway coffee Miss Langdon-Miles continued to read and, as I gazed out of the window, I recalled the last occasion on which I had used this restaurant car—on that ill-fated morning when I had met Miss Trubshawe prior to the episode at 'The Harrow'.

We reached Bristol at 10.20 a.m. The train had been standing at the platform for some minutes when I leapt up as if shot.

'Good God!' I cried, forgetting that I was in public, 'Good God! Look, Miss Langdon-Miles, it's Miranda!' There was Miranda, her long legs racing down the platform, her boater flying on its elastic. Then she was lost among the crowd which was leaving the station.

Restaurant car windows are notoriously impossible to open. I rapped on the glass with my knuckles but as I was wearing white kid gloves this was ineffective. I tried again with a coffee spoon.

'Miranda! Miranda!' I cried.

'Don't be a fool, Coppock. You're making us conspicuous. I can't think what the child is up to, but she's got a head on her shoulders. She won't miss the train. Sit down, Coppock.' It was all very well for Miss Langdon-Miles to talk in this fashion but it was clear that she was very badly rattled. She made her way to the door of the restaurant car and leaned out. I followed her and stood with my hand poised aloft ready to pull the communication cord the second the train began to move. What, after all, was £5 compared with Miranda. A nice home-coming for

Mr. and Mrs. Gladstone, I reflected, to be told that their only child had been mislaid at Bristol.

They were already slamming the doors when—at last!—she came sprinting up the platform, laughing, pink and all out of breath. Miss Langdon-Miles, leaning out of the window, saw her plunge safely into our compartment just as the whistle blew. So all was well. But as the train moved out I found that I was trembling all over.

I wanted to dash back to our compartment to find out what had happened, and why on earth Mr. Toplady had ever allowed such a thing. But Miss Langdon-Miles was firm and—for the second time that morning—told me not to fuss. So irritated had she been with Mr. Toplady's chatter that she kept me fidgeting in the restaurant car until we were past Maidenhead. If loyalty to the dead did not forbid I should be compelled to say that I thought she did it on purpose to annoy.

At last we made our way back along the swaying train. Miranda greeted us with a laugh.

'That was a narrow squeak,' she said, 'and I never found poor Mr. Toplady's friend for him after all —in spite of her red hat. . . .'

'My dear Miss Langdon-Miles,' Mr. Toplady chipped in, 'can you ever forgive me? I saw an old friend walking along the platform, a very dear lady friend whom I have not seen for years. I shouted after her, but in vain. My poor bad heart would not allow me to run, so Miss Miranda here most kindly came to my rescue.'

'Mr. Toplady said she had a red hat,' explained Miranda, 'but I couldn't find a red hat anywhere. I'm so sorry, Mr. Toplady.'

'It's for me to apologise, my dear. She must have

left the station before you could catch her. Of course, Miss Langdon-Miles, you know that I would never have allowed our young friend to have been left behind. I had a word with the guard, and, really, if it had not been for my bad heart, I would have run after the lady myself. . . .'

Of course I ought to have realised then and there that Mr. Toplady's heart was really the key to the whole Langdon-Miles tragedy.

It had been a disgraceful episode—an Easton Knoyle girl tearing about Bristol Station like that —but little good was to be served by saying more. We now seemed to be among London's outer suburbs, so I began to gather our things together in order not to lose a moment in securing a porter and a taxi. I lifted down a rug and some umbrellas from the rack—then I paused. How extremely odd, I said to myself. After we had left Exeter I had sat facing the engine, opposite Miranda. There was not the least doubt in my mind about that. Miss Langdon-Miles's dressing-case had been on the rack immediately above Miranda's head, and between Exeter and Taunton I had more than once observed the embossed silver monogram, P. L.-M. The dressing-case was still there, but the monogram was no longer visible. The dressing-case had been turned round!

9

'Hello! Aunt Philippa. It's simply years since I saw you.' We were all standing on the platform at Paddington and I was trying desperately to catch the eye of a taxi-driver, when a pleasant, cheerful voice sounded behind us. Although I had never met the young man, I knew, of course, that it must be Hallam from Cambridge, son of Fortescue, the Indian judge. As he kissed his aunt I thought how very good-looking he was—but then the Langdon-Miles were a good-looking family—with his fair hair and his dark twinkling eyes. So tall, too, like his aunt, but with just a touch of Langdon-Miles obstinacy about the chin.

'Don't you worry about a taxi,' he said, when Miss Langdon-Miles had introduced us all; Mr. Toplady, by the way, still seemed to regard himself as one of the party. 'I've got Uncle Harold's car here—a topping Bentley—and I can drop you at your hotel. But we must have lunch first and—oh! I say, Aunt Philippa, you will like Uncle Harold, he really is an awfully good chap.' Miss Langdon-Miles winced.

'I'm glad to hear it, Hallam. Well, Mr. Toplady, we must say good-bye.' But Hallam—if I may call him that—would have none of it; he could easily take anybody anywhere it seemed. I rather suspected that he enjoyed dashing about in that 'Bentley', and I began to feel nervous; London traffic is terrifying enough in any circumstances.

As the porter placed our luggage in the tonneau, I thought that it undoubtedly looked a most powerful vehicle.

'Miranda, you will sit between Mr. Toplady and myself; Miss Coppock will sit by Mr. Langdon-Miles.' But that was not what Hallam wanted. He smiled at Miranda.

'I expect that you'd rather sit in front, wouldn't you?'

'Oh! Yes. Rather!' said Miranda. I gasped, although I had noticed before how Miss Langdon-Miles's authority seemed to dwindle the further one got from Easton Knoyle.

So there we all were, threading our way through the Bayswater streets at a vertiginous speed; Mr. Toplady in a wideawake hat, sun-glasses and Van-dyke beard, perched on the edge of the seat between Miss Langdon-Miles and myself, and in front were Hallam and Miranda. What a really charming couple, I reflected. Somehow Miranda seemed so much more grown up that she had done at Easton Knoyle, and I am ashamed to say that my sentimental and foolish old heart was already manufacturing a romance. I can hear my readers laughing at me!

We were crossing the Serpentine and Hallam was driving more slowly so that Miranda could look at the Park—or so he said. They seemed to be enjoying themselves and Miss Langdon-Miles was looking extremely sulky. She was rather crushed between the side of the car and Mr. Toplady—to whom she had clearly taken a dislike—and she was fidgety about getting her costume creased. By the time we dropped the little artist at Victoria she was barely civil to him.

Then Miranda had to be delivered to her aunt at the Hyde Park Hotel, but before we knew where we were Hallam was driving round half London, showing Miranda the sights—or so he said—Buckingham Palace, Houses of Parliament and goodness knows what else. Miss Langdon-Miles was livid with fury, but was helpless. The last straw came when we pulled up outside Miranda's hotel.

'Miranda dear,' said Miss Langdon-Miles, 'you will give my regards to your aunt. Coppock, see to

Miranda's luggage.' But Hallam was already out of the car.

'Don't bother, Miss Coppock. I'll look after Miranda.' And before I could move, Hallam was up the hotel steps with the suit-case, Miranda at his heels. I really could not see why Miss Langdon-Miles should blame me. I hate injustice and we had quite a scene in the car while we were waiting for Hallam to return. I know that I must have gone quite scarlet, I always do on these occasions. At last he came running down the steps and jumped into the car.

'Nice girl, Aunt Philippa. I asked her to the dinner-party tonight, but her aunt had fixed up a theatre—a pity. But I'm going to have tea with them tomorrow before they go down to Tilbury.'

'Really, Hallam . . .' Miss Langdon-Miles was speechless, and—very wickedly—I felt the pleasures of revenge. My romance, too, seemed to be prospering. Hallam certainly hadn't wasted his time—but then both his father and his Uncle Edward had been highly susceptible to a pretty face when they were his age—and I suppose he took after them.

Miss Langdon-Miles was so upset that she declined Hallam's invitation to lunch, making what I thought was a very thin excuse about a headache. But he was a good-humoured fellow and took no offence. Unfortunately, when he said good-bye to us outside the Anglo-American Ladies' Club in Park Street—where we were to spend two nights—he made things no better by his parting remarks, although he meant well, poor boy.

'Well, good-bye, Aunt Philippa. I'll be seeing you this evening. It will be jolly. Uncle Harold is looking forward no end to meeting his new sister-in-law. I'm sure that he and Aunt Beatrice are going to be awfully happy together.' Considering that 'Aunt Beatrice' and 'Uncle Harold' had been 'married' at the Hampstead register office they were, if you thought it out, living in a state which was approximately the same thing as sin, and 'happiness' was not what one could or ought to wish for such a liaison. However, as I say, Hallam meant well and he was only twenty, far too young to understand such matters.

At last he left us and Miss Langdon-Miles and I were alone together in the elegant hall of the Anglo-American Ladies' Club. Miss Langdon-Miles had been a member of the Club ever since her visit to Boston. It was extremely refined and its residential arrangements enabled one to escape the publicity and unsavoury possibilities of the common hotel. Miss Langdon-Miles was very near collapse. Beneath a large marble bust of Ralph Waldo Emerson was a sofa, and on to this she subsided.

We spent a quiet afternoon resting on our beds. This is a practice of which normally I disapprove—in the Common Room I had always upheld a minority view on the issue—but I was very tired and Miss Langdon-Miles was positively prostrate with exhaustion. I had to administer a sedative before she could sleep. The Fishes' visit, the journey, the incident at Bristol, Hallam's conduct with Miranda and, above all, the prospect of the dinner-party—poor thing! she had made some sharp remarks to me but I could not help feeling rather sorry for her.

And yet, if Providence had seen fit to give us a glimpse of the future, how trivial all these things would have seemed. How utterly trivial and insignificant had we but known that Philippa Langdon-Miles had only twenty-four hours to live!

10

The arrangements for the dinner-party had been bungled from the start. Of course it was not dear Miss Langdon-Miles's fault, but it did seem ridiculous that the two sisters, after scarcely sending each other so much as a picture postcard for twenty years, should suddenly conduct a voluminous correspondence, lasting weeks, and all over a rendezvous for dinner.

Beatrice—with 'Harold' conniving I suppose—was entirely to blame. She kept a spacious and most extravagant house on the edge of Hampstead Heath —with several servants—and it would have been the easiest thing in the world for her to entertain us there in a proper and dignified manner. But no! There would be no time for dinner before the theatre, they were going north the next day and two of the maids were already on holiday, the house was being redecorated, it was a festive occasion—festive indeed! —and an evening at a theatre would be more in keeping, Hallam was there and would prefer an outing—and so on and so on, all very transparent. Clearly it was merely meanness, or possibly 'Harold' had had a twinge of conscience, though I doubted it, about playing host in a house purchased and maintained with Langdon-Miles money.

I rather gathered, too, that there was an acrimonious exchange between Beatrice and Philippa about my being present at the dinner; but on this point Philippa was adamant. Naturally I offered to stand down—never to push myself is my constant rule—but Miss Langdon-Miles stood her ground. Never, she said, would she face the newly married couple alone. If Beatrice was to have the moral support of Harold and Hallam, Philippa must have me at her side; clearly that was only fair. Beatrice retorted, quite irrelevantly, that it was a family party and that I should be an interloper. It was all very embarrassing and painful to me. However, Philippa issued her ultimatum—no Coppock, no dinner—and we carried the day. So, after all, I was able to pack my purple silk with the short sleeves, and I must own that I felt rather excited.

As to the choice of a piece: Miss Langdon-Miles had thought, very rightly, that there could be only one opinion on the matter; *The Trojan Women* was playing at 'His Majesty's' and was very highly commended in the journals. It would have been a dignified evening, and if by ill-chance Miss Langdon-Miles should be seen at the theatre by any Easton Knoyle parents, her position would not be compromised. But Beatrice was determined to be difficult. It would, she had written, mean a dull evening for Hallam. Then she added that there was a revival of *Lady Windermere's Fan* at the 'Globe'—and what could be more suitable or amusing! Fancy! How she could! Well, to cut a long story short, it all ended in a compromise. It was finally agreed that we should see *Macbeth* at—as it always seems to be called—the 'Old Vic'.

It was only some years later that it struck me as

rather a curious coincidence that it should have been *Macbeth*.

I *was* disappointed. I stand second to none in my admiration for the Swan of Avon, but this particular theatre, so Miranda told me, was away in the slums of South London, and rather dingy. I hope that I shall be thought neither skittish nor abandoned when I say that I had been eagerly looking forward to an evening in the West End—to the gay restaurant, to the sight of jewels and furs, to the lights and the glitter, and to the feeling that, just for once, I was mixing with the *haut ton*. I suppose that there is still a bit of the Old Eve in me for I never see Piccadilly Circus at night without getting that funny feeling which the French call *joie de vivre*. And now —I almost wept—we were to dine in the refreshment room at Waterloo Station! And 'Harold' —with Beatrice's money in his pocket—could so easily have entertained us on a really lavish scale. And even if it was called a 'Grill Room' I couldn't see that it made it any better—or not much. If we dined north of the river, said Beatrice—with her eternal excuses—it would mean such a rush, the theatre began early, the traffic might hold us up— and so on, *ad infinitum*. Well—the theatre had been more or less her choice, so it seemed to me that she had merely cut off her nose to spite her face. The whole outing now seemed very flat.

To be chattering on in this way about the restaurant and theatre world must seem trivial and heartless in view of the tragedy of the following day. The future, thank God, is veiled, but how often have I bitterly reproached myself for indulging in thoughts of gay and sensual pleasures when—had we but known—we were already within the Shadow. What a lesson!

Mr. and Mrs. Warburton—as I suppose I must resign myself to calling them—and Hallam were to call for us in the Bentley at the Anglo-American Ladies' Club. They were late, ten minutes late, which set me fretting and put both sisters in a temper. When, at last, they did arrive I had to rush round after cloaks and wraps and theatre tickets; consequently my first impression of Harold Warburton, standing in the hall of the Club all muffled up, was but a fleeting one. But it was more than enough, far more. I had expected a rake and a schemer, but it was a shock to meet a gorilla.

This great, gawky giant drove the car himself and to put Philippa next to him, on the front seat, all the way from Park Street to Waterloo, may have been intended by Beatrice as a conciliatory gesture. Actually it seemed to me to be neither more nor less than a gratuitous insult.

At dinner I had another look. It was only too true. I knew the fellow was an Australian but it had never occurred to me that Aboriginal blood might flow in his veins. To think that a vast fortune —which God had intended for His Church—was now securely in the grasp of those great hairy hands! Poor Miss Langdon-Miles! I could see, even from the other side of the table, that she was scarcely able to swallow her *hors d'œuvres*. My heart bled for her. What a brother-in-law!

His height alone amounted to a deformity, and he had such an ungainly stoop. How those hands ever managed to play the piano, I don't know. He had only been in England a few months, so I suppose his dress suit may have been made in Adelaide or Ballarat or somewhere, which would account for a good deal—but not for it being several sizes too small, nor for his tie being crooked. And his long moustachios were stained in a rather disgusting way by the evil-looking cheroots which he would chew all evening. Moreover, his ears were much too large and red.

That Hallam should have spoken of his uncle as 'an awfully good chap' could only be due to a chivalrous but wrong-headed loyalty to Beatrice. He said that 'Uncle Harold' might seem shy and clumsy when one first met him, but that really he was kind, intelligent and charming—as well as being a brilliant pianist. Hm!—I thought—the 'artistic temperament' again. Hallam laughed at my suggestion of a heathen ancestry, adding that his uncle and aunt had many interests in common and—if you please!—were deeply in love. This was too absurd. Beatrice was no chicken. Moreover, although I had never had anything but a low opinion of her idealism and 'good works', I reflected that, even for her, there must be a limit. No real *lady* could have fallen in love with this oddity. Clearly she had been trapped by an adventurer.

Hallam might say that Mr. Warburton was 'shy' —fancy, a big man like that!—but this was merely a kind-hearted attempt to excuse his uncle for being thoroughly *gauche* and inarticulate. Inarticulate! He grinned and smirked all through dinner—I suppose in his way he was an attentive host—but it was not until we were all pretending to enjoy a pêche Melba, and Beatrice had announced officiously that there would be no time for coffee, that he spoke up. Even then you could hardly call it speaking. He suddenly leapt from the table, without asking to be excused

—and made a dive for the cloak-room. I thought that perhaps he felt sick, the ragout had certainly been very rich, but he soon returned bearing two large boxes of chocolates—one with a purple ribbon and one with a green.

'I'd forgotten,' he said sheepishly, 'that these were in my overcoat pocket. One for you, Philippa, and one for Miss Coppock.'

'Thank you,' I said. 'Very kind.' I was too old to enjoy such frivolity but perhaps he meant it graciously.

'Why!' said Hallam, laughing, 'you might have given Miss Coppock the one with the purple ribbon, to go with her nice dress.'

'No,' Mr. Warburton cried. 'I bought that one for Philippa and this one for Miss Coppock, and we won't change them.'

We all laughed rather immoderately, a good deal more than the event justified, and I only record the incident to show how glad we were of such trivialities to help in breaking the ice. The strain of keeping up the conversation at dinner had been simply awful. Every topic was pregnant with danger, and one can't discuss the weather for ever. There had been at least six agonising silences. Family affairs, needless to say, were out of the question, and education, politics, religion, money, marriage, India, America and Australia were all sparks that might fire a mine. Philippa made one gallant effort to draw 'Harold' out on the subject of his musical career, but, except for the interesting fact that he had played in the Torquay Pavilion the previous winter, nothing came of this. Philippa remarked, rather pointedly, that he might have called on us at Easton Knoyle, to which Beatrice retorted that it was a pity that we hadn't been able to take tickets for at least one of his recitals.

When, at last, we reached our seats, and the curtain rose to reveal the blasted heath, the relief was indescribable.

It was in the second entr'acte that young Hallam hauled me off to the foyer in order, as he said, 'to stand me a drink . . .' what wicked nonsense! '. . . and to let the aunts and uncles get to know each other a bit.' It was then that I decided to tackle the lad. I don't know why I suddenly spoke out—perhaps I could bear the strain no longer, or perhaps Lady Macbeth's 'Screw you courage to the sticking place' was still ringing in my ears. Hallam could talk of nothing but Miranda, and it was some time before I could work round to my subject.

'Mr. Langdon-Miles,' I said at last, 'you must forgive me if I speak out. I will be frank. I am worried, very worried, about your aunt's marriage.'

'Oh come, Miss Coppock! You've got a bee in your bonnet about Uncle Harold. He's all right. Shy and awkward perhaps, but so nice really. What I call a beautiful smile.'

'Forgive me,' I said, 'but it's my duty to warn you. You are being fooled. You know nothing, absolutely nothing, of this Australian pianist. He turned up in this country—out of the blue—seeking concert engagements, and your aunt—with her usual quixotic attitude towards poverty-stricken genius—simply took him up. And now—as the vulgar saying goes—"he's hung up his hat in her hall." He's years younger than she is, and who can doubt but that he has more than half an eye on the Langdon-Miles fortune?' Hallam looked rather annoyed.

'Really, Miss Coppock, I do think Aunt Beatrice knows her own business.'

'It's not only *her* business,' I said: 'others are affected. When this Harold came over the horizon, your own prospects, for example, began to fade away.' I had appealed to him as to a grown man and I was hurt by his response.

'Thank you, Miss Coppock, but my father is in a position to look after me, and I shall earn my own living. Don't you think it would be better if you minded your own business?'

'It is my business,' I cried, getting rather hot. 'It's my solemn duty to protect Miss Langdon-Miles—not to mention the Church. For God's sake, let us urge your Aunt Beatrice, if it is not already too late, to refrain from making a foolish and wicked will!'

'Oh! Do leave the whole business alone, Miss Coppock. Damn money, anyway! It spoils everything. Why couldn't my grandfather leave the money to Uncle Edward—where it belonged—instead of being spiteful?'

'There were reasons,' I said.

'Why? Even if Edward's mill-girl did have a brat, he married her.' I was shocked to hear a young boy talking in such a flippant manner; I had thought, too, that that skeleton was securely locked in the cupboard.

'After all,' he went on, 'Uncle Edward could do with the money. This U.S. crisis is a ghastly business, and Aunt B. says that Uncle's firm—Langdon-Miles and Gabbitas—has gone down the drain with all the others.'

'Down the drain?'

'Yes, gone phut, bankrupt. His Rosie Sproggs

won't like it—if she's still alive. A case of "clogs to clogs." '

'It's your Uncle Harold,' I said, 'not your Uncle Edward, that I'm worried about. . . .' And then the curtain bell rang and we had to rejoin the others. I felt that I had made very little impression on the boy, and I was sorry that there should be any coldness between us. He was so handsome—if wrong-headed —and I was beginning to take quite an interest in his budding romance.

The aunts and Uncle Harold had been changing seats, and I now found myself next to the monster. It was very unpleasant having him so close in the dark, and his manners were deplorable. He had opened Philippa's box of chocolates and he kept picking them out and passing them to us in his fingers. They were rich liqueur creams, and I was afraid that they might give me an upset. The third act of *Macbeth* was, for me, absolutely ruined. The whole outing, about which I had felt so excited, had gone wrong from the beginning. And it might have been such a treat. Now everything was horrible; even the appearance of Banquo's ghost only served to remind me of the Easton Knoyle *tableaux vivants* at Christmas-time, and of the little ones at The Firs. All of a sudden I felt quite homesick—this London whirl was not for me—and in the darkness I wiped away a tear.

But the real trouble began in the Waterloo Bridge Road. It was raining and we all had to stand—for what seemed hours—on the steps of the theatre while Hallam fetched the car. If tempers were already frayed this did not improve them. Miss Langdon-Miles made an innocent remark about the car being large and comfortable—when it did come.

'I suppose,' said Beatrice, 'that you think it cost a lot.'

'I hadn't, but it obviously did. How fortunate that you can afford it so easily. Is it yours or Harold's?'

'It's ours,' snapped Beatrice.

'Now then, you two . . .' Harold was most irritating when he was trying to be jovial.

'I wasn't implying anything,' said Philippa.

'Then,' said Beatrice, 'I was wrong.'

'What should I imply?'

'Nothing. I thought you grudged Harold the car —that's all. I'm glad I was wrong.'

'Don't be so silly, Beatrice. It's nothing to me how Harold spends your money . . . father's money.'

'Come, come,' said Harold, which wasn't very helpful.

'Can't Beatrice and I talk?'

'Of course.'

'Well then.'

'Well what?'

'Nothing. Will Hallam be much longer? He is slow. I suppose Fortescue gives him a good allowance—or is he another of your protégés?'

'The poor lad is being as quick as he can. I'm sorry we haven't got a chauffeur.'

'Park Street isn't really on your way to Hampstead; Coppock and I had better get a taxi. Save Harold's petrol. . . .'

'Now please, Philippa,' said Harold, 'don't speak like that. We've only met today—and we are relations now.'

'Just.'

'What do you mean?'

'Nothing, only "just". . . that's all. For just a month.'

'Philippa, why can't you be nicer to Harold?'

'Well, really . . .'

'You're beastly to him. I'm afraid you're a snob, Philippa.'

'That's better than being a Bolshevik and an atheist. And I don't take penniless musicians out of the gutter—and live with them.'

'Anyway, he didn't woo me in the confession box. . . .'

'You beast!'

Well, of course, that did it. Voices were raised and people passing on the pavement began to stare. I got hotter and hotter—I simply didn't know where to put myself. I thought of the girls in bed at Easton Knoyle, and wondered what they would think. It was so dreadfully vulgar—and in those slummy sur-roundings too. Quite sordid! How impossible the Langdon-Miles were—except, of course, Philippa. I reflected that this sort of bickering had been going on, more or less, for three generations. Then, at last, Philippa cut the whole thing short. A taxi was pass-ing and she hailed it.

'Jump in, Coppock. Quick.'

Without so much as a 'good night' to the War-burtons we drove off. I began to cry, and when we got to the lighter streets of the West End I could see that Philippa was trembling all over and was quite white with passion!

11

I lay awake nearly all night wondering whether Miss Langdon-Miles's lecture would have to be postponed. Would she be fit for it? When I saw her the next morning I did not feel at all reassured. She was white and tearful, quite desperate-looking, and in a terribly emotional state. For a few minutes she would try to concentrate on her missal, then on Mrs. Meynell's poems, then she would get hysterical or lie back with her eyes closed. It was a distressing morning but she would not hear of her lecture being cancelled—so many, she said, would be disappointed. I had promised my Easton Knoyle colleagues that I would perform various errands at the Oxford Street shops but these had to go by the board; Miss Langdon-Miles clung to me and I could not possibly leave her.

By mid-day she had developed a splitting headache and I persuaded her to lie down until it was time to leave for the Cranmer Hall. I lunched alone in the large club dining-room, feeling very shy as well as miserable. After lunch I got out my invaluable spirit lamp and made her a strong cup of tea. I also gave her a couple of aspirins and was thankful to see her doze off.

I left her to sleep as long as I dare. The Cranmer Hall was only just off Victoria Street, but the traffic was very thick and we were a few minutes late. As she lay back in the taxi, her eyes closed, she told me that she thought she would get through all right. Looking back on it afterwards I realised that those were the last words she ever said to me.

As we entered the hall she was deathly pale. Her subject was 'The Place of Woman in the State', and I knew that she had some outspoken remarks to make about certain modern heresies. It was a distinguished company. Lord Huddersfield, the most ardent ritualist in the House of Laity, was the Chairman, and Dame Primrose was to propose the vote of thanks. At least two peers and a bishop were present and although I am anything but a snob I was very proud to have a seat—albeit a humble one—on the platform.

Lord Huddersfield's opening remarks were felicitous. Miss Langdon-Miles rose and took up her station bravely at the front of the platform. She always spoke without notes. After a few introductory words about the alarming decline of spiritual values in education she went on to condemn, in no uncertain terms, those who insisted, in season and out, that a Woman must have a career. She, Miss Langdon-Miles, was proud to uphold the banner of what our Bolshevik friends would call reaction. She was second to none in her desire to see Woman take her rightful place in the world, but it was in the religious field and as a gracious hostess that a woman could influence history, just as surely as if she sat in Parliament itself. Dame Primrose began to fidget a little. Miss Langdon-Miles then explained her ideal of the Christian English lady whose sphere was the home, and there was a murmured 'Hear, hear', from Lord Huddersfield. It was all familiar ground to me, but I was watching her very closely for she had been very white and shaky when she went on the platform and I was anxious to see how she would pull through.

Suddenly I realised that all was not well. She had

stopped in the middle of a sentence, her hand trying to grasp the air. Lord Huddersfield hurriedly poured out a glass of water, carelessly slopping it over the table. Then poor Miss Langdon-Miles gave a cry that must have been audible at the back of the hall —almost a shriek. She swayed, tried to clutch the table behind her, and fell with a horrible crash.

For a few seconds there was complete silence— we were all stunned. Then the audience was on its feet and Lord Huddersfield was calming them. But I knew nothing of that. I did not care what people thought; only one thing mattered—I was in a frenzy to get to my darling Miss Langdon-Miles. I fought my way forward from the back of the platform, pushing all aside. Then, at last, my arms were round her and I think she knew me. But she was in great agony; her face was twitching and she was doubled up with pain, arching her back and writhing on the platform. I was quite out of my mind but— for a fleeting second—I recalled with terrible clarity another occasion, and it was myself I saw, writhing and twitching in that stuffy little bedroom at Nether Fordington.

Lord Huddersfield—thank God!—kept his head. He asked for a doctor to come forward, but by a tragic mischance there was not one present.

'Will someone please telephone for an ambulance?' he said. 'I very much regret that Miss Langdon-Miles seems to have been taken gravely ill. Will you please all leave the building.'

It seemed a lifetime before the ambulance men came to carry poor Miss Langdon-Miles down the empty hall and out into the street. She was ominously still now. I followed, supported by Lord Huddersfield—so kind—and Dame Primrose—so efficient. I was in no state to know what was said to me or what I did; I only know that someone helped me into a car, saying that we would follow the ambulance to the Westminster Hospital. Once more, however, there was a strange moment of clarity; a few cars were still driving away from outside the hall and, as I looked up, I am sure—yes, I am quite sure —that among them, threading its way rapidly through the traffic towards Victoria Street, was a large canary coloured limousine.

I sobbed all the way to the hospital. They tried to comfort me—telling me that all would be well. But as I watched the stretcher being carried into the hospital I knew in my heart, beyond all doubt, that Philippa Langdon-Miles was already dead.

12

And at that point in my story I feel that I should really have passed on the pen to Mr. Muir, so that he might tell you of the sad events at the Coquet Hall Hotel, of the death of Mrs. Harold Warburton and of the coming of Mr. Stone—but first there must be a postscript to my story.

I leave it to my readers to imagine the state that I was in after my dear Miss Langdon-Miles's death. I felt quite alone in my sorrow. By the time the tragedy took place the Warburtons had set off in that Bentley for their holiday in the north, taking a perversely devious route so that it was two or three days before we could track them down. How ghastly to think of them gaily enjoying a motor tour in cold blood while Miss Langdon-Miles's corpse lay un-buried—but perhaps they would not have cared. When at last they did reach Coquet Hall, to find my telegram awaiting them, their conduct was certainly most extraordinary. My opinion of Beatrice had never been high but now it dropped to a very low level. She actually saw fit to absent herself from the funeral! True, by that time it would have meant a night journey from Northumberland to Devonshire, but what is a little thing like that when we are in the presence of the Great Leveller. As a result of her conduct not a single member of the Langdon-Miles family was present at the graveside. How shameful!

If the Langdon-Miles family was conspicious by its absence, sympathy and respect from other quarters was not lacking. There was a vast con-course, including many persons of high academic standing and several of the nobility. It did my heart good. The Bishop assisted Canon Fish in taking the service—and how that would have pleased dear Miss Langdon-Miles! The lawn outside the west door of the chapel was an absolute carpet of floral tributes, and it was a beautiful May morning when we bore that great English lady to her last resting place. I felt that it was a truly lovely ending to a terrible tragedy.

As it happened one advantage was gained by the delay in tracking down the Warburtons—though it was no credit to them. As soon as Beatrice heard the news she forced her husband to telephone to Easton Knoyle to say that, if possible, her sister was to be cremated. By that time—mercifully—other ar-rangements had been made and so this pagan idea, which would have been so repugnant to Philippa, was scotched. I remember that Harold Warburton was quite unreasonably vexed. In any case, although an autopsy had been performed immediately after death, I am not at all sure that the Westminster Coroner would ever have approved of cremation. I might mention, too, that Mr. Paston, the school solicitor, was Miss Langdon-Miles's executor and that he thoroughly approved of all the burial arrangements. The other executor was Canon Fish, and so Beatrice actually had no jurisdiction in the matter and Harold Warburton's vexation was quite out of place. Why could not the Warburtons mind their own business?

At first everything seemed to fall on my shoulders, and what made me feel even more lonely in my responsibility was that, on the very day of Miss Langdon-Miles's death, Canon Fish had succumbed to a severe chill—contacted, I fear, on that early morning train. At the last minute he most nobly rose from his sickbed to assist at the funeral service, but most of the time I really had no one to lean on except Mr. Paston who, though kind and sensible, was a little past it. Miss Wheelright, too, kept her grip, but was fully occupied deputising for Miss Langdon-Miles in the classrooms. The other members of the Common Room, it grieves me to say, were unaccountably indifferent to what had happened and there were even moments when I thought I detected flippancy. No one would have thought that the shadow of a great disaster had fallen across Easton Knoyle. However, the girls, I am almost sure, were altogether heartbroken.

Work was a great relief and I was glad to be busy replying to the hundreds of letters and telegrams which we had received. We had, of course, cabled to Fortescue in India and to Edward in New York.

I am sorry to say that Fortescue did not see fit to reply; perhaps he wrote to Beatrice—more probably not. It was all the more gratifying, therefore, when —two days after the funeral—the post-office telephoned through a cable from Edward: 'I share your deep sorrow and shall spare no effort to have the mystery sifted to the bottom: Edward Langdon-Miles.' After thirty years' silence it was very satisfactory to know that the wayward Edward had come to his senses, but I suppose Death draws us all nearer together. Philippa, I knew, would have been willing to forget and forgive—provided, of course, that he never brought his mill-girl back to England, for of his marriage one could never approve.

It was after tea, I remember, when I was relaxing in my room, that Parkinson called me down one day to the drawing-room to see Mr. Paston. As I passed through the hall the School House girls were just coming in from bathing and beach-cricket, and I could not help drawing a contrast in my mind between their innocent pleasures and the gross and evil business with which I was concerned. I found Mr. Paston very shaky.

'Ah! Dear Miss Coppock,' he began, 'you have been wonderful these last few weeks. I do thank you for all you have done. Easton Knoyle will always be grateful to you. . . .' This was gratifying but, I need hardly say, quite undeserved. I had done my duty— that was all—and looked for no reward, at any rate on this earth. I said as much.

'But I have one more shock for you, dear lady,' Mr. Paston went on. 'One more shock, and I don't understand it at all. Most puzzling, most terrible. A mistake, of course. It must be a mistake. But will the school survive it I wonder. Such a scandal, such

145

publicity. . . .' By now I was getting frantic and I almost snatched the telegram which he had in his hand. As I had suspected it was from his barrister brother who was holding a watching brief for Easton Knoyle at the inquest: 'Very much regret that the verdict is: "Wilful murder by person or persons unknown", death being caused by the administration of strychnine.'

I went into a dead faint.

13

I think that deep down in what Miss Trubshawe—in her odd modern way—would have called my 'subconscious self' I had known all along what the verdict would be. But to have my worst fears—those fears that had haunted my bewildering nightmares—confirmed in this uncompromising manner was a terrible shock. Mr. Paston and Canon Fish both urged me, in the most kindly way, to take a holiday—but how could I? What would Miss Langdon-Miles have said? Now, more than ever—if only to spite the villain who had done the deed—I must do all I could to take her place. A new headmistress would not be appointed until the following term—how I dreaded the thought of a stranger—and meanwhile it was the wish of the Governors that Miss Wheelwright and I should carry on as best we could.

It thus came about that a few days later I found myself in Cambridge. It had been Miss Langdon-Miles's habit, each year, to take up to Cambridge for a few days, those girls who were going to Girton after the summer vacation. Introductions were made and the girls were shown round so that when the autumn came they would not feel at a loss in a strange environment. Miss Langdon-Miles had always set great store by this pleasing arrangment and I was determined to act as she would have wished. Miranda Gladstone, Felicity Carhampton and Gay Clintock—what names parents do give their children nowadays!—were therefore spending two nights, under my wing, at the Trinity Arms.

I can't imagine how it came about, but that nice boy Hallam must have got wind of our visit. Surely he and Miranda had not been corresponding! On the very first evening just as the girls and I were chatting over our after-dinner coffee—the girls looking very charming in their best frocks—in walked the young man, as bold as brass. Miranda went very pink and then there must have been some winking and manœuvring behind my back, for Felicity and Gay were soon seated on the far side of the lounge, while Hallam became very thoughtful and considerate all of a sudden.

'Now, Miss Coppock,' he said, 'I bet you're worn out after your journey. If you feel like going to bed, don't mind us: we shall be all right.'

'I don't doubt it,' I said. Having a sentimental old heart, I felt rather a 'gooseberry' but I knew well what Miss Langdon-Miles's attitude would have been, and that, I decided, must be my guide. I got on with my knitting and left the young folk to chat. Suddenly I pricked my ears up.

'I say, Miranda,' Hallam was saying, 'do you remember that funny little artist we dropped at Victoria—that day I met you and poor Aunt Philippa? Well—would you believe it—he was here the next night, in this hotel.'

'Here!' exclaimed Miranda.

'Oh! Mr. Langdon-Miles,' I said, 'I think you must have made a mistake, because I distinctly remember Mr. Toplady saying that he was going down to Sussex.'

'It was Toplady all right, Miss Coppock. Aunt Beatrice and Uncle Harold came here for the night on their way up to Northumberland, which was nice for me. I had only been allowed two nights in Town and so we didn't motor to Cambridge until the evening—after I had had tea with you, Miranda. Naturally I wanted to have as long in Town as I could . . .'

'I should think so,' said Miranda. 'Who wouldn't?'

'. . . and when we got here there was old Toplady—what a name!—sitting on this very sofa. He was just behind Uncle Harold at the reception desk when they booked their rooms, and he and I had quite a chat.'

'It's very peculiar,' I said. 'I'm quite sure he said Sussex; besides, you can't get to Cambridge from Victoria.'

'I thought he was an awful bore, anyway,' went on Hallam. 'It must have been rotten for you having him all the way from Torquay.'

'Taunton,' I said. 'He had come from Simonsbath on Exmoor and had joined the train at Taunton.'

'Oh! no, Miss Coppock,' said Miranda. 'He came into our carriage at Taunton, but while you were in the restaurant car with poor Miss Langdon-Miles the ticket collector came along and I heard him say to Toplady: "Changed carriages I see, sir." So it seems to me that old Toplady was a bit of a fibber—

and I'm quite certain there was never a red hat on the platform.'

'Well, Toplady doesn't matter, does he, Miranda?' said Hallam. 'By jove! It will be simply grand to have you up here next term. You don't know Cambridge, do you?'

'No, but I very soon shall.'

'It's never too soon to begin. It's not quite dark yet; what about getting you first view of the "backs"?'

'Oh yes!' exclaimed Miranda. 'Can I, Miss Coppock?'

'Well, I don't know, I'm sure,' I began. I felt that Miss Langdon-Miles would have said 'No', but before I could get in another word Hallam was on his feet.

'We'll be all right, Miss Coppock. Don't you worry. Come on, Miranda.' These young people always take my breath away so. I tried to protest but they were gone. Gay and Felicity, in the other side of the lounge, began to giggle—which I thought was rather vulgar; I ignored them. As a matter of fact I had begun to do some hard thinking on my own account.

Suddenly I walked across to the hotel reception desk. I did hope that the clerk would not think it odd when I began to look through the register. I turned back the pages until I came to May 20th. Hallam had been quite right—and adjacent bedrooms too! There it was in black and white:

Room 121.
Mr. & Mrs. Warburton.   Hampstead.
Room 122.
Mr. F. Toplady.   Fowey.

'Well!' I said. 'Whoever heard of such a thing?' And then I sat down and wrote a long, long letter to Aunt Bertha. I had plenty of time before going to bed, because Hallam and Miranda came back disgracefully late.

Part Four

in which Mr. Adam Muir of Dalmellington tells how Lysander Stone came to visit Coquet Hall and how Mrs. Harold Warburton died in her sleep in the early summer of 1931

I

'Murder'—how strange that the word should ever have come into my life at all. My ways have always lain in quiet places. I am a solicitor or, as we say north of the border, a writer, and my practice, away in a little sleepy town in County Ayr, has always been a very humdrum concern. The family affairs of the local farmers and shopkeepers, a little conveyancing and an occasional appearance in the Sheriff's Court—that, for some thirty years, had made up my professional life. At the beginning of the century I had stepped into my father's shoes and after that things had been pretty comfortable in a quiet way. The firm of Muir and Maxwell, when I became a junior partner, was already a hundred years old, and since then the work has gone on behind the wire blinds of the small house in Cally Street, much as it had done since my great-grandfather had died—a good Jacobite to the end. Our aged clerk had spent nearly half a century in the service of the firm and there was little that could not be entrusted to him. As you may imagine, therefore, I had ample time for other pursuits.

I am a bachelor, my sister Janet keeping house for me in an efficient way. In 1910 I had purchased—very reasonably—the Little Doon Farm. Janet—more extravagantly—had made the interior pleasant with old furniture, china and chintzes—for all of which, it was said, she had a flair—while I devoted my abundant leisure to the breeding of a small Jersey herd, to fishing with the dry fly and to the study of Border literature. I always claim, in a modest way, that my collection of books and papers dealing with Sir Walter Scott and his circle is unusually complete. This collection had been most carefully acquired and it was ridiculous of Janet to say that I wasted money in the Edinburgh bookshops—or on one occasion at Sotherby's—for anyone but a woman would have realised that the whole thing was an excellent investment. A few, a very few, of my readers may recall a slim volume, *The Ettrick Shepherd*, which I ventured, very diffidently, to lay before the public some years ago. The sales were small, but the writing gave me much pleasure. I also play chess. But it was the brown trout and the scenes of the Border Ballads that brought me each year to Coquet Hall; Janet, meanwhile, visiting old friends in the south. It was not a bad thing, she used to say, for us to get away from each other for a couple of months each summer. Perhaps she was right.

Into this placid existence the Langdon-Miles tragedy came as an unwelcome disturbance, like a stone thrown into a still pool. Professionally I had never had anything to do with serious crime. As a law-student I had heard Crippen sentenced, the records of our firm showed that, some time in the 'eighties, old Maxwell had dealt with a nasty case of assault and, in my own time, there had been a very sad story of infanticide at an outlying farm—but to be intimately and personally concerned with murder, that was clean outside my experience. Janet, I remember, was annoyed with me; she said that I ought to have left Coquet Hall the moment things began to go wrong. That was all very well, but where was I to go? We had closed the house at Doon Farm for the summer, and to have gone to some other hotel would have been very costly. As Chairman of the little company which had founded Coquet Hall, I had a very equitable arrangement with Mrs. Soutar, her tariff for other folk being just terrible. Of course I should have been spared much trouble and horror if I had moved elsewhere but I am glad I did not do so, for I think that Mrs. Soutar was glad of my support in those trying days. At any rate it is to me that she has come, ten years later, for the writing of this narrative.

It was easy for Janet to be wise after the event, but had she been at Coquet Hall herself I doubt whether her inordinate curiosity would have allowed her to leave. Indeed, as a student of human nature, I could not help noticing that while everyone at Coquet Hall expressed their distaste at being involved in the scandal, none of them packed their trunks and left, which they could easily have done. I suppose they found the mystery irresistible and were fascinated by the horror. Even Miss Bunting who had been about to set off on one of those cruises, cancelled her berth on some flimsy pretext and stopped on at Coquet Hall for another month—with daily exclamations of dismay at being so close to such an unpleasant business.

If murder and intrigue had seemed grotesque in the sunny and bustling life of Easton Knoyle, how impossible they must at first seem in peaceful Coquet Hall—dominated by that reassuring, if silent, genius—Mrs. Soutar. And yet—looking back in after years—I sometimes wondered. Had I always felt quite comfortable, quite *sure* about Coquet Hall? True, I had gone there summer after summer, for the brown trout were plentiful, the border country never failed me in its romantic appeal and Mrs. Soutar's cuisine was unparalleled. It was only, as I say, in after years, that I began to realise that—sub-consciously I suppose—I had always had doubts, a curious kind of indescribable discomfort. The loneliness of the place and that odd collection of sophisticated and eccentric folk that had made up Mrs. Soutar's 'regulars', had they not sometimes seemed—what shall I say—rather unwholesome? There was the cynical and elegant Mr. Lacacheur, for instance, or poor Margaret Fish writing her lovely sonnets, or Mark Fanshawe in his invalid chair—and there was Hypatia Crowe, the dour chambermaid who so silently haunted those warm and carpeted corridors. And always, outside, for miles and miles, there was nothing but the brown moors and the clean skies. It was not a natural contrast.

Had there not also been moments, I have often asked myself, when Coquet Hall itself had seemed not only a little too remote, but even a little . . . queer? For all the warmth and comfort within there had, I decided, always been something quite grotesquely abnormal—but poetic too—about that

house, about the grey and mossy elegance of its age-
ing pilasters and its faded floral carvings, and
about the manner in which one came on it—so
suddenly always—in that great isolation. That
ten-mile track, rutted and stony—Coquet Hall's
link with the world—was it not just a little too
long? There was something startling, frightening
even, in coming over that last Cheviot spur
and discovering—set back a little at the head of
the burn—that strangely quiet and beautiful house,
so curiously urbane against its lonely group of
storm-torn elms? Yes, it was startling, weird, to find
such a house hidden in the very depths of those silent
hills—a silence broken only by the low whistle of
the wind in the grasses or, perhaps, by a stormy
night.

In fact, as Mr. Stone once pointed out to me,
Harold Warburton could hardly have chosen a
better place.

2

That year, I remember, I reached Coquet Hall very
late at night, and a dark night it was. In previous
years Mrs. Soutar had always sent the shooting
brake to meet me at Rothbury Station, but in 1931
Janet and I, after mature consideration, had purchased a car. That morning, after closing the house,
I had driven her into Edinburgh—where I had to
file some documents—and then we had gone on to
Newcastle. This made a long day, but also a considerable saving on Janet's fare to the south. At Newcastle I had seen her on to the night train for King's

Cross and had then set off by myself for Coquet Hall. There was no glimmer of moon or stars, but I enjoyed driving at night and I had the good feeling that I was at the very start of my holiday. The car was going fine and as I took the empty highroad through Morpeth—the telegraph post flicking by in the light of my headlamps—it was grandly exhilarating and I remember to this day how I sang 'Afton Water' to myself, while I let in the night air to play on my face and ruffle my hair. Morpeth and Rothbury were black and empty, for it was near midnight. I knew every inch of the way and I was soon twisting up the Coquet Valley, beyond Rothbury, into the very depths of the hills—the river now no more than a burn. Near Linbridge I had to stop the car while I drove a sleepy ewe and her lambs from the middle of the road, and through the darkness I could hear the water chuckling and babbling over the stones.

Then up and up into the heights of the Cheviots, almost to the border. We were not yet through the month of May and up there the air was sharp, once I thought I saw the last scrap of an old snow-drift, and more than once, above the drone of the engine, I heard the roar of the freshets which feed the Coquet in time of thaw. I could smell the peat, and all around, I knew, in the blackness were the great rotundities of the moors. Then suddenly, higher up still and far away to my right, was a wee light. So minute was it and so far above me that had there been a clear sky I might have thought it a bright star or a planet. But there were no stars and I knew —though it was past one o'clock now—that a light must be burning in a bedroom at Coquet Hall.

Now I began to look for the stone which bears Mrs. Soutar's post-box and marks the start of the ten-mile track. If I missed it my road would die out in the bogs and granite of the moor top; and all the time I had to keep a wary eye open for stray sheep. But my lamps were good and soon I had turned off and was bumping and bucking along the track, now shooting up to the top of a spur, now plunging down into a corrie; and twice there were stony fords to cross—first over Trow Burn and then over Usway Burn—and so on between High Bloodybush Edge and Cushat Law—sometimes losing that wee light but always getting nearer to it. Up and down went the track, but always more up than down.

At last, gaunt and queer in the light of the lamps, I saw the three lonely rowan trees which mark the start of the last mile, and I knew that straight ahead was high Cheviot itself and that, had it been day, I could have looked into Scotland. Down I went into the last little corrie, the lighted window again disappearing. Then I held my breath, for I was thoroughly startled. On the next spur, a quarter of a mile ahead, was a different sort of light—wobbling and swaying towards me. It stopped and then came on again down the opposite side of the corrie. What the devil!—I reflected—and at this hour! By the movement of the light and the speed of its approach I judged it to be a bicycle lamp. Then the cyclist, just before he came within range of my headlamps, must have wheeled his bicycle off the track into the heather, in order to make way for me. I never really saw the fellow—I could only think that he must have been out caring for a maimed sheep or something of the sort—but I stuck my head out of the car and yelled a 'good night'. If there was a reply the whir of the breeze in the coarse grasses must have drowned it—for I heard nothing.

I was not sorry when the car bumped over the last granite hummock and I could feel under my wheels the smooth paving of the Coquet Hall forecourt. The forecourt was open to the east and the wind was blowing bitterly cold now—at that height and at that hour. It came whistling across from the North Sea and had in it a hint of drizzle and damp sea-mist. I had turned off my lamps and put the car in a corner of the forecourt until morning, but as I rang the bell the light from the bedroom window just picked out the lichened edges of the great cartouche of arms, so luxuriantly carved above the panelled doors. The lighted window—queer as it was at that hour—gave a kind of promise of the warmth, the great fires, the thick carpets and all the delicious, familiar comfort within—all in such indescribable contrast with that lonely, cold, top-of-the-world feeling without.

It was Miss Amy Carlyle, Mrs. Soutar's little birdlike niece, who welcomed me. I apologised for the hour of my arrival—as well I might!

'It's of no consquence, Mr. Muir. My aunt has retired and begged you would excuse her. There is a little refreshment set for you by the library fire—for it is cold and tired that you will be after your ride. Crowe is about and will see to your things. There's a bonny fire in your room, Mr. Muir.'

I was not surprised that it should be Miss Amy, not Mrs. Soutar, who was there to welcome me. Until you came to know Coquet Hall well Mrs. Soutar was in the nature of a myth. For days on end she might not be seen, although, from behind the scenes, she was ruling with an extremely firm hand. These periods of retirement may have arisen from some lingering doubts about a minister's daughter turning hotel-keeper, a matter, I think, which always haunted her a little. Not that one was allowed to forget Mrs. Soutar. Miss Amy saw to the guests—but always with: 'My aunt says this . . .' or 'My aunt hopes that . . .'; it was Miss Bunting who had christened her 'the Grand Vizier'. Miss Amy followed me to the library.

For all his poverty, old Dr. Carlyle had lined his study at the Corstophine manse with a grand lot of books, and it was these brown-backed volumes that had found their way to the little crimson-and-white panelled 'den' beyond the big drawing-room at Coquet Hall. It was in this room, as the years passed, that Graham Lacacheur had so carefully compiled his two very unpleasant volumes on *Heredity and Crime*, and it was here, one wet summer, that I had corrected the proofs of *The Ettrick Shepherd*.

The fire was still blazing and set before it were my sandwiches, my favourite sherry and a hot 'night-cap'—one of the more mysterious concoctions from Mrs. Soutar's still-room. I sniffed . . . the familiar scent of those extremely expensive Turkish cigarettes was unmistakable.

'Mr. Lacacheur. . . .' I said to Miss Amy, 'already —so early in the summer.'

'He came soon after Easter, Mr. Muir, and he's not been out yet.'

'And the others? . . .' I asked. 'Is Mark here yet?'

'Both Mr. Fanshawe and his secretary—that awful Mr. Smith—came last week.' I never had thought that either Miss Amy or her aunt could have approved of John Smith—and really, you know, I couldn't blame them. It was not like Mark to have

159

chosen such a slimy creature; I often wondered why he had.

'Mr. Fanshawe looks forward to his games of chess with you, Mr. Muir. Now let me see . . . Miss Bunting has been here for a month. . . .' I nodded; I had seen the embroidery frame in a corner of the drawing-room.

'No tantrums, I hope.'

'Not yet, thank heaven! But no end of foolishness, Mr. Muir. She had suddenly convinced herself, if you please, that Mr. Lacacheur is a *ci-devant* Russian prince, and has set her cap at him. Fancy! After all these years! I suppose, Mr. Muir, she's not . . . is she?' Miss Amy tapped her forehead significantly. I laughed.

'Not far off,' I said, 'but Mr. Lacacheur does rather encourage romantic theories, doesn't he? So elegant *and* mysterious. Secretive too. But I suppose she's fifty if she's a day.'

'It's all very well to laugh, Mr. Muir, but there *are* the tantrums. Crowe was up two nights with her last summer.'

'Well,' I said, 'she's not quite ripe for a mental home yet. Who else is here?'

'Sir Harry McQueen. . . .'

'Oh dear! And the boys?'

'Yes. It's a pity. We have decided not to allow it next year. It upsets the others and, after all, they would be happier at Gleneagles. Then the Canon and Mrs. Fish will be here on Monday. I do hope it will be all right. We should hate to refuse them, Mr. Muir; Miss Coppock would be so hurt. But the Canon had a dreadful row with Mr. Fanshawe after you had left last year.'

'Theology?'

'Transubstantiation—and all that. Of course as a Presbyterian one had to agree with Mr. Fanshawe, but he needn't have said the things he did—quite blasphemous. Aunt Nellie was very cross and Mrs. Fish—strange, sensitive creature—broke down, poor thing. However, the others all enjoyed it enormously.'

'And Mrs. Bradford?' I asked.

'She came a month ago, with entourage—maid and chauffeur as usual. She has been in her room all the week. Crowe tells me that the old thing is feeling her back, but of course it mustn't be mentioned—Mrs. Bradford must never be ill. She was eighty this year.'

'Her niece will be coming later?'

'Miss Coppock will join her when the term ends at her Torquay school—as unpaid companion, I suppose. Poor Sophie—so put upon, between you and me, Mr. Muir. And speaking of Sophie reminds me . . . although I didn't mean to trouble you tonight . . . we are in rather a difficulty about the newcomers.'

'The newcomers!' I exclaimed. I was surprised; it was many years since Mrs. Soutar had accepted a new client without very careful enquiry. If any of my readers have been imagining that they can visit Coquet Hall, demanding dinner and a bed—as in more ordinary hotels—they are very much mistaken. Mrs. Soutar would never allow that. It might upset the others.

'They are not altogether strangers,' Miss Amy explained. 'Poor Sophie—so well-meaning—always sending us her friends and acquaintances . . . her aunt, then the Canon, and now the Warburtons. Mrs. Warburton was a Miss Langdon-Miles.'

'What—not the Torquay woman?'

'No, her elder sister. But it's the "Torquay woman", Mr. Muir, that has died—quite suddenly. . . .'

'That will be a blow for Miss Coppock,' I said. 'She was always so full of Miss Langdon-Miles.'

'Yes, I suppose she will be upset,' said Miss Amy, 'but, you know, Mr. Muir, Sophie's good nature was taken advantage of at Torquay, as well as by "dear Aunt Bertha". I'm told, too, that Miss Langdon-Miles was wrecking that school with her snobbery and High Church practices. But of course Sophie would never admit that.'

'And the Warburtons . . . is their visit cancelled?'

'On the contrary, Mr. Muir, that's just the trouble. Miss Langdon-Miles died suddenly in London on Tuesday afternoon. It's Thursday now—or Friday rather . . .' Miss Amy glanced at the clock, '. . . and, so far as we know, the Warburtons haven't heard a word about it. Of course they may see it in *The Times*—but such a shock to learn of it in that way—and if they had, then surely we should have heard from them—postponing or cancelling their visit. It's very annoying. Sophie telegraphed them here, but they are motoring north in a leisurely way and we don't know where they are—nor does anyone else apparently.'

'Very awkward,' I said. 'But you needn't worry; it's not your fault, Miss Amy. And no doubt they'll see it in the papers.'

'In that case, Mr. Muir, as I say, they should have got in touch with us.'

'I don't know about that,' I said. 'I once gathered from Miss Coppock that the Langdon-Miles family are an odd lot. This Mrs. Warburton may not let her sister's death spoil her holiday after all.' Miss Amy was a little shocked at this.

'Blood is thicker than water, Mr. Muir. That telegram has been lying on the table in the hall for well over forty-eight hours now, and there is nothing we can do about it. Mr. and Mrs. Warburton are not due here until Saturday evening; meanwhile they may be anywhere in England almost. But I didn't intend to worry you at this hour. If you'll excuse me, Mr. Muir, I'll be wishing you good night. It's your old room—the green and gold—Crowe will see to the lights. Good night, Mr. Muir.'

'Good night, Miss Amy.'

I relaxed luxuriously in the big maroon leather chair. How quiet the house seemed now! I had demolished the sandwiches and the sherry while we had been chatting, and now I began to enjoy the 'nightcap'. After the cold air, the sherry had made me a trifle muzzy. I could hardly keep my eyes open as I lay back, looking up at the little shameless boys and plump goddesses who floated around the old ceiling —those Coquet Hall ceilings which sent Mr. Lacacheur into such ecstasies. I decided that, if I didn't go to bed, I should fall asleep where I was, so I made my way across the big, half-darkened drawing-room and up the great staircase.

Crowe—dark, sallow and tragic-eyed—was at the head of the stairs, her starched apron and capstrings gleaming curiously white in the gloom. She had parted the heavy curtains and was looking out into the black night. The wind had risen and the rain was lashing the glass. She cannot have heard my step in the heavily-carpeted stair, for when I said good night to her she gave a little cry, caught her breath and let the curtains fall quickly.

'Oh! Mr. Muir. I'm sorry, sir, but you did startle me so. Is there anything you require, sir.'

'Nothing, thank you, Crowe. You're up late.'

'I always am, sir. I can't sleep. I can't sleep. Good night, sir.' And then—through some door in the panelling—she was gone.

I made my way down the corridor, past Mrs. Bradford's suite and then past Mark's door—poor Mark was having one of his fits of coughing—and so to the little square room, the one with the powder closet, in the south-east corner of the house. There was, as Miss Amy had promised, a 'bonny fire' burning, and Crowe had laid out my things. I undressed and then pulled back the high, green brocade curtains and folded the shutters into their deep embrasures. How the rain did drive across from the distant sea! It was black as ink, but away to the right a light was moving and swaying, disappearing and reappearing like a will-o'-the-wisp. My cyclist must have turned and be coming back again, towards the house. That any sane person should cycle up and down that lonely track, and on such a night as this, was quite beyond explanation. The light had disappeared for a moment, then it went on—and off; on, off; on, off—five times—sharply, as though controlled by a switch, or perhaps a hat was being used as a sort of shutter. In the darkness one could not be sure, but I guessed that it might be about a mile away—somewhere by the three rowan trees.

Then—quite suddenly—my face was pressed against the glass and I was breathing hard. Far, far away, miles away—somewhere, I reckoned afterwards, on the Great North Road above Alnwick—

two car headlamps had appeared, two sparks at that distance. On, off; on, off—five times. I put my watch on the table by the bed; it was precisely three o'clock.

In spite of the 'night-cap' and my former drowsiness, I lay awake a long time. Cough, cough—very faintly, through the thick walls, I could hear poor Mark. There would be a long silence, then again—cough, cough. Ever so faintly. Grey Cushat Law was taking shape against the grey sky of a grey dawn before—at last—I fell asleep.

3

' ". . . And so she married an Aldwinkle of North Mimms, in the county of Hertfordshire. . . ." '

Mr. Lacacheur waved his thin white hand towards me. He was the only person in the small breakfast-room; the McQueens had gone off—hours ago —on some expedition, the 'others' would be down in ample time for lunch. Mr. Lacacheur's table was almost completely occupied by a huge volume from which, as I poured the cream on to my porridge, he continued to read aloud.

' ". . . survived to see the Great Exhibition at the Crystal Palace, and died, leaving fifty-six grandchildren behind her." How charming! '

'Really! ' I said. 'What on earth are you talking about. And—by the way—good morning.' He looked up at me, smiling; one forgave Mr. Lacacheur when he smiled. He seemed, I thought, a trifle older than a year ago, a little more white in the dark, sleek

hair—always so carefully brushed across the high
forehead of that thin, grey, Semitic face.

'Good morning, my dear Muir, good morning—
and a million apologies. How thoughtless I am! But
in this place one picks up the threads so easily from
summer to summer, that really for the moment I
quite forgot that you were not with us last night.
You see—you belong. But how delightful, my dear
fellow, how very delightful to see you once again.'

He sugared the canteloup which, with excessively
strong coffee, was his breakfast.

'Thank you,' I said. 'It's delightful to see you. But
what is all this nonsense?'

'For ten summers, ten summers, we have been
coming to Coquet Hall, and it was only over our
coffee cups last evening that we found, to our shame,
that not one of us knew the story of this . . .'
he waved his hand towards the Adam fireplace
'. . . this really beautiful house. Absurd! They
motor to Melrose, Abbotsford—God knows what
ghastly haunt of sham romance—while here, under
their noses, is this feast of delicious palladianism.
A trifle faded perhaps, but how much better that is!
And we knew nothing of its story—not one of us.'

'Melrose is delightful,' I said, 'and as for . . .'

'Forgive me, my dear Muir. You have a weakness, I know, for the ivy-clad ruin, complete with
owl and moon; "Groves of caverned Hawthornden
. . ." and all that kind of thing. You are a pursuer of
the Gothick—what?'

He could pull my leg if he wished. I gave a shrug
and passed on from porridge to trout in silence. Mr.
Lacacheur, I reflected, might be a very clever fellow—at least the 'others' seemed to think so—but I
would sooner have written *The Ettrick Shepherd*

166

than *Heredity and Crime*. He ran on, undeterred by my silence.

'And so I gave our dear Miss Bunting an undertaking that, by lunchtime today, I would have for her the complete story of Coquet Hall. And here, all the time, it lay buried in Roger's *County History* —the tale of that delectable admiral, Patrick Brophy.'

'You needn't have wasted your time,' I said. 'I could have given you all the details. As for your "delectable admiral", he was a drunken, sordid brute. Only a lunatic would have built a house here, anyway . . . "Brophy's Folly". And when it was finished he tried to burn it down—in a fit of pique.'

'I know; the whole affair is too charming. But you don't mean to say that you have had the story in your secretive breast all these years, and have kept it to yourself. What an odd chap you are, Muir, upon my soul!'

'The less the story is known, the better pleased Mrs. Soutar will be.'

'Oh! I find Brophy quite too fascinating,' declaimed Mr. Lacacheur. 'True, he usually finished the evening under the table—but the eighteenth century was, after all, the eighteenth century. He may have flogged at least one groom to death and, of course, he was wont to assert his *droit de seigneur* over the shepherds' daughters, but since he was an Irishman of the Ascendancy—what would you? . . .'

'The decent border folk hounded him out of the county,' I said, 'and quite right too.'

'And to think that for twenty years he searched for the Alchemist's Secret, in the cellar—here, beneath our feet. Ah! What romance! And then there were his three glorious lily-white daughters who—

until Brophy locked them up—broke the hearts of half the squires in the north of England. Anna, Delilah and Grace. Ah! What romance, what romance!' Mr. Lacacheur gave an absurdly deep sigh. 'It was Grace,' he continued, 'who had the fifty-six grandchildren. I picture her as a very, very lovely old lady—a kind of mid-Victorian Mrs. Bradford.'

'Mrs. Bradford,' I said, 'would at any rate have kept the squires in their place. As for your romantic and delectable admiral—he died in a padded room.'

Mushrooms and bacon replaced my trout. Mr. Lacacheur rose and made his way towards the tall French window and the sunlit forecourt.

'Last night's storm,' he said, 'has given way to a most benign morning. I shall take the air. Perhaps you will join me on the terrace—or are you going fishing?' I was not 'going fishing' and so, after my third slice of toast and marmalade, I went out to him.

There never had been a garden at Coquet Hall. One the eastern side was the paved forecourt and to the south was the terrace. A huge curved flight of steps led from one to the other; the peat and the heather sweeping up to the very plinth of the balustrade. Mr. Lacacheur had put on his long, straight black overcoat, the one with the Astrakhan collar—so long that only three inches of the minute but decisive check of the trouser was revealed. As a comical and bizarre gesture to the moors, he had acquired a tweed cap equipped with ear flaps. The flaps were, at the moment, buttoned out of use on to the cap's crown. When I came upon him he was standing by the crumbling and bramble-covered Sarty which marks the eastern corner of the terrace. He was blowing tobacco smoke distastefully towards the distant Dale.

'This place,' he said, 'gets more like Blackpool beach every day.'

I merely smiled at this 'Lacacheurism'. For some thirty miles not a human being was to be seen. To the east one could, with difficulty, discern faintly a plume of smoke from some collier off Blyth; to the south, winding away past Bloodybush Edge, were the rough poles which marked our track and carried our telephone line to the world. Every other sign of the human race was conspicuously absent.

'Look!' he exclaimed. 'Look! Campers!' He raised his thin ebony cane and pointed. He was right; about a mile away was a very small white triangle.

'Boy Scouts,' I suggested.

'The excellent Miss Amy,' he said, 'informs me that it is a female painter who has thrust herself upon us. We shall soon have char-à-bancs and orange peel in the forecourt!'

'You exaggerate,' I said. 'Besides, the artist . . .'

'Artist! Artist!' he interrupted rudely. 'I told you that she painted; not having seen her work by what right, pray, do you call her an artist? There are only four in Europe. Moreover,' he added, 'Miss Amy tells me that she is fat and wears tweeds.'

'Well,' I said, 'she's not likely to trouble you.'

'My dear Muir, you think that I am being absurd, but listen. How often have I told you that the twentieth century—and everything that it stands for —is to me utterly repellent, utterly. I regard the fall of the Bourbons and the discovery of coal as the two most deplorable events in human history. I have— with great care—arranged my life so as to avoid the present; eight months of the year I spend at my modest villa below Pisa—in the lush, coloured meadows Shelley loved—and four months at Coquet Hall. Thus I savour the two poles of our civilisation —the Latin south and the grey north. The vulgar present I shut out. I live, however, in a state of constant terror lest this so-well-balanced arrangement should be destroyed.'

'But really!' I said, 'one little tent—and a mile away.'

'It is symptomatic,' he cried, 'symptomatic—and at Coquet Hall one had thought oneself safe. And then there's the moss man.'

'The moss man?'

'Certainly—the moss man. Why not? It's a positive invasion!'

'I've never heard of him.'

'He lives,' said Mr. Lacacheur, 'at Galbraith Farm....'

'Well, well, that's twenty miles away.'

'It's the nearest house. And he cycles all over Northumberland, apparently, putting mosses in a black tin.'

'An innocent micologist...'

'... with a most evil propensity for hunting down his miserable lichens under the very shadow of Coquet Hall. Do you think,' he added as he gazed dreamily into the distance, 'do you think that she was cruel to her grandchildren?'

'Who?' I asked. Mr. Lacacheur had a most disconcerting way of changing the subject.

'Who! Why, Grace of course—Grace Brophy. The enchanting admiral was a sadistic brute and *his* father ran West Indian slave-ships. The laws of nature compel me to abandon my illusion of the kind and lovely Victorian lady. She probably invited her grandchildren to North Mimms and tortured them —one by one. Pain, my dear Muir, pain! I feel sure that she enjoyed it!' As I watched his little glittering eyes and the glee on his grey face I felt rather sick.

'You are obsessed,' I said, 'with your "Heredity and Crime" theories. After all, Lacacheur, most of us, I suppose, have a cruel or dishonest ancestor somewhere in the remote past, but we haven't all got criminal tendencies.'

'Are you sure?' He shot the question at me. 'Are you sure? Don't you ever feel it in yourself? I do. Often. Ambition, greed, jealously—these three! One fine morning . . . and one of them has you in its grip . . . the long hidden passions rise to the top and, behold! —you have an enemy of society. Today it may be a mild, little man like Crippen, a genius like Wainwright, a respected citizen like Major Armstrong, a pious Sunday-school teacher like Lizzie Borden, or—yes—even an innocent child like Constance Kent . . . and tomorrow you have a monster of iniquity, wading through blood and cruelty to achieve his ends.' I had been sitting on the stone balustrade, and as he spoke his grey face came down and down until it was very close to mine.

'And think, think of the thousands and thousands who go undiscovered . . . and die in their beds.'

'Now what on earth are you two awful men gossiping about?' It was the voice of Miss Bunting. She was coming up the steps to join us. I breathed a sigh of relief; the evil spell of Mr. Lacacheur's talk was broken.

Above Miss Bunting's withered complexion were mountains of straw-coloured hair. Trailing behind and around her were: a Paisley shawl, an orange silk cushion with appliqué flowers, *These Charming People*, *Vogue*, a box of charcoal biscuits, a huge raffia bag, an absurd parasol, a small, white pom called Binks, a medley of handwoven scarves and wraps—and a deck-chair. We hastened to relieve her. After a complex discussion on the direction of the breeze and the potential path of the sun, I got her settled in front of the south wall, while Mr. Lacacheur, to his intense fury, was sent hunting for a small plank to keep her Tyrolean sandals from the damp paving.

'Now tell me,' she said when he returned, 'what were you two talking about?' She looked at us over her tortoiseshell rims. 'You both looked most guilty. Binks agrees with me.'

'Crime,' said Mr. Lacacheur. Miss Bunting gave a little shriek, and closed her eyes.

'You ogres! Aren't they, Binksey?'

'And other things,' I said. 'Lacacheur dislikes this tent which has appeared on the horizon.'

'Oh, that!' said Miss Bunting, extracting a long jade cigarette holder from the raffia bag. 'Quite a harmless creature. A schoolmarm acquaintance of Mrs. Bradford—or of her niece. Her name is Trubshawe and she paints. Dreadful things! Mrs. Soutar said she could camp down there on the edge of the estate; an extraordinary thing to allow—I think we should have been consulted, after all we do pay—but I suppose, coming from Mrs. B., it was a royal command. By the way, Mark is not down yet.'

At Coquet Hall, for many years, the latter half of the morning had been invariably dominated by the burning question of whether Mark was, or was not, 'down'. The ceremony and ritual surrounding the passage of the invalid chair from the bedroom to the drawing-room was something of an epoch in the day.

'But there were signs . . .' went on Miss Bunting, 'that odious slug John Smith had been arranging things in the drawing-room, and Crowe was on the landing—hovering.'

'I stopped in my first morning,' I said, 'specially to see Mark. How is he?'

'Fat and rosy as ever. It's very mysterious; I suppose there *is* something the matter with him.'

'My dear Maisie!' said Mr. Lachacheur, 'how can you?' It was some three years since the word had first gone round that her name was Maisie, but I had no idea that she and Mr. Lacacheur had reached that stage.

'And Mrs. Bradford?' I said. 'Miss Amy tells me she's feeling her back.'

'So she says. She hasn't been seen for a week. No bulletin has been issued this morning, but as the court chamberlain hasn't cleared the staircase, I presume that "we" are remaining in our room.'

'My dear Maisie! How can you?'

'Thank God the insufferable McQueen youths have gone off with "Dad" for the day. They're more gauche than ever.'

'Miss Amy tells me,' I said, 'that it's going to be prevented next year.'

'I should think so. Definitely one of Mrs. Soutar's major blunders—definitely. I'm like a wet rag by bedtime.'

'Another blunder,' said Mr. Lacacheur, 'is having the telephone in the hall.'

'Look!' I cried. 'The moss man!' My gaze had wandered from Miss Bunting to the distance, and there he was—bumping along the track on a bi-

cycle. He had passed the three rowan trees and one
could see his black 'plus-four' suit and his white
panama hat. He stopped, propped his bicycle against
a telephone pole, and plunged into the heather.

'I saw a bicycle lamp last night,' I said, 'but it
can't have been his. What would a micologist be
doing at three a.m.?'

'Visiting Miss Trubshawe in her tent!'

'My dear Maisie! How can you?'

'Really!' I exclaimed.

'Well, he's a dark horse about women—is the moss
man,' Miss Bunting prattled on. 'He's living at that
dreadful farm; God knows why—it must be filthy,
but he manages to meet his flashy friends in Newcastle.'

'Oh come!' I said.

'Mrs. Soutar let me have the shooting brake
yesterday—to go and buy silks. And there was the
moss man—outside "The Royal", with a scarlet
woman in a yellow Rolls!'

Above our heads there was the sound a a sash win-
down being thrown open.

'That's Mark's room,' I said. 'He must be down,
or they wouldn't open the window.'

Just then, too, the lunch gong sounded. As Mr.
Lacacheur and I, leaving Miss Bunting to her charcoal biscuits, made our way down the steps, I
noticed that the panama hat was still visible in the
heather and that, lower down the Dale, a substantial figure in brown tweeds was laboriously making her way from the tent to the hotel.

4

It was Sunday afternoon and Mr. and Mrs. Warburton had arrived.

'His moustache,' said Miss Bunting, 'is far worse than darling Binks's whiskers. Now that they are married perhaps she'll trim it for him.'

'My dear Maisie! How can you?'

'She looked extremely ill . . .' I began.

'He's a great ungainly creature,' interrupted Miss Bunting, 'isn't he, Binksey? What Mrs. W. was thinking of I can't imagine!'

'My dear Maisie, you have never even met them.'

'That, Graham dear, is where you are wrong. Mrs. Soutar introduced both Mr. and Mrs. Warburton to me and Binks—only two minutes ago, as we were crossing the hall for lunch. They had enough luggage for a lifetime.'

'Well anyway,' I said, 'she looked ghastly and now, poor thing, she has to face the news of her sister's sudden death. I must say, Miss Bunting, that I am sorry for them.' But Miss Bunting was invariably critical and snappy on Sunday afternoons and there was no reasoning with her; she had made up her mind to dislike the Warburtons—and that was that.

'If,' went on Miss Bunting, 'she's socialist and progressive and all that nonsense—as she claims to be —then she has no right to be going about in that huge car, let alone stopping in a ruinous place like this. It's the grossest hypocrisy—isn't it, Binkseywinksey diddums?'

'Possibly,' said Mr. Lacacheur, 'it's the bewhiskered Harold who has the money.'

'On the contrary,' I said, 'I believe that in marrying a Langdon-Miles he did very well for himself. Miss Amy tells me he was a poor Australian pianist —quite unknown in this country—and that she took him in hand and made a sort of protégé of him.'

'There!' exclaimed Miss Bunting triumphantly, 'What did I tell you? She makes subversive speeches to dockers, just as a cloak for her wealth, and all the time she's pouring out money on this untidy oaf. She's old enough to be his mother too— isn't she, Binksey? And fancy marrying an Australian!'

'My dear Maisie! How can you?'

We had expected the Warburtons the previous evening but—somewhere in the Lake District— Mrs. Warburton had had a 'nasty attack', whatever that might mean, and they had stayed on at Keswick for another night. When the big Bentley had pulled up in the forecourt, below the dining-room windows, Sunday lunch was barely over. The odious John Smith had not yet appeared to wheel Mark's chair into the smoking-room, and Mark and I, lingering over our dessert, had seen Harold Warburton almost carrying his poor wife into the hotel.

'That woman,' said Mark, 'looks as if she might die.'

You know I liked Mark Fanshawe—really. I admit it was curious, and I never felt quite comfortable about it. If I had ever taken it into my head to invite him to the Doon Farm, I believe Janet might have been rather shocked. But he had his attractions Not, of course, to look at. He was dreadfully fat, but that, I suppose, was because he could never take any exercise. Again, he had red, bright red, curly hair—

masses of it—but you couldn't really hold that against him. Nor was it his fault that he should have had what Miss Bunting so rudely called 'a rush of teeth to the head', and a slight lisp. His tastes were necessarily sedentary and I admit that the 'horsey' checks and yellow waistcoats which he affected were perversely out of place. But one forgot so easily that he was only thirty.

Twice I had seen traces of bad—uncontrollable—temper. The valets and secretaries were always leaving. John Smith was a recent acquisition. There was much that one had to forgive but, on the whole, he was a pleasant fellow, jovial even at times, and full of subtle fun and all sorts of odds and ends of curious learning. He would polish off Miss Bunting's most difficult crossword puzzles in no time, and yet —unlike Mr. Lacacheur—he was free from the more absurd affectations of the erudite. It was not fair of Miss Bunting to say that 'Mr. Fanshawe couldn't be pleasant without gushing.'

Of course one was sorry for him. He told me once that the thing he regretted most was being debarred from foreign travel. And yet he was always moving about in search of health. He would have liked to have wintered on the Riviera or in Egypt, but the journey was out of the question and I think that he was always glad when the spring came and he could get back to Coquet Hall—and to his games of chess; he got so bored, he said, with the Torquay hotel to which his doctors sent him each year.

Mark had been rather a nuisance at lunch that day, raving about an early Ming pot—'pure white and slightly translucent'—which 'his man' had just 'picked up' for him in Paris. He had the pot on the table all through lunch. This sort of thing meant very little to me and, for once, I almost agreed with McQueen—bounder though he was—when he said that he couldn't see why there should be such fuss 'just because Fanshawe had paid far too much for a perfectly plain vawse.' We all knew that Mark was fabulously wealthy but the Ming pot rather surprised me because his real passion was Italian primitives. The big house in Palace Green—where the blinds were down for so great a part of the year—had, I believe, whole rooms full of Ucellos, Bellinis and so on. It really was a consuming passion with poor Mark. I remember one year, just after he had arrived from Torquay, he told me that when one had a lot of money it was only the unobtainable that mattered. There were pictures, he told me, in galleries and private collections, over which he had often gloated—'gloated' was his word—but which no money could buy. 'It's just those pictures that I want,' he said; 'it drives me nearly mad to think that they belong to someone else. I would go through fire and water to get hold of them—I would do anything, anything.' And oddly enough, you know, he meant it.

For ten years—every summer—I saw Mark and in all that time he never told me what was the matter with him. None of us knew. I suppose it was his own business but Miss Bunting was right, in a way, when she said that it was very mysterious.

He was rather like a spoilt child. I am not a bad judge of chess and I regarded him as an excellent player. At any rate, whereas I could beat everyone in our little circle at Dalmellington, Mark could nearly always beat me. I was not altogether sorry for I am afraid that he was a bad loser.

The game which had been broken off the previous

autumn was to be resumed, that Sunday afternoon, in the smoking-room. The smoking-room—once, long ago, the salon of Admiral Patrick Brophy—was rather gorgeous. As I came through the mahogany doors from the dining-room, John Smith was 'arranging' Mark—his cushions and what not—before the centre window, and Mark himself was setting out the Indian chessmen.

It was a queer picture: the sleek and white Smith —so slug-like in his black clothes—and Mark— *outré* in ratcatcher and stock; and behind them the high, gilded pilasters, the maroon and purple curtains, the draped organdie, the delicate pattern of the thin window bars—echoed and distorted in the shadow and sunlight on the carpet—and on either side the two vast urns *à la Grec*. Before the dim browns and purples of all this faded magnificence Mark's red hair, a dramatic discord, glowed like orange fire.

It was as we began our game that Miss Bunting had—so rudely—criticised the Warburtons. Miss Bunting had, as a matter of fact, no real business in the smoking-room at all. Her excuse was that in the drawing-room she would have been alone—except for Binks—and she hated being alone. It made her nervy. Mrs. Warburton was ill and Mrs. Bradford, suddenly recovering from 'feeling her back', had that morning, before breakfast, set off in her large Daimler for the Northern Choirs Festival at York. It was a way Mrs. Bradford had. Coquet Hall was never, for her, more than a headquarters whence—after keeping her chauffeur kicking his heels for days on end—she would suddenly depart on some weird expedition, often stopping away for a week or more. And so without apology, Miss Bunting had taken up her position in the smoking-room, arranging her embroidery frame, her table of silks and herself not inartistically before the fire. She always liked to 'set the scene'. On the hearth was Binks's basket, and on the silk cushions of the sofa was Binks.

Away at the far end of the room, in the recess, Mr. Lacacheur reclined—save for the bizarre Sunday afternoon carpet slippers, incredibly elegant. Against a small circular window his long Semitic head was silhouetted like a primitive saint against his aureole—so inappropriately. Even in 1931 he had begun to contemplate and take notes for his *Crimes of the Popes*, and it was from the gastronomic and sexual orgies of the Early Fathers that he looked up, now and again, to interpose some remark into 'Maisie's' interminable chatter.

The afternoon ran its course. Between two and four o'clock Mark moved his queen, I moved my bishop—and it was Mark's move again. From time to time we could hear the distant click of the McQueen billiard balls and the 'baaing' of moorland sheep beyond the balustrade. Binks snored. Miss Bunting passed on from being rude about the Warburtons to the more ancient theme of her operation, and Mr. Lacacheur threatened to take himself and his books to the little white-and-crimson 'den' beyond the drawing-room. At last it was the hour for the dumb waiters to be wheeled in and for Miss Amy to dispense tea. It was only when Alice was passing round the cups that Mr. Warburton left his wife and joined us.

He *was* ungainly—six feet four at least, if it had not been for an awkward stoop. And so painfully shy and gauche. His tailor must long ago have despaired of ever making his suits sufficiently large, for wrists and ankles were displayed, thick woollen socks all down over the latter. The ends of his straggling moustache, as well as his big hairy hands, were stained with nicotine and even now a long thin cheroot—unlit—hung from one corner of his mouth. His eyes were strangely wild and he seemed harassed. As he sat down near the chess table he smiled—and was not without charm.

'May I look on?' he said. I nodded.

'Of course—it's Fanshawe's move. I'm sorry to hear that your wife is unwell.'

'Thank you, thank you.' How shy and nervous he was—all on edge. 'It's very worrying. She had what appeared to be a heart attack. Really, I wondered whether we should get here. And she's never had heart trouble before—in her life.'

'Very trying for you both,' I said. 'Is she better now?'

'A little, I think. But there was sad family news awaiting her here. Most unfortunate, on top of the heart attack.' He looked around him. 'I don't know many English hotels but this is an unusual room, isn't it? For a hotel I mean.'

'It's an unusual hotel,' I said.

'Really. Shooting and fishing folk mainly, I suppose.'

'No. They faded out years ago. I fish a little, and there are the McQueens—who seem to have got in by mistake—but most of the people here . . .' I lowered my voice '. . . are really rather peculiar.'

'Peculiar?'

'Well—eccentric. There are some thirty bedrooms, but they have nearly all been made into suites. The dozen "regulars" pay through the nose—between you and me—to have the place to themselves.'

'Is this . . .' he made a gesture to the room '. . . everyone then?'

'Nearly. There's an Exeter parson and his wife due this week. And of course there's Mrs. Bradford who is away for a few days. She isn't often seen downstairs. That's pretty well everyone, and they'll all be here until the autumn.'

'It must be a very well run place.'

'Oh! Extremely so! I can recommend the light sherry and all the Rhine wines, if you're interested in such things. The late Colonel Soutar knew what was what.'

'Thank you, thank you. . . . Ah!' Fanshawe had moved a pawn. Alice wheeled the cakes and sandwiches in our direction. Mark took the largest cream éclair—what a child he was! Mr. Warburton, with his charming smile, turned to Alice.

'Would you,' he said, 'kindly do something for me. Ask the hotel office, please, to get me a trunk call to Torquay. I'm afraid I don't know the number, but I want Easton Knoyle School. I'll speak to a Miss Coppock, if she's there. Can you remember that?'

'Oh yes, sir. We know Miss Coppock quite well here, sir.'

'Of course, I forgot. And one other thing: I told the manageress—Mrs. Soutar, I mean—that my wife would have supper in her room. I ordered a very light meal—just dry toast and a little minced chicken. Will you give instructions, please, that I am to be told when the tray is sent up. My wife may get some sleep and I am most anxious that she shall not be disturbed. I will take the tray to her myself . . .'

There was a clatter on the parquet, and a little growl from Binks. Mr. Lacacheur had dropped his thin gold pencil.

That night Mark was coughing again. It was faint but persistent and it must have wakened me. I thought of going to him—poor chap—but I heard a murmur of voices through the wall and remembered John Smith—and that he had a bed in Mark's dressing-room. I looked at my watch; it was one minute to three. A queer thought came into my head and I went to the window. How different it was from the stormy night of my arrival. In that clear air every star glittered. A gibbous moon hung far out over the North Sea, but below me all the country lay in darkness. I leaned out and the cold reminded me that it was not yet June. Somewhere in the four ragged elms behind the house an owl hooted, and then Mark started to cough again.

On my left a beam of light was shining out from the wall of the house into the darkness. The same light, the same bedroom window, as four nights ago—the little light which I had seen from so far away down the Coquet Dale. Mentally I counted up windows and corridor doors; it was very odd, it must be Mrs. Bradford's sitting-room. But Mrs. Bradford, with her chauffeur and her little, pale twittering maid, was over a hundred miles away, in York. I turned and looked out along the track; I could hear the telephone wire singing on its poles, even in that light breeze.

Then it came—the bicycle lamp by the rowan trees—on, off; on, off—five, six, seven, eight, nine, ten. Surely, I thought, it was five last time. Then, far away—it must have been on the Great North Road for one could see the little lamps of night lorries on the move—came the reply, on, off; on, off—ten times. I waited. I was shivering with cold, but by the rowan trees a dark figure—just visible—had begun to move in the direction of the hotel. He—if it was a he —was walking as briskly as the rough track would allow. He had extinguished the lamp and he had no bicycle. When he was, I reckoned, about a quarter of a mile away, he left the track—as if to avoid being seen from the front windows of the hotel—and the corner of the building soon hid him from view. I waited, listening for every sound. I wished Mark would stop coughing. The light in the bedroom went off, and made me start. I was getting nervy. The clock in the hall chimed the first quarter, and I jumped so that I had to tell myself not to be a fool.

At last—after what seemed hours but must really have been about five minutes—I heard the ghost of a noise, and there was my man in the forecourt— right under my window. He must have climbed the balustrade of the terrace and tiptoed down the curved flight of steps. What a commonplace figure he looked with all the mystery and spaces of the night around him. He wore a bowler hat and mackintosh, and he carried an unlit bicycle lamp. From directly above him that was about all I could see. The great carved cartouche of arms, projecting from the wall, again hid him from view as he pushed open the front door. I never even got a glimpse of the fellow's face. The door must have been unlocked for I heard just the faintest click as he let down the night latch and closed the door behind him.

Mark, John Smith, Mr. Lacacheur, Harold Warburton, the three McQueens—and myself—that was all the men in the hotel. I could still hear the murmur of voices, so John Smith and—of course—Mark could be counted out. It was not really my business —the front door had obviously been left open for the fellow—but I slipped on my dressing-gown and went out quietly into the corridor. There was a shaded light away at the far end, near the turn to the staircase. I stood back, hidden between the deep door jambs, and waited. Then came the surprise.

I don't quite know, to this day, what I expected. I suppose I hoped that the man with the bicycle lamp might come up to bed and that I would then know who he was. What I didn't expect was what happened. There was the sound of a door opening and from Mrs. Bradford's sitting-room there came—on tiptoe—a stout woman in tweeds and brogues, with ash plant and Burberry. Down the corridor to meet her—from somewhere beyond the shaded lamp— came a figure in black. It was Crowe. Without the white starched cap how dark her hair seemed— drawn tightly away on either side of her long tired face. How silently she came along that carpeted corridor. She nodded to the woman in tweeds.

'He's in now, Miss Trubshawe. I'll come downstairs and lock the front door behind you.'

I stepped back into my room. At last Mark had stopped coughing and the night now seemed very quiet. I was glad to be in bed again for I had got cold leaning out of the window.

5

Lysander Stone was the most extraordinary man I have ever met. For twelve hours Mrs. Soutar kept his presence at Coquet Hall a secret, but when I came down to breakfast that morning it was clear that all was not well. Mr. Lacacheur, a slim volume

propped against his coffee pot, and Sir Harry Mc-
Queen, hidden behind the *Financial Times*, were
carefully ignoring each other. That, so far as it went,
was normal. 'The others' were not yet down. It was
only when I asked for porridge and got melon—
which I loathe—that I knew something must be
seriously wrong. Mistakes of that sort were simply
not made at Coquet Hall. I glanced at Miss Amy,
who was in command at the sideboard, and saw that
she had been weeping. She came over to me and said,
in a low voice, that 'Aunt Nellie' would like to see me.

Mr. Lacacheur had on his table a white rose. By
twisting my head round I could just see that it was
labelled: 'To my prince, from Maisie'. This irritated me intensely, but what annoyed me even more
was that Mr. Lacacheur gave me no help whatever
in coping with Sir Harry's conversation. Sir Harry
McQueen, who never stopped talking, went through
life light-heartedly forming and reforming vast cartels and combines. His tweeds—ostentatiously 'for
the moors'—as well as his cars and salmon rods,
were extremely expensive, or so he had often told
us. His Glasgow schooling had been sound, but he
and the late Lady McQueen had decided that they
would do the right thing by 'the boys'. 'The boys'
who, at that moment, were practising mashie shots
in the heather, had been sent to a public school which
—since it is possible that someone may have heard
of it—I will not name. They were rather more
illiterate than their father, but looked down on him,
since he made *gaffes* which they avoided. Everything
possible was done for 'the boys'; their sports cars
and other impedimenta—like Sir Harry's—came
straight from Jermyn Street and Piccadilly. But that
was not all; their parents, determined to do what was

right, had even called them Antony and Michael.

It is only fair to say that Antony—like 'Dad'—was going through the mill from the bottom, and that it would be at least six months before he got anywhere near the top. Later he might go into Parliament; 'Dad' could afford it, and British Alloys Ltd. hadn't got a good man there just now. But you mustn't think that Sir Harry was a millionaire. Oh dear me, no! He merely knew a few. He was a modest man, and he once told Mark that he considered himself in the Rolls, but not the yacht, class. Both the boys had now left school and as they seemed prepared to spend most of the summer—and not merely August—at Coquet Hall, it was generally agreed that Mrs. Soutar would really have to make it the last time.

I was in a hurry to finish my breakfast and see Mrs. Soutar, so Sir Harry, of course, was simply bubbling over. He had been fishing Lord Legge's loch.

'A magnificent day, old man. A grand day. Gave the boys a taste of the real thing. Never enjoyed ourselves so much.'

'I'm glad,' I said, 'that you had such good sport.'

'I don't know about that, old man. We didn't catch anything at all—not a bite. But it was a wonderful day. The gillie had the P.M. in the boat last year. What do you think of that! Same gillie, same boat. And Legge's house—never seen such a place, never. He was away but we had a look round. Legge told us to go where we liked. You see—he's United Refrigerators and I'm Alloys, so he couldn't very well refuse—not just now anyway. Never seen such a place. Three hundred and sixty-five windows, one for each day in the year. There's a clever idea for you! And the dining-room—copied from the Taj Mahal . . .'

Mr. Lacacheur choked, and cleverly avoided an accident to his coffee.

'. . . and the dahlias, simply miles of them, old man. And then, on the way home, we were able to do Mrs. Soutar a good turn . . .' Sir Harry McQueen, to do him justice, was always glad to do anyone a good turn '. . . . we picked up this Mr. Stone at Rothbury Station and saved the shooting brake a long journey.'

'Who is Mr. Stone?' I asked. I was rather surprised; Canon and Mrs. Fish, I knew, were due in a day or two, but I had heard of no other guests being expected. Miss Amy would have told me.

'I forgot,' said Sir Harry, putting a finger on his lips. 'Very hush-hush.'

Mr. Lacacheur, having completed his meagre breakfast, picked up his white rose and his book, and left us.

'I expect you'll be in on it,' said Sir Harry as soon as Mr. Lacacheur had gone. 'This Stone is an amazing fellow. He's a private 'tec. He told me a thing or two, old man, and—I don't mind telling you—it's pretty awful. But I mustn't say any more; I'm sworn to secrecy, more or less.'

Mrs. Soutar awaited me upstairs in her little parlour. It was almost the first time, that year, that I had seen her. Ever since my arrival she had been in almost complete retirement. I have said before that she was a woman who commanded respect. Never, for one moment, did she forget that she was a daughter of the manse, and it was difficult for anyone else to forget it. She was square in build, round and red of face. Until 7 p.m. she invariably wore a black skirt and a white silk blouse, the collar being kept in position, well up the neck, by vertical whalebone props. After 7 p.m. she wore black velvet, a cameo brooch and a similiar collar. I had not seen her outside Coquet Hall for over ten years, so it would be unfair to describe her hats.

In the great stately rooms of Coquet Hall the *décor* was superbly correct, but here—in what had once, long ago, been the panelled sitting-room of Admiral Brophy's poor housekeeper—the ghosts of Corstophine and Dalmeny had been allowed to run riot. The little room was thick with the relics and household gods of the Soutars and Carlyles. Over the fireplace was the big oil painting of old Dr. Carlyle—his right hand resting on the Book of Books; on the bureau was a silver-framed photograph of the late Colonel Soutar—last year's Flanders poppy still perched above it. Shells, fretwork, tartan boxes, cases of butterflies and photographs—endless photographs—were everywhere. The great dining table from the manse, with its plush cloth, filled the room; it was now the hotel 'desk'. On the far side sat Mr. Stone.

Mrs. Soutar was looking grim, very grim, but she had left the weakness of tears to Amy.

'This,' she said, 'is Mr. Stone. Mr. Stone, this is Mr. Muir, my solicitor.' Then she turned to me. 'Mr. Stone had better tell you his business himself. It's all beyond me . . . but, of course, whether we have the police in or not, it's the end of Coquet Hall. . . .' And, chin up, she marched out of the room.

I found myself face to face with Lysander Stone.

I am almost sure he wore corsets. He undoubtedly wore a monocle. His very pale, dove grey suit was exquisitely cut, if slightly foreign. It might, perhaps, have come from Paris or Geneva. His collar was what used to be known as a 'choker', and his tie was just one shade paler than his suit—almost silver. His hair was close cropped, very close cropped, and this—combined with his monocle—gave him the air of the traditional Prussian officer. Not that he looked a bully, only that he expected to be obeyed without question. His mouth was hard, and mercy —one thought—was not part of the character of Mr. Stone. He adjusted his monocle and fixed me with a stare—his lips pursed and his eyes half closed. He watched me while I sat down, then he rapped out a question.

'Does the name "Langdon-Miles" convey anything to you?'

'Practically nothing,' I said. 'A lady who comes here each summer is—or rather was—secretary to a schoolmistress of that name. But really, Mr. Stone, before we go any further may I, as Mrs. Soutar's representative, ask why your presence in the hotel last night had to be kept secret, and what your business may be. The gentleman who brought you from the station tells me that you are some sort of private enquiry agent. If you are seeking evidence for some divorce case I warn you that we can have not truck with people of your kidney. All our clients are well known to us and . . .'

'Divorce case!' he shouted, 'divorce! I am Lysander Stone, sir, and am not to be trifled with. I am investigating a peculiarly horrible case of murder!' I thought that perhaps I was dealing with a madman, and I decided to humour him a little.

'Well, well. In that case had not the police better be called in?'

'The police, sir, are running after a mare's nest

at the other end of the country. Idiots!'

'You had better explain yourself,' I said, 'but I warn you, Mr. Stone, that in fairness to Mrs. Soutar I shall require the fullest credentials. . . .' He whipped a letter out of a despatch case and threw it across the table. While I read he again fixed me with his monocle. I reproduce the letter here:

Langdon-Miles and Gabbitas,
Stockbrokers & Financiers,
5 Wall Street, N.Y. City.

Lysander Stone, Esq.,
  2b Pall Mall,
    London, Eng.

Sir,—Your name has been given to me by Pinkertons, the American detective agency, as being the most suitable person in Europe for my purpose.

My younger sister, Phillipa Langdon-Miles, of Easton Knoyle, Torquay, died suddenly on the 20th inst. in mysterious circumstances. Reports in the Boston Press suggest that her death may have been due to foul play. I have been out of touch with my relatives for many years but, for the sake of the family honour, I request you to investigate and report. I have no faith in the English police, and owing to the economic crisis I am unable to cross the Atlantic myself.

My sister was emotional, but virtuous, and I doubt whether sex played any part in the mystery. It was probable that she would in the course of time inherit a considerable fortune. My father's will can, no doubt, be inspected at Somerset House. In this connection I suggest that you

investigate the antecedents of one Harold Warburton, formerly of Melbourne, and now married
to my elder sister, Beatrice, of Wildwood Road,
Hampstead.

All other relevant information is more likely to
be available in England than here. I have arranged
with Chases' Bank for the payment of your fees
and expenses and should be obliged if you would
cable your acceptance or otherwise of this com-
mission.

I am, sir, yours truly,

Edward Langdon-Miles.

Mr. Stone had stood up and was lighting a cigar,
but he still had his eye fixed on me.

'Well?' he said.

'Mr. Stone,' I replied, 'I think that perhaps it
would be best if you told me the whole story.'

6

My nerves arc as sound as those of most people—
I managed, at any rate, to pick up my share of
decorations in the last war—but I confess that when
Mr. Stone had finished his story I was in a pretty
bad state. I suppose that facing a Hun barrage needs
one sort of courage, but that quite a different kind
of self-control is needed to sleep in the next room to
an arch-poisoner. And at Coquet Hall, too, we were
so many miles from help of any sort—just that one
telephone wire, nothing else; and twelve miles to a
house.

'I have not,' began Mr. Stone, 'allowed the grass to grow under my feet. That, sir, is not Lysander Stone's way! Miss Philippa Langdon-Miles died last Tuesday—today is Monday. She had Boston connections and the case was reported there on the Wednesday. Her brother, being a stockbroker, had access to rapid means of communication—"teleprinters" and the like. By Saturday morning I had had his letter and immediately—by cable—put my services at his disposal. That evening I had three minutes' conversation with brother Edward on the trans-Atlantic telephone. By then I had already interviewed the deceased's secretary—a Miss Coppock—at the Anglo-American Ladies' Club. A most fruitful interview, most fruitful. I spent Saturday in the British Museum and at Somerset House The whole of Saturday night I spent in my own unique library of criminological newspaper files. Throughout those three days my brain was working at very high pressure. It is a first-class instrument, sir, a first-class instrument. My conclusions have now been formed and my case established. There is no mystery left—none at all.'

'Indeed,' I remarked. I was tickled as well as irritated by the little man's vanity.

'Yesterday,' he went on, 'I caught the midday train from King's Cross—and here I am!' He puffed out his chest. 'In view of the—er—unsavoury nature of my enquiry it was at Mrs. Soutar's request that I was so to speak—ha, ha—kept in quarantine, until I had had the pleasure, sir—the great pleasure—of explaining matters to the good lady's eminent solicitor.'

Mr. Stone bowed from the waist in a slightly

ridiculous manner. I gave him a curt nod, and he went on with his tale.

'Even now, sir, at this hour, Miss Langdon-Miles's mortal remains lie unburied. The funeral is, I believe, this afternoon. You will agree, sir, that it has been smart work, very smart work, on the part of Lysander Stone—what?'

'Mr. Langdon-Miles seems to have acted pretty promptly too,' I said.

'Oh! Quite, quite.' Mr. Stone gave me rather a nasty look. 'I shall explain that in a moment. He, of course, was expecting something of the kind, although unable to foresee precisely where the blow would fall.'

'You amaze me, Mr. Stone. *The Times*, I think, said that the headmistress of a well-known school had collapsed and died at the Cranmer Hall . . . but premeditated murder, if that is what you are implying, is a very different matter. Come, come, sir, such things don't happen . . . not, at least, in our class. And what has the Coroner got to say?'

'The Coroner's Court, Mr. Muir, was adjourned, but the autopsy established strychnine poisoning as the cause of death. Beyond doubt. Two or three times the fatal dose. A painful death, Mr. Muir, a very painful death. One retches and writhes.'

'If the Coroner has come to no conclusion,' I said, rather nettled by Mr. Stone's manner, 'I can see no reason why we should do so. In my opinion your action is premature. It is, surely, a police matter. . . .' For the second time that morning Mr. Stone went purple with anger.

'If your object is to persuade me to behave like a cold-blooded monster, Mr. Muir, than I am afraid I must decline. . . .'

'Well, really,' I said, 'I had no intention. . . .'

'The police are dithering. In fact they are in the process of making up their minds whether there is anything to dither about. They—and the virtuous Coppock—are obsessed with a crazy notion that there is a plot to steal an old Italian picture from the Torquay school. Idiots! Idiots! I ignore them. A life is at stake, sir, and you—yes, you—would have me do nothing. While Scotland Yard and the Devon Constabulary entangle themselves in their own red-tape, a noble woman is in peril of her life—and you would have us sit back as mere spectators of the tragedy. . . .'

'Very well, very well,' I said. 'Come to your point.' I had, after all, agreed to listen to his fantastic story, and I had better do so with a good grace. In silence he opened his despatch case and laid before me on the table a series of newspaper cuttings. In my mind's eye I can see them now, lying there on Mrs. Soutar's plush table-cloth, half a dozen of them—old, yellow and with the small type and narrow columns of thirty years ago. The first, from the *Melbourne Sun* of July 10th, 1910, was a photograph of a young man; beneath were the words: 'HENRY WASHWOOD, "THE BUNDABERG MONSTER." '

'Bundaberg,' explained Mr. Stone, 'is on the coast of Queensland; a very one-horse place in 1910, I imagine.'

The photograph, which might have been re-produced from a daguerreotype—there was a hint of a potted palm in the background—showed a youth with the braided jacket, high collar and crimped hair of the period. It meant nothing to me, and I turned to the next cutting, from the *Sydney Star* of a month later. In 1910 the Australian Press still had something to learn from America in the matter of sensational headlines. The column of close and faded print was headed simply: 'THE WASHWOOD CASE.'

'At the forthcoming Assize, public interest will naturally centre upon what is already being called, rather sensationally, 'The Poisoned Brides Case'. The accused, Henry Washwood, was born at Bundaberg in 1885—the son of a barber. He is of extraordinary physique, and in his native town he was dubbed 'the monster', the children fleeing at his approach. He is excessively tall, with huge ape-like arms and a shambling gait. When Washwood was charged in the magistrates' court, however, he seemed very mild, and even cowed by his surroundings. He reserved his defence.

'Apparently he is not without a streak of genius and, in his childhood, was regarded locally as something of a musical prodigy. An extreme example, perhaps, of the unbalanced artistic temperament. On leaving the town school he drifted to Perth, where he set up, without much success, as a teacher of the pianoforte. In Melbourne he had better luck and a number of young ladies from respectable homes went to him for musical instruction. He even became fashionable in a small way. It was at this point—if the allegations against the accused are well-founded—that the trouble began. In 1904 he formed a liaison with one of his pupils, an Alice Lucas. She had the reputation of being something of a belle. Her father was a farmer, and would have nothing to do with her after her association with Washwood. Upon Miss Lucas becoming *enceinte* the accused insured her life, in his own favour, for the sum of

£5,000. In due course she gave birth to a still-born child, and some six months later she died in her sleep; the cause of death being certified as heart failure.

'Washwood, with his £5,000, then moved to Sydney where he again set up as a music teacher —this time in some style. One of his pupils was a Miss Mabel Priestley, heiress to a wealthy New South Wales farmer. On this occasion the accused, with more regard for the proprieties, married the girl. About a year later her father died, and at the beginning of the following year, 1908, Mrs. Washwood was stricken with the first of a series of painful and inexplicable illnesses. To the last of these, about nine months ago, she succumbed, leaving her entire fortune to her husband. Mr. and Mrs. Washwood are said to have lived in a rather eccentric manner. They kept no servants and throughout her illness Mrs. Washwood was tended only by her husband.

'It is also rumoured that between the death of Miss Lucas and his marriage to Miss Priestley, Washwood lived with another young woman. She is said to have died very suddenly while consuming an almond cake, but on this point we are unable to establish the facts, and they did not emerge at the magistrates' hearing. Whatever the truth may be—and it is not for us to comment on a case which is *sub judice*—Washwood seems to have had an extraordinary attraction for a certain type of young woman, and that not necessarily the loose or the abandoned.

'Some two months ago local gossip, both in Melbourne and in Sydney, busied itself with the affairs of Henry Washwood. On visiting his native town of Bundaberg he found himself in grave danger of being lynched. Eventually the authorities took action and the remains of Alice Lucas and of Mrs. Washwood were exhumed. In the former case a very large dose of heroin was found in the body, and in the case of Mrs. Washwood an altogether abnormal quantity of arsenic —as one police officer remarked, "enough to kill a regiment." A warrant for arrest was then issued.

'Next week Harry Washwood will stand his trial, and it is not too much to say that Sydney, and indeed the whole country, looks forward to a *cause célèbre* of the most sensational and horrible kind. The names of counsel on both sides give promise of a first class forensic battle.'

I looked up to find Mr. Stone regarding me quizzically, with just the trace of a triumphant smile.

'Good God!' I said. 'What on earth are you driving at? It can't really be that Warburton is . . .'

In reply he merely waved his hands towards the other cuttings on the table. They were lengthy. The report of the last day of the trial occupied a whole page of the *Sydney Star*. In August, 1910, Henry Washwood, aged twenty-five, had been tried before the Hight Court of the Commonwealth of Australia, charged with wilful murder on three counts, that he did cause the death of Alice Lucas by the administration of heroin, of Olive Righton by the administration of cyanide, and of Mabel Washwood, *née* Priestley, by the administration of arsenic. The trial was conducted on the basis of the latter charge only. It took ten days, a large number of witnesses being called both for the prosecution and defence. Many 'fashionably dressed women' were, needless to say, present in the public gallery. In spite of the ghastly nature of the story which I was reading I could not help smiling a little as I envisaged the Australian 'fashions' of 1910. The jury retired for only twelve minutes and then returned a verdict of guilty. The Bundaberg monster—said by the *Sydney Star* to be 'umoved' and by the *Melbourne Sun* to be 'in a state of collapse'—was sentenced, under Australian law, to twenty years' penal servitude. A later newspaper cutting reported that an appeal to the Privy Council had failed.

I was dazed—the whole idea was so incredible and terrifying. Yes—I was terrified! I turned again to the old, faded photograph of the youth. It showed only the head and shoulders but it might, I thought, be the head of a giant. The straggling, nicotine stained moustache was missing, but—beyond doubt—there were the restless, wild eyes.

'It's impossible,' I said, 'I simply can't believe it —and at Coquet Hall of all places. . . .' I put my hands to my head for, to tell the truth, I felt stunned. Mr. Stone thrust towards me the last of his documents. The white and shiny page, with its modern type, was in almost dramatic contrast with the old, yellow slips on the table. Somehow it made them look pathetic—symbols of a far-off tragedy, a tragedy which must have struck deep into the simple life of Edwardian Australia. I looked at Mr. Stone's latest 'exhibit'. It was—of all things—a recent copy of the *Tatler*. A paragraph in a gossip column had been marked.

'Popping into the Chilean Embassy the other afternoon for one of those *thés musicales* which His Excellency has made famous, I found that the main subject of conversation was the Australian pianist, Harold Warburton—the latest find of the *avant garde* of the musical world. His rendering of Debussy, just before I arrived, had caused something of a sensation. Mr. Warburton, with whom I had a chat, is a shy, middle-aged man of extraordinary physique, quite unlike the popular idea of a musician. A couple of months ago he was absolutely unknown, and quite new to this country, but now—he tells me—he has a whole string of concert engagements. It is no secret that he is engaged to Beatrice Langdon-Miles, the well-known Fabian and social welfare expert. They are to be married in the spring.'

I pulled myself together; this thing must be dealt with. I still had a faint hope that Mr. Stone might be mad.

'You say, Mr. Stone, that the police are acting slowly and that, so far as the murder of Miss Langdon-Miles is concerned, they are running after a mare's nest, but all this . . .' I pointed to the newspaper cuttings on the table '. . . would surely convince them.' Mr. Stone smiled.

'I am not a fool, Mr. Muir. I may criticise the police but I know that in this country, in the long run, one cannot act without then. On Saturday evening I presented at Scotland Yard the whole of the evidence which I have laid before you. . . .'

'And . . .' I said.

'And they are writing to Australia about it. I suppose we may expect an answer before Christmas. Damned fools! Damned fools!' It was, at any rate, something of a relief to my mind to know that the police had been informed. Mr. Stone suddenly stepped across the room and stood by the window, looking down into the forecourt.

'Look! Look!' he said. In the sunshine Mrs. Warburton, very shaky, was walking slowly, leaning on her husband's arm. She was a tall woman, but she did not come up to his shoulder.

'There,' said Mr. Stone solemnly, 'there goes the Bundaberg monster . . . and his next victim!'

I felt rather sick, but I was determined now to thrash the matter out. I owed it to Mrs. Soutar.

'Assuming,' I said, 'that your fantastic and revolting thesis is correct—that Henry Washwood is Harold Warburton—I still fail to see why Miss Philippa Langdon-Miles, the revered headmistress of an English school, should go the same way as Alice Lucas and those other poor girls.' Mr. Stone made a gesture of impatience.

'Mrs. Warburton,' he said, 'is a wealthy woman. Not a millionairess perhaps, but very wealthy indeed. She may have made a new will when she married. She may not. I don't know. If not, then her entire fortune would probably have gone, one day, to her sister and—on *her* death—to the Church . . . out of reach, for ever, of Harold Warburton *alias* Henry Washwood, or any other human being. That contingency, at any rate, Harold has staved off. On the other hand, if Mrs. Warburton did make a new will she might still, of course, leave a large proportion of the money to Philippa—since Harold's position as a successful pianist was well established. That, I am inclined to think, is what she did do. If so, he must have been furious—*it meant two murders instead of one*. Philippa, obviously, had to die first. If he had killed his wife first, and then Philippa, the money would simply have ended up in the coffers of Philippa's favourite convent. Little Miss Coppock gave me some useful information on that score. Now, of course—with Philippa dead—Harold Warburton stands to gain the whole of the Langdon-Miles fortune.'

'Very well,' I said, still completely bewildered, 'I admit that there was a motive for the murder of Miss Langdon-Miles. But what about opportunity, Mr. Stone? Strychnine is not so easily administered.'

'Ah!' Mr. Stone replied with a smile. 'That again is where the little Coppock comes in. She tells me that on the evening of May 19th, Miss Langdon-Miles went to the theatre—the old Vic—with Miss Coppock, Mr. and Mrs. Warburton and a nephew. Miss Langdon-Miles had not seen her sister more than once or twice in the last twenty years—they seem to have been a quarrelsome family—and Miss Coppock says that this theatre party was intended as a sort of reconciliation. As such it was a complete failure. It finished up with a violent quarrel in the Waterloo Bridge Road.'

'But the strychnine?' I said impatiently. Mr. Stone gave a little chuckle which, in the circumstances, I found rather revolting.

'During the evening,' he went on, 'Mr. Warburton presented his sister-in-law with a box of chocolates. They were very rich liqueur creams, Mr. Muir. Admirably chosen for concealing a bitter flavour. In the third act—the play was *Macbeth*—Mr. Warburton sat between Miss Coppock and Miss Langdon-Miles, passing them chocolates, *in the dark, one at a time in his fingers*. Less than twenty-four hours later Miss Langdon-Miles was dead.'

'My God! Mr. Stone, this is simply awful . . .

do you mean to say that we are simply going to sit here and wait for Mrs. Warburton to die too?'

'And what the devil, sir,' cried Mr. Stone rudely, 'do you think I have come to Coquet Hall for—if not to prevent such a tragedy. I was close on the Warburtons' heels.'

'And how,' I asked, 'will the blow fall? Strychnine again, I suppose.'

'You may have observed, Mr. Muir, that Henry Washwood of Bundaberg was careful to avoid the traditional blunder of the great poisoners. He varied his poison from time to time. Alice Lucas died in her sleep from a dose of heroin; Olive Righton collapsed suddenly through taking cyanide in an almond cake; Mrs. Washwood's distressing sickness was due to arsenic. In fact "variety" became Washwood's hallmark just as surely as any single poison might have done. And now, twenty years later, Miss Langdon-Miles dies in agony—great agony—as the result of taking strychnine in chocolate creams; Mrs. Warburton will, unless we can prevent it, die from some other cause. I think that I know what it will be, but I am not sure—yet.'

'And when,' I asked, 'do you expect Warburton to act?'

Mr. Stone had been standing by the window while he talked, watching the Warburtons as they strolled in the sun. Now he came over to the table again and, once more, fixed me with his monocle.

'From what Mrs. Soutar has told me,' he said slowly, 'I understand that poor Beatrice Warburton had her first heart attack at Keswick, the night before last.'

7

Mrs. Soutar had always been a brave woman, but when she rejoined Mr. Stone and me in her little parlour I think that she was very nearly at breaking point. As for Miss Amy—her aunt and I packed her off to bed. I think it was less the beastliness of Mr. Stone's fantastic tale that had upset them—for they had, as yet, hardly grasped that—than the conviction that Coquet Hall would never survive the publicity. It was agreed that Mr. Stone should now appear among the guests and should pose as an acquaintance of mine, sharing my table in the dining-room. I confess that I found this rather annoying but if we did not do something of the kind the others might wonder why Mrs. Soutar had suddenly accepted a stranger as a client. In the appalling circumstances I could hardly object to anything, and my holiday was now ruined in any case. It was to be understood that Mr. Stone was visiting the moors as an amateur water-colourist. We could probably buy a box of paints in Rothbury, and amateur water-colourists in hotels are never expected to be anything but bad.

Mr. Stone's story and my study of the Washwood Trial had taken up most of the morning, and when he and I went downstairs the others were on the terrace waiting for the luncheon gong to sound. As Mr. Stone and I crossed the black-and-white marble floor of the great hall we had to step aside for a moment. A ceremony was going on. Mrs. Bradford had returned, rather unexpectedly, from York, and was on her way to her room. It was a Royal Progress.

She was a wonderful woman—Mrs. Bradford of

Bath. Eighty, if she was a day, and over forty years a widow, she was as straight as a ramrod—even if, at times, she did find it convenient to 'feel her back'. As she sailed past in her mink mantle I was honoured with a kindly smile. Mr. Stone, of course, was ignored. Mrs. Soutar, one felt, would be called upon later to explain his presence. A glimpse of glorious white hair and magnificent pearls—gleaming in the dark hall—and she was gone. Two of the Coquet Hall maids flanked the foot of the staircase and Mrs. Soutar herself—shaky as she was—had followed us down in order to welcome the old lady, who had after all been away for only one night. For anyone else Miss Amy would have deputised, but Mrs. Bradford was different. She always had been. In Mrs. Bradford's wake came her own maid, a poor, white creature, hung around with rugs and cushions. Mr. Stone's glance followed Mrs. Bradford until she had disappeared round the bend in the great staircase.

'Who is the Archduchess?' he whispered.

'That,' I said, 'is Mrs. Bradford. Bertha Bradford. A surgeon's widow and aunt to the little Coppock. Not to be trifled with.'

Mr. Stone and I passed out into the forecourt. On the far side—gazing out over the moors—were the Warburtons. I could not help shuddering. By the front door was Mrs. Bradford's big black Daimler. Old Jennings, the 'boots', was on the top of it, passing luggage down to the chauffeur—also rather ancient, for once, long ago, he had driven his mistress's victoria. I was accustomed to the ritual of Mrs. Bradford's outings. There were two or three each summer.

Somehow Mrs. Bradford, at that moment, symbolised for me the solid, respectable peace and comfort of Coquet Hall, as I had known it for so long. It was in a half-dazed condition that I escorted Mr. Stone up the curved stone steps and past the green Satyr. I found it difficult to believe that in a few days the end might have come and that Coquet Hall would be invaded by police, reporters and Heaven knows who else! It had occurred to me that Sir Harry McQueen would be severely tempted to chatter about his 'private 'tec', and I was anxious to warn him. But as we came on to the terrace it was clear that even the intriguing Mr. Stone would receive but little attention.

Miss Bunting was having tantrums.

She was lying in a *chaise-longue*, and the others were gathered round trying to calm her, without the slightest effect.

'Oh! Oh! Oh!' she screamed, the heels of her Tyrolean sandals beating a tattoo on the paving. The entire mass of her straw-coloured hair, *en bloc*, was awry. I had often wondered whether it was not portable. The tears were coursing down her withered cheeks, making runnels for themselves in her makeup—just like our moorland freshets. Her charcoal biscuits were scattered about the terrace.

'Come, Maisie, come! Don't cry.' Mr. Lacacheur was clearly out of his depth. He might as well have told the Coquet to stop flowing.

'You brutes'—gasp and a sob—'you horrible, cruel brutes'—another sob—'but men are all the same. Poor, darling little Binksey Winksey.'

'Now, my dear Miss Bunting,' began Sir Harry, 'really, you know, it's nobody's fault.'

'It is, it is,' she shrieked. 'Your horrible son accused poor Binksey of stealing and it broke his dear, little heart. He was always a sensitive doggy. Just an innocent, dumb lamb.' And the sobbing began all over again.

'Dear me,' I said. 'What is the matter?' Miss Bunting looked up and saw Mr. Stone, gazing at her through his monocle. She gave a shriek, and fell back with her eyes shut.

'Oh! My God! The sleuth!'

'Now, Miss Bunting,' I said, for I knew her of old. 'Stop this nonsense immediately. We don't want to have to fetch Crowe to you. Stop sobbing and tell me what it's all about.' She stopped. Once upon a time, when the tantrums were bad, Crowe had thrown cold water in her face. Miss Bunting had not forgotten.

'It's Binksey! Poor, wee, mumsie's darling. They put the tray on the mat'—a sob and a gasp—'those horrible Warburtons. I knew they were bad. That horrible mous'—a sob—'tache! If you put minced chicken on the mat, of course a poor, innocent little doggy-woggy will think it's for him. And why shouldn't he have a little bit of chicken anyway.' Another sob and gasp. 'And then all you beastly men accuse the little lamb of stealing . . . you brutes!'

'Oh! come, Maisie. Nobody said that.'

'They did. They did. They did. I distinctly heard that beastly McQueen boy say that the "nasty little pom had stolen Mrs. Warburton's supper." Of course it broke the poor lamb's heart—being spoken to like that. I could bring an action. . . .' And then the sobbing started again. I turned to Mr. Lacacheur.

'What has happened?' I asked. He pointed to the step of the French window behind us.

There, stretched out stark and stiff, with glazed eyes, was the corpse of Binks.

'Poor Crowe,' I said, 'she will probably have to cope with more tantrums in the night. But . . .' and I lowered my voice, ' . . . I must say that I'm not sorry Binks has gone. Nasty, snappy little beast.'

The luncheon gong sounded. The unpleasant John Smith had already wheeled Mark into position at his table in the window. Not, of course, the centre window. Mrs. Bradford always had that. Mark was devouring olives with his sherry. There was, I thought, a slight hum of surprise as Mr. Stone took his seat at my table. Well, introductions could come later.

'I see,' I remarked conversationally to Mark, 'that Mrs. Bradford has returned.'

'I,' replied Mark, 'have had an audience, on the landing. The Northern Choirs seem to have given satisfaction, but whom do you think the old girl saw —yesterday afternoon—poking round York Minster?'

'Who?'

'Why, the moss man—complete with collecting tin. I suppose he's left Galbraith Farm.'

'And who is the moss man?' asked Mr. Stone. I told him.

Mrs. Bradford entered the dining-room. It was some weeks since she had appeared in public at Coquet Hall, so the visit to York must have done her back good. It wouldn't do, however, to mention it. Mr. Lacacheur rushed to pull back her chair; one maid relieved her of her black stick, a second maid waited for her order, and a third hovered. If you had looked very carefully you might have seen Mrs. Bradford bow to those with whom she was acquainted. This, of course, excluded Mr. Stone and the Warburtons. A morsel of *soufflé*, a carefully chosen pear and half a glass of the late Colonel Alexander

Soutar's best Montrachet: that was Mrs. Bradford's lunch. Consequently she had vanished upstairs again before Mark—always on the gluttonous side—had had time to pass on from his trout to his game-pie. She might reappear for dinner, on the other hand it was more probably that she wouldn't.

When speaking on the telephone in public I always feel a fool. As Mr. Lacacheur had once said, it was one of Mrs. Soutar's few blunders—putting the telephone in the hall. But it was really Admiral Brophy's fault. He had made his entrance hall impressive, but funereal. In contrast with the whites, golds and crimsons of the big rooms, it was panelled in black marble. The stairs themselves were white, and on either side were niches. In the right-hand niche the Admiral had placed a life-size Venus de Milo—also in white marble. In the left-hand niche there had once been an Apollo of the Belvedere. Mrs. Soutar had tolerated the Venus, but she had drawn the line at the Apollo. The symmetry was completely ruined and, when it was decided that the telephone might well replace the Apollo, it was barely restored.

It was particularly annoying that the telephone should ring just as we were all coming out of lunch. Of course it was not really my business to answer the telephone, but I knew that Mrs. Soutar and Miss Amy were more than worried—so I dealt with it. As I say I felt a fool. The others were passing through the hall and Mr. Stone stood at my elbow, waiting for me. It was the Rothbury post-office, with a telegram for Mrs. Bradford. That was not, in itself, surprising; Mrs. Bradford habitually sent the most lengthy telegrams, and she expected telegraphic replies. 'I never,' she once said to me, 'write a letter if a telegram will do.' It would not have mattered if the girl in Rothbury post-office had not made me repeat the whole thing after her. It sounded so silly. It went like this.

'Totterdell has found it in the bottom of the pew. Lincoln, London and New York. Take care of your poor back. Much love, Sophie.'

I scribbled it down so that one of the servants could take it to Mrs. Bradford's room. We were going on our way to the smoking-room when Mr. Stone beckoned to me to follow him out into the forecourt. We strolled about in the sun.

'Mr. Muir,' he said, 'you know the habits of this hotel. What, in your opinion, would be the best time of day for us to ransack the Warburtons' bedroom.'

8

It was a long time before I could reconcile myself to Mr. Stone's suggestion. It went against the grain. I had the gravest legal doubts about hunting through the private rooms of a fellow guest in a hotel. Although Warburton and Washwood might be the same person, the whole business was so fantastic and improbable that I felt very strongly that we ought to have absolute proof before we took the law into our own hands. It was evident that when Mr. Stone had visited Scotland Yard—where, apparently, he was known and respected—the police had admitted a *prima facie* case for an enquiry and had, accordingly, written to Sydney; but they weren't going to make fools of themselves by arresting a perfectly innocent man for no other reason than that he stood six foot four in his socks and came from Melbourne.

There was, however, a good deal to be said for Mr. Stone's point of view. One had to admit it. The musical ability of both Washwood and Warburton and the sudden death of Miss Langdon-Miles, added to Warburton's stature and Australian origin, made a quadruple coincidence which it was difficult to ignore—however horrible the implications. Above all there was a life at stake. Nobody knew how many days Mrs. Warburton had to live.

I eventually gave way when Mr. Stone pointed out that the whole object of going through the Warburtons' possessions was to find that very proof which we needed to clinch our case. It was that, more than anything else, which influenced me. After a rather sleepless night spent in weighing the 'pros and cons' and in generally contemplating the awful cloud which hung over us, I finally agreed. I made a proviso—Mrs. Soutar must be consulted.

'Oh! I could never dream of allowing anything of that sort, never!' That was her first response, and then—incongruous as it may seem—she almost laughed. What, after all, was the ransacking of the Warburtons' bedroom compared with the real issue.

Finally it was decided that Mr. Stone and I should enter the Warburtons' room during dinner. We were to bath and change before the dressing gong sounded and then, the moment the Warburtons went down to the drawing-room, we were to do our dirty work. If the Warburtons were dressed in good time it might even be possible for Mr. Stone and myself

to hunt through their room and appear at dinner ourselves, not too conspicuously late. The difficulty was
Crowe. The other staff would, in one way or another, be concerned with the serving of dinner.
Crowe, however, usually had a supper tray in her
room at about eight o'clock. It was at last decided
that she should be sent in the shooting brake to
Rothbury to perform an 'urgent' errand for Mrs.
Soutar. Mrs. Soutar herself would be in command
at the sideboard that evening, while Miss Amy stood
guard for us on the landing.

I didn't like it. I didn't like it a bit. But if our
marauding expedition produced something, anything,
which we could lay before the police, and which
might thus end the awful suspense, then I was prepared to face it. I don't know what I expected to find
in the Warburtons' room; I wasn't very optimistic
about the result but Mr. Stone felt sure we should
find something worthwhile.

The next morning Mr. Stone gave me a few instructions in the art of hunting efficiently through
drawers and wardrobes without leaving signs of a disturbance, and I then spent a thoroughly miserable
day—waiting. By half-past six I was sitting in my
bedroom, dressed for dinner, and trying to concentrate on a trashy novel which Miss Bunting had
insisted I should read. I had already seen Crowe,
clothed in black, setting off on her errand to Rothbury—old Jennings driving her. About twenty past
seven, three knocks came at my door—the signal as
planned with Miss Amy. The Warburtons must be
safely downstairs.

I went quietly out into the corridor. There, at the
far end, Lysander Stone was awaiting me. In the dark
corridor only the gleam of his shirt front and the

twinkle of his monocle were really visible. He carried Mrs. Soutar's master-key. The Warburtons had a small suite—a bedroom with a bathroom opening off on one side, and a dressing-room on the other. The dressing-room also had its own door on to the corridor, which was rather a comfort since it gave us a chance of escape if we were caught red-handed. It had been agreed that I should start work in the bedroom, while Mr. Stone dealt with the dressing-room.

I felt horribly guilty as I systematically went through Mrs. Warburton's possessions. Everything showed that she had taste, as well as money. Clothes, shoes, books—everything—were severely plain but of superb quality. The dressing-room, Mr. Stone told me afterwards, was an absolute bear-garden compared with the tidy bedroom. 'Master Harold,' he said, 'was evidently in need of a good wife.' In the circumstances the *double entendre* of this remark left rather a nasty taste in the mouth. I had rummaged through the top drawers of the dressing-table, not quite knowing what I was looking for, when Mr. Stone came into the bedroom on tiptoe.

'We've finished,' he said. 'These are more than enough to cook his goose.' He held up a green leather diary and a large fountain-pen. 'We'll have a squint at them in your room, and then put them back. The second gong hasn't sounded yet.'

Mr. Stone sat on the edge of my bed, rather cocky about his 'find'.

'The diary may be useful,' I said, 'if he's fool enough to give himself away. But I can't see the object of the pen.'

'If Harold Warburton had left this pen on his dressing-table,' said Mr. Stone, 'I admit that I might have passed it by, but when you find a fountain-pen hidden in a pile of summer pants—then you begin to wonder. Listen!' He shook the pen close to my ear and there was the faintest possible rattle. He unscrewed the cap and the case and drew out the ink container. He held it upside down and I expected to see the ink flow out on to the green silk eiderdown. Instead there dropped out twenty little pellets—very small and quite globular. I gave a long, low whistle.

'Phew! What on earth are they?'

'I'm not sure,' said Mrs. Stone. 'Heroin probably. We'll keep one for the analyst and one for Scotland Yard. The others can go back. Let's hope he doesn't count them. Now for the diary—also from under the pants.'

I found the diary even more frightening than the pellets. It showed not only cold-blooded premeditation, but suggested a certain fiendish glee. It was a 1931 pocket diary. The entries were very brief; most of them mere memoranda, I think, made before the events to which they referred. It was written in pencil, very neatly and precisely. Half a dozen entries, however, were in red ink, and these were the most significant of all. After the tragedy the little book came into my possession with the other documents, and in its faded greeen leather cover it lies before me now. I will give the entries for that fatal week, although a few of them refer to events with which my readers are familiar.

Mon., May 19. Aeolian Hall 2.30. B. has a welfare committe at home so had tea at Club. Call from Philippa at Park St. 6.30. Old Vic. An unpleasant evening. P. is evidently difficult and a snob. It ended in a row. CHOCS.

The word 'chocs' was scrawled in red ink, in capital letters and had a red circle round it.

Tues., May 20. Lunch at home and a quiet afternoon. B. exhausted after last night's ructions. Call for Hallam at Hyde Park Hotel 5.30. His new flame is pretty but far too young. Calf love. Cambridge in time for dinner. 'Trinity Arms'. Interesting chat with an artist.

And then, at the end of this entry, again scrawled in red ink, was the symbol + and alongside it the capital letter P.

Wed., May 21. Hallam came over to 'Trinity Arms' for breakfast. Began our zigzag tour up England. Bentley ran well to York. Speedometer just 150. 'Black Swan' comfortable, but B. very headachy.

Thurs., May 22. My first view of the English Lakes. Good time of year; no 'hikers', etc. B. prostrate with headache. Aspirin and so on not much use. The 'Dragon' at Keswick rather poor. No. 1.

The letters and figure—'No. 1'—were in red ink with a red circle round them. This rather puzzled me.

Fri., May 24. B. very ill indeed. Local doctor says 'heart'. Rather alarming. Wired to Coquet Hall postponing our arrival. No. 1 HAS GONE SPLENDIDLY.

Once again, the last words were in red ink, with a red circle round them.

> *Sat., May 24. B. is rather better. Decide to go on tomorrow if possible as this hotel is a mere pub. Hallam wires to say he is engaged. Absurd! He has only met the girl once. B.'s RECOVERY RATHER QUICK. MUST STRENGTHEN DOSE FOR No. 2.*

Again the last words were in red ink.

> *Sun., May 25. Wonderful ride but B. unable to enjoy it. Speedometer 106. Reach Coquet Hall in time for late lunch. B. went straight to bed. Very beautiful hotel and well worth the price. It was recommended by P.'s secretary. Very remote, out on the moors—a good thing. Queer lot of folk here. A decent little Scotch solicitor named Muir, but all the others odd. Telegram awaits us saying P. died suddenly on 20th. Had to 'phone Torquay about cremation, etc. B. going to funeral is quite out of the question. No. 2 FAILED.*

'No. 2 FAILED' was in red ink, with a red circle round it.

'That,' said Mr. Stone, 'was Binks's doing.'

> *Mon., May 26. B. able to stroll in the sun for an hour this morning. This is a beautiful spot and a lovely house. Late 18th century. Had a long chat after lunch with a fellow called Lacacheur—rather a flaneur. His speciality is crime. CAVE.*

'No doubt,' said Mr. Stone, 'you used the expression as a schoolboy; *'cave canem'* as the Romans had it, or 'beware of the dog'. He seems afraid lest Lacacheur's diligent researches may have included the Washwood Trial. I doubt it, I doubt it. Friend Lacacheur impresses me as being the veriest amateur.'

There were only two more entries, both in red ink. One was for that very day, May 27, and was simply —'No. 3,' and the other, for June 1st, was again the sign + and the capital letter B.

'We have,' said Mr. Stone quietly, 'just four days left in which to persuade the police. There is a train to London tonight; I could go to Scotland Yard tomorrow. . . .'

'For God's sake!' I cried, 'explain what it all means.' I had glimpsed the truth, but there were still one or two things that puzzled me. I will say this for Lysander Stone, that—unlike some of the detectives I have read about—he made no mystery of his craft. He explained.

'You see,' he said, 'it was all very well to kill Phillippa off suddenly like that—but it was a bit obvious. The chocolate-cream dodge may or may not emerge at the inquest. But, in any case, I expect the verdict will be "wilful murder". Now, if Beatrice died in a similiar manner and Harold was left with the cash—well, that would be a bit thick!'

Mr. Stone had a curiously flippant, and sometimes callous way of speaking, but I said nothing. He went on with his explanation.

'Two violent deaths—and questions would be asked. Philippa might even have to be exhumed. You note that he tried to arrange for cremation. Fortunately he failed. Remember, Henry Washwood has already done twenty years' hard—and all through neighbours' gossip. The old lag isn't making the same mistake again. *For Beatrice there must be something more subtle.* Hence the heroin. She has already had heart attack No. 1. Heart attack No. 2 was scheduled for last Sunday evening—but Binks's partiality for minced chicken rather spoilt the scheme. The comparatively mild dose of heroin which would have given poor Beatrice an unpleasant —but not fatal—heart attack, quite finished off Binks. Really, you know, our friend Maisie wasn't far wrong when she said that her poor little doggy died of a broken heart! No. 3 heart attack is clearly planned for tonight.'

'Well! But, good heavens!' I cried, 'can't we do anything about it?'

'Oh!' said Mr. Stone, 'it won't be fatal. But I expect she will suffer . . . quite a lot. Each attack is, I expect, worse than the one before. And poor Harold does get so distressed when his wife is ill. A brilliant actor, you know—in his way.'

'And June 1st . . .'

'Ah!' said Mr. Stone solemnly. 'That, obviously, is the Ides of March—for poor Beatrice. But we still have four clear days.'

You can imagine the state of mind in which I followed Mr. Stone downstairs to the dining-room. I hardly knew what I was doing or where I was going. My last doubt—and with it, my last hope—had vanished. Miss Amy was still mounting guard at the top of the stairs, but when making our plans there was one person we had forgotten. It was most unfortunate. Mr. Stone had put the pen and the diary back among Harold Warburton's pants and was just coming out of the dressing-room door when—a little way down the corridor—there emerged from Mark's room that unpleasant, white slug—John Smith.

Mark always called him 'secretary', but I think really he was more a valet than a secretary. At any rate he always dined upstairs, and very glad we all were to have him out of the way. But it was a bit of a shock when he suddenly appeared in the gloom of the corridor—about a yard away from us. A nasty, supercilious smirk passed across his pallid features —and he went on his way.

Dinner was drawing to a close when we entered the dining-room. Mrs. Bradford was about to leave for her room, and Miss Bunting—still dabbing her tear-stained cheeks—was making for the drawing-room. Mark was toying with his cognac and Mr. Lacacheur was not there at all. I don't know why. The McQueens were eating oranges. To see the two Warburtons dining together, *tête-à-tête*, made me feel so sick that I could hardly eat a thing. She still looked very ill. I don't know whether anyone felt curious about our being late—and, frankly, I was beyond caring.

After dinner I mooched about a bit and then— feeling indescribably wretched—I decided to go to bed. I told myself that Mr. Stone could probably be trusted to see that everything was all right—but time seemed precious short. As I undressed it was— in that northern latitude—still broad daylight. It was a perfectly still evening and quite cloudless. About three miles away, near Cushat Law, I could see a car —bumping its way along the track towards the hotel.

Before I was ready for bed the car pulled up in the forecourt below my window, and I could hear Mrs. Soutar greeting the new arrivals.

'So pleasant to see you both again. I trust you are not too tired. . . .'

'Rather, I am afraid. But it's nice to be back at

Coquet Hall. Miss Coppock said we were to be sure to give you her kind regards. Poor thing—such a shock for her. My husband had to take the funeral service yesterday . . . and we've come through from Exeter in the day. I *am* rather tired, Mrs. Soutar.'

Of course—I had forgotten. Mrs. Soutar had expected them earlier in the day . . . Canon Fish and his poor wife.

9

It was not until the next afternoon that it dawned upon me that almost everyone at Coquet Hall knew all about the Bundaberg monster and of the fate that hung over poor Beatrice Warburton.

When I came down that morning, May 28th, Canon Fish was already breakfasting. I had never liked him. He was considered, according to his own lights, to be devout and a sound theologian, but the aura of nasty priestliness with which he managed to surround himself, not to mention his Papistical hocus-pocus, grated on my Wee Free soul. He also took cold baths—or so he informed us—and was consequently even pinker at breakfast than at other times. He was genial; some people called it gush. His wife, now, was altogether different. We all liked her in a way. By conventional standards she was very plain, even ugly, but with dear Margaret Fish that didn't matter. The inner light shone in her eyes. She was shy—terribly and painfully shy—but then it was not among people that she sought her happiness; as 'Michael Lechlade' she had written some of the loveliest sonnets of our time—although her identity was known to very, very few. Poor thing—she suffered from insomnia, and I believe that her best work was done in the small hours of the morning.

For nearly ten years the Fishes had been coming to Coquet Hall so I suppose it was natural for the Canon to greet me rather effusively. But he did gush so. Perhaps my nerves were on edge—but he irritated me beyond description.

'Poor Mrs. Soutar,' he said, when the greeting was over. 'I am distressed more than I can say by this horrible affair. Of course the police will be in time—but it's a wretched business. I don't want to desert Mrs. Soutar in her hour of need, but I really don't know whether we ought to stop. So degrading. I suppose the others will be going. . . .'

Well, well, if Nellie Soutar had seen fit to confide in the Canon, it was none of my business. She always had had an exaggerated respect for his cloth, but I must say that I was surprised.

Mr. Stone was demolishing his last piece of toast as I sat down. I was in an agony of suspense. His first words relieved my mind, although I knew that relief could only be temporary.

'Mrs. Warburton has got through the night,' he said. 'No. 3 heart attack hasn't come off. Crowe tells me that she is, if anything, rather better this morning.'

'Thank God!' I murmured.

'I'm not so sure about that. I'm worried. Something has upset Harold's timetable. He may have smelt a rat. Tell me—who is this John Smith who found us in the corridor? An unpleasant specimen; where did Fanshawe pick him up?'

I couldn't tell him much about John Smith; he

had been with Mark only a couple of years, but then Mark's secretaries or valets—or whatever they were—were always coming and going. On the whole I didn't think it very likely that John Smith—for all his evil aspect—would 'spill the beans' to Harold.

'Well,' said Mr. Stone. 'I must be off; the shooting brake is waiting. I shall see Wuthersby at the Yard this evening and—if I can—bring him back with me some time tomorrow. Good-bye—and keep your eye on Master Harold.'

Outwardly the day at Coquet Hall was more or less normal. Mrs. Warburton had been given another lease of life—although we all knew that it might be only for a matter of hours. The McQueen boys spent the morning racing their cars into Newcastle and back, and the afternoon in losing an extravagant number of golf balls in the heather. Although the heat wave of 1931 had begun early, Mr. Lacacheur spent the day by the fire—in the little 'den' beyond the drawing-room—completely absorbed in his *Crimes of the Popes*. Mark came down very late. Margaret Fish—after her tiring journey—spent the morning in bed. Mrs. Bradford appeared for only a few minutes at lunch. Miss Bunting wandered about, within half a mile of the hotel, looking for white heather for Binks's grave. The Warburtons strolled in the sun.

As for me I spent an utterly miserable morning. I hadn't the heart to go fishing, and it was too bright anyway. It might have been better for me if I had done, but somehow I felt that I was keeping guard over Mrs. Warburton—although I didn't quite know what I could do for her. For a time I wandered aimlessly about, and then made my way to the little white-and-crimson 'den'. It was hard to realise that here it was that I had spent so many contented evenings over *The Ettrick Shepherd*, and that here Mark and I had enjoyed so many games of chess. They had been pleasant holidays—and it was melancholy to think that this might be the last. I tried to concentrate on some notes which I had made that winter on the Scott-Hogg letters, but the room was like an oven and Mr. Lacacheur looked furious when I wanted to open the window. I decided to try the smoking-room. As I was going Mr. Lacacheur looked up from his manuscript.

'A Botany Bay ancestry, I suppose.'

'Good God!' I said. 'Do you know too?'

'Naturally. My subject is crime and Mr. Stone was evidently glad to consult me.'

'And the Washwood Case . . .'

'Oh dear me, yes! I've known of it for years. I gather that Stone has gone up to see them at Scotland Yard. Let us hope that he is in time. He impresses me as being a smart fellow. Only eight days since the Langdon-Miles death; he hasn't let the grass grow under his feet. Mark, by the way, is putting up a sort of façade of intellectual superiority; says that he doesn't believe a word of it and that Stone is certifiable. Its pure jealously, of course. Mark always did resent anyone but Mark taking the centre of the stage.'

'Mark is always sceptical,' I said, 'but the diary . . .'

'Ah! Yes—the diary; that ought to have convinced him. You, I understand, have actually seen it. I must say, Muir, that it is extremely gratifying to find my theories on criminal heredity working out so well in practice.'

'Gratifying!' I gasped.

'Oh! Of course one is sorry for the poor wife, but

if—say a century ago—one of Washwood's ancestors was deported to Botany Bay, how utterly fascinating that would be! An investigation of the Washwood genealogy may prove very fruitful. I look forward to it.'

I went off—rather disgusted. Lunch was a nerve-racking meal. My own appetite had gone completely. A servant dropped a fork, whereupon Miss Bunting gave a scream. So she knew too! Mark was annoying; he sneered at our 'nerves' and ostentatiously read The *Connoisseur* throughout the meal. But, as he drank his cognac, I could see that his hand was shaking. Mr. Lacacheur also had a book propped up in the table, but he didn't notice that it was upside down until he had finished his soup. The Canon and poor Margaret never spoke; I think that she was quietly crying. Mrs. Bradford alone seemed quite unmoved—but perhaps she alone did not yet know. And—worst of all—the Warburtons looked so happy.

Alone in the big smoking-room, after lunch, I thought I might get a little sleep. But as the afternoon wore on the atmosphere in that strange and beautiful house became terrifying. It was so lonely —and so silent. Even that white tent, a mile away in the heather, had—since the incident in the corridor —become rather sinister; not, as it had once seemed, a comforting link with the world, but rather the out-post of some besieging army of evil. We were sur-rounded by evil—and over it all was a fog. And the fog was the worst part. Even inside the hotel—in fact most of all inside—it all seemed so . . . so un-wholesome, as if everyone was just a little ab-normal. I told myself that it was all nonsense—for Harold Warburton, surely, was the only truly, horribly, abnormal one . . . and then Mr. Stone, surely, surely, would be in time. And then the police would quietly take Harold away—and everything would be all right again. But . . . in those sleepy, warm afternoon hours . . . it was so deathly quiet. The others were in their bedrooms, but God knows what was happening behind all those closed doors. So quiet—but so dangerous. That sophisticated life, the soft luxury and the wealth . . . and those queer, twisted minds, each with their secret thoughts. Mark, for instance, or Mr. Lacacheur; Margaret Fish—so pathetic, or John Smith—so repulsive. And the Cañon. Yes, and even the dark, dour Crowe— haunting the silent corridors. And there were the signals in the night, there was strychnine and heroin, and a fashionable funeral at Torquay. . . .

The telephone rang. I leapt out of my chair with a little cry. I told myself not to be a fool, and I was glad that I had been alone in the room. But the spell was broken. Alice came in.

'Please, sir, I'm sorry to trouble you, but it's a telegram for Mrs. Bradford, and there's a word, sir, that I can't make out at all. Something about "tricks".'

It was actually a relief to go to the telephone in that black marble hall. Momentarily it gave one something to do. It was the Rothbury postmistress with one of Bertha Bradford's silly telegrams, but this time there was only Alice to hear me make a fool of myself as I repeated the message.

'Yes, MacTaggart says large cicatrix on the right leg. Miranda's mother has given way at last. Newcastle 4.0 p.m. tomorrow. Very dear love, Sophie.'

I scribbled it down—neither knowing nor caring what it meant—and told Alice to give it to Mrs. Bradford's maid—the poor creature who was bullied so. Then I wandered out to the forecourt. I had decided to take the car out for a couple of hours. I couldn't bear that beautiful, silent house for another minute.

10

In the afternoon sun the moors lay warm and still. Somewhere at the back of the house were faint noises from the kitchen, and once I heard the distant crack of a golf ball—where the McQueen boys were playing, far out in the heather. I passed through the great arch—all flourishes and carving—that led from the forecourt to the old cobbled stable yard. Here—long ago—had stood Admiral Patrick Brophy's four lumbering coaches, with sundry chariots and gigs. Here, too, long ago, the three lily-white daughters—Anna, Delilah and Grace—had stabled their Arab mounts. Once there had been loose boxes for forty, and you could still see the mangers on the wall. But now, today, there was Mrs. Bradford's big black Daimler, covered with dust sheets. Then came Mark's gorgeous vehicle—crammed with expensive luxuries—and the Canon's car, mud stained from its long journey. Next there was a gap where Miss Trubshawe from the tent was allowed to keep her little Austin Seven. Then, all chromium and vermilion paint, were the McQueen boys' sports car —one on either side of 'Dad's' big blue limousine.

226

Next to them was my own car—very modest because my sister Janet had been dead against 'launching out'. Then the Warburtons' huge grey Bentley, and—last in the line—the invaluable house shooting brake.

It was with an enormous feeling of relief that I drove out of the yard and across the forecourt. I knew that that relief could only be very temporary, but—for a couple of hours—I was going to get away from Coquet Hall. I left that grey house sleeping in the sun, and—with the car windows open so that I could breathe the good moorland air—I bumped off along the track—past the rowan trees and under the shadow of Bloodybush Edge. This was the first time I had used the track since the dark night of my arrival. That had been less than a week ago . . . and yet it seemed like months and months.

I had crossed the two burns, and as I came up the slope from the bottom of a small corrie, a fair stretch of the track lay open before me. A quarter of a mile ahead, cycling slowly in my direction, was the moss man—black 'plus-fours' suit, white Panama hat, and collecting tin. It seemed odd. Mrs. Bradford had seen him poking around York Minster—so she said—as recently as Sunday afternoon . . . and now here he was again. Of course if he chose to add Gregorian chants or archæology to his other hobby of moss-collecting—he was at liberty to do so. But it was, nevertheless, distinctly odd. According to Maisie Bunting's gossip, the lad who came over with the eggs from Galbraith Farm had reported the moss man's final departure—and now here he was, cycling towards Coquet Hall.

The moment I emerged from the corrie he dismounted. Then he turned his bicycle round and started to pedal off, as hard as he could go, in the opposite direction. This was getting odder and odder, but—unless I was prepared to break the springs of the car—a bicycle on that track, picking its way along the ruts and round the projecting lumps of granite, actually had the advantage of me. Long before I could catch up with him he had reached the end of the track—where it joined up with the road down the Dale. He propped his bicycle against the stone to which Mrs. Soutar's post-box was fixed, and then—on foot—he plunged into the heather and peaty bog on the other side of the road. That way lay Galbraith Farm.

I might have followed him, but you can imagine that I was in no mood for a chase through the heather. And, after all, why should I? His behaviour was peculiar—he may even have been a little mad—but it was no business of mine. I turned down the Dale towards Rothbury, thankful to put a few more miles between myself and the horrors of Coquet Hall.

Beyond Harbottle I turned south, and then in a few miles I doubled back through Otterburn to join that great highway that sweeps up from England to Carter Bar. The car went like a bird and I think that the sixteen odd miles from Otterburn to the border helped to clear away some of the cobwebs and enabled me to see things in better perspective. They were bad enough—however you looked at them— but Mr. Stone, I reflected, would be back in time. Scotland Yard, after all, knew its job. The British police might be slow—but they were sure. Mr. Stone had an overwhelming case—since we had found the pellets and the diary—and the police would surely come with a car and—quite quietly—take Harold

Warburton away. After that there might be reporters and a good deal of fuss. But, with firm handling, the name of the hotel might be kept out of the case altogether. The only tragedy—so far—had been in London, at the Cranmer Hall. Coquet Hall might lose one or two good clients—the Canon perhaps, or Mrs. Bradford . . . and then, after a time, things would go on as before. Miss Langdon-Miles was dead, but Mrs. Warburton could be, and must be saved. Already, it seemed, Harold Warburton was frightened and had altered his timetable. And—even if we accepted the dates in that terrifying diary—there were still three days to go. Scotland Yard seemed a long way off, but Mr. Stone might come back on the night train—that very night—and be with us before morning . . . or at worst, some time tomorrow. As I argued with myself I felt a little comforted. It had been a good thing to get away from that house for an hour; at lunchtime I had almost lost my nerve, and that would never do.

At Carter Bar I had turned the car off the road—to be alone with my thoughts, while I looked down into Scotland and away to the Pentland Hills, all golden and clear in the sunshine. It was strange to think that Coquet Hall, and all those queer people, were just a few miles away, as the crow flies, beyond that great Cheviot ridge. Then, with a heavy heart, I turned the car south, and began the long run down to Otterburn and the foot of the Dale. On the road ahead of me were two lorries and a big car. I passed the lorries but was in no hurry to pass the limousine—a canary-coloured Rolls Royce. Suddenly—somewhere near Rede Water—a smaller car shot out into the road. I had to jam on my brakes—hard. There was no side road for miles and the little car must have been standing in a roadmenders' quarry. It was a typical piece of woman's driving—just the sort of thing Janet did. It was so close to me that I could recognise the driver . . . the fat schoolmarm from the tent.

Ahead, for miles, one could see the telegraph posts swinging away across the moors—down into England. Half a mile in front was the yellow Rolls, with Miss Trubshawe in its wake. Somewhere close behind me were the two lorries. At the fork above Otterburn the Rolls and the little Austin bore away eastwards towards Rothbury and the Coquet Dale. I followed, but a moment later I saw that the two lorries had left us; and for a while I could watch them far away, following the telegraph posts to the south.

Where the Grassless Burn joins the Coquet the road forked again. To the right it ran on to Rothbury, to the left up the Dale and so back to Coquet Hall. The yellow Rolls stopped, so did Miss Trubshawe. Then, out of the bushes, jumped the moss man. There was no mistaking that black 'plus-four' suit and that white Panama hat. He had no bicycle now. In a trice he had leapt into the Rolls. It drove off towards Rothbury—Miss Trubshawe following. I took the left-hand road. I drove slowly homewards up the Dale and along the track, in a sadly puzzled frame of mind.

As the house came into sight again all the nervous horror came rushing back. I began to wonder whether I could bear it for another night. Of course I knew that I couldn't really desert Mrs. Soutar. And also—in a way, you know—there was an evil and altogether inexplicable fascination about it all. That was the queerest part of the whole business.

We all felt it. Often, in those last days, one or other of us considered packing up and going . . . but none of us did.

As I crossed the forecourt I heard, faintly, the sound of the dressing gong; but there was not a soul to be seen. In the stable yard, however, the two McQueen boys were fiddling with their cars. They rushed out to me with pale, frightened faces. Antony was as white as a ghost, and poor liitle Michael was actually blubbering.

'Mr. Muir, Mr. Muir,' they cried, 'can you come a minute—quick. Something dreadful has happened!'

'What on earth . . .' I began as I climbed out of the car.

'Come and see,' they almost whispered—and there was real terror on their faces—'come and see. It's something awful . . . at least we think so.'

Either 'Dad' or Maisie Bunting, with her clacking tongue, had told the boys about the Warburton business. It seemed a mistake . . . but I supposed that they would have to know sooner or later. Their nerve seemed to have gone already—pretty completely. I follow them towards the Warburtons' grey Bentley.

'We didn't mean any harm,' explained Antony, 'but it's such a topping bus that we thought we would just have a look over it, and . . . and'—I thought that, like his brother, he was going to break down—'and . . . look what we found!'

He opened the door of the Bentley and there—still half covered with the rugs and coats which had hidden it—was a large, new, shiny spade!

'Does it?' stuttered, Michael. 'Is it . . .? I mean, is he going to dig with it? Is he going to dig a . . .?'

'Don't worry,' I said, putting my hand on his shoulder, 'don't worry, old man. Mr. Stone will be back here tomorrow, with the police. Then it will be all over—and everything will be all right again.'

As as matter of fact I was quite wrong. That night —quietly and painlessly—Beatrice Warburton died in her sleep.

II

She was buried in the little grey churchyard at Galbraith, under the slopes of Crigdon Hill. Harold Warburton never even suggested cremation. There was no inquest; the doctor at Keswick had attended the poor woman only three days before she died, and old Dr. Ritchie from Rothbury certified 'cardiac failure', without asking awkward questions. Canon Fish refused to take the burial service if Harold Warburton was present, so a curate from a village in the next dale was brought over in the shooting brake. A nephew, Hallam Langdon-Miles, came from Cambridge for a few days, to be with his uncle; he seemed a decent lad and I felt sorry for him. A terrible disillusionment awaited him. I attended the funeral, representing Mrs. Soutar and the hotel. Harold Warburton gave one the impression of being a completely broken man . . . as Mr. Stone said: 'a brilliant actor to the very end.'

Mrs. Soutar had broken the news to us after breakfast—very quietly, to each of us in turn. All she said to me was: 'Mr. Muir, I am afraid that Mr. Stone is too late. Murder has come to Coquet Hall. Now, I suppose, we shall have to sell up.'

There was an extraordinary calm in the hotel, in those days between the murder and the funeral. Mark was rather sulky. He had been sceptical about Lysander Stone's story and had laughed at the Bundaberg monster . . . well, of course, nobody likes to be proved wrong. Mr. Lacacheur was aloof and superior. By some extraordinary piece of confused thinking he seemed to imagine that he shared in Mr. Stone's brilliant exploit. Now and again Miss Bunting was a trifle hysterical, but the greater part of her grief was still reserved for Binks. The McQueens, very wisely, went off on long expeditions, remaining away from the hotel all day. We weren't sorry; they grated. And anyway it was better for the boys to be out of it all.

Mrs. Bradford, except for one unaccountable outing in the Daimler, never stirred from her room. All her meals were served upstairs, and the schoolmarm from the tent paid her several visits. We had always understood that they were old acquaintances. Poor Margaret Fish appeared to feel the whole situation intensely.

As for Mr. Stone—he took a typically brilliant and unexpected line. He had got back to Coquet Hall a few hours after Mrs. Warburton's death. Mrs. Soutar had rather old-fashioned ideas about death, and Mr. Stone told me that it was a great shock to him to discover, as his taxi approached the hotel, that the blinds were drawn in every window of the old house. He blamed himself bitterly, he added, for being too late. He came alone. Scotland Yard had remained incredulous—although, said Mr. Stone, they had gone so far as to cable Sydney for information concerning Washwood's present whereabouts. I rather gathered that Mr. Stone had left Scotland Yard with something of a flea in his ear. The official view, apparently, was that the Northumberland County Constabulary were a competent body, and that the matter should have been dealt with through the 'usual channels'.

'Idiots!' said Mr. Stone. 'Do they expect me, Lysander Stone, to negotiate with the village "copper".'

The vital thing now, explained Mr. Stone, was to lull Harold Warburton into a state of complete self-confidence; then—sooner or later—he would give himself away . . . and we could strike. Meanwhile a plain-clothes man was expected from Newcastle, to make 'preliminary enquiries'. Harold had aimed at producing every appearance of a perfectly natural death, and was—no doubt—convinced that he had succeeded absolutely. And how ingenious he had been! Twice his wife had had a severe heart attack, and twice he had played the part of the distressed husband. An inquest had been avoided, and so confident was he that he had not even bothered to suggest cremation. And now, presumably, the Langdon-Miles fortune would be his.

Ingenious—yes. But how much more ingenious had Mr. Stone been. *Harold Warburton was now living in a hotel where every single person knew that he had poisoned both his wife and his sister-in-law . . . and he hadn't the remotest idea that they even suspected him.* The situation, for Harold, was fraught with danger at every point. Lull him into false confidence, said Mr. Stone, and he will convict himself.

It was not an easy situation. In fact those three

234

days were crammed with difficult and embarrassing moments. We were all watching a guilty man, watching every movement and noting every word he said; and all the time, under Mr. Stone's direction, pretending to show some sympathy for the bereaved husband. Unlike Harold Warburton, we were not all brilliant actors and, in actual fact, I think that most of us rather funked the situation and left him severely alone. He and the nephew went a good many lonely walks together on the moors, but —as Mr. Stone pointed out—the very last thing Harold Warburton would do now would be to run away. His position must have seemed—to him— very secure. But how perilous it really was! Oh yes —Mr. Stone had been very ingenious.

'Soon,' he said, 'friend Harold will give himself away. If not . . . then I shall call a conference and we —all of us in this hotel—will demand that the Home Office shall order the exhumation of Beatrice's body. I—yes, even I, Lysander Stone—have failed to convince the police, but, if necessary, the force of public opinion must be brought to bear. . . .'

Well, in the end that was what happened; Mr. Stone called us together one evening in the drawing-room. It was a strange meeting—with the shadow of the gallows across it—but, first, I must say something about Mrs. Bradford's most peculiar expedition in the big Daimler. It really was most peculiar.

It was the day after the funeral. We were all on the terrace waiting for the luncheon gong to sound. Miss Bunting was on the *chaise-longue*; the odious John Smith had just appeared, ready to wheel Mark's chair into the dining-room. How Mark's hair did glow in the sun—bright orange. A little apart, Harold Warburton and the nephew were sitting on the stone balustrade; while Mr. Lacacheur—tactless idiot—was chatting pleasantly to Mr. Stone about the Webster case. The Canon's efforts to be cheerful were not being appreciated. There was an awkward silence; there had been many awkward silences of late. Then Maisie Bunting made a remark.

'Mrs. B.,' she said, 'is off.'

'Permanently?' I asked.

'I don't know, but the luggage is going on the Daimler now, piles of it. The first rat, I suppose, to desert the sinking ship.'

'Sh!'

'Oh! Sorry. I forgot.'

Then Mrs. Bradford herself came through the French window behind us. She bowed to one or two of us . . . and spoke.

'I am,' she said, 'going away for a few days, and I wish to say good-bye.' This unexpected descent to the normal human level produced suitable responsive murmurs. A precedent had been broken. Mrs. Bradford's expeditions usually just happened . . . we were not informed.

'I shall be back,' she announced, addressing herself to the company in general, 'in a few days, but I am going a considerable journey. I shall spend at least one night at the 'Trinity Arms' at Cambridge, and I may then go on to the 'Stag Hotel' at Simonsbath . . . on Exmoor, you know. Good-afternoon. . . .' and she sailed down the steps to the waiting Daimler in the forecourt.

That night Harold Warburton fled.

In his evening clothes Mr. Stone looked more cor-
seted than ever. He stood, his little legs apart and
his chin thrust out, glaring at us through his
monocle.

In front of him, on a small Pembroke table,
were the 'exhibits'—the old, faded, yellow cuttings
from the *Melbourne Sun* and the *Sydney Star*, that
week's reports of the Langdon-Miles inquest, the
little green leather diary, the fountain-pen and
seventeen pellets of heroin. The diary and the
pellets—what remained of them—Harold Warburton had left behind him. His flight had, apparently,
been precipitate. He had last been seen, just before
sunset, walking hatless on the moor. Then—that
morning—Crowe had reported that his bed had not
been slept in.

How right Mr. Stone had been when he said that,
sooner or later, Harold Warburton would convict
himself. Apparently the strain had been too great—
even for that monster. Something in his brain had
snapped . . . and he had gone in terror. Could there
be more overwhelming proof of the miserable
creature's guilt. Harold Warburton's flight completed
Mr. Stone's case—beyond doubt.

Mark's chair had been wheeled close to the fireplace. His red mop glowed, against the white marble,
even more fiercely than in the sunshine. His sulks
had given way to nervousness, and he kept plucking
at his black pearl studs. Twice he rang for another
of his eternal cognacs. By the end of the evening he
was just a little drunk. Behind him, in the shadow,

white and trembling, was the loathsome John Smith.

From time to time, as Mr. Stone brought out the more horrific points of his story, Maisie Bunting, would give little shrieks and close her eyes. Mr. Lacacheur, as he patted her hand, would nod sagely at Mr. Stone's reasoning—as if to say that he and Lysander Stone were really very clever fellows. The McQueen boys and 'Dad' spent the evening in a state of frozen terror. Antony went out once—to be sick. Cartels and combines were child's play compared with this.

What a sad figure was Margaret Fish. How willingly she would have been elsewhere. God knows what her thoughts were, but she never even seemed to hear what Mr. Stone was saying, and never once did she raise her eyes. The Canon put a brave face on things but was very bewildered . . . 'so completely outside my orbit' . . . and the pink had all gone from his cheeks. His cigar went out and remained out, unnoticed.

For two hours, point by point, remorselessly and ruthlessly—like a trained advocate—Mr. Stone told his story . . . much as he had told it to me in Mrs. Soutar's parlour. From one trembling hand to another the faded, yellow cuttings, the diary and the heroin pellets were passed round the room.

'I blame myself,' said Mr. Stone in conclusion, 'I blame myself bitterly for that poor lady's tragic death. It is not Lysander Stone's habit to make mistakes, but I should have foreseen—yes, yes, I have foreseen that Harold Warburton might alter his plans in order to forestall me. Something or someone . . .' and here Mr. Stone glared straight at the trembling John Smith '. . . something or someone, I say, must have aroused his suspicions. He guessed, I

think, that I had gone for the police. Be that as it may
—it is certain that he originally intended to poison
his wife on the night of June the first, but that—for
some reason—he altered his plan and—as you all
know—she died in her sleep on the night of May
the twenty-ninth. For that I blame myself—most
bitterly.'

Of course, to most of us, the story was not new.
But it sounded much more terrifying and macabre
when it was told—as Mr. Stone told it— point by
paint, in cold blood, and with a purpose. To Hallam
Langdon-Miles, however, it was a complete and absolute shock. He nearly collapsed and twice during
the evening Miss Amy had to fetch him a brandy.

Mr. Stone had paused. Away on the far side of the
house I could hear a car pulling up in the forecourt.
It was getting dark now, but the servants had been
told to keep away and nobody seemed to think of
turning up the lights or of drawing the curtains. Outside, against a pale green sky, Bloodybush Edge was
purple-black, and the evening star hung above the
ragged elms. The play of the firelight on Mr.
Lacacheur's thin, grey face was rather ghastly. Mrs.
Soutar had just whispered to me that she thought Mr.
Stone had finished, when he stepped forward
dramatically.

'Twenty years ago,' he cried, 'that foul monster,
Henry Washwood, was brought to justice because
the simple citizens of Sydney and Bundaberg
insisted upon it. Now, today, it is our duty, the duty
of every one of us here, to see to it that—this time—
he does not escape the hangman's rope. Beatrice Warburton's body must be exhumed and . . .'

He had stopped. He was glaring at the door,
furious at being interrupted in the middle of his

239

peroration. Mrs. Bradford had entered the room. There was a little stir of surprise. We had imagined that she was at Cambridge, or even Simonsbath.

'My programme,' she said as she walked across the room, 'had to be rearranged at the last moment. I must apologise to Mr. Stone for my rudeness in being so late for his dissertation. Pray continue, Mr. Stone. . . .'

Then our surprise at seeing her was changed into absolute amazement. I wondered whether I was not going just a little mad. In Mrs. Bradford's train there had entered into that darkened, firelit room, not only her maid with the usual cushion, but a most bizarre and extraordinary procession of femininity.

Mrs. Bradford—in black velvet and wearing her famous brown diamond choker and earrings—was followed by an odd, twittering little female. Pointed nose to the fore, and flat-heeled, she marched forward in a determined manner—very grim. She was garbed in purple silk with short sleeves. There was a black velvet band at her throat and a black watered ribbon to her eye-glasses.

'Sophie,' said Mrs. Bradford, 'you will sit here.'

Then—still wearing her tweeds and brogues— came the fat schoolmarm from the tent. On her arm, in a long white evening frock, was the loveliest young girl I have ever seen—dark-haired and with glowing rosy cheeks—but looking rather solemn just now.

'Miranda—you of all people! What on earth are you doing here?' It was Hallam Langdon-Miles who had leapt forward. I was finding it all more and more inexplicable. He evidently knew the girl!

'Miranda dear,' said Mrs. Bradford, 'you will kindly sit there, next to Mabel Trubshawe. You and

Mr. Langdon-Miles will have plenty of time to talk later.'

Finally, most astounding of all, came the dark and dour Hypatia Crowe, her starched cap and apron gleaming strangely in the firelight.

'Now,' went on Mrs. Bradford when we were all seated again, 'now, Mr. Stone, I want to congratulate you on your ingenuity.' Mr. Stone bowed in a rather ridiculous manner. 'You had a very difficult and complex problem to solve, and you have —it cannot be denied—solved it in a most ingenious and original manner. I am in complete agreement with what you said just now, as I came into the room. The remains of Beatrice Warburton must be exhumed. A very distasteful but very necessary step. Very necessary.'

I looked up sharply. Had I detected a strange tone, an ominous tone, in Mrs. Bradford's voice? Then she spoke again.

'But I think, Mr. Stone,' she said quietly, 'I think that it would be most helpful if—before we go any further—*you told us exactly what you and Mrs. Carberry have done with poor Harold Warburton's body.*'

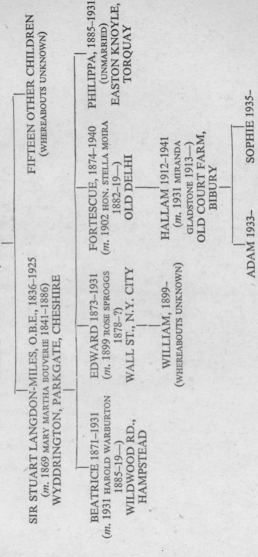

WILLIAM MILES 1795–1850
(m. 1830 JANE LANGDON 1800–1851)
16 BARNET'S RENTS, GATESHEAD, CO. DURHAM

SIR STUART LANGDON-MILES, O.B.E., 1836–1925
(m. 1869 MARY MARTHA BOUVERIE 1841–1886)
WYDDRINGTON, PARKGATE, CHESHIRE

FIFTEEN OTHER CHILDREN
(WHEREABOUTS UNKNOWN)

BEATRICE 1871–1931
(m. 1931 HAROLD WARBURTON
1885–19—)
WILDWOOD RD.,
HAMPSTEAD

EDWARD 1873–1931
(m. 1899 ROSE SPROGGS
1878–?)
WALL ST., N.Y. CITY

WILLIAM, 1899–
(WHEREABOUTS UNKNOWN)

FORTESCUE, 1874–1940
(m. 1902 HON. STELLA MOIRA
1882–19—)
OLD DELHI

HALLAM 1912–1941
(m. 1931 MIRANDA
GLADSTONE 1913—)
OLD COURT FARM,
BIBURY

ADAM 1933–

SOPHIE 1935–

PHILIPPA, 1885–1931
(UNMARRIED)
EASTON KNOYLE,
TORQUAY

Part Five

In which Mrs. Joseph Bradford, of Sheridan Crescent, Lansdown, Bath, describes the methods used by Lysander Stone in solving the Langdon-Miles problem.

I

If Dr. Plummett of Nether Fordington had thought rather more of his patients, and rather less of the whisky bottle and fox-hunting, then the Langdon-Miles mystery might never have been solved. 'It's an ill wind . . .'—but clearly the man was a fool. And as for the other man—Dr. Parker from the village—Sophie as good as said that he was suffering from senile decay. But the proper place to begin a story is at the beginning.

My name is Bertha Bradford. I am over ninety now, and I was eighty at the time of the tragedy. My friends consider that ninety is a great age. Nonsense! One is as old as one feels, and I am in full possession of all my faculties. I sometimes feel my back—but I always have, so that can have nothing to do with my years. A few weeks ago Jenkins, my maid, had the impudence to tell me that I was getting slightly deaf. Nothing of the sort! If I don't always hear what people say, that is solely because the younger generation are not taught to articulate their words correctly. I have entirely given up going to the theatre; the actors mumble so atrociously that I can't hear a word. Now when my husband used to take me to the Lyceum, Sir Henry enunciated every syllable perfectly. In any case, most modern plays are indecent. It is quite ridiculous for Jenkins to say that I am deaf; she has been with me over thirty years and I am afraid that she is beginning to take liberties. I shall have to speak to her.

Obviously Dr. Plummet was an incompetent fool. But then Sophie always said that—coming from a medical family—I am hypercritical where doctors are concerned. Maybe I do regard doctors with a critical eye, but at bottom I am nothing if not charitable in my judgment of my fellow men. My father, Archibald Coppock, was a laryngologist of high repute in Aberdeen, and a childhood spent in that admirable city imbued me with my share of common sense—if it did nothing else. My brother, Tertius Coppock, sometime in the 'eighties, set up in general practice—away in Nithsdale, near Dumfries—on the other side of the country. Why, I could never imagine; but then Tertius was always wilfully independent. His marriage to Jane Fairweather, for instance, was altogether beyond me. I had quite a different type of girl in view for him. Jane was a poor, feeble sort of creature . . . she never bore him more than one child—Sophie. That was quite enough for Jane.

My husband, Joseph Bradford, was a brilliant and successful gynæcologist, and we kept up a large Town establishment in Portland Place, which was a very pleasant street in those days. By a curious coincidence poor Joseph died on the same day as Queen Victoria. After Joseph's death I had to live on a very reduced scale, quite humbly, keeping only one house.

When I found that I had been left so poor I decided to leave the West End altogether, making my home at Landsdown, the only bracing part of Bath. Even then I had to face the fact that I could not possibly afford more than five servants. And during the last war, when—thanks to Mr. Lloyd George's scandalous incompetence—income tax rose to such terrifying heights, I was compelled to reduce this number to four. I have sincerely tried, as a good Christian, to meet all my troubles courageously.

My very modest fortune—or such of it as remains when I have been mulcted on all sides—will one day go to dear Sophie. Sophie is an orphan. Tertius, her father, was killed in an accident. His gig was upset in the snow, one New Year's eve, when he was returning from a confinement. He was always a very reckless driver. Competent nursing might have saved him, but Jane Fairweather invariably went to pieces when there was trouble. So when Tertius died she had only herself to thank. However, I have always had some regard for Sophie. Except on one occasion, when she made me very angry, she has—on the whole—been a thoroughly sensible girl, standing no nonsense from anyone—and, Heaven knows, she was surrounded by fools at Easton Knoyle. Fortunately she was a Coppock, not a Fairweather. She had had to make her own way in the world as, of course, after poor Joseph's death I was in no position to help her. But Sophie had her head screwed on, and she was also fortunate in her friends. The Carlyles of Corstophine showed her some kindness and it was the old minister who used his influence to secure for her the post at Easton Knoyle. My father would have been very shocked to think that one of his grandchildren had to earn her own living

—but times change, and since I was so poor there was no alternative—Sophie had to go to work.

The Carlyles were sensible and pious folk, and when Mrs. Soutar turned hotel-keeper in such an extraordinary manner I was very glad to lend her my patronage. Her charges are simply outrageous—and I have often told her so—but, try as I would, I could find very little at Coquet Hall of which to complain. Naturally I took Jenkins and the chauffeur with me and—as an unprotected widow—I was always forced to have my own sitting-room; otherwise hotel life—even at Coquet Hall—would have been quite unbearable. I might go there more often, but it is expensive and I also find, if I am away from home for too long, that the servants get lazy.

Sophie usually had a proper sense of duty and gratitude, and has always responded in a becoming manner to anything I did for her. With the passing of the years a real affection has arisen between us—we are both Coppocks through and through—and I have made it a habit to invite her to Coquet Hall each summer for a few weeks. This solved a problem for Sophie. She had little in common, I am glad to say, with the flibberty-gibbets whose pose as school-teachers in these days, and her holidays would have been lonely if I had not stepped into the breach. Sophie welcomed the opportunity of seeing something of Nellie Soutar, her old school friend. In spite of the financial sacrifice I was glad to give Sophie this pleasant holiday each year, and she was able to relieve Jenkins of some of her tasks—altogether a most satisfactory arrangement.

Although Sophie's handwriting has recently become less legible, I cannot really reproach her with being a bad correspondent. For over forty years she has written to me every week, giving me a full account of her doings. Since, one day, she is to enjoy my money it is, of course, only right and proper that she should satisfy me as to her way of life, but her letters also gave me an insight into the daily round at Easton Knoyle and into the disgraceful way in which that autocratic snob, Philippa Langdon-Miles, mismanaged the place . . . and all those goings-on with the Canon. I was always telling Sophie what I thought about it, but where Miss Langdon-Miles was concerned Sophie had a blind spot.

I have heard it said that I do not suffer fools gladly. I am, in actual fact, most forbearing. There are so many fools about that I have to be. But I was certainly astounded at the ease with which Lysander Stone twisted all those silly sheep at Coquet Hall round his little finger. Mr. Mark Fanshawe alone— to his credit—remained sceptical about all that Bundaberg monster nonsense. But even he was so lazy-minded that he hadn't the *nous* to see the true state of affairs. I must say that I think Mr. Muir ought to have known better, and as for that popinjay, Graham Lacacheur—well, he deserved what he got. However, it is only fair to them all to point out that, on account of the very lengthy letters which Sophie wrote to me, *I—and I alone—could know what was going on both at Torquay and at Coquet Hall*. I was the only person who could possibly be familiar with life in both places . . . and this was something which Mr. Stone could not even suspect. Sophie's letters to me were the link between Northumberland and Devonshire . . . and it was that which was his undoing.

2

Throughout the whole of the Langdon-Miles affair I found Mabel Trubshawe an invaluable ally. Her views on Art were, no doubt, quite ridiculous—but who cares about Art—and in every other way she was a level-headed creature . . . thoroughly reliable. That she should quarrel with Miss Langdon-Miles was, in my opinion, very much to her credit; the best thing Mabel Trubshawe ever did was to shake the dust of Easton Knoyle from her shoes. Mind you, I don't approve of gallivanting off to village inns, still less do I approve of sleeping in the open. It stands to reason that a tent must be oppressively hot in warm weather, and positively dangerous at all other times. But I can't think of anything else that I have got to hold against Mabel Trubshawe.

As soon as I heard that Sophie was lying in the shadow of death at the 'Harrow Inn', I wrote to Mabel Trubshawe demanding a full account by return of post, since Sophie—poor child—could hardly scrawl her name on a post-card. I could see that something was very wrong indeed; both doctors were clearly incompetent—grossly so. Dr. Plummett ought to have been an inmate in his own asylum, but I suppose that if Sophie had died he would have got off scot free! There is something very wrong with the law.

The instant it was known that Sophie had swallowed strychnine a most ruthless enquiry should have been conducted—without regard for anyone's feelings—although I should have thought that the solution of the problem was as plain as a pikestaff. But this young man—who drank like a fish and openly boasted that it was the hunting that had brought him to the district—contented himself with asking Sophie a lot of idiotic questions about what she had eaten on the day she was taken ill. Utter waste of time! Even a child knows that strychnine acts very quickly and that what you have eaten hours before is quite beside the point. Moreover, Sophie had been very sick indeed, as the result of her bilious headache, and anything she may have eaten during the day was vomited from her stomach just before the strychnine caused her collapse.

To give the Devil his due, Dr. Plummett did say: '. . . it beats me. Here's a patient who's violently sick and half an hour later I have to empty the stomach all over again to save her life.' But there the scamp left the matter.

In any case, if we must consider what Sophie had eaten that day, we find that her meals had been very simple—she never had a strong stomach—and that she had taken nothing in which the bitter flavour of strychnine could have been hidden. For breakfast, before she left Easton Knoyle, she had a very lightly boiled egg and a pot of China tea. I admit that weeks later, when Miss Langdon-Miles died, it did strike me as curious that both she and Sophie should have drunk black coffee in the restaurant car, just outside Taunton, a few hours before they were taken ill. My mind toyed with this idea for a time, but I finally rejected it as a mere coincidence . . . the governing factor being the speed with which strychnine acts. Dr. Plummett—I suspect on Mabel Trubshawe's initiative—had the remains of the potted meat analysed . . . the potted meat which the two women had eaten in their sandwiches on the hill above Broadway. The analysis was negative, and in any case Mabel Trubshawe, as well as Sophie, had eaten the sandwiches. All these enquiries were really beside the point, and as soon as I brought my wits to bear on the problem the solution seemed to be self-evident. It stared one in the face, and how Plummett missed it, I don't know . . . fuddled I suppose.

After a day of quite unnecessary stress and strain, and threatened with a sleepless and flea-ridden night, Sophie herself was not surprised to find that she was suffering from one of those bilious headaches to which she is so prone. They must be a Fairweather inheritance. I never get headaches. It was plain that Sophie's headache was quite natural and usual; in the circumstances it was even to be expected. It was also plain that the mere sight of the cold mutton and pickles, which 'the Harrow' provided for supper, was—together with the crimson finger-nails of the barmaid—more than enough to bring Sophie's bilious attack to its climax. She fled to the bedroom and was sick. Now this supper of cold mutton and pickles was the only meal in which strychnine could have been taken, which was also sufficiently near in time to the ultimate attack. Pickles, too, is one thing in which the flavour of the strychnine might have been hidden. But another thing, even more certain, is that Sophie never touched either the mutton or the pickles.

No—the strychnine, odd as it may seem, must have been taken by Sophie during the ten minutes which elapsed between her being sick and the moment when her shrieks rang through the inn. What happened in those ten minutes . . . Mabel Trubshawe boiled the spirit-kettle for the hot-water bottle, and

Sophie took two tablets of aspirin. A few minutes later she was apparently dying, and Trevor was rushing off on his motor-cycle to get the stomach pump from the asylum.

There was one good thing about it; it taught Sophie a lesson. She now spends Christmas and Easter sensibly at 'The Balmoral' at Leamington—knitting and listening to the band—instead of escapading around the country imperilling her life.

As soon as I realised what had happened I telegraphed to Mabel Trubshawe to send me all the remaining aspirins. She was rather surprised but she did as she was told. I then ordered Jenkins to grind up two of the tablets and put them in Josephine's water dish. When Jenkins took the green baize cover off the cage next morning, Josephine was lying dead with her legs in the air. I am told that twenty-two is a ripe age for a budgerigar, so this didn't matter—but, of course the other aspirins had to be sent off to the chemist. It was then found that, of the thirty tablets still left in the bottle, there were six which each contained more than a fatal dose of strychnine. Here was a pretty how d'ye do! I am not a murder expert, but it seemed to me most ingenious. It quite tickled my fancy. I remember that Jenkins wondered what on earth I was chuckling at. I didn't tell her . . . and that made me chuckle even more.

I never have headaches myself—I don't believe in them—but I find that most elderly people—especially if they lead sedentary lives—do take aspirin, phenacetin or some such drug—I suppose, on the average, four or five times a year. Insert a few poisoned tablets into the bottle—and there you are! Sooner or later your victim will suffer from a headache, neuralgia or some other *malade imaginaire*—

and will take one of the poisoned tablets. Meanwhile, months may have gone by and the murderer may be on the other side of the world—and, of course, quite unsuspected. Oh yes, it did make me chuckle!

If only one poisoned tablet was put in the bottle it would be impossible—except by a process of really intelligent deduction such as I applied in Sophie's case—to discover in what form the poison had been administered. Most people, being fools, would think all about the food which the victim had eaten and ignore the aspirin altogether. Moreover, the ordinary headache which led to the taking of the aspirin would probably be looked upon as the first onslaught of the fatal attack—thus confusing the issue still further. Indeed, the aspirin—since it would be taken *after* illness had begun—would probably be regarded, if it was thought of at all, as being the one thing which *couldn't* have caused that illness.

There were, however, grave drawbacks to putting only one poisoned tablet into a whole bottle full of harmless ones. It might be months, even years if the victim happened to be free from headaches, before the fatal tablet was taken . . . especially if it had worked its way down to the bottom of the bottle. Also, since aspirins are often available to more than one member of a household, the wrong person might die and the intended victim escape. Another drawback—the murderer would be under a great strain, waiting week after week, month after month, for news of his victim's death.

If half a dozen or more of the poisoned tablets were put in the bottle, the chance of killing the wrong person would be increased, but so would the chance of killing the right one—quickly.

If it was considered desirable that death should

take place as soon as possible—say within a month —the bottle could be entirely filled with poisoned tablets—provided that the murderer was indifferent to the risks of an all-round massacre. As we shall see, it was this method—the method of the full bottle—which was used in the case of Miss Langdon-Miles. One poisoned tablet, half a dozen poisoned tablets, or a whole bottle full. . . . I must say that— had I been the murderer—I should have derived a good deal of amusement from weighing up the merits and risks of the different methods.

By the time I had experimented on Josephine and obtained the chemist's report, Sophie—small thanks to Dr. Plummett—was well on the road to recovery. That there should have been a stomach pump within a hundred miles of that outlandish spot, was a piece of good fortune for which Sophie ought to have been very grateful. Perhaps she was. Sophie had, of course, brought the bottle of aspirins with her from Torquay, and it immediately occurred to me that this ingenious fiend might have played his tricks on other pills and medicines at Easton Knoyle. Philippa Langdon-Miles, I imagine, was one of those emotional, overwrought women who resort to drugs on the least provocation, and the medicine cupboard was probably full of all manner of concoctions. As soon as I heard from Sophie that she was back at Easton Knoyle I telegraphed her, ordering the instant destruction of all the drugs in the house. It is not often that Sophie disobeys me but, on this occasion, she seems to have imagined, for some inexplicable reason, that I had taken leave of my senses . . . which only shows how ill she must have been. Sophie must have suffered a good deal, for strychnine poisoning is very painful, and I cannot but regard her pain as Divine punishment for disobedience. When she ignored my telegram she assumed a very grave responsibility . . . although I suppose that *they* would in any case have murdered Miss Langdon-Miles in one way or another, sooner or later—and of course nobody, except Sophie, shed any tears over that.

The next question that presented itself to my mind was: who on earth could possibly have wanted to murder that harmless creature—Sophie Coppock?

3

I had established the method, but who was the murderer and what was the motive? In Sophie's case there was no answer.

It would be difficult to imagine anyone more harmless or having fewer enemies than that odd little spinster—Sophie Coppock. I had known all about Sophie from the day she was born, and I knew that there were no skeletons in her cupboard. Of course the child had faults—I frequently had to speak to her about them—but no enemies. She always held firmly to her opinions and expressed them bluntly—not that I count that a fault—and she often found it most necessary to reprove and set right some of those loose-thinking young women in the Common Room. She was also suspected by the other mistresses of currying favour with Miss Langdon-Miles—for this Sophie had only herself to thank; I had warned her. All this did not make Sophie popular . . . but murder—that was a very different kettle of fish. And there was no evidence that there was anyone at Easton Knoyle—fools as most of them were—who was on the verge of insanity or likely to run amok. Of course, an unsuspected homicidal maniac is always a possibility—even among the girls. I had taken a strong dislike to that Mac-Taggart woman, but there was nothing in Sophie's letters to suggest that she was actually certifiable.

No . . . Sophie's colleagues must be ruled out. Having disposed of this point to my satisfaction I then asked myself—what motive could anyone have for killing poor, innocent Sophie? I have said that there were no skeletons in her cupboard. Passion had played no part in her sheltered and virtuous life. I should never have allowed such a thing. Some thirty years ago, when Sophie was working for the London School Board, a young chemist's assistant started running after her. He was a feeble and penniless youth and I had had to put my foot down most firmly. Sophie still has an old dance programme at the bottom of her jewel box. Really there are times when I have no patience with the girl. Anyway, that is all very ancient history; the story had no complications and could have no bearing on the present.

As for money . . . well, Sophie is as poor as a church mouse. Humble as my circumstances are, I'm the goose that lays the golden eggs. Nothing was to be gained by killing off Sophie, unless I was murdered first . . . and I should never permit that.

The more I thought of it, the more impossible and improbable it seemed that Sophie should have been the object of foul play. It was not a bad thing, of course, that Sophie should have had such a narrow shave since it had enabled me to discover the murderer's method—that ingenious method which had caused me to chuckle so. It had been well worth it. Finally I was forced to the conclusion that the poisoned aspirin had gone astray, that it had never been meant for poor Sophie at all. As I have pointed out, there was always that risk inherent in the method, the risk that there might be, so to speak, a miscarriage of death.

Almost any member of a household may resort to a bottle or aspirin. But Sophie did not belong to an ordinary household, and at first I thought that in trying to find the *intended* victim I should have to consider everyone at Easton Knoyle. Then it occurred to me that the field was much narrower than that—that it was indeed exceptionally narrow. If the poisoned tablets had been placed in one of the bottles in, say, the matron's store cupboard, my task would have been hard indeed. But it stands to reason that the murderer would do nothing of this kind since his chance of killing the right person would be very remote—although he might kill several wrong ones. No—at Easton Knoyle the risk of a miscarriage of death had been only two to one *. . . Sophie's drugs were all kept in the medicine cupboard in that bathroom which she shared with Miss Langdon-Miles—and which nobody else was allowed to use.*

The poisoned tablets which Sophie had taken from Torquay to Nether Fordington must have been inserted into a bottle, in the medicine cupboard, in the bathroom. Therefore . . . they must have been intended for either Sophie or Miss Langdon-Miles. When I thought of this I felt much more cheerful. For Miss Langdon-Miles surely had more enemies, more dark places in her life, than had innocent little Sophie. Oh! undoubtedly I concluded, the tablets had been meant for Miss Langdon-Miles.

The murderer had failed once—Sophie nearly paying the price of his failure—and he would try again. I now felt certain that, sooner or later, Miss Langdon-Miles would die—quite suddenly.

I was the only one who knew, the only one who had been clever enough to discover the poisoned aspirin. I didn't breathe a word to a soul, not even to Jenkins. I had never met Miss Langdon-Miles, but I hated her. I am never jealous, but after all I am Sophie's sole benefactress, and the whole of Sophie's affection and respect ought to have been kept for me . . . but soon, quite soon now perhaps, there would no longer be a 'dear, dear Miss Langdon-Miles' to steal that affection away. I thought of Josephine lying on the bottom of her cage, and I remembered how painful strychnine poisoning would be. Miss Langdon-Miles would writhe and cry out, just like Sophie at 'The Harrow'.

4

Oh yes, it was plain that Miss Langdon-Miles had got to die. Nothing could prevent that! But I still didn't know why, nor did I know—for certain—who the murderer could be. Of course, I had my suspicions, for there was—you will agree—only one obvious person.

But, oddly enough, it wasn't until the very day of Miss Langdon-Miles's death that my suspicions were confirmed. It must have been in the afternoon, just about the hour when Miss Langdon-Miles was dying in agony on the platform at the Cranmer Hall, that I got Sophie's letter giving me her impressions of *Macbeth*—I had always insisted on a full account of sermons and plays—and describing that hilarious dinner-party at Waterloo Station. Then of course everything became quite clear. That young jackanapes Hallam Langdon-Miles, when he was talking to Sophie in the foyer at the Old Vic, had let the cat right out of the bag. I had had my suspicions all along, but that settled it.

Well, the Langdon-Miles had all been cruel and sadistic beasts. Just think what a heartless creature Philippa was, stealing away Sophie's affection . . . from me, a poor, lonely widow—almost penniless. For three generations the Langdon-Miles have been beating and torturing each other, and as for their greed—it's been simply monstrous. Sophie had frequently told me the history of the family, and to an old lady like me, who wouldn't harm a fly, it was a truly dreadful story. It made my blood boil. And then there was that little gold-digger on the Mersey ferry . . . oh! a dreadful story.

A hundred years ago William Miles, the County Durham miner, had thrashed his wife and sixteen brats soundly, every Saturday night. Mind you—I believe in thrashing children. If I had had any children I should have thrashed them . . . but his wife! Why—the man must have been an inhuman monster. Nobody knows what happened to the brats, they seem to have been thrashed into insignificance —all except Sir Stuart Langdon-Miles. Heaven knows where he got the 'Langdon' from—perhaps it was his poor mother's name. It was snobbery and greed—greed for money, and vanity—that brought Stuart to the top. My goodness—how rich he was!

It was all very well for Sophie to say that he wasn't really a millionaire . . . but he had pots, simply pots. And to think—that 'dear, dear Miss Langdon-Miles' would sooner or later have the lot. Except that, of course, she was going to die.

And Sir Stuart was no better than his coal-mining father—worse in fact. Sophie had always told me that there were stories going around Liverpool a generation ago, of how cruel—physically cruel—he had been to his two sons . . . out in that gaunt and lonely mansion on the Wirral. If it hadn't been for his pride, his determination to keep up appearances he would have driven them out of the house without a penny.

Not that the sons were immaculate. Oh dear me—no! There was Hallam's father, for instance—Fortescue the Indian judge—who was just as cruel as *his* father and grandfather had been before him. He had—according to Sophie—been sent down from Oxford in connection with some unsavoury story about torturing a dog. Then, as soon as he got to India, he passed savage sentences on the niggers. The beast! I have always been so kind to Josephine, my budgerigar, that you can well imagine that I am stirred to the depths by cruelty to dumb creatures. The niggers were different—they probably deserved it. With such an unpleasant father it's a miracle that Hallam is so presentable. But I expect that the Langdon-Miles inheritance will come out one day— and then Miranda can expect the worst!

The whole lot of them were so ruthless too— ruthless in their hunt for money. And I can't bear people who think too much of money. Edward would have done anything for money—simply anything! He threw up his career in the Church just to make money in insurance or stockbroking or something. And Edward was no fool—he could probably have been a bishop in no time. Then along came the golden-haired mill girl, and the fat was in the fire. Sophie, poor innocent, had thought that that skeleton was well locked in the cupboard, and was rather shocked when Hallam referred to it. I suppose that, being squeamish about that sort of thing, she thought it was all rather indecent. But if people can drag unpleasant skeletons out of other people's cupboards, they will. It's only human. I always do when I can, just for the fun of seeing how embarrassed my friends get.

You might think that it would ruin Edward—especially in those days—to marry a creature of this sort. After all, he had more or less picked her up out of the gutter, or—to be accurate—off the ferryboat. Edward was out, just then, to make his way in the world, and he would—you may be sure—have thrown the girl over heartlessly if there had not been something unusual about her. She must have had, as Sophie said, all the wiles of the little gold-digger, but she must have had something more, some force of character or strange fascination, for the sake of which Edward—ambitious though he was—was prepared to risk his whole career. In view of what came to light later, I am inclined to think that—so far from wrecking his career—the little mill girl was the driving force behind it—some might have called her his evil genius. Edward, when he married, must have known that his father would ship him out of the country. Perhaps he didn't care. America was a land of promise in those days, and a land, too, where a mill girl wife would be no handicap. No—I am inclined to think that if there were any gaps in Edward's ruthlessness, any weakening in his avaricious hunt for money, that Rosie Sproggs—or Rosie Langdon-Miles as we must call her—more than made up for it.

But Sir Stuart had his revenge. When both the sons were safely established—one on the Indian Bench and the other in Wall Street—he cut them clean out of his will . . . and told them nothing. Of course they were both well off by the time Sir Stuart died, but to Edward, at any rate, it must have been a shock. A will is a pretty powerful thing. I frequently order my solicitor up to Lansdown, and then I have great fun toying with the different clauses. If Sophie has misbehaved . . . if, for instance, her weekly letter has shown too much affection for Miss Langdon-Miles, then I add a thousand pounds or so to one or two of my many charitable legacies. I can understand Sir Stuart's feelings, and his desire for posthumous revenge—while preserving in his own lifetime all the outward appearances of paternal benevolence. A clever old man . . . in spite of his cruelty I think that I should have got on well with him.

When Edward heard of his disinheritance he must have danced with rage. The fact that he was a rich man didn't affect his feelings in the very least. He had always regarded himself as 'the Langdon-Miles heir' and now he felt cheated and insulted; although, of course, he ought to have expected it. I can picture Edward throwing things about the room in a real Langdon-Miles manner. It would have done old Sir Stuart's heart good to see him. As for the wretched Rosie . . . her feelings must have been indescribable. A poverty-stricken girl off the streets in the first place, she must always have been haunted by the 'clogs to clogs' legend . . . the dread of a return to the poverty she had once known.

But it was not in the nature of either Edward or Rosie to take a blow of this sort lying down. There was, in the breasts of both, an insatiable lust for wealth. It had dominated their lives. But that was not all. . . . Edward had within him all the cruelty and sadism of the Langdon-Miles clan. I have nothing but contempt for Graham Lacacheur—with his affected ways—but he wasn't altogether wrong about crime and heredity; he was just completely taken in by Mr. Stone, and hunted up the ancestry of the wrong man.

Above all . . . if Edward ever faltered in his cruel and evil design, then Rosie was there at his elbow to urge him on and screw his courage to the sticking place—his 'Lady Macbeth'. Hatred and cruelty in Edward, a desperate and haunting fear of poverty in Rosie, ruthlessness in both . . . here were elements which, in combination, created a couple who were barely sane.

Then the crash came—the great American economic crisis of 1930 and 1931. With thousands of others the stockbroking firm of Langdon-Miles and Gabbitas went under. This was unknown to me until Hallam told Sophie about it, that night at the Old Vic—the night before Miss Langdon-Miles's death. The dreaded poverty, which had always haunted Rosie, was now a stark reality.

It must have been in the autumn of 1930 that Edward and Rosie arrived in Europe. It was the first time in thirty years. I have often wondered whether their first sight of the old country was from the Mersey. I think that when they came their plans were only half formed. Edward, at any rate, can hardly have dared to face the true and awful implications of their journey. Sometimes, perhaps, he was even terrified by Rosie's dark hints. I suspect that she taunted him with cowardice, and gradually he accepted the whole idea. After all, he was a ruined man, convinced of his moral right to the Langdon-Miles fortune—a fortune securely in the hands of Beatrice—and convinced that he had been insulted and cheated by an irascible old madman. But it was Rosie who, in desperation, plotted and schemed, and urged him on at every turn. It was Rosie who worked out all the details.

If Graham Lacacheur cares to look up the ordinary, common records of the criminal classes in Lancashire, for the last two hundred years, I dare say he will find some utterly fascinating information—under the name of Sproggs.

They were both ruthless, both desperate, both cruel . . . but I am convinced that Rosie was the force behind it all. He was the instrument which she used for carrying out those plans. He was not an altogether unwilling instrument, and he was certainly a very skilful and cunning one. Not that he didn't make some mistakes . . . he did—damning ones. By the beginning of December, 1930, Rosie was already in Torquay and—as the mysterious and obnoxious Mrs. Carberry—had made her first scouting expedition to Easton Knoyle.

5

The problem which Edward and Rosie—Mr. and Mrs. Edward Langdon-Miles—had to solve was complicated. In simple terms it was to transfer the Langdon-Miles fortunes from Beatrice to themselves.

They must have known before they left the U.S.A. that they were committed to crime, almost certainly to murder. My enquiries to the shipping authorities showed that a 'Mr. and Mrs. Carberry' had reached this country from New York in November, 1930, but—needless to say—there was no record of a Mr. and Mrs. Langdon-Miles having arrived. I am inclined to think that Mr. and Mrs. Carberry did not travel alone. In 1900, when they had left Liverpool, Rosie was going to have a child . . . the chauffeur of the canary-coloured Rolls was probably their son. As an ultimate beneficiary of the murder he was the only person on earth to whom they could entrust their dreadful secret.

Rosie no doubt amused herself on the voyage in working out all the details. I should have enjoyed that. She must have known, however, before leaving New York what, in a general way, she intended to do. Undoubtedly the poison was obtained and the aspirins prepared in America, for one cannot, of course, go around England buying quantities of strychnine and heroin as though they were so many pounds of tea.

One difficulty confronted Edward and Rosie from the first. They didn't and couldn't know the exact contents of Beatrice's will. However, when they first arrived Harold Warburton had not yet come on the scene . . . his presence was later to complicate matters enormously . . . and so it might be assumed, and indeed it was generally known in the family, that Beatrice had left the greater part of the Langdon-Miles fortune to Philippa. *It was clear, therefore, that Philippa must die first.* The murder of Beatrice alone would achieve nothing . . . it would actually make matters worse. If Beatrice died the money would go to Philippa, and on her death to the Church . . . out of reach for ever of even the grasping hands of a Sproggs. Yes, Philippa must die first—that was quite plain.

I suspected nothing, you must remember, until after Sophie's illness at Nether Fordington, in the Easter of 1931. But once I had deduced the poisoned aspirins and the inevitabliity of Miss Langdon-Miles's fate, I began to study the letters which Sophie had written to me just before Christmas, at the end of the Winter Term—those letters which described Mrs. Carberry's visit to Easton Knoyle, and that absurd 'Mr. Pym' escapade in the chapel. Miss Langdon-Miles, by the way, has only herself to thank—in my opinion—for her own murder; any competent headmistress would have set the police on to that 'Mr. Pym' as soon as he started accosting the girls . . . in the café or on the pier or wherever it was. Edward must have played the part of 'Mr. Pym' with a good deal of glee—he had always had a way with him where young females were concerned. As I again read Sophie's account of those events I already knew, by then, that 'dear, dear Miss Langdon-Miles' was doomed, and how very painful her death would be, but what I did not know was, who either Mrs. Carberry or 'Mr.

Pym' really were. Mind you—I had had my eye on Master Edward—as the aggrieved heir—but I still thought of him as a rich man. Hallam had not, at that time, let that particular cat out of the bag.

On re-reading Sophie's letters I felt but little doubt that it was Mrs. Carberry—whoever she might be— who had put the aspirins ito the medicine cupboard. The whole thing was very transparent and ought to have been spotted . . . but then, as I have said before, most people are fools. The daughter, Jennifer, was of course pure fiction, but she was a good enough excuse for Mrs. Carberry to worm her way into Easton Knoyle. It was probably a scouting expedition to discover the best method of depositing the aspirins—although Edward—masquerading as 'Mr. Pym' had possibly already acquired a good deal of miscellaneous information about the ways of Easton Knoyle. In actual fact, Mrs. Carberry saw her opportunity and it became much more than a mere scouting expedition. Once she had seen that double suite, with the common bathroom, her way was plain. The temptation must have been irresistible. A fainting attack, a fit of giddiness, followed by the necessity of lying down on the nearest bed . . . and, with the mistresses and girls safely at lunch, Mrs. Carberry *alias* Rosie Langdon-Miles *née* Sproggs had the whole suite to herself for half an hour.

The bathroom medicine cupboard was a risk—a two-to-one risk that Sophie instead of Miss Langdon-Miles would take the aspirins; but Rosie was not above a risk on odds of that sort. Into the medicine cupboard the aspirins went . . . eight of them well dosed with strychnine. Of those eight we know the history. The first was taken, the following Easter, by

266

Sophie at 'The Harrow', the second by poor Josephine, my budgerigar, and the remaining six were analysed by my chemist in Milsome Street . . . a history which neither Edward nor Rosie—for all their ingenuity—could possibly foresee. Mrs. Carberry felt, I imagine, profoundly satisfied with her morning's work. She could afford to be affable to poor Sophie as they went downstairs to rejoin the waiting chauffeur and the pug. The fictitious Jennifer's claim to a vacancy the following term need no longer be pressed, and Mrs. Carberry, of course, was not known at The Sheldon.

6

Rosie, in her Mrs. Carberry escapade, had made a valuable discovery—the slype. It was this passage between Miss Langdon-Miles's suite and the chapel which tempted them, and led them on into the fiasco of the 'Mr. Pym' expedition.

The medicine cupboard—with only a two-to-one risk against poor Sophie—had been a Godsend, but the slype—leading from the semi-public chapel to the corridor—must have seemed to present an even more golden and attractive opportunity. Mind you —to this day I am not quite certain why 'Mr. Pym' hid in the chapel that night . . . But I can picture 'Mr. Pym' and Rosie talking the matter over, and deciding that the medicine cupboard and the slype combined offered such an opportunity that a bottle in which every tablet had been dosed must be substituted for the comparatively mild weapon which Mrs. Carberry had left behind her. Why—they must have said to each other—it may be weeks, months even, before Miss Langdon-Miles has had a sufficient number of headaches to work down the bottle, to one of the eight lethal tablets. Actually, as we know, it was over three months before one of those tablets came poor Sophie's way. The strain of waiting must have loomed too large for Edward and Rosie to tolerate it.

So they decided—since Mrs. Carberry could hardly, in decency, visit Easton Knoyle a second time—that Edward should go there on the night of the Christmas play . . . an event of which the girls must have told him so much. With so many 'fathers' about he would not be challenged . . . and indeed if Sophie had not seen his 'trousered leg' slipping up the stairs in the interval between the first and second acts of that dreadful Congreve play, the plan might have gone well. But that was not the only reason for its failure. When 'Mr. Pym' arrived up-stairs he found the medicine cupboard empty and both Miss Langdon-Miles's and Sophie's luggage packed, in readiness for the Christmas holiday. As I read of this in Sophie's account I realised what a bad set-back it must have been for Edward. In his disappointment he probably did not realise that here was a wonderful chance to put the bottle into Miss Langdon-Miles's dressing-case; that idea only came to him later—to be developed. Perhaps, however, it was with the idea of returning to Miss Langdon-Miles's room later in the evening, possibly even with the idea of committing some bloodier kind of murder that night, that Edward went on through the slype and hid himself in the back pew of the dusky, candle-lit chapel. It is a fascinating point, and I never quite cleared it up with Mr. Stone.

But Sophie and Miss Wheelwright—the latter an admirable female—were more than a match for Edward . . . and his daring expedition ended in fiasco. Miss Wheelwright chased him across the snow-covered lawn—I had to rebuke Sophie for her timidity on this occasion—and only by stealing that MacTaggart woman's bicycle was he able to escape. His subsequent interview with Rosie was probably unpleasant . . . I don't suppose she spared him.

When, three months later, after the Nether Fordington business, I re-read Sophie's letters, I noticed one thing. 'Mr. Pym' was last seen pedalling down the back drive—hatless. I was still at that time, you must remember, hunting for the identity of the Pym-Carberry couple and so I immediately telegraphed to Sophie for the name of 'Mr. Pym's' hatter. Sophie again had the impertinence to think that I was going off my head—the very idea!—and I had to make a second demand after I had gone up north for the summer. The result was very unsatisfactory. Totter-dell, it was true, had found the hat—as I thought he would—at the bottom of the back pew, but the well-known firm of Lincolns', the hatters, gave their address simply as 'London and New York'—a most irritating ambiguity. I felt furious and gave Jenkins rather a bad time. A purely American hatter would have enabled me to get on the track of 'Mr. Pym's' identity very much sooner than I did . . . and a whole heap of trouble could have been prevented.

After the failure of this escapade in the chapel, Edward and Rosie settled down—if 'settled down' is the right description of the awful state of suspense in which they must have been living—to await Philippa's death from one of the eight poisoned aspirins. But Easter came and went, and still Philippa lived on. Considering that the aspirins were, by then, safely in my keeping, this was not surprising. As for Sophie's illness, I think it unlikely that Edward and Rosie ever heard of it.

Then came the blow. The engagement of Beatrice Langdon-Miles to Harold Warburton was announced. Considering that Beatrice was sixty, it was not unreasonable that Edward and Rosie should have failed to foresee such a contingency. But it was a blow—nevertheless. It must have thrown all Rosie's carefully laid plans into frightful confusion. *They simply didn't know whom to murder next.*

It was probable that Beatrice would, on her marriage, make a new will leaving the entire Langdon-Miles fortune to Harold. This probability, by the way, seems to have depressed 'dear, dear Miss Langdon-Miles' almost as much as it did her brother Edward; fundamentally I don't suppose she was one wit better than he was, the nasty creature. On the other hand it was possible, in view of Harold's age and his well-established position as a pianist, that Beatrice might still leave a great part of the money to her sister.

The situation was now terribly complicated, and —worst of all—full of uncertainty. If the original plan could have been adhered to, and Philippa and Beatrice both disposed of before the marriage—then all would have been well. Edward, as next-of-kin, would have inherited the Langdon-Miles fortune. But it was now extremely doubtful whether this plan could be safely carried out. Two factors were working against Edward and Rosie. First: Beatrice and Harold had no use for long engagements; as Sophie remarked, the marriage was rushed through in a most indecent fashion. Second: there was the very uncertain time element inherent in the poisoned aspirin method. They were very loth, I imagine, to abandon the aspirin scheme; it was—from their point of view—so safe. Why—they might even be back in New York, and nobody a penny the wiser, before the first of the lethal tablets had been swallowed.

But now things must have looked rather black to Edward and Rosie. Suppose Beatrice did make a new will, leaving everything to Harold . . . then the murder of Philippa—and she might die at any moment now—would have been superfluous. That in itself might not have mattered, but the whole scheme had crashed. On Beatrice's death—natural or otherwise—the Langdon-Miles fortune would go to Harold, and on his death to . . . well, to whoever his ultimate beneficiaries might be, and out of the Langdon-Miles line of succession for ever. Even if Beatrice, in her new will, still left a portion of her fortune to Phillippa, things would be no better; for on Philippa's death Beatrice, obviously, would revise her will and leave everything to Harold, and poor Edward and Rosie would be back where they were!

They must have felt desperate. They had come so far and made such careful plans . . . and now the possibility of failure stared them in the face. However, beneath her mink coat and her Fifth Avenue coiffeur Rosie was still a Sproggs, her roots reaching back into the dark and sanguinary places of Liverpool's dockland slums. She was not beaten yet. She made a new plan, a terrible and ghastly plan. As I watched it slowly working itself out to its awful and predestined conclusion . . . I often chuckled to my-self.

Three murders, Rosie must have said to herself, would be a little too much . . . they might attract attention, and that would never do. Anyway, it was no good. What would be the use if, after all their troubles, the Langdon-Miles fortune simply passed out of their reach . . . into the hands of some distant sister or nephew of Harold's. No—Rosie had a much better plan than that. Philippa and Beatrice must die, just as it was originally intended they should. Philippa first and then Beatrice . . . as soon as possible after Philippa, just on the off chance, the remote chance, that she had delayed making her new will in Harold's favour. But Rosie wasn't banking on that chance. Oh yes—Philippa and Beatrice must be murdered, but—and how cunning Rosie was—they must be murdered by poor, shy Harold War-burton . . . or so everyone must think. And then poor, shy Harold would no longer be able to inherit the Langdon-Miles fortune from his wife, for poor Harold would be a murderer. He would die on the gallows or—yes, that would be better still—he must disappear in fleeing from justice. Much better that, much better . . . for if there was a trial awkward things might crop up, and Harold—there was just a chance—might not be found guilty. But if Harold, the load on his conscience proving too great, were to flee, and never be heard of again, why then—and how right Rosie was—why then nobody would doubt his guilt, not for a moment. He would be a murderer and all his rights of inheritance would be null and void, and then—why then Sir Stuart Langdon-Miles's eldest son would come into his own again. It was hard on poor Harold, of course, but then old Sir Stuart really had been very unfair . . . shipping Edward and Rosie out of the country like that, insulting and robbing them. It had rankled with Rosie for thirty years. But now everything was to be put right once more . . . it might be illegal, it might be hard on poor Harold, but really Rosie thought—it was nothing more than bare justice.

7

I find that it was on May 20th, a few hours before Miss Langdon-Miles's death, that Sophie wrote to me—from the Anglo-America Ladies' Club, describing the party at the Old Vic and that astonishing journey to London in the company of Mr. Toplady. It was this letter which enabled me to start piecing together a satisfactory explanation of the poisoned aspirins.

First, of course, there was Hallam's interesting— and indeed decisive—remark about 'Langdon-Miles and Gabbitas' having gone crash in the American crisis—without which invaluable piece of information I might never have found the true explanation of everything. The reason ' for the association of a woman of vulgar origin with 'Mr. Pym' and all the goings-on at Easton Knoyle were now clarified, and became in themselves evidence of the most circumstantial kind.

Then, clearly, Mr. Francis Toplady, R.A., was an awful liar. In putting her new and more terrible plan into operation Rosie had evidently decided that, so far as Philippa was concerned, her patience was exhausted, and that Philippa must be eliminated —without delay. Hence Mr. Toplady.

There was—or so Rosie thought—very little risk in Edward assuming his new role. As 'Mr. Pym' he had been seen at close quarters only by old Totterdell and a few of the girls. Miss Langdon-Miles had never seen him, and Sophie only in the darkened chapel—by candlelight. Even then he had—as she drew near to him—been careful to cover his face with his hands. Poor, simple Sophie really did think he was saying his prayers by the Christmas crib. Edward of all people . . . Edward, who had abandoned the Church years ago for stockbroking and murder. How I did laugh as I read Sophie's letter.

In the five months between Christmas and the end of May, Edward had sported a neat little Vandyke beard. And dressed in his Norfolk suit and his foulard tie he looked quite the part. In fact, as even Sophie spotted, just a little too much so. Fowey, too, as an address for an artist was only less obvious than Chelsea . . . although it had the advantage of accounting for Mr. Toplady's presence in the West of England. Then, too, the 'R.A.' was such a clumsy blunder; Academicians, I imagine, don't often hire themselves out as copyists, and on making an enquiry I was informed that Mr. Toplady was not known at Burlington House. Lie No. 1. I had begun to feel an almost vicarious affection for little Toplady, but I fear that he really was a wicked liar. Extraordinary, when you consider how strictly the Langdon-Miles boys were brought up.

It also struck me that Mr. Toplady was just a trifle too accommodating and obliging. You couldn't possibly copy Bellinis in the dim, religious light of that hideous Easton Knoyle chapel. But, of course, it was very convenient for Mr. Toplady to be left there alone . . . so near to the slype and to that private suite. Once could so easily slip along to Miss Langdon-Miles's bedroom when she was not there; or even, perhaps, when she was there . . . for poisoned aspirins are not the only weapon, there are others—more direct but rather messy. No wonder that Mr. Toplady was content to set up his easel in that dark and gloomy Lavers Memorial Chapel—so anxious was he not to give trouble. It would, he said, be an admirable place in which to work on the Bellini. Lie No. 2.

Then, quite suddenly, he changed his tactics, Miss Langdon-Miles mentioned that in four days she would be travelling to London. It was at this point that Mr. Toplady postponed his work on the Bellini in favour of a strenuous walking holiday on Exmoor—at Simonsbath. It must have been just then, I think, that the dressing-case plan evolved itself in Mr. Toplady's active mind.

When four day's later, he popped into Miss Langdon-Miles's carriage at Taunton, he must have had a nasty shock—finding Miranda there. It was something that he could not have foreseen and—as I shall describe later—it was his undoing. I need hardly say that he had never been to Simonsbath . . . a very few moments' study of Bradshaw showed me that there was no train from Minehead which would have enabled him to catch that very early morning connection to Paddington. Besides . . . Miranda told Sophie later that she distinctly heard the ticket collector say to Mr. Toplady: 'Changed carriages, I see sir.' I doubt if he had risked being seen at Torquay that morning . . . he probably joined the train at Exeter. But, in any case, the visit to Simonsbath was Lie No. 3.

When Miss Langdon-Miles took Sophie off to the restaurant car for coffee . . . her fate was sealed. It was a fairly transparent device which Mr. Toplady used in order to send Miranda tearing off down the platform at Bristol—after 'a friend in a red hat'. Really, Mr. Toplady, you might have thought of something a little more subtle than that. And it was clumsy, Mr. Toplady, very clumsy to say that it was your bad heart which prevented you running after the red-hatted lady yourself. Very clumsy indeed, for a man who had boasted four days before of his twenty-mile tramps over the moor. Lie No. 4.

But the device served its purpose. It gave Mr. Toplady two minutes alone in the railway carriage, with all the suitcases and other impedimenta . . . and in those two minutes the fully loaded aspirin bottle went into the dressing-case. No mistakes this time, no danger for Sophie. The dressing-case was clearly marked with its silver monogram, P. L.-M., and when Mr. Toplady saw Miss Langdon-Miles looking so pale and distraught, so obviously in need of an aspirin, he must have thought that things were moving quickly. It was a pity that Miranda ran so fast down the Bristol platform—after the lady with the red hat—and was back so soon. Mr. Toplady got flustered, and put the dressing-case on the rack the wrong way round. However, nobody noticed—except Sophie, just as the train was running into Paddington.

It amused me to ponder on what Miss Langdon-Miles's emotions would have been, had she known that the little artist in the other corner seat, was her

276

brother—once her favourite brother—Edward. But that had been thirty years ago . . . and it was Miranda, not Philippa, who was his undoing.

8

During the next few days Edward and Rosie must have been very busy . . . much coming and going in the yellow Rolls and in taxis . . . much meeting and consulting at various rendezvous. Miss Langdon-Miles had looked so ill on the train that they must have felt almost certain that their plan was coming to fruition; surely in the next day or so—what with the lecture and the dinner party—surely she would suffer from a headache. Edward and Rosie were taking no chances, but they must have lived in hope that Beatrice—at the time of her marriage—had neglected to make that new will. It was unlikely, but it was possible, and so it was vital that her death should follow very swiftly upon Philippa's.

A woman's husband is not, of course, her next-of-kin in the eyes of the law. If Beatrice had, therefore, by some lucky chance, neglected that will or decided not to leave her fortune to Harold, then she would die virtually intestate . . . provided Philippa had succumbed only five minutes before her. And then . . . Edward would come into his own! It is a credit to Rosie's stage management that only a week should pass between the death of one sister and the death of the other.

Edward, in the role of Mr. Toplady, had acquired a good deal of valuable information. He must have discovered, for instance, while chatting in the train, that Miss Langdon-Miles and Sophie were to spend two nights at the Anglo-American Ladies' Club, that Miss Langdon-Miles was to lecture at the Cranmer Hall the next afternoon, that they were all going to *Macbeth* that evening, and—while driving in the Bentley from Paddington to Victoria—he must have heard Hallam telling Miranda that Aunt Beatrice and Uncle Harold were going to the 'Trinity Arms' the following night, after which they would, by stages, be going north to Coquet Hall. All this was—as I believe they say in the Army—useful intelligence work by little Toplady.

From that moment I doubt whether Miss Langdon-Miles was ever out of their sight for long. Rosie, Edward or the chauffeur-son must have constantly 'shadowed' her until the hour of her death . . . although it was not until the very last moment, the moment when her body was being placed in the ambulance, that Sophie saw the yellow Rolls gliding swiftly away from the Cranmer Hall. That little incident, of course, had finally disposed of any doubts which I still had concerning my whole theory . . . although Mr. Toplady's wicked lies had really settled it.

Philippa was dead . . . now it was the Warburtons' turn. Speed was essential. If that will in Harold's favour had not already been made by Beatrice, it almost certainly would be as soon as she heard of her sister's death. On the evening of May 20th—only four hours after the tragedy at the Cranmer Hall—Mr. Toplady was awaiting the Warburtons at the 'Trinity Arms'. Rosie was probably in the offing, perhaps at another hotel. The War-

burtons walked straight into the trap. Mr. Toplady was just behind them at the reception desk, and
he secured the adjoining bedroom. Some time during the evening he must have slipped into the Warburtons' room and deposited his dosed aspirins. It
was almost too easy. But this time it was heroin—
not strychnine. Two sudden and agonising deaths
from strychnine—and in the same family—might call
attention to themselves. It would, if it could be arranged, be so much more convenient for Beatrice to
die from heart failure. And if, later, it should become necessary to exhibit Harold's guilt to the
world . . . well, the use of two different poisons
would merely increase the cunning and the premeditated fiendishness of that uncouth giant. There
should be no difficulty about that.

Early next morning the yellow Rolls was streak-
ing up the Great North Road. That chauffeur-son
knew how to get the maximum speed out of the huge
limousine, and I can picture Edward and Rosie re-
clining luxuriously on the back seat. Rosie, in her
mink or leopardskin coat and in her toque of
violets, lolling back in the fast canary-coloured car,
must have looked indescribably vulgar, but anyone
who saw them can hardly have suspected the
emotions that stirred their hearts. Edward—full of
greed and hate for the whole Langdon-Miles clan,
but perhaps a trifle tremulous; Rosie—ruthless and
efficient, screwing his courage once more to the
sticking place, reproaching him with having too
much of the milk of human kindness . . . although,
Heaven knows, he had little enough; and both of
them—rather satisfied that the first part of the plan
had gone so well, and both feeling very safe.
Philippa was dead, and somewhere in Beatrice's suit-

case were sixty tablets of aspirin, each dosed with heroin . . . not a fatal dose, but enough to give poor Beatrice quite a nasty heart attack. The final, culminating dose could come later—at Coquet Hall. As for Mr. Francis Toplady, R.A.—somewhere on the road between Cambridge and Newcastle he disappeared for ever into the blue. The neat little Vandyke beard, the Norfolk suit and the foulard tie faded away, and their place was taken by black 'plusfours', a white Panama hat and—curiously enough —a micologist's collecting tin.

Then, like the rest of us, Edward and Rosie lost sight of the Warburtons for five days. I don't think that this worried them very much; the Warburtons were making their way slowly north, Harold getting his first view of the Lakes and other 'sights', and it might be that they would not hear of Philippa's death until they reached Coquet Hall. Certainly Beatrice wouldn't make a fresh will in the middle of a motor tour. In actual fact, as we know, the Warburtons did not hear the news of the Cranmer Hall tragedy until they found Sophie's telegram awaiting them.

Long motor rides did not agree with Beatrice, and it was a great piece of luck for Edward and Rosie that the first headache should have come so soon—on the road from York to Keswick. It was— as might be expected—followed almost immediately by a rather severe heart attack. The plan was going almost better than could have been hoped. Incidentally the heart attack at Keswick was later to provide an alibi for everyone at Coquet Hall.

Edward and Rosie made no attempt to 'shadow' the Warburtons all up England. There was no need; their final destination was known. Just as Mr. Top-

lady had awaited them at the 'Trinity Arms', so—in
some other role—would either he or Rosie await
them at Coquet Hall. Then came a nasty set-back
. . . not fatal, but maddeningly inconvenient. Mrs.
Soutar never, on any account, receives clients unless they are either recommended or personally
known to her—a most proper procedure. And on this
occasion Rosie's strident and vulgar 'Mrs. Carberry' accent over the telephone was not likely to
persuade the excellent manageress of Coquet Hall to
relax her rule.

There was nothing else for it—Rosie and the
chauffeur-son went to the 'Royal' at Newcastle,
while Edward, as a collector of moorland mosses,
obtained a dirty and uncomfortable room at Galbraith Farm—rather nearer to the scene of impend-
ing action. Rosie and Edward were a little careless
about being seen together, but then they must have
felt so safe. True, they took some trouble in the
matter, but twice they blundered. The first time was
at Torquay, when the school was closed for Christmas holidays and the girls and mistresses were all
away. . . . Edward and Rosie must have felt that
they could meet for a stroll on the prom on Christmas
morning, without undue risk, but they had reckoned
without old Totterdell. The second blunder was in
Northumberland . . . again it must have seemed safe
enough for the moss man to meet Rosie so many
miles away—in Newcastle, and it was just a piece of
bad luck that that scatter-brained gossip, Maisie
Bunting, should—on one of her silk-buying expeditions—have seen them together in the yellow Rolls
outside the 'Royal'. Just a piece of bad luck but—
as it happens—it was fatal, quite fatal, because it
gave me my first warning that Edward and Rosie

were in Northumberland . . . awaiting their victims.

Although I now knew a large part of the truth, there was still a great deal that I did not know. The whole situation—as the Warburtons drove nearer and nearer to their doom—was pregnant with danger. If both Rosie in Newcastle and the moss man at Galbraith Farm were to be watched—night and day—I must, I decided, have a trustworthy ally. I decided against Sophie . . . I should have had to pay her bill at Coquet Hall. Mr. Muir was an estimable little fellow—but no backbone. The others at Coquet Hall were clearly hopeless. I therefore telegraphed to Mabel Trubshawe, since she had behaved so admirably at Nether Fordington, ordering her to drop all her work instantly and come north. Of course Mrs. Soutar's extortionate charges would have been out of the question for a humble schoolmistress, but I remembered that tent which had once made Sophie so nervous, and I arranged with Mrs. Soutar that Mabel should camp a short distance from the hotel. I also took completely into my confidence that excellent female—Hypatia Crowe.

9

People who live in tents may say that they sleep soundly, but personally I have never believed it. Anyway Mabel Trubshawe spotted the signalling with the bicycle lamp the very first night.

Rosie and Edward were now separated by some forty miles, and at Galbraith Farm there was, of course, no telephone. It would hardly have been wise for the yellow Rolls to have appeared in such a remote spot as the head of Coquet Dale. It would be noticed and remembered. For Rosie—whiling away the hours at the 'Royal'—it must have been another week of suspense. She knew that the Warburtons were on their way to Coquet Hall, but she did not know when they would arrive. They might, possibly, spend weeks making their way up England. But it was essential that action should be taken to eliminate Beatrice at the earliest possible moment. And so, each night, the pre-arranged signal went out from the rowan trees, to be acknowledged by a flash from the headlamps of the Rolls—somewhere on the high road above Alnwick . . . five flashes if the Warburtons had not yet arrived, ten flashes when they had. It looked very mysterious at first, but it was really very simple.

I once sent Mabel Trubshawe up beyond Alnwick in her Austin Seven, at three o'clock in the morning, in order to verify the fact that it *was* the yellow Rolls which acknowledged the signals. She also spent a very cold but, no doubt, exciting night when I ordered her to hide behind a boulder close to the rowan trees . . . just to make sure that it really was the moss man who had sent the signals. It was a damp night and she very foolishly caught a chill, which annoyed me considerably as it might well have made her *hors de combat*, this causing me inconvenience. As for me, I often sat up reading so that I could watch the signals from my window, but I made Jenkins keep up a roaring fire, and Crowe brought me a fresh hot-water bottle at 3 a.m. I have always prided myself on being a good organiser.

Moreover I had no intention of allowing the sordid affairs of the Langdon-Miles family to interfere with my normal life or with my very simple pleasures. That would have been foolish. I invariably pay an annual visit to the Northern Choirs Festival at York. It thus happened that I was away from Coquet Hall on that Sunday afternoon when the Warburtons arrived, and also in the evening when Mr. Stone so cleverly fooled Mrs. Soutar into giving him a bed for the night. That was also the night when I very kindly allowed Mabel Trubshawe to use my sitting-room as a vantage point from which she could watch the rowan trees.

My visit to York was full of interest. The choirs sang most beautifully, and I was able to send a message to the Dean saying that they had given me satisfaction. Very gratifying. But the really amusing part of my visit began just as I was going down the nave towards the West Door. Whom should I see ahead of me among the crowd but—of all unexpected people—the moss man! Of course I couldn't be sure; he had always been extremely careful never to come withing fifty yards of anyone at Coquet Hall, and I had only seen him cycling along the track. But the black 'plus-four' suit was there, and he carried, in addition to a small suitcase, his white Panama hat and—what seemed conclusive—the collecting tin. Jenkins was waiting for me in the Daimler outside the Minster, but this little adventure was not to be missed. I am still—at ninety—a fast walker and in those days I had no difficulty in following the moss man round the streets of York.

My peregrinations were well rewarded. The moss man started by going to a large hairdressers. I was very angry at being forced to walk up and down outside, but after about a quarter of an hour I went in and, by taking ten minutes to choose a hair-net, I was able to catch a glimpse of the moss man—without his Panama—as he emerged into the outer shop to pay his bill. A glimpse was enough. When Mr. Stone turned up at Coquet Hall, looking just like a German general, I had no difficulty in recognising him immediately.

I then followed the moss man down the hill to the station. I easily got behind him at the booking office and when I heard him ask for a single ticket to Rothbury I wasted no further time. I went straight to the post-office and put through a trunk call to Crowe, telling her to warn Miss Trubshawe of what I had seen. Then I went back to the Daimler. Jenkins, who is really very fond of me, was in a terrible fidget, wondering where I had go to . . . but I only smiled. Altogether a most profitable hour.

That night on the train the black 'plus-fours' and the collecting tin must have disappeared and—presumably in the lavatory—their place was taken by the exquisitely tailored dove grey suit, the monocle and the corsets . . . such a wise move to alter one's figure a trifle. Edward never indulged in the crude disguises of the theatrical costumier. Once, indeed, he had donned a pair of sun-glasses, but that was when—as Mr. Toplady—he was at close quarters with Philippa, between Bristol and Paddington. Even then it was only an extra precaution, for the risk of Philippa recognising him was extremely slight—after thirty years. Generally speaking it was Edward's rule that those who had seen him in any of his many manifestations should never see him in any other. Philippa never saw 'Mr. Pym' or the moss man. Beatrice never saw 'Mr. Pym', Mr. Toplady or the moss man. Sophie, it is true, saw both 'Mr. Pym' and Mr. Toplady, but then she had never seen Edward as a young man, and 'Mr. Pym'—as I have said before—was seen by her only when he was praying by candlelight. As for Rosie—none of us ever saw her at all, except of course Philippa and Sophie in their interview with the obnoxious Mrs. Carberry; and I doubt whether Philippa, as a girl, had ever been allowed so much as a glimpse of Miss Rose Sproggs, the golden-haired mill girl. In the whole of this matter Edward and Rosie showed considerable ingenuity . . . and it was only Miranda who was their undoing.

And so the ingenious Mr. Stone, having left Galbraith Farm that morning as the moss man, travelled to York—probably in the Rolls. At York he had his hair cropped and then boarded the London-Newcastle train, *en route* for Rothbury. Why, after all, trouble to go further south than York in order to arrive on the London train. And why should the word of Lsyander Stone be doubted when he said that he had come post-haste from his chambers in Pall Mall . . . solely to save Coquet Hall from a grave scandal. Were not his credentials above suspicion—even in the eyes of Mrs. Soutar, always so careful in such matters. An authentic letter from the New York office of Edward Langdon-Miles instructing Mr. Stone to investigate the untimely death of poor Philippa . . . what more could one ask? No doubt it was all very horrifying and unusual, but eminently correct. And then Lysander Stone himself . . . a trifle aggressive perhaps, but such a reassuring and respectable figure, quite a gentleman. No wonder that poor Mrs. Soutar and poor Miss Amy—both so terrified of scandal—fell straight into the trap.

That night I spent at York. But Mabel Trubshawe, sitting at my window, saw ten flashes go out from the rowan trees, and ten answering flashes from the high road above Alnwick. Ten flashes, not five, for that afternoon the Warburtons had arrived. But this time it was not the moss man who manipulated the bicycle lamp, for he had disappeared into thin air for ever, somewhere between York and Newcastle. No —it was Mr. Stone, in a mackintosh and a bowler hat, who—watched from the shadows at the head of the stairs by the dark and dour Hypatia Crowe— slipped quietly out of the hotel into the mooonlight . . . to flash the news to Rosie across twenty miles of moorland.

10

When I got back from York I found that all those idiots at Coquet Hall had been completely bewitched by Mr. Stone. I naturally expected nothing but foolishness from Maisie Bunting, and little else from that affected *flâneur*—Graham Lacacheur. But Nellie Soutar and little Mr. Muir really ought to have known better—I was surprised at them. Canon Fish, I found, had simply collapsed into a state of bewildered incredulity . . . much good his Christian fortitude was to him! As for his wife . . . well, tears have never solved problems yet, and I can't tolerate neurotic poets. The McQueens, of course, I know nothing about, they are not the kind of people who come into my purview.

But I remember one extremely diverting lunch. The nervous tension was terrific. I recall that one of the maids very carelessly dropped a fork, whereupon

Maisie Bunting screamed, this being followed by what, in my childhood, were called 'vapours'. Graham Lacacheur had his book upside down, and Margaret Fish, as usual, was quietly weeping. Mr. Mark Fanshawe alone had preserved something of his normal phlegm but he was very sulky. I was the only one who was unmoved, and I am afraid that Mr. Muir thought me heartless. Actually I was enjoying myself trying—not very successfully—to trace facial resemblances between Mr. Stone on one side of the room and his sister Beatrice on the other.

Mr. Stone had told his story to each of them in turn—each, of course, being under a pledge of secrecy—and they were all suffering from a curious mixture of sheer terror at what was to come and pride at being in the know. Not one of them had had the gumption to see even the glimmerings of the truth . . . but then, to be fair, I was the only one who knew what had happened at Easton Knowle and Nether Fordington. In less horrible circumstances I should have regarded the situation as delicious.

Naturally, having told all the others his story, it was not long before Mr. Stone came to me. I granted him an interview. Indeed I invited him to take tea in my sitting-room, being careful to put Sophie's photograph in the drawer. I listened to him very patiently . . . in fact with great interest. As soon as he began it was clear that he and Rosie were taking no chances about Beatrice having made—or not made—a new will. Beatrice was evidently going to die quickly—probably in a day or two—and Mr. Stone's story was simply an impertinent and far-fetched attempt to establish Harold's guilt in advance. What was more sinister was that public opinion at Coquet Hall was being rapidly and—

such is human gullibility—very successfully organised against poor Harold.

Bundaberg Monster indeed! Not—mind you—that there was no such person . . . there was. He died at a penal settlement in Tasmania in 1916. At first, like Mr. Mark Fanshawe, I refused to believe that Henry Washwood of Bundaberg had ever existed. Edward and Rosie made several bad blunders, but they had one colossal piece of good luck . . . the discovery of a criminal giant in the Australia of twenty years before. They must have been so delighted with this that they made it the very core of their plot. I only discovered that Washwood was a real person when I sent Mabel Trubshawe off that night on a flying visit to the British Museum, with instructions to dig the whole story out of the newspaper files . . . if indeed there was a story to dig out. Not that she found an account of the Bundaberg case; what she did find was that all the relevant paragraphs had been neatly cut from the *Melbourne Suns* and *Sydney Stars* of 1910. This filching from the dusty files of the Museum would inevitably be discovered sooner or later . . . probably sooner, for Mr. Stone, when Harold had duly 'fled', would no doubt draw attention to it as being Harold's last, desperate attempt to wipe out all traces of his past.

As soon as Mr. Stone had laid out his gruesome little array of exhibits on my sitting-room table I was struck by the fact that the photograph of 'Washwood' was on a separate slip of paper, not an integral part of one of the cuttings. But it was not until some months later that I discovered it had been reproduced from one of Harold Warburton's very early Australian programmes. The real Bundaberg

Monster was quite a different type—a brutal, leering, sensual half-wit. Harold, on the other hand, for all his clumsiness, obviously had a shy and rather indefinable charm . . . as indeed his nephew Hallam had always insisted.

Edward and Rosie then had what they must have regarded as a second piece of colossal luck—almost too good to be true. As it happens it was quite fatal for them. Within twenty-four hours of Miss Langdon-Miles's death Edward had temporarily assumed the role of Mr. Stone—just for a few hours —and had what he called a 'most fruitful interview with Miss Langdon-Miles's secretary' at the Anglo-American Ladies' Club. Silly Sophie! She was so overcome at the death of her 'dear, dear Miss Langdon-Miles' and so bemused at finding herself in the presence of a real, live detective, that she never even thought of Mr. Francis Toplady being concealed behind the aggressive personality of smart Mr. Stone. She swallowed his story—hook, line and sinker. Her prejudice against Harold had always been patently absurd, and in Mr. Stone she found a ready listener. She told him all about Harold's 'disgusting manners' at the Old Vic, and how he had so rudely doled out the chocolate liqueur creams with his fingers. Sophie was most particular about such things . . . actually, of course, it was not an unnatural gesture for a shy and self-conscious man trying to be friendly and informal under difficult conditions. But Mr. Stone, I imagine, could hardly believe his ears; he and Rosie leapt on that chocolate cream story so eagerly that they never stopped to think. They seized it and worked it into their general plot. From their point of view, of course, it was a pity that nearly twenty hours had elapsed between the time when Philippa ate the chocolates and the time when she fell dead at Cranmer Hall; a pity, too, that when the Nether Fordington affair cropped up I had enquired so closely into toxicological matters and was so well aware of the rapidity with which strychnine attacks its victims. I also knew that Miss Langdon-Miles—prostrate from her quarrel with Beatrice the night before—had taken two aspirins before leaving the Anglo-American Ladies' Club for the Cranmer Hall. It would in fact, have been better for Edward and Rosie if they had left those chocolate creams severely alone.

Not that they were fools . . . you mustn't imagine that they were ever so naïve as to expect to see Harold Warburton in the dock, charged with wilful murder. That was quite unnecessary. For the purpose of creating at Coquet Hall an atmosphere violently hostile to Harold, for creating that condition of affairs in which we were all waiting for him to poison his wife, for fooling us all . . . for all that Mr. Stone's story was overwhelmingly adequate. In court, clearly, it would have stood no chance . . . the truth about the Bundaberg Monster and about the chocolate creams would soon be laid bare. But suppose that all of us—all of us at Coquet Hall— were soon convinced of Harold's guilt that we should feel it our duty—with a little urging from Mr. Stone —to demand Beatrice's exhumation, and then suppose that Harold was to disappear in his flight from justice. Why—then the case against him would surely be overwhelming. There would be no trial, but guilt would be assumed without too many pettifogging enquiries, and Harold and his heirs would be duly deprived of their right to benefit from Beatrice's will. After all—who else could have administered the heroin of which such a large dose would be found in Beatrice's body. By that time, too, Mr. Stone—with the newspaper cuttings, the pellets and the diary—would have faded away . . . and Edward Langdon-Miles would be back in his New York office ready to express becoming surprise on being informed of his good luck in inheriting—in such a devious way—the famous Langdon-Miles fortune.

One rather adroit move by the ingenious Mr. Stone was the manner in which he kept all the Coquet Hall crowd quite inactive. One or two of them, at least, would have done what they could to save or to warn poor Beatrice . . . but Mr. Stone saw to it that they should be impotent. They might be horrorstruck, but they need do nothing . . . for was not Mr. Stone —a professional detective—keeping in touch with the police. True, the police, according to Mr. Stone, were slow and incredulous, but he assured us all that they would be in time . . . Lysander Stone would see to that! Just a little more evidence, and the case which he would take to Scotland Yard would be incontrovertible. Then the diary and the pellets turned up . . . here was the evidence, said Mr. Stone, for which he had been waiting, and off he rushed to Scotland Yard. I need hardly say, perhaps, that in actual fact he never went near the place.

On that nerve-racking day when they all believed that Mr. Stone was in London, and were all anxiously waiting for him to return with a couple of stalwart policemen, Mr. Stone was actually spending his time in quite a different manner. You see he had begun to have just a very faint suspicion that I might know something that I ought not to know. The summer sky of Edward's and Rosie's security was still clear and serene, but on the horizon there was just the very faintest cloud; I was Sophie Coppock's aunt. With a gossip like Maisie Bunting about the place it wouldn't take Mr. Stone long to find that out. Also, he must have heard from the same source that I had seen the moss man in York Minster. Thereupon he almost panicked, and once again played into my hands. He tried to establish a sort of alibi to show that Mr. Stone and the moss man were two persons and not one. His visit to Scotland Yard gave him the chance.

Having been deposited by the shooting brake at Rothbury Station, on the first stage of his journey, he got out of the train at Newcastle and came back to the Coquet Dale in the yellow Rolls. Inside the car he once again assumed the black 'plus-fours', the white Panama hat and the collecting tin of the moss man. Having reached the head of the Dale he proceeded to cycle along the track towards Coquet Hall. If he was seen from the windows of the hotel it would be quite sufficient for his purpose . . . the news that the moss man had returned would spread. It was just bad luck that Mr. Muir—unable to bear the nervous strain a minute longer—should have chosen to set off in his car for a run to Otterburn and the border. They very nearly came to close quarters and the moss man had to flee. He still had Mrs. Stone's close-cropped Teutonic hair, and a meeting might have been disastrous. It was a narrow squeak and when he rejoined the Rolls I suspect that Rosie gave him a good curtain lecture. By now, of course, almost as a matter of routine, Mabel Trubshawe was constantly 'shadowing' the yellow Rolls, wherever it went. . . . Rosie was her care, Edward was mine.

One of the curious things about Mr. Stone's story was that so much of it was true. Almost all the reasons he gave as to why Harold Warburton should commit murder applied with equal validity to himself. The motive—the Langdon-Miles fortune—was the same in each case; so were many of the details. The need, for instance, to eliminate Philippa first and Beatrice second—so as to avoid the money slipping away into the hands of the Church—existed equally whether the murderer was Harold Warburton or Edward Langdon-Miles *alias* Mr. Stone. The desirability of varying the poison—the change from strychnine to heroin—in order that Beatrice might die a 'natural' death . . . all that, too, was just as Mr. Stone explained it to me and to Mr. Muir. I suppose that the Langdon-Miles children had been brought up to have a strict regard for truth, and Mr. Stone did not lie unless he had to. On the whole, in fact, his story was true . . . except for the trifling discrepancy that it was Harold Warburton and not himself who was the murderer.

The diary which turned up so conveniently was, however, Mr. Stone's clumsiest and most transparent advice. I was amazed at Mr. Muir's gullibility. As soon as Mr. Stone told me about the diary I sent him off to get it from beneath that pile of summer pants in Harold's dressing-room. The Warburtons were strolling in the forecourt at the time, so there was no difficulty about Mr. Stone entering their suite. Summer pants indeed! The diary and the pellets must have been in Mr. Stone's pocket all the time. Little Mr. Muir had been busy ransacking Beatrice's possessions when Mr. Stone had originally 'found' them in the dressing-room. And after I had inspected the diary and the pellets, and Mr. Stone had 'returned' them to their nest among the pants, I sent Crowe into the dressing-room and she couldn't find them anywhere.

I suppose, by the way, that it was when Mr. Stone and Mr. Muir were ransacking the Warburtons' rooms that Mr. Stone substituted the aspirins with the full dose of heroin, for those with a mere 'heart-attack dose'. I am inclined to think, too, that in addition to heroin the aspirins contained a dash of opium . . . just to make sure that Beatrice suffered from a sufficient number of headaches. Rather a cruel murder on the whole. . . .

I found the diary itself most unconvincing. To start with, the entries had been filled in since the beginning of the year, but a small adhesive label inside the back cover showed that this particular pocket-diary had been bought at a large stationers in the Strand, whereas in January Harold Warburton had been in mid-Pacific. I pay exorbitant rates in order to support a police force and had no intention of turning myself into a professional sleuth; I therefore took it for granted that the entries were made in a tolerable imitation of Harold's handwriting . . . sufficiently so at least for the purpose of fooling and gulling the occupants of Coquet Hall. The point that really interested me was that up to May 25th—the date when Mr. Stone had finished writing the diary—all the entries, both the normal ones and the sinister red-ink scrawls, were an accurate record of events, but what we may call the 'prophetic' entries, those dealing with events yet to come, were all falsified in due course by what actually happened.

Of course Mr. Stone knew that this was bound to be so, for with all his ingenuity he couldn't control the exact dates on which Beatrice should have heart-attacks or die. And so he devised various ways of showing why Harold's 'timetable' should have gone awry. The minced chicken episode was one such device. According to the diary Beatrice was due for a heart-attack on May 25th. When Mr. Stone happened to see the supper tray on the hot-plate at the head of the stairs, he seized his opportunity. He stole some of the chicken—probably shovelling it off into an envelope—and then put the tray on the mat outside the Warburtons' door. Once again his eagerness had betrayed him for Crowe told me that the maids were never allowed to put trays down in that crude manner—they were always placed either in her room or on the hot-plate. Mr. Stone then gave that nasty little dog a good stiff dose of rat poison, and told the McQueen boys that Binks had stolen Mrs. Warburton's supper. Of course Mrs. Soutar would never have allowed anything of that sort to happen at Coquet Hall, but Binks was a most unpopular dog and the McQueen boy eagerly passed on the tale.

When Beatrice Warburton died on the night of May 28th, it was a great shock to us all. If it had been a natural death it would still have been a shock, for she was an estimable and progressive woman, or so I am told—I never knew her. Nobody in the hotel had thought that death would come before the date in the diary—June 1st—and they had all expected Mr. Stone to come back with the police on the morning of the 29th. They all had great faith in Mr. Stone. Even he, I think, was surprised at death coming so soon; he said he was shocked when he saw the blinds down on his return from 'London'. He adroitly attributed this early death to Harold having 'smelt a rat'. That odious John Smith might—Mr. Stone suggested—have told Harold of the ransacking of his rooms . . . and so Harold had speeded things up.

Beatrice Warburton's death was a shock for me too. I must say that I had not thought it would occur while Mr. Stone was away for the night. I should have realised, of course, that Mr. Stone's absence from Coquet Hall could have no possible bearing on whether Beatrice happened, or did not happen, to take an aspirin. Poor Harold Warburton! He was obviously a broken man . . . and Mr. Stone had to spend the day of the funeral going round to each of us in turn asiduously insisting that 'Harold was a brilliant actor to the end.'

When the McQueen boys found that new and shining spade hidden under the rugs in the Warburtons' Bentley, I decided that the time had come for me to act. At first I had dismissed that spade as being the most stupid and, indeed, the silliest of Mr. Stone's devices. It might serve to throw the McQueen boys or Maisie Bunting into a state of hysterical panic . . . but really it was quite meaningless. All Edward's and Rosie's energies had been devoted to arranging matters so that Beatrice should, above all things, appear to die from natural causes. Any attempt to dispose of the body in a clandestine manner would completely wreck this scheme. And the funeral must be as 'natural' as the death; although I suspect that Mr. Stone was rather disappointed when Harold failed to ask for cremation. The spade, if it was intended to implant in our minds the idea of a secret grave, simply didn't make sense.

Then suddenly I saw the whole meaning of it. I had assumed that we had been *meant* to know of the spade hidden in Harold's car, just as we had been meant to know about the Bundaberg Monster and the diary. I had been wrong. With Beatrice ill or dead the Bentley was unlikely to be used and it was therefore—if it had not been for the inquisitive McQueen boys—an excellent hiding place, at any rate for one night. The spade was meant to be hidden and it must have been a blow for Mr. Stone when it was found, for whereas it had no connection whatever with Beatrice's 'natural' death, it was a most essential implement for bringing about Harold's disappearance during his flight from justice. In purchasing that spade Edward and Rosie were already preparing for the final act of the drama; it was for digging, not of Beatrice's grave, but of Harold's.

11

It would have been too absurd to have allowed Mr. Stone to cause me any discomfort or to let him upset the tenour of my well-ordered life. Without ceasing to enjoy my moorland holiday I could quite easily deal with Mr. Stone in my stride. I therefore felt that it was slightly ridiculous that my plan of action should involve me in the worry and disturbance of leaving Coquet Hall for the night. It was only a few days since I had returned from York. It was most annoying to have to uproot myself a second time. The thwarting of Mr. Stone might be an agreeable change from playing patience and watching my investments, but the Langdon-Miles family were, after all, nothing to me . . . and it does no good to bonnets and mantles to keep taking them in and out of the trunks. However, the matter had gone so far that it would have been a pity to hand it over tamely to the police. I was enjoying the feeling of power which is derived from knowledge. In any case packing and unpacking gave Jenkins something to do, and she had been getting very idle of late. There is a small but expensive private hotel in Edinburgh which always makes me very comfortable . . . and from there I could keep in touch by telephone with Mabel Trubshawe. I telegraphed for my usual rooms.

The morning after the funeral I summoned Harold Warburton to my sitting-room. He was with me nearly three hours. Poor fellow . . . he was quite frantic by the time I had finished my story, and Mabel Trubshawe and I had the greatest difficulty in dissuading him from taking the law into his own hands . . . he wanted to deal with Lysander Stone there and then in accordance with his deserts. For a few minutes I was quite fearful lest Harold Warburton should go off his head. He was a very strong man and if Mr. Stone had been in my room at that moment I tremble to think what might have happened. It was not until Mabel Trubshawe had administered a sedative that Harold was able to discuss my little plot in a rational manner.

I must say, to his credit, that he didn't care a button for his own peril; his anger was aroused by the pain which Beatrice had had to suffer, I think that he really did want to kill with his own hands the man who he kept referring too—oddly but correctly —as his brother-in-law.

When Harold Warburton had become a little calmer he showed me a letter which he had received that morning. It bore the Rothbury postmark, and was a clear indication that we were acting only just in time. Harold was in very great peril.

Meanwhile Jenkins had been packing in the adjoining room, and just before lunch the trunks were ready. I went downstairs to find an uneasy and embarrassed company on the terrace, gossiping as usual. Gossip and meals, gossip and meals . . . that was the daily round at Coquet Hall. Naturally I never took any part in their chatter. I had never felt called upon to explain my comings and goings to every Tom, Dick and Harry in the hotel . . . they got to know far too much about other people's affairs as it was. But on this particular occasion I had a motive. . . .

As I emerged on to the terrace from the French window there was an awkward silence. I then spoke.

'I am,' I said, 'going away for a few days, and I wish to say good-bye. I shall be back in a few days, but I am going a considerable journey. I shall spend at least one night at the "Trinity Arms" at Cambridge, and I may then go on to the "Stag Hotel" at Simonsbath . . . on Exmoor, you know. Good afternoon.'

Then I went down the steps to the waiting Daimler in the forecourt . . . and started on my short ride to Edinburgh. I don't like telling lies, but I had no qualms of conscience this time. As my car swerved and bumped over the rough track Jenkins must have wondered yet again why I was chuckling so. I was thinking of the terrible and ghastly panic which I had left behind me, seething in the breast of Lysander Stone.

12

How right I had been! Things soon came to a head and I had to spend only one night in Edinburgh. Since I was simultaneously paying Mrs. Soutar for my suite at Coquet Hall, this was a good thing. On the day after my arrival I was called from my lunch to speak to Mabel Trubshawe on the telephone. Mr. Stone, she said, had reacted just as we had expected he would . . . complete panic! Crowe had told her that within an hour of my departure 'for Cambridge and Simonsbath' he had packed and unpacked his suitcase four times. Then, at 3 a.m., from the window of my room, Mabel Trubshawe had seen seven answering flashes from the headlamps on the Great North Road. . . . 'Danger!' presumably.

Above all, Harold Warburton, and the Bentley, were missing. Crowe had reported to Mrs. Soutar that his bed had not been slept in.

I think that the most infuriating part of the business for Mr. Stone must have been the impenetrable fog in which he now found himself. How much did I know? Everything had seemed to him so serene and secure . . . and now there was this ghastly doubt. This, of course, was precisely what I had intended. If I had said more, if I had allowed Mr. Stone to think that I knew the whole truth . . . then he and Rosie would have known what to do—precipitate flight would have been their only course. But by merely issuing the 'Cambridge and Simonsbath' canard I had reduced their schemes to chaos. Of course I should never have dreamt of putting myself to the expense and inconvenience of tearing from one end of England to the other. The mere mention of Cambridge and Simonsbath was sufficient for my purpose. It showed them that I knew something . . . that the scent was hot. Inevitably—they must have thought—that old woman will find that Mr. Francis Toplady was at the 'Trinity Arms' on the same night as the Warburtons, and that never, in his life, had he been near Simonsbath at all. But if I knew enough to be on the track of Toplady— how much more did I know? That was the question which must have haunted them. In the end they decided that something must be done before my return. . . . Exmoor was a good way off and they probably thought that they had a clear four days. The elimination of Harold Warburton must be speeded up . . . the plans were already laid for that. And then if necessary I, too, must be eliminated. Murders, it would seem, are rather like lies . . . one leads to another.

Meanwhile—so Mabel Trubshawe told me—Mr. Stone had called his drawing-room meeting for that evening. Everyone at Coquet Hall, of course, was well aware of the agenda of that meeting. It would be an almost formal monologue by Lysander Stone. He would conclude by holding Harold Warburton's sudden disappearance before them as the crowning proof of guilt; and all that remained for Mrs. Soutar and all her guests to do would be to demand that the Home Office should exhume poor Beatrice. Indubitably heroin would be found. How perfectly the ingenious Mr. Stone had evolved his complex plan. It had all gone with the greatest precision . . . until my little Simonsbath trick had thrown a monkey-wrench—as I think the vulgar phrase goes—into the works.

I gave Mabel Trubshawe a few necessary instructions and then I telephoned to Laburnum Cottage, Otterburn, where Sophie and Miranda Gladstone had been living for the last two days—*incognito*. Mrs. Gladstone had made an unpardonable fuss about her dear Miranda being involved in such a gruesome scandal, and to appease her I had taken some quiet apartments where Miranda could continue her studies while Sophie did some fine sewing for me. A pleasant little holiday for them both.

After I had partaken of a substantial high tea at my Edinburgh hotel, the trunks were again put on the car and I proceeded south. It was a cloudless and very lovely evening and I found the ride most exhilarating. Mabel Trubshawe, with Sophie and Miranda tucked in the back of her Austin Seven, was waiting for me as we arranged, where the road forks above Otterburn. After a useful visit to Rothbury Police Station we held a rather crowded counsel of war inside the Daimler. By the time we finally bumped our way along the track to Coquet Hall the light was failing, and the evening star was hanging in the sky above the ragged elms.

Hypatia Crowe was waiting for us by the big log fire in the hall. We had timed it well. Crowe, on my instructions, had been eavesdropping at the drawing-room door. Mr. Stone's 'lecture', she said, seemed to be coming to an end. I waited for a rather breathless moment, with my hand on the door-knob, and then, when Mr. Stone seemed to be launched on his peroration, I entered.

It was a queer sight. Nobody had troubled to turn up the lights, and the fire threw strange shadows among that strange company. It flickered in a rather ghastly fashion on Mr. Lacacheur's thin, grey face.

How orange Mark Fanshawe's hair looked against the white marble of the fireplace, and how pallid the face of the odious John Smith seemed in the gloom.

Lysander Stone of Pall Mall, *alias* the moss man of Galbraith Farm, *alias* Francis Toplady, R.A., of Fowey, *alias* 'Mr. Pym' of Torquay, *alias* Edward Langdon-Miles of Wall Street, New York, was demanding that the remains of his sister, Mrs. Harold Warburton, be exhumed in order that the guilt of her husband might be placed beyond all reasonable doubt.

As I crossed that shadowy room, followed by my maid, Jenkins, and by my niece, Sophie Coppock, by Mabel Trubshawe and Miranda Gladstone, and by the dark, dour Hypatia Crowe . . . there was a deathly silence. The quiet sobbing of Margaret Fish was the only sound.

Of course I had to agree with Mr. Stone that the remains of Mrs. Warburton should be exhumed. That was most necessary. But I also felt bound to ask him what he and his wife had done with poor Harold Warburton's body.

And then . . . why, then—as the room grew darker and darker—I told them my story . . . very much as I have written it down in these pages.

13

After that it was plain sailing. As I finished the long story of how—with Sophie's bilious headache as my starting point—I had been able to build up my case against Edward and Rosie, I noticed that all eyes had turned from me and were now directed upon Mr. Stone. It was rather difficult to see in the flickering firelight—and it was now quite dark outside—but I am sure that Mr. Stone had gone green, and he was running his finger round the inside of his collar as though it had suddenly become too tight for him. He sat down and gripped the edges of the little Pembroke table on which the green leather pocket-diary, the pellets and the faded cuttings from the *Melbourne Sun* were still lying.

Then, you know, I am afraid that Mr. Stone was very rude to me. He had suddenly become rather hoarse and I couldn't hear anything he said, but I distinctly heard the words 'doddering and senile old bitch!' This was not at all nice. I was also surprised because I had always thought of the Langdon-Miles children as having been very carefully brought up. I can only suppose that it was the influence of his vulgar wife.

Hallam Langdon-Miles—such a nice looking boy —and little Mr. Muir had each taken a large silver candelabrum from the mantelpiece. They were fine eighteenth-century pieces—rather early and heavy —and I hoped that they would not have to be used as weapons. Hallam and Mr. Muir had closed in on Mr. Stone, and were standing on either side of him. I had arranged with Mabel Trubshawe that if there was any trouble of that kind she was to take Miranda out of the room.

Except for Mr. Stone's ill-mannered outburst I was the only one who had spoken since our arrival. I had been listened to in complete silence . . . indeed, Mr. Lacacheur, Maisie Bunting and Mark all seemed quite petrified. But now Hallam spoke up, addressing himself to Mr. Stone.

'And where, you filthy swine, is my uncle?' Mr. Stone's answer was a mere croak. . . .

'I don't know, really I don't. I swear I don't.'

'I had quite forgotten,' I said, 'to explain about Mr. Warburton. How stupid of me . . . you must have all been quite anxious. But of course I should never have allowed him to be murdered; once one knew the truth, that would have been too ridiculous—wouldn't it?'

'But he's gone,' said Hallam, 'he's been gone for over twenty-four hours . . . and the Bentley. Where is he?'

'Your Uncle Harold,' I explained, 'received a letter yesterday morning, from Miss Lettice Howe of Liverpool . . .'

'Never heard of her . . .'

'Don't interrupt,' I said. 'Naturally you have never heard of her. There is no such person. In this letter Miss Howe explained that she had been governess to the Langdon-Miles children, and that she had always kept up a friendship and correspondence with dear Beatrice . . . her favourite pupil. She added that she had heard of Beatrice's death too late to attend the funeral, but that she was now in Rothbury for the night . . . and would your dear uncle care to meet her in that—er—very lonely moorland churchyard. She wished to visit the grave and was anxious, most anxious, to hear of something of Beatrice's last hours. It was not the kind of invitation which, normally, a man would refuse.'

'And he went . . .'

'No. In spite of a certain risk I sent my niece, Miss Coppock, in his place. Sophie, you had better tell us what happened. . . . Speak up, child.'

'Well,' said Sophie, 'it was the most extraordinary

thing, and I do hope that I shall tell it right. You must all forgive me if I don't. It was yesterday morning; Miss Trubshawe and I set off in her little Austin Seven. The last time I was in that car was when we drove away from "The Harrow". How stupid it was of me not to spot those aspirins for myself . . . but then I was feeling so ill, and who would think of anything so wicked. There I go, getting away from my tale already. Miss Trubshawe and I arrived at the little grey churchyard under Crigdon Hill—such a lonely spot—just at the time when this Miss Lettice Howe had asked Mr. Warburton to meet her. She was there first—or so we thought. A large yellow Rolls was standing outside the lych-gate, and she herself was standing by the grave . . . such a peaceful spot and the wreaths were still looking quite fresh. Miss Trubshawe and I walked up the path together, but—do you know—it wasn't Miss Lettice Howe at all. It was someone I knew quite well.

' "Why, Mrs. Carberry," I said. "What an unexpected pleasure. I haven't seen you since you visited us at Easton Knoyle last winter. . . ." And then the most extraordinary thing happened. Mrs. Carberry dropped the little black pug which she had in her arms, and ran—yes, ran—as hard as she could go, down the path to the lych-gate. The young man who acts as chauffeur must have been watching us, for he had got his engine going. Mrs. Carberry leapt in and they were off and out of sight round the bend before Miss Trubshawe and I could recover our wits. And we couldn't very well leave the black pug behind in the churchyard, so we had to bring him with us. . . . Did you ever hear of such a thing?'

When Sophie had finished speaking she was quite

breathless. The events of the last few days had been too much for her and, to tell the truth, she hadn't quite grasped it all. She never did—quite. I had had qualms about sending her to that very lonely churchyard, but I thought that the sight of Miss Coppock of Easton Knoyle would strike terror into the breast of Rosie Langdon-Miles more than anything else. I don't know what fate had been intended for Harold Warburton . . . a prick from a hypodermic, perhaps, or a shot from a revolver—for it was a very lonely spot indeed. And I expect that that new and shiny spade was inside the Rolls. But the exact nature of the death which had been planned for Harold was one of those questions upon which Mr. Stone never would enlighten me. He never would tell me either, whether he had intended to murder Philippa —there and then—that night when he hid in the chapel at Easton Knoyle. The Langdon-Miles were always very obstinate folk.

Hallam was really a very impatient youth. He still seemed dissatisfied and wanted to know where his uncle was.

'Don't fuss,' I said; 'your uncle is perfectly safe. I granted the use of my suite to Mabel Trubshawe last night, while I was in Edinburgh.' They all looked very surprised at that. . . . 'Yes, Edinburgh,' I went on, 'not Simonsbath, or even Cambridge. And, for the last twenty-four hours Harold Warburton has been in Mabel Trubshawe's tent. Rather uncomfortable and very boring, but he had some detective stories with which to while away the time. You see, it was the one place where no one would think of looking for him . . . and if he had been found before I got back from Edinburgh, Mr. Stone would have fled. But as long as Mr. Stone thought that

Rosie had disposed of Harold, and that I was on my way to Exmoor . . . why, he carried on with his plan. That is so, isn't it, Mr. Stone? Isn't it? . . . Very well, if you won't answer, you won't.'

'And where is the Bentley?' Hallam asked.

'In a quarry, half way to Rothbury,' I said. 'I am afraid that it is unlikely that you will ever see your wife again, Mr. Stone, unless . . . but we won't probe just now into the very unpleasant future. Is there anything that you wish to say.'

If anyone in that room had imagined that Lysander Stone would go down without a struggle, they were very much mistaken. His hands were clutching convulsively at the sides of the table, and he was swearing. Then he stood up.

'It's all a lie,' he shouted, 'a bloody lie . . . this old bitch is over eighty; she's senile, I tell you, mad! It's all a figment of her diseased imagination . . . a crazy story. Why, Edward Langdon-Miles is in New York. I told Mr. Muir that. I told him that I had spoken to Edward on the telephone—the trans-Atlantic telephone . . . only a few days ago.'

'Well,' I said, 'we might try to do so again—but it's very expensive.' There was a little laugh at that, and then Mr. Stone went on with his angry speech.

'This crazy old witch can prove nothing . . . absolutely nothing. All these absurd people—"Pym" and Toplady—who are they? We have only the old woman's word for it that they ever existed . . . and if they did, what has it got to do with Mrs. Warburton's death . . . or Miss Langdon-Miles's. It's all a damnable lie, I tell you. She can't prove a thing. Who was this creature "Pym"? Why, she doesn't even know his real name. And I have never been near Torquay in my life.'

Really, the man was getting quite violent, shouting and foaming at the mouth and leaning on the little Pembroke table until I thought it would break. And I have left out some of his obscene language. It was quite dreadful. I can only hope that Miranda didn't understand it.

'Mr. Stone,' I said, 'you mustn't be silly. Of course I can't produce "Mr. Pym"—because you are "Mr. Pym".'

'Prove it then, prove it! '

'Very well then,' I said, 'I will. Miss MacTaggart, the English mistress—a young woman whom I have never met—met you on the beach, Mr. Stone . . . at the time when you were masquerading as "Pym". She had taken the little ones from The Firs down to bathe, and you too, Mr. Stone, had on only your bathing-dress. If Miss MacTaggart's memory is accurate we shall find a large cicatrix on your right leg. Pray, Mr. Stone, raise you right trouser a trifle. . . .'

'I shall do nothing of the sort,' retorted Mr. Stone; of course I have got a scar on my leg—or cicatrix if you prefer the word—if I hadn't you wouldn't have invented one for "Mr. Pym", whom you also invented. Besides, there is not a soul here who ever saw this fictitious "Mr. Pym".'

'Now that,' said Miranda, 'is where you are wrong.'

Everyone looked at the child in amazement. She was rather flushed and solemn, but her eyes sparkled and she spoke with a very firm voice.

'That,' she said, 'is where you are quite wrong. Surely, "Mr. Pym", you remember taking me and Prudence Lloyd to Paignton on the tram. I am going to Girton next term and I should never dream of doing anything like that now, but don't you remember how we all giggled . . . and then we used up all your pennies in the slot machies on the pier. Surely you remember that, "Mr. Pym".'

'No, I don't,' he snapped. 'first it's old women, and now it's schoolgirls.' But Miss Amy had turned up the lights, and I found that I had been right . . . he had gone green, a rather nasty sort of green.

'Well,' went on Miranda, 'I am surprised that you don't remember that. We used up all your pennies, and then we wanted you to get change for the William and Mary florin—on your watch chain. . . .'

'Ah!' I said, for—like a shot—Mr. Stone's hand had gone to his waistcoat pocket.

'Why!' cried Hallam, 'there were two William and Mary florins. They were dug up years ago in the garden of the old house on the Wirral . . . my father has one in India, and he always said that Uncle Edward had the other.'

After that there was not much more to be said. Mr. Stone tried to say something. I think he was blaming Rosie for it all . . . but he choked, and Miss Amy had to fetch him a brandy. Then I turned to Nellie Soutar.

'Mrs. Soutar,' I said, 'you will kindly telephone to the Rothbury Police Station. The sergeant in charge knows all about it and he will send up a car immediately—and the warrant—if you just mention that you are speaking on behalf of Mrs. Joseph Bradford.'

Part Six

being an epilogue by Mr. Adam Muir

July is a very hot month in Provence. Graham Lacacheur and I subsided gratefully into our chairs in the shade of the big walnut tree. From the terrace of the little café at Villeneuve we could look back the way we had come ... along the white, dusty road, past the tower of Philip the Fair and across the luminous shallows of the Rhône to where the walls of Avignon and the ramparts of the Papal Palace stood clear against the steel blue distance.

Mrs. Soutar had closed Coquet Hall immediately. It was really the only thing to do, the only way to deal with the growing army of reporters and photographers. But we insisted that she should open it again the next year ... and we nearly all went back, for it was a most unusual hotel. Canon and Margaret Fish said that they would never go near the place again, and indeed they never did; the McQueens, as was sooner or later inevitable, found a natural refuge at Gleneagles. But the rest of us were loyal. Maisie Bunting was quite annoyed at being turned out even for one summer; she had cancelled her cruise, she said, in order to be in at the kill ... although that wasn't exactly the way she put it. Poor Mark, I fear, was reduced to Bournemouth for the rest of the year, and was very irritable about it.

Miss Coppock, of course, returned to her work at Easton Knoyle. She is, to this day, very critical of

the new Headmistress and she never can quite grasp
that the awful man who accosted the girls in Mellor's Café was really Miss Langdon-Miles's brother.
After all it was, as she said, 'Such a complicated story,
such a maze,' and it was all rather too much for her.
She was never quite the same again, but at Easton
Knoyle they are very kind to her.

Graham Lacacheur was convinced that the 'disgusting publicity' would make England quite unfit to
live in. Actually the newspapers weren't in the
least interested in Mr. Lacacheur, but inevitably he
saw himself as the central figure of the case, and
suffered from a delusion that the reporters were waiting to pounce on him in order to obtain his views.
However, he really had wanted to do a little re-
search, on the spot, for his Crimes of the Popes, and
so he had persuaded me to accompany him to Avignon. We should have to be back before the end of
the month for the Newcastle Assizes, but meanwhile
I was not sorry to get away. My sister Janet had been
most unreasonably crotchety about my getting mixed
up in such a gruesome business . . . although I
couldn't, for the life of me, see that it was my fault.
I wasn't keen on spending three whole weeks with
Lacacheur but, frankly, I thought that the Doon
Farm would be better without me for a time.

As Mrs. Soutar's solicitor I had had to wait in
England until after the exhumation. Crigdon Hill
Churchyard is such a very lonely spot that the
authorities dispensed with the usual jiggery-pokery
of lanterns and moonlight. A constable, with his bicycle, kept guard at the top of the lane while we
hoisted the coffin into a Black Maria . . . it was all
very simple, but the quantity of heroin found in the
body was terrific.

Very quietly, almost secretly, Hallam and Miranda had got married. Girton had been abandoned. Of course Miranda was very young, and Mrs. Bradford had expressed the very strongest disapproval. But really there was nothing against it. Poor Beatrice Warburton, in that notorious will of hers which had caused so much blood and tears, had remembered her nephew in a very handsome fashion, and Hallam and Miranda had bought a lovely old farmhouse in the south Cotswolds. The neighbouring villagers, they thought, would be unlikely to connect young Mr. and Mrs. Miles with that sordid tragedy of the Northumberland moors. At that moment they, too, were on their way south, and it was at the café at Villenueve—where, said Lacacheur, they served the best bouillabaisse in Provence—that we had arranged a meeting.

As they joined us on the terrace, a little out of breath from climbing the hill, I thought that Hallam seemed rather older than when I had first met him . . . only six weeks ago. But when I looked at Miranda I told myself, once again, what a very fortunate young man he was.

Graham Lacacheur had arranged a superb lunch —he loved doing that sort of thing—but I admit frankly that I would have been just as happy with Janet's bannocks and Scotch broth. As we sat there, the sunlight filtering through the leaves of the walnut tree, we talked quietly of many things, mostly of the future, but not at all of that one thing of which we were all thinking.

It was not until an old man began to play the fiddle in the street below us, and Miranda had gone to the edge of the terrace to watch him, that Hallam turned to me and asked if there was any 'news'.

315

'*The car was found,*' I said, '*gutted in a side road, somewhere in the Welsh mountains. It was identified . . . it was hired last November from a firm in the West End.*'

'*And was there . . . I mean was there anyone . . . any remains?*'

'*No, nothing at all. And I think, somehow, that we shall never hear of Rosie again . . . nor of the chauffeur.*'

Miranda was still watching the old man with the fiddle, so I pulled a letter out of my pocket and threw it across the table to Hallam.

'*That,*' I said, '*reached me this morning . . . it seems to be the best way out . . . for us all.*'

Paston & Paston,
Solicitors,
Torquay.
12th July, 1931.

Messrs. Muir & Maxwell,
  Writers to the Signet,
    Cally Street,
      Dalmellington, Ayr.

Dear Sir,

    in Rex v. Langdon-Miles.

We are given to understand that you are acting on behalf of the Coquet Hall Hotel in the above, and that you have accordingly instructed counsel to hold a watching brief in the forthcoming trial. We therefore beg to state that we are informed by the Governor of Newcastle Gaol that, on the 5th inst. the accused, Edward Langdon-Miles, did succeed in extracting from the ink container of his fountain pen—when preparing documents for his solicitor—two tablets of aspirin. Fifteen minutes later the accused was found dead on the floor of his cell. He had succumbed in considerable pain and the prison authorities certified death as being due to strychnine poisoning. . . .

Miranda rejoined us, and over our coffee and cognacs Graham Lacacheur and I drank to her and to Hallam. Then, after a few moments, Hallam gave us a parting toast.

'. . . a commanding old woman,' he said, 'but the only one of us who was even more ingenious than Mr. Stone.'

And then Graham Lacacheur and I said good-bye to them. We left them sitting under the big walnut tree, while we walked slowly back to our hotel . . . along the hot, white, dusty road.

If you would like a complete list of Arrow books please send a postcard to P.O. Box 29, Douglas, Isle of Man, Great Britain.

Here are some *Arrow* books that will be of interest

THE HOMICIDAL COLONEL

ROBERT PLAYER

No one knew what would happen next. No one knew who would fetch that will from the little bureau—the bureau in the bedroom where, awaiting the undertaker, Delia Pangbourne lay beneath the sheet. No one stirred, everyone was waiting for someone else. And then, sweating with excitement, Suzanne Beaunier came in, to lay a Western Union Cablegram before the Doctor. He read it twice. Then he turned gravely to them all.

'I am sorry to tell you that another member of the family, yet another of Mrs. Pangbourne's children, is dead—a violent death, I fear. This may make a great difference to us all. . . .'

OH! WHERE ARE BLOODY MARY'S EARRINGS?

ROBERT PLAYER

Eddy had hardly recovered from the shock when there was a sound behind him. He whirled round. A door had opened— the door to one of the dining-rooms. A head appeared; a black face beneath a yellow turban. It was the Munshi. The colour drained from Eddy's face. His choker collar almost strangled him. His long cuffs shot out from the gold-laced sleeves. His hands twitched even more than usual. His face twitched. He took a step towards the onyx table and towards the tiara which, by some unwanted oversight, Sir Henry Ponsonby had left unguarded.